LONG TIME COMING

www.**rbooks**.co.uk

LONG TIME COMING

Robert Goddard

BANTAM PRESS

LONDON · TORONTO · SYDNEY · AUCKLAND · JOHANNESBURG

TRANSWORLD PUBLISHERS
61–63 Uxbridge Road, London W5 5SA
A Random House Group Company
www.rbooks.co.uk

First published in Great Britain
in 2010 by Bantam Press
an imprint of Transworld Publishers

A CIP catalogue record for this book
is available from the British Library.

ISBN 9780593060254 (cased)
9780593060261 (tpb)

Addresses for Random House Group Ltd companies outside the UK
can be found at: www.randomhouse.co.uk
The Random House Group Ltd Reg. No. 954009

The Random House Group Limited supports The Forest Stewardship
Council (FSC), the leading international forest-certification organization. All our
titles that are printed on Greenpeace-approved FSC-certified paper carry the FSC logo.
Our paper procurement policy can be found at
www.rbooks.co.uk/environment

Typeset in 11/14pt Times New Roman by
Falcon Oast Graphic Art Ltd.

Printed and bound in the UK by
CPI Mackays, Chatham ME5 8TD

4 6 8 10 9 7 5 3

LONG TIME COMING

1976

ONE

My mother surprised me when she announced that my uncle was staying with her. It was the first of many surprises that were shortly to come my way. But of all of them it was probably the biggest. Because I'd only ever had one uncle. And I'd always been told he'd died in the Blitz.

I'd phoned her from Heathrow, to give her an idea of when I'd be arriving. I didn't have the change for a long call. 'We'll have to make this quick,' I said. Maybe that was what prompted her to spring it on me. We'd spoken a couple of times over the previous week, while I was still in Houston. She'd said nothing about Uncle Eldritch then. Maybe her nerve had failed her. Maybe she'd doubted if I really was abandoning what she regarded as my glamorous existence in Texas. If not, I could be spared the revelation, at least for a while, that the old man wasn't dead after all. But I'd gone ahead and left. So now I had to be told. And the lack of immediate opportunity for cross-questioning was a bonus.

'I ought to have mentioned it sooner, dear. You uncle's come to stay.'

'My *uncle*?'

'Eldritch. Your father's elder brother.'

'But . . . he's dead.'

'No, dear. That's what your father always insisted we should pretend. But Eldritch is very much alive.'

'How can he be? Where the hell's he been all my life?'

'In prison. In Ireland.'

'*What?*'

'I'll explain when you get here.'

'Hold on.' But already I was talking over the pips. 'Let's just—'

'See you soon, dear,' my mother shouted. And then she put the phone down.

Perhaps I should have been grateful. But for Mum's bombshell, I'd probably have spent the journey down to Paignton, as I had the overnight flight from Houston, wondering just how I'd allowed a disagreement with the corporate finance director at Sanderstead Oil to become a resigning issue, with disastrous consequences for my engagement to his daughter. Because I'd wanted to would have been the honest answer. Because the job and the engagement were both too good to be true and I was young enough to find worthier versions of both. But naturally I had my doubts about that. Part of me was gung-ho and optimistic. Another part reckoned I'd been a damn fool.

I was pretty confident, nonetheless, that I'd be able to get back into the oil business whenever I chose. With the North Sea fields coming on-stream, there were plenty of openings for a geologist with my qualifications. First, though, I planned to spend a few weeks in Paignton, unwinding and taking stock. I hadn't seen as much of my mother as I should have in the two years since my father's death. The guesthouse kept her busy, at least in summer, but I wanted to reassure myself that she was coping as well as she claimed.

After the news of my uncle, all such thoughts went out of my head, of course. My mother's matter-of-fact tone couldn't disguise the enormity of what she'd actually said. Eldritch Swan of the exotic Christian name and raffish reputation had *not* been among the thousands of Londoners killed by the Luftwaffe in 1940. His death was a lie. And it soon occurred to me that his life might be a lie too. Nothing I'd been told about him accounted for several decades of imprisonment in Ireland. Evidently my father had decided I was better off not knowing the truth about his brother.

Or maybe he'd decided *he* was better off by my not knowing. A dead relative is more socially acceptable than an imprisoned one. I might have shot my mouth off to the neighbours about dear old banged-up Uncle Eldritch. And that would never have done. Grandad might have insisted on blanking his son out of the family, of course. That was a distinct possibility. But he'd been dead for more than twenty years. And the record had never been set straight. Until now.

My paternal grandfather, George Swan, was an engineer who rose to the higher echelons of management with the East African Railways and Harbours Administration, first in Kenya, then Tanganyika. His eldest son was christened Eldritch on account of his mother's maiden name. His second son, my father, received the more conventional Neville as his label in life. The difference turned out to be prophetic, since Eldritch 'racketed around Europe', according to Dad, until the outbreak of war forced him to return to his homeland, only for a German bomb to score a direct hit on the Mayfair gambling den where he happened to be hunched over the baccarat table one night in the autumn of 1940. Meanwhile, my father, favoured, he'd often point out, with a less expensive education than his brother, worked for a shipping agent in Dar-es-Salaam and fought for his country with the Eighth Army in north Africa and Italy. At the end of the war, he transferred to the agent's London office, where my mother was working as a typist. Courtship, marriage, parenthood and suburbia duly followed.

My earliest memories are of our house in Stoneleigh. It backed on to the railway line and on fine mornings Mum would take me into the garden after Dad had left for the station so we could wave to him as the Waterloo train rumbled past. The scene changed for good when Grandma and Grandad died within a few months of each other the summer I was eight. Dad inherited what he'd never describe more specifically than 'a tidy sum'. It was enough for him to quit the shipping business and buy a guesthouse in Paignton, the seaside resort where we'd spent several summer holidays. He needed a lot of persuading by Mum to take the plunge, though. She was always the more enterprising of the two. My father was a cautious man, fretful with the slightest encouragement. But deceitful? I'd never have said so. Until now.

Paignton was a wonderful place to be a child. Zanzibar, as Dad named the guesthouse, was only a few minutes from the beach. Sun, sea and sand were my summer-long companions. The sideshows on the pier; travelling fairs on the green; open-top bus rides to Torquay; rock-pooling at low tide: the real winner from the move to Devon was me.

Ordinarily, I'd have needed to fix that thought firmly in my mind when I got off the train in the middle of a chill grey March afternoon. Torbay Road, running between the station and the Esplanade, is a depressing drag to the adult eye of bucket-and-spade shops and slot-machine joints. A walk along it, rucksack on back, suitcase in hand, had promised to test my spirits. Never were the oily charms of Houston likely to seem more bountiful.

As it was, though, I barely noticed my surroundings as I made my way towards the seafront. A dead uncle was waiting for me at Zanzibar. And a mother with a lot of explaining to do.

Zanzibar started life as one of a terrace of Victorian houses in a cul-de-sac off the Esplanade. Like most of its neighbours, it subsequently acquired the standard trappings of the local tourist trade: dormer window in the roof, striped awnings over the other windows and porch, palm tree out front (supplemented in the season with pot plants and hanging baskets), AA and other accreditations prominently displayed, illuminated vacancies sign suspended in the ground-floor bay. It had been my home from the age of eight to eighteen and in many ways still was. It was stuffed full of memories. It held a part of me, however far or long I strayed.

The awnings were currently retracted. The palm wore a weather-beaten look. And the fully lit NO VACANCIES did not signal brisk business. But it did have one guest, of course – one very special

6

guest. Unless you regarded him as a member of the family, which I wasn't sure I did.

My mother must have been looking out for me. The front door opened as I approached and she appeared, pinnied and permed as ever, smiling her wide, toothy smile at the sight of her only child. 'There you are, dear,' she called. 'Come along in.'

We hugged in the hallway, the lingering fragrance of her lily-of-the-valley soap summoning the past with instant ease. How had the journey been? Was I hungry? What could she get me? It was the usual home-coming litany, recited with no reference to the news she'd broken over the phone. I opted for tea and a slice of Dundee cake and followed her into the kitchen, which Bramble, the waste-of-space cat she'd acquired since my father's death, vacated as we entered, with the hint of a glare in my direction.

'Where is he, then?' I asked as she switched the kettle on, sensing she might launch blithely off into a series of questions about my career and the former fiancée she'd never met (and now never would) if I didn't set the agenda.

'You mean Eldritch?'

'No, Mum. I mean the other ex-con you've taken in.'

'There's no need to be sarcastic.' She spooned tea into the pot. 'And don't call him an ex-con.'

'But that's what he is, isn't it?'

'He's not here at the moment. He goes to Torquay most days. I think he finds it more . . . sophisticated . . . than Paignton.'

'I suppose he has a lot of sophistication to catch up on.'

Mum sighed. 'I'm sorry it had to come out of the blue, Stephen. I really am. It's not my fault. Your father was adamant. So was your grandfather. They were ashamed of Eldritch. And what was I to do? I'd never even met him. I had no idea what it was all about.' The kettle had come to the boil as she spoke. She poured water into the teapot and rattled the lid back into place. 'They said he'd never be let out. So, it was better to pretend he was dead.'

'But now he *has* been let out. Unless you're going to tell me he's on the run.'

'Don't be ridiculous, dear. He's an old man.'

'How did he wind up here?'

'He had nowhere else to go. I wrote to the Irish Prison Service when your father passed away, asking them to let Eldritch know. That's how he was able to contact me. He wrote just before Christmas, saying they were going to release him and could he come and stay here until he'd found his feet. Well, I couldn't turn him down, could I?'

'That depends.'

'What on?'

'What he was in for, to start with.'

'Well, I really don't know.' She spoke airily, as if the nature of Eldritch's offence was a trivial matter. But I'd mulled it over on the train and couldn't see him serving such a long stretch for anything short of murder. 'Your father never said. I'm not sure he knew either.'

'He must have done.'

'You'd think so, I agree. But . . .'

'But what, Mum? Tell me you're sure you haven't got a mass murderer living under the same roof.'

'Oh, he didn't murder anyone, dear. I can set your mind at rest on that. Now, cut yourself a slice of cake and bring it into the sitting-room.' And at that she set off with the tea tray.

The gas fire was wheezing into action when I caught up with her, the tea already poured. I took a sip and swallowed a mouthful of cake.

'What kind of food do they have in Texas, dear?' Mum casually enquired as she stroked Bramble, who'd plonked himself on the sofa and showed no sign of moving on this time.

'Don't try to change the subject, Mum. How do you know Eldritch didn't murder anyone?'

'He told me so.'

'Just like that?'

'Well, he obviously thought I might worry about it, so he made the point in his letter. "I didn't kill or injure anyone."

His exact words. You can read the letter if you want. I kept it.'

'I'd like to see it, yes. But how can you be sure he's telling the truth, since apparently he didn't go on to say what he *had* done?'

'Well, they censor prisoners' correspondence, don't they? They wouldn't have let him lie to me.'

My mother knew as much as I did about the Irish Prison Service's censorship policy, of course: precisely nothing. But there was nothing to be gained by pointing that out. I tried an appeal to reason. 'Doesn't it seem odd to you that he won't say what he did to land himself behind bars for . . . however many years it was?'

'Thirty-six, dear. Well, nearly. July 1940 until this January. A long, long time.'

'Exactly.'

'Your father and grandfather were never informed of the particulars, you see. Only that Eldritch had been imprisoned indefinitely for . . . offences against the state. Your father thought . . . well, he was afraid . . . his brother might have been . . . spying for the Germans.'

'What put that in his mind?'

'I don't know. He never said.'

And my mother, with her undentable insouciance, had evidently never asked. 'Ireland was neutral in the war, Mum. What would Eldritch have been spying on?'

'I can't imagine.'

I couldn't suppress a sigh of exasperation. 'For all you know he could be a member of the IRA.' I didn't really believe that, but I reckoned the suggestion might snap Mum out of her complacency. The papers I'd read on the train had been full of IRA bombings and shootings. I'd forgotten while I'd been away just how murderous their campaign was.

She shook her head. 'Nonsense.'

'How can you be so sure?'

'I'm not quite as naïve as you seem to think, Stephen,' she replied. 'I was actually intending to press him on the question of his offence once he'd settled in, but he . . . dealt with the subject before I could raise it.'

9

'How, exactly?'

'He explained it was a condition of his release that he say nothing about the circumstances leading to his imprisonment.'

'*What?*'

'He explained it was a condition of—'

'I know. I heard you. I just . . . don't believe it.'

'Really?' Mum frowned at me in puzzlement. 'Why on earth not?'

'Because . . .' I broke off and raised two hands in mock surrender. 'I'm only thinking of you, Mum. How can you trust this man? You know nothing about him.'

'I know he's your father's brother and needs a helping hand. I've given him the use of the attic room until Easter. He's promised to move on by then. I think he's looking for a flat in Torquay. Meanwhile, he keeps himself to himself and causes me no problem. So, I hope you're not going to *create* a problem, dear.' She gave me a stern look. 'I really do.'

TWO

I took a long, hot bath that I badly needed and would have found relaxing in normal circumstances. I debated with myself whether I was overreacting and concluded that, even if I was, my mother was certainly *under*reacting. I'd refrained from asking her whether she thought Dad, if he'd still been alive, would have taken Eldritch in. Pretending he was dead as he had, I seriously doubted it. But maybe Dad had had the advantage of knowing what those mysterious '*offences against the state*' were. Maybe he'd feigned ignorance on the point because he couldn't bear to admit to his wife what his own brother had actually done.

While I was soaking in the tub my mother had dug out the letter Eldritch had sent her from prison. It was waiting for me on the bed-side cabinet in my room. I read it as I dressed.

It was written in copperplate ballpoint on lined paper, under the printed address *Portlaoise Prison*.

21st December 1975

Dear Avis (if I may),
You were so good as to write to me when Neville died. I should have acknowledged your letter and offered you my condolences, but, to tell the truth, I have survived these long years of incarceration by ignoring the existence of the

11

outside world, since there appeared to be no prospect of my ever rejoining it.

That state of affairs has now changed. I am told, to my surprise and bewilderment, that I am to be released early in the New Year. This seems only to confirm what a fellow convict who had been here even longer than I have once averred. They free you only when freedom is no longer of any use to you.

I have, to put it plainly, nowhere to go and no one to turn to but your good self. If you could see your way to accommodating me for a few weeks after my release, I would be deeply grateful. You wrote that you run a guesthouse. I wonder therefore if at this time of year you would be able to spare me a room. I could pay you rent, though I should tell you that my means are severely limited.

You should also know that my imprisonment has not been on account of any violent crime committed by me. I did not kill or injure anyone. I can say no more than that. Perhaps Neville acquainted you with the circumstances of my con-finement. I am not aware how much or how little he knew.

If you prefer not to reply to this letter, I shall entirely understand your position and will make no further contact. I hope, however, that you may feel able to help me.

Sincerely yours,
Eldritch

The old fellow had a nice line in self-pitying ingratiation. There was no doubt about that. Though he had never met my mother, he had pitched his appeal to her softer instincts perfectly.

I caught my first sight of him while I was unpacking. I passed the window and glimpsed a figure in the street. I knew it was him before I'd even stopped to look down. There was something in his build and posture that reminded me of my father. And surely, yes, the raincoat he was wearing had belonged to my father. Mum must have kept it, though hardly with this contingency in mind. It was another reason to dislike the man, to add to all the other reasons to distrust him.

He was walking slowly towards Zanzibar, one hand thrust into a pocket of the raincoat, the other busy with a cigarette. I couldn't see much of his face beneath the brim of his hat – a jauntily angled fedora that certainly wasn't my father's. He was thin and slightly stooped. He stopped at the pavement's edge as I watched to take a last drag on the cigarette before tossing it into the gutter. My mother abhorred smoking and used to banish Dad to the back garden to indulge the vice. It looked as if she'd made no concessions to Eldritch on that point at least.

He stood where he was for a moment, apparently lost in thought. Then he raised his head and looked straight up at me. His face was grey and lined, the tendons of his neck stretched like cords beneath the skin. His eyes remained in shadow, but I sensed them meeting mine. There was the faintest of acknowledging nods. Then he pressed on towards the house.

I heard the front door close down in the hall. My mother was in the kitchen. Whether she was aware of his arrival I couldn't tell. He started up the stairs, climbing slowly, but treading lightly. I wondered if he meant to carry straight on up to his room and decided to leave him no choice in the matter. I stepped out on to the landing and watched him as he reached the top of the first flight of stairs, his hand grasping the acorn cap on the head post for support. He was breathing heavily and wheezily.

'Hi,' I said expressionlessly as he turned and saw me.

He didn't reply at first, either because he didn't have the breath or because he wanted me to understand he wasn't about to let me intimidate him. I could see his eyes now, the same washed-out hazel as my father's. His face was even greyer than I'd first thought. He looked as weary as he was wary, an old man with an extra decade or so loaded on to him by long-term imprisonment, a ghost in more ways than one on account of his eerie resemblance to my father and his recent return from the supposedly dead.

'You must be Stephen,' he said at last, in a low, cultured

voice that somehow sounded as if it had spoken from the past.

'That's right.'

He took off his hat, revealing a sparse covering of oil-darkened hair and a deeply furrowed forehead. Then he stepped towards me and extended a hand. 'Eldritch Swan. Your uncle. Pleased to meet you.'

There seemed nothing for it but to shake his hand. His grip was surprisingly strong, though dismayingly cold. 'They told me you were dead,' I said, aware that he couldn't have judged from my tone whether I regarded the news that he wasn't as either good or bad.

'I might as well have been.' He released my hand. 'I never thought they'd let me out.'

'Why did they?'

He shaped a crooked little half-smile. 'Bit of a shock for you, was it, son? Finding out I was still in the land of the living.'

'Don't call me son.'

'Fair enough.' He nodded a restrained apology. 'I don't want to upset anyone.'

'Mum says you're here till Easter.'

'Unless she asks me to leave sooner.'

'I doubt she will. She has a soft heart.'

'I expect you could talk her into it, though, Stephen.'

'Why would I do that?'

'I don't know. How long are you here for, yourself?'

'A few weeks at least.'

'Right. So, we'll have to . . . rub along, won't we?'

'Apparently.'

A brief, heavy silence. Then he said, 'Come up to my room. There's something I want to show you.'

'What is it?'

'Nothing really. But you should see it even so.'

The attic room had the lowest ceiling but the finest view in the house. From the dormer window you could see the whole expanse of the bay towards Berry Head. It was furnished simply, with its own tiny en-suite bathroom. At first glance, it would have been hard to tell anyone was staying in it, apart from the fact that the bed was made up and my father's old dressing-gown was hanging on the hook behind the door. Eldritch hadn't exactly stamped his personality on the room. I wondered if that was what he wanted me to see: visible proof that he wasn't trying to put down roots.

But no. As it transpired, that wasn't quite the point he was anxious to make.

Breathless again from the climb, he took off his raincoat and opened the rickety wardrobe. The only item of clothing already hung up was an old brown and gold pinstripe suit. The jacket had wide lapels and there were turn-ups on the trousers. He hung the raincoat beside it and slid his hat on to the shelf above. Then, leaving the door open, he moved away and sat down on the chair by the dressing-table.

I recognized the tweed jacket he was wearing as another hand-out from Mum's hoard of my father's clothes. The shirt and trousers looked new, though I couldn't be sure. The tie was a narrow, striped number, possibly contemporary with the suit. Likewise the ancient brogues. It was more obvious now how thin he was, little more than skin and bone, driven falteringly on by some stubbornly functioning mechanism.

He was seven years older than Dad, which made him sixty-eight. And every one of those years had left its mark. But then I didn't imagine Portlaoise Prison had been an easy place to grow old in.

'Tell me, Eldritch,' I said, 'if Dad had still been alive, would you have asked him to take you in?'

'Certainly,' he replied. 'But I wouldn't have known where to find him. He never wrote to me. And I wouldn't have expected a welcoming answer even if I had.'

'But still you'd have asked if you could?'

'Oh yes. Thirty-six years in prison sucks all the pride out of you.'

'What did you want to show me?'

'That suit in the wardrobe.'

'What about it?'

'The suit and the hat – and this tie and these shoes – are what I was wearing when they arrested me. The sixth of July, 1940. They gave them back to me when they discharged me two months ago. Plus one wristwatch.' He raised his left arm to show me the watch. 'Along with my cigarette case and lighter.' He took them from his pocket, then dropped them back in. 'Also my fountain pen.' He tapped its clip where it was hung inside his jacket. 'And a quantity of cash that was no longer legal tender.'

'Why are you telling me this?'

'Because I want you to understand. That was it. The sum total of my possessions, parcelled up and waiting for me. And it wasn't a very big parcel. I didn't want to leave, you know. I *had* wanted to, of course, more than I'd wanted anything in the world. But at some point – I can't say when exactly – I gave up dreaming of freedom. And at some other point – also indefinable – I realized I preferred to stay where I was. It was safe in its way. The outside world was strange and vast and . . . frightening. It's the final phase of institutionalization. The victory of the system over the individual.'

'Is that why they let you go? Because they knew they'd beaten you?'

Eldritch chuckled drily. 'Good question, Stephen. Actually, no. There was a more specific reason. But I can't tell you what that was without explaining why I was imprisoned in the first place. And I gave them a written undertaking I wouldn't tell anyone. A breach of that undertaking could land me behind bars again. And I couldn't bear that. Strange and vast and frightening as it is, this world I don't belong in is preferable to the one I reluctantly left behind.'

'This undertaking you gave is very convenient, isn't it?'

He frowned. 'How so?'

'Well, it neatly relieves you of the need to admit what you did, doesn't it?'

He smiled thinly. 'As a matter of fact, I did nothing.'

'You're an innocent man?'

'Not particularly. Something of a rogue in my day, to be honest, as I'm sure your father must have told you. But I wasn't guilty of what they said I did in Dublin. I was fitted up.'

'Of course.'

'You don't believe me?'

'I don't know you, Eldritch. And apparently you can't tell me what happened to you in Dublin back in 1940. So, how am I to believe or disbelieve you?'

'Good point.' He nodded thoughtfully. 'I can't argue with that.'

'Excuse me.'

I turned to leave, exasperated by his hangdog evasiveness. I was already through the door when he called after me, in a curiously antique turn of phrase, 'Hold up.'

I stopped and turned round. 'Yes?'

He waved me back into the room. I went as far as the threshold. 'Could you do me one favour, Stephen?'

'What?'

'If anyone – any stranger – asks you about me, could you tell them . . . you don't know anything . . . about my past . . . or my plans for the future?'

'Of course.' I treated him to an openly sarcastic grin. 'After all, it'd be nothing less than the truth.'

THREE

Conversation didn't exactly flow fluently over dinner. My mother filled the silences with babble about recent events in Paignton which only made it obvious there hadn't been any. Eventually, Eldritch seemed to take pity on her and started asking me about life in the United States. It soon became clear he'd seen more of the country than I had, though naturally his knowledge of it was about forty years out of date.

'I've stood in Trafalgar Square on both sides of the Atlantic,' he remarked as he fiddled unenthusiastically with Mum's rice pudding. 'How do you suppose I managed that?' The answer, it transpired, was that a replica of the square had been constructed at the Twentieth Century-Fox studios in Hollywood for a film (*Cavalcade*) in 1933. And he'd been there at the time.

'You were inside the studios?' I asked.

'Yes,' he replied cautiously.

'On business?'

'You could say so.'

'And what business was that?'

He smiled. 'I forget.'

As this exchange made apparent, it wasn't only his disastrous run-in with the Irish authorities back in 1940 that Eldritch was reluctant to discuss. Hard information about virtually any aspect of his life was off-limits. Anecdotes culled from his many travels –

climbing pyramids in Egypt, playing polo in India, shearing sheep in Australia – were his stock-in-trade. But they revealed nothing about him, even if they were true, which I wasn't at all sure they were.

It wasn't mere curiosity that made me want to find out more. I was genuinely doubtful he'd move out when Easter came and feared Mum might allow him to stay on. I resented this elderly cuckoo in the nest and decided to put my career on hold until I'd done my best to ease him out.

Volunteering to redecorate the dining-room before the tourist season began (the three of us could easily eat our meals in the kitchen) was partly a ploy to delay my own departure, though there was no denying it needed doing. It meant I was at home most of the day for a week, then another week when I moved on to the equally shabby hall. Eldritch generally took himself off to Torquay from mid-morning to mid-afternoon. Mum quoted a neighbour as saying she'd seen him in the reference library. That was the only clue to his activities.

During one of his absences, when Mum was out shopping, I gave his room a discreet once-over. But he'd certainly been telling the truth when he described how little he'd left prison with. And he didn't seem to have acquired any possessions since. There were skeletons in his cupboard, I didn't doubt. But there was nothing in his wardrobe.

On another occasion when I was alone in the house, I answered the phone to a woman who asked the rather strange question, in an Irish accent to boot, 'Is that the household of Mr Neville Swan?' I sensed a connection with Eldritch right away.

'You mean my father,' I said guardedly. 'I'm afraid he died two years ago.'

'I'm sorry to hear that.'

'How can I help you?'

'Well, it's actually Mr Neville Swan's brother, Eldritch Swan, I'm enquiring after.' (Surprise, surprise.) 'That would be your uncle.'

'Indeed.'

'Have you heard from him since . . . his release?'

'He's out, is he?' I wasn't going to give her anything for nothing.
'He is so.'

'And you are?'

'Moira Henchy. I'm a freelance journalist, Mr Swan, based in Dublin.'

'What's your interest in my uncle?'

'I believe he has a story to tell. I'd be willing to pay to hear it. If not from his own lips, then from those of someone close to him.'

'What story did you have in mind?'

'The obvious one, Mr Swan. *Have* you heard from him?'

'I don't think so. I'd have to check with my mother, but I don't believe we've heard anything. He and my father . . . lost touch.'

'I see. Well, could I give you my phone number and ask you to contact me if you do hear from him? Or if your mother knows anything?'

'All right.' She reeled it off and I jotted it down.

'Remember there could be a payment for information I can use, won't you, Mr Swan? Could I ask your first name?'

'Stephen.'

'Thank you. I hope to speak to you again, Stephen.'

'One thing, Miss Henchy.'

'Uhuh?'

'Can you tell me what my uncle was convicted of that put him in prison for thirty-six years?'

A pause. Then she replied, 'No, Stephen. I can't.'

'Why not? Is it such a big secret?'

'Yes. That's exactly what it is. A big secret. So, let me know if you think you can help.'

Eldritch habitually stepped out into the garden for a smoke after dinner. That evening I joined him. It was a cold, still night. The sea running in the bay was barely a murmur. The scent of his Sobranie hung in the air.

'You want one?' he offered, the silver of his cigarette case catching the light from the kitchen window.

'No, thanks.'

'What, then?' He coughed. 'I suspect you didn't come out here to judge how bad my lungs are.'

'An Irish journalist phoned here today.'

'Really?' He didn't sound particularly surprised. 'What did he want?'

'*She* was asking after you. Had we heard from you? Did we know where you were? That kind of thing.'

'What did you say?'

'I said no: you hadn't been in touch.'

'Good. Thanks, Stephen. That was kind of you.'

'She offered money for your story.'

'Did she?'

'Aren't you going to ask how much?'

'No. Whatever the figure, I can't afford to sell. But tell me if you want.'

'Actually, she never specified an amount.'

'Ah. Right. Negotiable, I suppose. As most things are.'

'Her name's Moira Henchy.'

'Henchy?' Now he did sound surprised.

'Yes. Do you know her?'

He seemed to have to mull the point over before replying. 'Never heard of her.'

'Are you sure?'

'Absolutely.'

I gave him a moment to reconsider his answer. But he didn't. So then I said, 'It won't end with one phone call, will it?'

'No.' He drew on his cigarette. 'It assuredly won't.'

'I don't want Mum bothered on your account.'

'Don't worry. I'll make sure she isn't.'

'How will you do that?'

'I'll think it over. And let you know.'

There seemed to be only one way Eldritch could keep his word. That was by doing what I'd been willing him to do all along: move out of Zanzibar. He'd been dead to us all my life. I saw no

21

good reason why he shouldn't revert to that status. Mum would forget him soon enough. I was his only blood relative. And I was confident I wouldn't miss him, sly old relic of a chancer that he was.

I decided to give him a few days to come to the obvious conclusion before putting it to him bluntly. But before the few days were up, something else happened.

The hall was an organized chaos of dust sheets, stepladders and paint pots, with the front door wedged open to aid drying, when an early-afternoon caller pressed at the bell.

'Hold on,' I shouted, balancing my brush on an open pot before threading my way along the hall.

I eased the door open and found myself looking down at a short, tubby, middle-aged man in a dark overcoat that was far too heavy for the springlike day, and a black Homburg. His round face was framed by a cushion of fat, emphasizing the smallness of his features, which he'd complemented with tiny, round-framed glasses and a smudge of moustache. A surprisingly vivid bow-tie peaked out between the raised lapels of his coat.

'Good afternoon,' he said with a smile. His voice was soft and precise. 'I'm looking for Mr Eldritch Swan.'

I was tempted to say, '*Join the queue*'. Instead, I replied, accurately enough to my mind, 'He doesn't live here.'

The smile stayed in place. 'Is he in?'

'Like I just said, he—'

'Excuse me, young man,' he interrupted, 'I don't want to waste your time or mine. I assume you're Mr Swan's nephew, Stephen.'

'How do you—'

'Let me finish.' He cautioned me to do so with a raised leather-gloved finger. 'I have a proposition to put to Mr Swan. A potentially very lucrative proposition. On behalf of a client. My card.' He plucked a card out of an inside pocket and slid it into my hand. I glanced down at it.

F. J. Twisk
Solicitor
3 Ely Court
London EC1
Telephone 01-278 6296

'You've come a long way, Mr Twisk,' I said noncommittally.

'I'm putting up at the Redcliffe, Mr Swan. Your uncle can find me there. I know he's been staying here since his release from prison. Impecuniousness is the curse of many an ex-con, if you'll pardon the term. I'm in a position to solve that particular problem for him. The solution might even be described as overkill.' His smile had tightened. 'I'm here to do my client's bidding. Your uncle would be well advised – and certainly well rewarded – to do the same. Tell him it concerns this.'

Another pluck at an inside pocket produced a newspaper cutting, which he laid gently in my palm. Under the headline **Pick of American tycoon's collection comes to London** was a screed of prose about some new exhibition at the Royal Academy. I caught the name Jay Brownlow, along with a jumble of artistic greats: Monet, Cézanne, Picasso, Matisse and the like. Brownlow I remembered as an American food-canning dynasty, Jay as its public, party-going face of earlier in the century. I'd never heard of his art collection before. But it was no surprise he had one. It went with the territory.

'What's this supposed to mean?' I asked. But, looking up, I saw that Twisk had no more to say to me. He was already making off along the street at a brisk, short-paced clip. What he'd come to do he'd evidently done.

According to the newspaper cutting, Jay Brownlow had taken up art collecting as he had charitable giving after a misspent youth that had made no discernible dent in his family fortune: a Jazz Age bon viveur turned middle-aged connoisseur-cum-philanthropist. He had died in 1972, decreeing the wider world should have a chance to see the Impressionist and Post-Impressionist master-pieces adorning the walls of his Baltimore mansion. Hence the

23

touring exhibition that had just arrived at the Royal Academy. The *Daily Telegraph*'s art critic gave it top marks. '*An extraordinary concentration of high-quality painters' highest-quality work.*' The Picassos were singled out for particular commendation. Someone, Twisk presumably, had underlined the phrase '*A roomful of glittering Cubist gems*'.

What Eldritch had to do with this was likely to prove impenetrable unless I could wheedle it out of him. But I was actually more interested in using Twisk's visit to hasten my uncle on his way. He was welcome to keep his secrets if we could be rid of him.

I told Mum what had happened and was gratified to see how disturbed she was. The mystery of what crime Eldritch had committed was beginning to cast its shadow over her, admittedly with a lot of encouragement from me. In the circumstances, his reaction to the news was every bit as suspicious as I might have hoped.

'You told him I've been staying here, Stephen?'

'He already knew.'

'How could a solicitor from London know that, Eldritch?' Mum asked.

My uncle shrugged. 'I have no idea.'

'But you must have an idea what the lucrative proposition is that he wants to put to you,' I said.

Another shrug. He produced a pair of glasses that looked as if they had probably been Irish Health Service standard issue circa 1960 and proceeded to skim-read the cutting. 'Who's his client?' The question was barely more than a rhetorical murmur.

'He didn't say.'

'You mentioned a card.'

'Here.' I handed it to him.

'Ely Court.' He shook his head. 'Someone's playing games with me. Do you have a map of London, Stephen?'

'An A to Z, yes. You want to know where Ely Court is?'

'Confirmation . . . would be useful.'

I fetched the *A–Z* from my room and looked up Ely Court in the index as I wandered back downstairs. It was so small it wasn't actually shown on the map, listed merely as '*off Ely Place*', a cul-de-sac running north from Holborn Circus.

Mum caught my eye as I re-entered the sitting-room. Eldritch was staring into space – or, rather, into a past he had no wish to revisit. He looked older and frailer than ever, hunched in an armchair, dressed in his dead brother's clothes, a shaft of sunlight revealing every line and crevice on his haggard face.

'The A to Z,' I said, holding the book in front of him, open at the listed page. 'Ely Court is off Ely Place.' I pointed. 'There.'

He put his glasses back on and peered at the map, then took the book from me and peered some more. 'Damn it all,' he said under his breath.

'What's wrong?' I asked.

'It's close to Hatton Garden,' he replied. 'Too close to be a coincidence.'

'Hatton Garden? The diamond district?'

'Exactly.' He passed the book back to me and took another look at Twisk's card. 'Journalists and lawyers. You know it's time to worry when you have both of them on your trail.'

'Do you intend to see this man, Eldritch?' my mother asked.

He sighed. 'It seems I may have to.' He levered himself out of the chair and plodded towards the door. 'Excuse me. I need to . . . consider my position.' In the doorway, he stopped and gazed around the dust-sheeted hallway. 'It's a pity you can't just . . . redecorate a life,' he mused. Then he started slowly up the stairs.

FOUR

Eldritch went out an hour or so later, telling Mum he wouldn't be back for dinner. He didn't say where he was going, but it seemed obvious. He wasn't exactly the centre of a wide social circle. I didn't see the going of him myself. But I planned to be on hand when he returned. And to find out, if I could, whether he had taken on the 'lucrative assignment' Twisk was offering him. As it turned out, I got my chance to do that long before he returned.

Mum was engrossed in some TV cop show when the phone rang late that evening. She signalled for me to answer it. To my surprise, the caller was Eldritch.

'I'm at the Redcliffe Hotel, Stephen,' he announced.

'I thought you might be.'

'Do you think you could join me here? There's something I'd like to put to you. Man to man.'

'What about Twisk?'

'He's toddled off to bed. But I've . . . reached an agreement with him. That's what I want to discuss with you. Meet me in the bar, there's a good fellow.' His unusually avuncular tone suggested he'd already spent some time in the bar. 'I'll buy you a drink. Well, Twisk will. Or, rather, his client. We really should talk, Stephen. Do say you'll come.'

*

26

I'd spent one university vacation working at the Redcliffe. It maintained the palm-court tradition in the teeth of changing fashion, though it looked more like a maharajah's seaside retreat thanks to its Indian-style architecture. That was a legacy of its original owner, Colonel Robert Smith, who'd retired there after making pots of money building roads, bridges, houses and palaces all over the subcontinent. Torbay's mild climate had always attracted well-heeled Britons returning home after long years abroad. In that sense, Eldritch fitted in perfectly, bar the well-heeled part, of course.

Dancing was in progress in the ballroom, the band doing its brassy best to fill the floor. Eldritch was at a central table in the adjoining bar, in the lee of a pillar, sipping whisky and apparently lost in thought. He was wearing his brown pinstripe suit and smoking one of his Sobranies with an air of half-remembered decadence. All in all, the hotel could have done worse than hire him to enhance the mood of a bygone age.

He looked up as I approached and nodded to the barman, which sufficed to get me whatever I wanted to drink. I settled for a beer and joined him at his table.

'Cheers,' I said, with less than wholehearted enthusiasm.

'Your good health, Stephen.' He took another sip of whisky. 'I haven't tasted Scotch in thirty-six years, you know. Thanks to Twisk's client, I've been able to break my drought with a particularly fine malt.'

'Who is his client?' I asked in a casual tone.

'He won't say. But evidently no skinflint. Twisk didn't stint himself when it came to ordering wine with our dinner. I haven't tasted Chambertin in thirty-six years either.'

'I take it from all this generosity on his part you've agreed to do what his client wants.'

'Yes.' Eldritch winced. 'Which I'll no doubt come to regret.'

'Why do it, then?'

'No choice. I can't stay on at Zanzibar. And, as I'm sure you've already come to suspect, I haven't the means to move anywhere . . . tolerable. So, I need money. Enough to take me somewhere . . .

where I can die in comfort. The Riviera, perhaps. Cannes. Nice. Somewhere like that.'

'Sounds good.'

'Indeed.'

'Are you planning to tell me what you have to do to fund your Mediterranean dotage?'

'Yes. I am. That's why I asked you here. But let's go somewhere quieter.' He glanced towards the ballroom. 'I can't compete with a saxophone.'

The first-floor lounge, Colonel Smith's old ornately ceilinged drawing-room, was where guests often retired for coffee after dinner. They'd all been and gone by the time we walked in, though coffeepots, drained cups and chocolate-crumbed plates remained on several tables. We sat by one of the windows that looked out into the bay, with the lights of Torquay twinkling in the distance.

Eldritch was breathing hard but shallowly after climbing the stairs, a smoker's cough rumbling away in his chest. It didn't stop him lighting another Sobranie, though.

'I reckon my lungs are shot,' he said when he'd recovered his breath. 'Smoking was about the only pleasure there was in prison. On the other hand, my liver's probably A1 on account of the enforced sobriety. The way I was going in 1940, cirrhosis would probably have got me long since if the Garda hadn't felt my collar. It's not much of a consolation for spending all those years inside, but maybe I should be grateful. What do you think?'

'I . . . don't know.'

'No. No more you do. No more does anyone who hasn't gone through it. Buried alive. That's what I was. Entombed. Walled up. After a few months at Mountjoy, they sent me to Portlaoise. And there I stayed until January of this year. I first saw the town the day I was released. I'd arrived at night in the back of a van. And you could only see sky from the cells or the exercise yard. Just a patch of sky. Grey, usually. Grey and blank. Like wadding inside a box. You have no idea, Stephen. You can't imagine what it's like. I couldn't, unless I'd been through it. And if I *had* been able to, I couldn't have imagined surviving it.'

'How *did* you survive?'

'I'm not sure. By not counting the days, I suppose. By not expecting it to end. By not hoping. But I'm hoping now. That's the worst of it. That's what happens when people offer you money. I can't sell my story to Moira Henchy or anyone else. But I *can* do what Twisk's client is asking. It's a calculated risk. But I have to take it.'

'And what is it?'

He sighed and drew on his cigarette. 'He – or she – wants me to prove the Picassos in the Brownlow Collection were stolen from a man called Isaac Meridor. In 1940.'

'Were they?'

'Certainly.'

'How do you know?'

'Because I helped steal them.'

I stared at him in silent astonishment for a moment. His responding gaze was sardonic, almost mischievous.

'It's not what the Irish put me away for, Stephen. Ironically, I was innocent of what *they* accused me of. But innocent of all wrong-doing?' He smiled. 'Hardly.'

'Why are you admitting this to me?'

'Because I need your help. And because, as Neville's son, you've shared to some degree in our family's ill-gotten gains.'

'What the hell's that supposed to mean?'

'Let me explain. According to your mother, Neville used a bequest from our father, *your* grandfather, to fund his early retirement and the purchase of Zanzibar. It was a lot more than he might have expected to receive. And not just because he didn't have to split it with me. The old man was as big a rogue as I am in his own way, you see. I don't suppose your father ever told you that. Well, maybe he never knew, though I find that hard to believe.'

Dad had always attributed Grandad's unsuspected affluence to shrewd investment. I'd suggested it might have had less respectable (or more interesting) origins myself a couple of times, much to his annoyance. Naturally, I wasn't about to admit that to Eldritch. But I did want to know where his claims were leading. 'What kind of rogue exactly?' I prompted.

'The bribable kind, Stephen. Isaac Meridor was a Belgian diamond merchant, one of Antwerp's wealthiest. A Jew, as almost all the merchants were, and are, I dare say. Unlike most of them, however, Meridor had stakes in several mining companies in the Belgian Congo, where the diamonds actually came from. He'd been out there as a young man, employed as an agent by one of the companies. Ever read *Heart of Darkness*?'

'Yes, I have.' And who, having read it, could forget it? Conrad's defining vision of horror and brutality in the Congo of the late nineteenth century was as powerful as it was forbidding.

'Enough said, then. Meridor was a part of the system that ran that charnel house. But he didn't go mad like Kurtz. He went another way: into business. The mining companies made handsome profits. Costs are low when labour's free, when all's said and done. But King Leopold, and later the Belgian government, after he sold the colony to the state, held half the shares in all the companies and added on a load of taxes and fees as well.

'The profit margin wasn't big enough to satisfy Meridor. So, he arranged a little secret trade on his own account. Some diamonds, instead of being sent down the Congo to Leopoldville for shipment to Antwerp, found their way out to the east, by rail through Tanganyika to Dar-es-Salaam, where they were officially recorded as originating in Rhodesia. They eventually reached Antwerp via London as consignments purchased direct by Meridor. But he was buying them from himself. And keeping all the profit, except what he had to pay in bribes, of course. He needed someone well placed in the British East African Railways and Harbours Administration to smooth his diamonds' passage through Tanganyika – someone to look after the paperwork. And I'm sure you can guess who that was.'

I didn't want to believe it, though instinctively I did. Suddenly, I was tainted by association. Slave labour in Congolese diamond mines long before I was born had indirectly furnished my father with his shabby little inheritance and his seaside retirement. All those massacres and mutilations I'd read about; all those decades of oppression and exploitation: I'd thought until now they didn't involve me. But I'd been wrong. Oh so wrong.

'The Belgian Congo, they call it Zaire these days. And the Americans approve of the Mobutu regime, so everything's fine and dandy, unless you look too closely. Which naturally I didn't, during the years I worked for Meridor.'

'You worked for him?'

'Oh yes. I travelled the world and lived on my wits after I was sent down from Oxford. But eventually my luck turned and I was forced to ask the old man if he could bale me out. He offered to fix me up with a job he reckoned would suit me. Well, I have to hand it to him, he read me right. Running errands for Isaac Meridor was something I really was cut out for. Lots of variety and plenty of perks. Not to mention a generous salary. Meridor was a good employer, as long as you didn't mind cutting a few corners on his behalf. It helped that he liked me, of course. I reminded him of himself as a young man, apparently. He referred to me as his secretary, though the job went well beyond that. I liked him too. I respected him.'

'But that didn't stop you stealing from him.'

'I didn't steal from *him*. Not exactly.'

'Meaning?'

Eldritch stubbed out his cigarette and studied me through a plume of residual smoke. 'Twisk's client wants me to try to find proof that Brownlow's Picassos are rightfully the property of Meridor's daughter. The client seems to know I need no convincing of that. But the outside world does. The family's already lost one lawsuit in the United States. Now, with the pictures on tour, outside American jurisdiction, they have a chance of reopening the case.'

'This daughter must be Twisk's client, then.'

'You'd think so, wouldn't you? I'm not sure. What I *am* sure of is that fifty thousand pounds would see me out in handsome style.'

'*Fifty thousand?*'

'The reward, if I succeed.' He smiled. 'Tempted?'

'What's it got to do with me?'

'I need a young pair of legs – and lungs. I need someone to help me. You're a bright boy, currently with time on your hands. I'll offer you ten per cent to do some running around – and whatever else crops up – on my behalf. Twisk will cover all our expenses. What do you say?'

'I say I'd need to know a lot more about this before I could consider getting involved.'

'And there's the painting to finish, of course.' He held my gaze, letting me see and understand that he would regard turning him down as somehow unmanly. The offer was also a dare. Did I have what it took? 'Listen to me, Stephen. I'll tell you everything you need to know *if* you agree to help me. Not otherwise. And even that probably won't be everything you *want* to know.'

'What makes you think I want to know anything, Eldritch?'

'The fact that you came here tonight. The fact that I would, in your shoes. The money would clinch it, of course, as it always has for me. But perhaps you're above such things. Or perhaps not.' He raised his glass, as if about to propose a toast. 'Yes or no, Stephen. Which is it to be?'

1940

FIVE

It is a bright spring morning in Antwerp. The SS *Uitlander*, a double-funnelled four-masted liner, stands loading at the Quai Van Dyck. Stevedores are busy transferring cargo from the sheds that flank the dockside railway line, watched by passers-by on the terrace above. Gulls wheel and shriek in the clear, cool air. Sunlight sparkles on the rippling waters of the Scheldt. It is a scene that could have been witnessed on countless occasions in recent decades, outwardly calm and seemingly orderly. It is the last day of April and the *Uitlander* sails for New York on the morrow. It has made the crossing many times, as one of the Red Star Line's best-equipped ships. But Red Star are no longer its owners and no one will be joining the voyage for pleasure or leisure. Since the outbreak of war between Germany and the British and French in September 1939, U-boat attacks have made transatlantic travel hazardous as well as expensive, though many, for various reasons, have been willing to pay for their passage and take their chances. And this, though no one here knows it, is one of the very last such chances. In eleven days, the German army will cross the Belgian border. In less than a month, King Leopold will have surrendered. The world is about to change.

A man who has been in conversation with an officer on the foredeck of the *Uitlander* concludes their exchanges with a handshake and heads down the gangway to the wharf. He is slim and smartly dressed in a brown and gold pinstripe suit, a grey fedora shading his eyes. He looks to be in his late twenties or early thirties, a pencil moustache adding a note of maturity to his open, confident features. There is something more than confidence in the way he carries himself, however. The flick of the wrist as he raises his cigarette to his lips and the hint of a swagger in his gait suggest cocksureness amounting to arrogance.

As he reaches the wharf, he glances up, as if studying the manoeuvrings of the crane currently lowering a large crate into the hold of the vessel he has just left. But his gaze is actually directed elsewhere, to a man of about his own age, dressed in similar style – though it would be clear to a discerning observer that he has used a cheaper tailor – who is leaning against the railings up on the terrace, watching the loading operations. They acknowledge each other with a nod. A moment passes, sufficient for both to draw reflectively on their cigarettes. Then the man on the wharf taps himself on the chest with his thumb and points to the terrace. He will join the other. They have something to discuss.

Eldritch Swan was neither pleased nor surprised to see Pieter Verhoest that morning. He had half expected the fellow to be loitering around the quay, reassuring himself that all was going according to plan. Swan would have much preferred to ignore him, but knew he could not afford to do so. Verhoest must be given no cause to doubt his terms were being complied with.

He was thin, alert and slope-shouldered, a year or so Swan's junior. His luxuriant blond hair was currently concealed beneath his hat, tilted forward against the riverside breeze. He was irritatingly good-looking and the predatory gleam in his pale-blue eyes escaped many, Swan not among them. He spoke English, French and Dutch with equal facility and gave no impression of underestimating himself. He was, in short, a man Swan instinctively disliked as well as distrusted. And Swan suspected the feeling was mutual.

'Verhoest,' Swan greeted the other off-handedly as he joined him by the railings.

'Meneer Swan.' The courtesy was undisguisedly sarcastic. 'A fine morning.' The beaming smile seemed hardly more genuine.

'Indeed. You're here to take the air?'

'Yes. Also checking that loading is on schedule.'

'I'm assured it is.'

'Excellent.'

'Tomorrow we'll be on the high seas.'

'I look forward to it. Belgium's too . . . small for me.'

'Well, I'm sure you'll find the United States . . . suitably large.'

'Yes. I'm sure I will.' Verhoest slipped a small flask out of his coat pocket and unscrewed the cap. 'Some brandy for you, Swan? To toast our voyage to the New World?'

'No, thanks. Too early for me.'

'As you please. *Prost!*' Verhoest took a sip. 'I never drank a drop till I went to the Congo, you know. But the things I saw there . . . and the fevers I caught . . .' He shrugged. 'It's served me well, though. The Congo. Better than I ever hoped.'

'What will you do in America?' Swan asked, daring the other man to proclaim some imaginative vision of a new life beyond the Atlantic.

'I'll think about it on the crossing. You?'

'I'll go on working for Mr Meridor.'

'Ah. Our . . . benefactor. Meneer Meridor. We have a lot to be grateful to him for, you and I. First-class liner tickets. United States visas. He's a generous man.'

'Very.'

'For a Jew.' Verhoest's smile vanished. 'I expect he'll go on being generous, don't you?'

It was a more or less open declaration that a feather-bedded exit from Europe would not be the last reward Verhoest expected for keeping to himself all he knew about Isaac Meridor's diamond dealings in the Congo. Blackmailers always came back for more, of course. It was in their nature. There was only one sure way to stop them.

'Tell Meneer Meridor, would you, Swan, that I have some . . . ideas for investments . . . I'd like to put to him . . . during the voyage.'

37

'I'll be sure to.' Swan smiled tightly. 'Well, I must get on. There's a good deal still to attend to. You'll have to excuse me.'

'Certainly. Until tomorrow, then.'

Swan nodded. 'Until tomorrow.'

A quarter of an hour later, Swan was sitting on a number 2 tram, rattling along the streets of Antwerp, bound for the Gare Centrale. He gazed out benevolently at the shop fronts and wandering specimens of humanity as the tram wound its way through the old town, bidding them all a private adieu. He had enjoyed his few years in Antwerp. He had no wish to leave. But the international situation – and his employer's particular need to place himself beyond Hitler's reach – left him no choice in the matter. It was time to go. Part of him wanted to head for England. This was the old country's hour of need. And he was a patriot of sorts. But another part saw following Meridor to New York as much the better bet. Life in the diamond merchant's household had been duller since the departure of his wife and daughter the previous autumn. The pair had been despatched to New York as soon as war broke out. Swan missed the daughter, Esther, in particular, and had good reason to believe she missed him. It would be a pleasure, a very distinct pleasure, to see her again. It might also be financially beneficial to his future, something he always tried to look to.

The tram reached Meir, the main shopping street, and stopped beneath the Gratte-Ciel, Antwerp's one and only skyscraper, to take on passengers – women with children, laden bags and harassed looks; men in frayed suits with pipes and rumpled copies of the *Gazet van Antwerpen*: a random sample of the city's populace, going about their business, conspiring to pretend, as best they could, that the war was not about to come to their door.

One passenger, who looked thoroughly inconspicuous in a shabby jacket and trousers, tieless dark shirt and flat cap, took the seat next to Swan and mumbled an apology for falling against him as the tram started away with a jolt.

'That's quite all right,' said Swan. He had no doubt the other man would understand English, for they had met before. He and

Smit, who was almost certainly born with some other surname, had entered into a confidential agreement which was shortly to be implemented. Their meeting that morning, though it might have appeared to be, was not a matter of chance.

'Is there anything I can do for you, meneer?' Smit asked in an undertone.

'Yes,' Swan replied.

'Tonight?'

'Yes.'

Smit nodded. 'It will be done.'

'Thank you.' Swan leant up and pressed the bell. 'Excuse me, will you? I'm getting off at the next stop.'

'*Tot ziens, meneer.*'

As Swan moved towards the door, he saw from the corner of his eye Smit slide across the seat he had just vacated. The plain brown envelope he had left behind was neatly pocketed before any other passenger could have noticed it. The deal was done.

Swan walked the rest of the way to the Gare Centrale. He never ceased to be impressed by the magnificence of the structure, standing like some Baroque cathedral at the end of Avenue de Keyser. It was where he had arrived, tired and uncertain of what lay in store for him, at the outset of his engagement as Meridor's secretary. Even in his distracted state, he had been amazed by the scale and grandeur of the station. Later, he had realized that its construction, like so much else in the city, had been financed from the riches of Belgium's vast African colony: the Congo. Meridor would not have become a wealthy man without that resource to draw upon, and Swan would not have become a wealthy man's well-rewarded employee. Above the entrance to the Zoo, next to the station, stood a statue of an African boy on a dromedary, gazing down at the comings and goings of his latter-day imperial masters. But the statue was too high for anyone to be sure of the expression on the boy's face.

The Gare Centrale itself was not Swan's destination today. He was heading for the diamond district – the complex of streets to the south and west of the station, where Isaac Meridor and his kind held tight commercial sway. Their clients tended to come and go by train and had no wish to wander the streets of Antwerp with pocketfuls of diamonds. Meridor was a founding member of the Beurs voor Diamanthandel, housed in grandiose neoclassical premises close to the station's side-entrance. Swan was not a member of any kind, of course, and stepped no further inside than the reception desk. But he was a familiar face, well known as Meridor's secretary. A message was swiftly passed to the great man up on the dealing floor. And, hardly less swiftly, he descended.

Isaac Meridor disdained the overt orthodox costume of many of his fellow Jewish diamond dealers. True, he was heavily bearded and usually dressed in black, but there was nothing otherwise to distinguish him from the rest of the city's business community. Indeed, the three-piece suits he favoured, with the usual addition of a gleaming loop of gold watch-chain, were very much the Antwerpian norm. He only wore the yarmulke on Fridays and attended synagogue more out of habit and convention than anything else.

He was a short, stout man in his mid-sixties, balding and bland-faced, but possessed of a mischievous gaze and a ready smile that were the keys to his genius as a bargainer. He was everyone's friend, blessed with an elephantine memory and an encyclopaedic knowledge of the small and lucrative world he moved in. His reputation was for fairness and reliability, an irony Swan secretly found hilarious. Meridor was in reality a ruthless manipulator of other people's credulity. His most precious gift was his opacity. No one ever saw through him. Unless he wanted them to.

'What you must understand about diamonds, Eldritch,' he had said once during Swan's first few months as his secretary, 'is that they have no value except what we in the trade can persuade people to believe they have. It is a confidence trick, you see? Like so much commerce. It is all about confidence. Which some call trust. And I call . . . opportunity.'

*

40

Meridor the confident opportunist signalled with a bob of the head for Swan to accompany him outside. They stood in the sunshine by the columned entrance to the Bourse, Meridor puffing cigar smoke into air already made smoky by the arrivals and departures of trains on the elevated tracks opposite. The noise of trains and trams and carts and cars was cacophonous. It was so hard for them to hear each other speak that they could be sure no one could conceivably *over*hear them.

'All is well at the quay, Eldritch?' Meridor asked in his thick, gravelly voice.

'Everything's loaded.'

'Good.'

'Except . . .'

'What we will bring ourselves. Yes, yes.' A flap of his cigar-hand indicated that Meridor quite understood that. 'And our friend?'

'It's arranged.'

'Also good.'

'You realize—'

'Of course. Of course.' Another flap. 'He brings it on himself. I recommend . . . an early lunch. Champagne to settle your nerves. Yes, yes. I very much recommend it. Then you can take the afternoon off. You will need to pack, of course. So, where shall we go? The Café des Arts?'

The decision apparently made, Meridor set off along the street. Swan followed. 'Sir,' he began, 'I—'

'I know what you think, Eldritch. That we are too drastic with him. But he will not let go unless I . . . remove him. You see? In business, you must know when to attack and when to retreat. Our friend is outmatched. As the Belgian army is by the German. So, I deal with the two threats very differently. But enough of that. We will enjoy our lunch and talk of other things. It will be our last lunch in this city. For many years, I fear. When we return, it will be a different place, I think. Very different. But not us, eh?' Meridor laughed throatily, as if to defy the unpredictability of the near future. 'We will be exactly the same.'

41

SIX

The Zurenborg district of Antwerp began its development as a treasure trove of exotically varied domestic architecture when Isaac Meridor was a young man. He saw the exuberant flights of fancy taking shape in brick, mortar, rooftree and gable in the triangle of land enclosed by the embankments of the railway lines leading from the south and east into the Gare Centrale and the redundant fortifications built in earlier centuries to defend the city. He saw; he admired; he envied; he coveted; and soon enough, returning from the years of toil in the Congo that were to be the foundation of his success in the diamond trade, he possessed.

The Cogels-Osy family, owners of the land and founders of the company that conceived and carried through the area's transformation, bestowed their name on the central avenue where the most extravagant and expensive properties were built. For Meridor, only an address in Avenue Cogels-Osy would fulfil his ambitions. This he eventually acquired in the form of a pair of semi-detached residences, which he converted into a single large dwelling for himself, his wife and the numerous children he expected to have, but of whom, in the end, there was only one. The houses, mirror images of each other, bore the name *Zonnestralen* – Sunbeams. This was a more or less direct statement of the architect's intent. High, wide windows filled the building with light, while cleverly located panels of rainbow-hued stained glass cast watery visions of sunrises and sunsets across the interior. When the sun shone, Zonnestralen glowed.

This, its high ceilings and deep rooms made the house ideal for the display and admiration of Meridor's art collection. While Mevrouw Meridor might fail to supply him with the quantity of offspring he had hoped for, the dealers of Paris, Brussels and London could be relied upon to satisfy his taste in modern art ad infinitum. And perhaps the fracturing of light in Zonnestralen's stained-glass images is what gave rise to his particular enthusiasm for Cubism.

The exterior of the house was Art Nouveau with a decadent edge. Wrought iron curled like vine. Balconies and window surrounds drooped like wax on half-burnt candles, as if some unseen giant had held up a magnifying glass to melt them with the concentrated power of those eponymous sunbeams. Porches and canopies hung low, like a sunbather's sleepy eyelids. The bohemianism Isaac Meridor stood a pole apart from in his soberly suited business life was waiting, in finely dressed stone, to receive him at the end of every day.

That, it was clear, was as he wanted it. By 1940, he had long been wealthy enough to buy a country estate – or two – beyond Antwerp's grimy reach. But he never showed any inclination to do so. A modest villa at Het Zoute satisfied his wife and daughter's liking for seaside air. He seldom went there himself. Zonnestralen was the only home he wanted, which only the threat of German invasion could force him to abandon.

Quite apart from its comfort and status, the location was also convenient: a short tram-ride from the diamond district, not to mention the Gare Centrale, starting point for Meridor's periodic art-buying expeditions. Eldritch Swan walked from the Café des Arts to Zurenborg that afternoon, to clear his head and aid his digestion after a long, unstinting lunch. The architectural *richesse* of the neighbourhood no longer amazed him. It was simply part of the scenery. He suspected the clean lines and soaring spaces of New York would come as something of a tonic after dwelling amongst so much ornateness, but he could happily cope with either. He was not a prey to his surroundings. They neither enchanted nor oppressed him.

Zonnestralen still possessed its two original front doors, with complementary stained-glass sunburst panels. The right-hand door, number 84, led to the family rooms, while the left, number 86, led to those Meridor used as art-hanging and entertaining space. Several archways had been knocked through the dividing wall, but a degree of separateness still prevailed. Swan entered to the left. It was, in fact, the only door he had a key to. His room was on this side of the house. And that was where he was heading, to pack his belongings for the voyage.

Meridor had returned to the Bourse after lunch. He had farewells to make. And he also had someone to do his packing for him: Jean-Jacques Nimbala, his Congolese valet, the only one of the servants who would be accompanying him to New York. The others – a cook, two maids and a chauffeur-gardener – were staying on to maintain the house. Meridor insisted – and badly wanted to believe – that he would be back as soon as the international situation had resolved itself.

Nimbala, known to his master and to Swan as J-J, was in the first-floor salon, where Meridor's pride and joy, his collection of Picassos, had hung until recently. Swan caught sight of him as he reached the landing, a tinted and fractured sight thanks to the crisscrossing shafts of multicoloured light from windows above and around him that were so characteristic of the house. He stepped into the room, which seemed even larger than ever now its walls were bare, its furniture dust-sheeted and crowded into one corner. The doors to the balcony were wedged half open, allowing soft, spring-scented air to fill the salon. The light cast angular shadows across the wall to Swan's left, where empty picture frames leant in orderly stacks. Nimbala's work, it was clear, was almost done.

He was a tall, thin, slightly stooped man of forty or so, with flecks of grey in his hair and a sadness in his eyes that was somehow part of his dignified bearing. There were a good many Congolese in Antwerp, but none Swan had come across possessed Nimbala's poise and percipience. Meridor had chosen him well. His latest task, the removal of the Picassos from their frames, had been accomplished with his customary efficiency. The paintings had been wrapped and packed in the specially partitioned trunk that stood in the middle of the room. Nimbala's long, slender fingers slid across their felt-covered edges as he rose from a crouching position by the trunk and turned to greet Swan, whose footfalls on the uncarpeted boards he could not have failed to hear.

'Meneer Swan.' He glanced down and flicked a speck of dust from his wasp-striped waistcoat. 'I did not think you would return so soon.'

'I have to pack, J-J.'

'Of course.' There had never been any question of Nimbala extending his valeting duties to Swan. He was the servant of one man only, grateful, presumably, for being plucked from a life of squalor and privation in Leopoldville, though of that gratitude there was little sign beyond his loyalty. And yet, it sometimes occurred to Swan, what greater sign could there be?

'All's well at the quay.'

Nimbala nodded. 'The master will be pleased.'

'He is. We lunched together.'

'You lunched well, I hope, sir?'

'We did, thank you.' Swan gazed at the empty walls. 'Tell me, J-J, do you think one day you'll rehang those pictures in this room?'

'Who can say, sir? The future is an unknown land.'

'True enough. But it's a nice thought, isn't it? Putting it all back as it was.'

'Indeed, sir. Very nice.' If faintly childish, Nimbala's expression, though not his tone, implied. He was a man obliged to deal in practicalities from his earliest years. Nice thoughts were an indulgence he had no time for.

'I'll see you later, J-J,' said Swan as he wandered back out of the room.

Packing would have to wait, Swan decided when he reached his room, high up in Zonnestralen's artfully windowed eaves, where an oculus with an iris of stained glass gave him a bird's-eye view of the neighbourhood. He needed a doze, not least because he suspected he might not sleep well that night. He hung up his jacket and hat, kicked off his shoes and lay down on the bed. He felt tired enough to sleep for a week.

But tired or not, his mind was active. Meridor had been franker than usual over lunch in his assessment of his prospects. 'Many of my fellow diamantaires think I am foolish to be leaving, Eldritch. They think Belgium can stay neutral. Or, at worst, that it will be like last time. A few years of turmoil, then . . . business as before. But it will not be. Hitler hates us. The Jews, I mean. We have to go. Thank God I got Esther and her mother out early. I didn't understand then that there would be danger for neutral ships. So, as my friends see it, I am being reckless as well as cowardly. You can't win.' He had laughed. 'You can only survive. The New York Diamond Dealers' Club will welcome me. There will be many . . . opportunities. There will be a future. We shall drink to that.' And Swan had drunk. But now, in the mid-afternoon silence, he wondered if he should have clung so long to Meridor's coat-tails. The Verhoest affair was a shadow he could not step out from. Maybe he should have gone back to England. Maybe—

There was a tap at the door. It opened before he could answer. 'Eldritch?' The soft voice belonged to Marie-Louise, one of the maids. She was a pretty, dark-haired girl – also firm-bodied and affectionate, as he had occasion to know.

He sat up and swung his legs to the floor as she crept into the room. She closed the door gently behind her. 'What's wrong?' he asked. Her eyes were red. It looked as if she had been crying.

'You ask what's wrong? *Mon Dieu.* You leave tomorrow.'

'I'll be back as soon as I can.'

'Will you?'

He rose and put his arm around her. 'Of course I will.' He kissed her forehead. 'Don't worry.'

'But I do. The master says we are to stay here and the bank will pay our wages. But what if the Germans come?'

'They won't.'

'The master thinks they will. That's why he's leaving. That's why *you're* leaving.'

'He pays my wages too, Marie-Louise. I have to do as he says. Just like you. At times such as these, it's best not to think too much.' It was only a pity, he reflected, that he could not follow his own advice.

'I can't help it.'

'Well, maybe I can take your mind off it.' He smiled. And, eventually, she smiled back. 'Later.'

'You are such a bad man, Eldritch.'

'I know.' He slid his hand down her back and squeezed her bottom. 'But that's what you love about me, isn't it?'

Late that night, Pieter Verhoest made an unsteady exit from his favourite restaurant, A l'Ombre de la Cathédrale, in the Marché aux Gants, and headed across the moonlit cobbles of the Grand Place, confident that a kilometre or so's walk through the old town would hone his one still unslaked appetite of the evening to a suitable pitch. He had eaten and drunk well. And he proposed to indulge himself no less fully at his favourite brothel to round off a fitting farewell to Antwerp. The years of drudgery as a junior administrator in the Congo had finally been rewarded. His tenacity in following the paper trail of Isaac Meridor's diamond-smuggling racket would bring him a handsome and regular dividend for as long as he cared to claim it. He had Meridor – along with his smug English errand-boy, Swan – at his mercy. And mercy was not his strong suit.

The Grand Place was quiet, like the city as a whole. Belgium might be neutral in the European conflict that had been under way since the previous autumn, and that conflict might so far have been singularly uneventful, but Antwerp's night life had undoubtedly been affected. The decline in shipping meant there were fewer carousing sailors on the street, for one thing. And the locals ventured out to bars and restaurants less readily. Verhoest had the square to himself.

Or so he thought. But, as he stopped and turned for a farewell look around at the Hôtel de Ville and the Brabo Fountain, smiling as he did so at the similarity, in his own estimation, between Silvius

Brabo's legendary victory over the giant Antigonius and his over Isaac Meridor, he was surprised to see two men almost at his shoulder, ambling soft-footedly across the cobbles. They were darkly clad, with caps worn low, and were clearly not merrymakers of any kind.

At almost the same moment, he heard a car pull into the square behind him. There was a squeak of rubber on stone as it braked to a halt. Instinctively, he turned towards it. Then something hard and heavy struck him at the back of the neck. He fell, hitting the ground with a thump that drove all the breath from his lungs. He groaned and rolled over, glimpsing a blurred vision of the cathedral spire before a figure blocked the view and another blow descended.

A few seconds later, the cathedral clock began to strike midnight. But Verhoest did not hear it. He lay unconscious in the boot of the car as it drove out of the Grand Place and away into the night.

A few seconds later still, the clock of the Eglise Saint-Norbert in Zurenborg also began to strike midnight. Eldritch Swan was likewise deaf to the sound, but in his case because he was in the powerfully distracting midst of an orgasm, as his ever more urgent thrustings into the gasping, bucking Marie-Louise reached a deliciously protracted climax. For the moment, Pieter Verhoest was far from his thoughts.

SEVEN

The SS *Uitlander* cast off on schedule the following morning and eased serenely away from the quay, falling in behind the pilot's launch that would lead it downstream towards the sea. It had been fully booked for weeks, but there were fewer people seeing it off than would once have been the case, perhaps because entire families were leaving, with no close relatives left behind to wave a hanky-clutching farewell. Nor had the sailing been much, if at all, advertised. It was as close to a non-event as the departure of such a large vessel could ever be. There was an impression of tail-between-the-legs about it, a hint of desperation.

Certainly many of those on board, especially the large Jewish contingent, were desperate, though they did not care to show it. Were they fleeing prematurely – or just in time? No one knew the answer. But they were fleeing nonetheless.

Isaac Meridor, muffled up in an astrakhan coat and homburg, watched the city of his birth slip slowly away behind him from the spacious vantage point of the first-class deck, puffing glumly at a cigar. Nimbala was below, preparing his cabin. Of Eldritch Swan there was no sign.

Meridor was still standing there, gazing into the middle distance, when the *Uitlander* began to round the first westward bend in the river, carrying it out of direct sight of the city. It was then that Swan made his appearance on deck, breathless from a swift ascent of the companionways. He moved to Meridor's side.

'Confirmation from the purser, sir,' he announced. 'Verhoest is a no-show.'

'On the contrary, Eldritch,' Meridor responded, 'show is all Verhoest was.' The significance of his use of the past tense was lost on neither man. 'But thank you.' He took one more puff at his cigar, then tossed the generous butt over the rail. It hit the silt-clouded water as a distant speck. Meridor studied the point of its disappearance as if it possessed some metaphorical force, then nodded in evident satisfaction. 'I'll go below now,' he murmured.

Swan went below as well, to unpack. But he was back on deck an hour or so later to take in the scenery as the ship passed Flushing and headed out into the North Sea. It was a fine, breezy day. If the weather held, they would have an easy crossing. They were due to call at Dover that afternoon and he was looking forward to seeing the White Cliffs once more.

Nimbala materialized at his shoulder as he stood by the rail, to report a summons from their mutual employer. 'The master wishes you to join him in his cabin, sir.'

'Can't it wait till lunch, J-J? We'll be meeting then anyway.'

'No, sir.' The ghost of a smile on Nimbala's lips implied to Swan that he already knew what Meridor wanted – and why it could not wait. 'I don't believe it can.'

Meridor's cabin was the finest on the ship – a luxuriously appointed stateroom with its own sundeck and views to the stern. He was seated at a large marble and gold desk of an ornateness more suited to a Bourbon monarch, sifting through a sheaf of forms that Swan recognized as diamond reports, each one complete with a listing of precise dimensions and a diagram of the stone's facets. Meridor was still in the black suit he would have worn to the Bourse. He was evidently intent on pursuing his trade even at sea.

'Sit down, Eldritch.' He waved to the vacant sphinx-armed chair on the other side of the desk. 'There's something we need to discuss before lunch.'

Swan sat down and lit a cigarette. 'I'm all yours, sir.'

Meridor smiled fleetingly at Swan's choice of words. The turn of phrase was, after all, almost literally true. He pushed the diamond reports to one side. 'Why do you think I collect art, Eldritch?'

'You enjoy it.'

'And fine art is a fine investment. Yes, yes. But there's more to it. More to my Picassos, in particular. I'm not sure I enjoy his paintings. They're too . . . raw. But I admire them. Oh yes. I appreciate them. More, I understand their . . . historical importance. I think I understood it the day I walked into the Kahnweiler Gallery in Paris and saw them on show for the first time. 1908, that would have been. More than thirty years ago. They're the art of this raw century, Eldritch. A lot of people have said such things recently. Especially since he produced *Guernica*. He's become more than an artist. He's become . . . a symbol of the times.'

'That must make your collection very valuable, sir.' Swan glanced over his shoulder at the trunk containing Meridor's Picassos, which stood in the far corner of the room.

'Yes, yes. Very valuable. Financially and . . . historically.'

The preoccupation with history was new in Swan's experience of his employer. The need to flee Belgium had clearly prompted him to take a broader view of the world. 'You must be glad to have them close by you.'

'Yes. But they cannot remain close by.'

'They can't?'

'No, Eldritch. Most certainly not. Too many neutral ships have been sunk by the Germans for me to risk taking them across the Atlantic. I have to go. I have no choice. And the rest of my collection, in the hold, I *will* risk. But not the Picassos.'

'I don't understand. They're here, with you. They *are* going.'

'No. We put them off at Dover. And I want you to get off with them.'

'*Me?*'

'Take them to London. To this man.' Meridor slid a business card across the desk. 'Geoffrey Cardale has a gallery in St James's. I trust him. He will look after the paintings until it is safe for me to

51

collect them or have them sent to me. You have a British passport, so there will be no problem for you entering the country. Cardale is expecting them. There will be no problem there either.'

If Cardale was expecting the paintings, Meridor must have made the arrangement with him some time previously. This was no snap decision. But only now, at a few short hours' notice, was Swan being told of it. His mind raced to deduce why this might be. An obvious and sickening answer presented itself. Meridor had needed his unquestioning loyalty in neutralizing the threat posed by Verhoest. The revelation that he was to be cast adrift in this fashion might have caused him to question his loyalty – as indeed he was now doing.

'I did not tell you before because I was waiting for a message from Cardale. It arrived this morning.' That sounded just a little too convenient to Swan, as Meridor seemed to sense. 'You will con- tinue in my employment on the existing terms.' He placed a small velvet bag on the table and loosened the drawstring to give Swan a glimpse of the diamonds it contained. Their colour suggested low to moderate value. But still the bagful might represent a tidy sum, on which point Meridor was the expert. 'These are worth the amount of three months' salary,' he went on. 'Take them to Levi Burg in Hatton Garden. Mention my name and he will pay you the correct price. I will cable you with further instructions when I reach New York.' He paused. They looked at each other. Then: 'Any questions?'

'As an able-bodied Englishman,' Swan said slowly, 'I might consider it my patriotic duty, finding myself in London with time on my hands, to offer my services to my country.'

Meridor steepled his fingers. 'I would appreciate warning, Eldritch. But, of course, I would understand it if you . . . took such a decision.'

Indeed, he might even be grateful. Swan could easily persuade himself to read as much into Meridor's expression. A fresh start in New York: off with the old; on with the new. Swan had been use- ful to him. But he was not indispensable. And there was Esther's fondness for him to be taken into consideration. If Meridor knew of it, as he probably did, a clean break at this stage might have commended itself to him as the safest policy all round. He certainly would not want Swan coming between his daughter and any eligible son-in-law he cared to select.

'This will give you a chance to see your parents, of course. You must give them my very best wishes.'

'I'll be sure to.'

'A holiday is how you should see this period, Eldritch.' Meridor smiled. 'A well-deserved spell of leave, shall we say?'

'Yes.' Swan returned the smile, hoping it appeared as genuine as did Meridor's. 'Let's say that.'

And so Eldritch Swan found himself back on dry land much sooner than he had expected – high and dry, as it seemed to him. He was received in Dover by grim-faced customs officials and assorted posters declaiming wartime regulations that he had no wish to become familiar with but suspected he would have to. By the time various forms had been completed in triplicate relating to his trunkload of fine art, the SS *Uitlander* had left the harbour. His last sight of it was as a parallaxed speck on the south-western horizon, viewed through the salt-grimed windows of the customs shed.

Half an hour later, he was standing on the platform of Dover Marine station, waiting with a miserably dressed and generally downcast crowd of other travellers for the next train to London. The trunk and his suitcase stood beside him on a barrow, a porter having been promised half-a-crown to load the trunk in the guard's van when the train arrived. Swan was leaning against the barrow, smoking a cigarette and trying very hard to stave off depression. He would not have refused a nip from Verhoest's brandy flask now. He had begun to realize just how much he had been looking forward to revisiting New York. Glamour, bright lights and the best of everything were not, he felt certain, to be found in wartime London.

'Mr Swan?'

The voice had carried from some distance. As Swan turned in its direction, he saw a man in a well-cut suit, trilby and brightly striped tie striding towards him along the platform, capped brogues ringing on the asphalt. He was grey-haired, with a moustache and the rugged, ruddy looks of a hard-drinking man of the world. Swan would have put his age at sixty or so and reckoned his profession as something on the dodgier fringes of finance – but for an instant suspicion that he was actually an art dealer with a gallery in St James's.

'Cardale's the name. Geoffrey Cardale.' He extended a hand as he approached. 'You *are* Eldritch Swan, aren't you?'

'Yes. I . . .' They shook. 'I wasn't expecting to be met.'

'I thought I'd drive down and spare you the anguish of transporting Meridor's pictures on whatever wreck of a train Southern Railways deign to lay on for you. Travel's generally become a nightmare since they brought in petrol rationing.' This begged the question of how Cardale had been able to drive to Dover, but it was not a question Swan had any intention of asking. 'What say we track down a porter to stow this trunk in my car and see if there's anything to overtake on the way back to London?'

Naturally, Swan raised no objection. Soon they were speeding north through the Kent countryside on an eerily empty road in Cardale's Lagonda V12, sunlight flashing on its burnished bonnet. It was a perfect spring evening. Swan's depression was beginning to lift. And it was about to vanish altogether.

'I imagine you'll be kicking your heels until you hear from Meridor,' said Cardale as he began to give the car its head. 'Unless you're planning to enlist right away.'

'Well, I . . .'

'They'll keep you waiting even if you do. There's quite a queue, so they tell me. Especially for chaps your age.'

'Is that so?'

'Yes. So you might consider helping me out at the gallery pro tem, in return for the use of the flat above, currently lying idle. My young assistant's gone off to train as a pilot in the RAF, lucky dog, leaving job and flat both vacant. Meridor evidently rates you highly, which is good enough for me. Interested?'

Swan's reply was a masterpiece of understatement. 'I think I might be, yes.'

EIGHT

Swan persuaded himself that Meridor would have wanted him to accept Cardale's offer on the grounds that it meant he could keep a close eye on his Picassos. Not literally, of course, since Cardale promptly deposited them in the bomb-proof vault of his Piccadilly bank. There had not actually been any bombing yet, but the National Gallery had evacuated its collections long since – to north Wales, so rumour had it – and as Cardale said: 'We must take good care of your employer's property for him, mustn't we?'

Unsurprisingly in the circumstances, Cardale's gallery in Ryder Street was thinly stocked. It was made clear to Swan that his commitments there would be far from onerous. 'The show must go on, old man, but don't expect any full houses.' Nor was he required to discharge any of those commitments until the following week. 'You'll need a few days to find your feet.'

The use, free of charge, of a comfortably furnished flat in St James's greatly eased the process of feet-finding, as did the large cheque Swan obtained from Mr Levi Burg of Hatton Garden in exchange for his diamonds. Burg confessed himself envious when he heard of his friend's departure for the United States. 'New York will soon be the only place where our business can flourish, Mr Swan. I would go there myself if I could obtain a visa. Isaac must know more influential people than I do. But why am I surprised? He's always been gifted in that department.'

Swan opened an account at Cardale's bank with the money and

judged he could afford to live as well as wartime conditions allowed for some time to come. The London he had returned to was not, of course, the London he remembered. Eros had left Piccadilly Circus. Barrage balloons floated in the sky. Many statues were boarded up, many buildings sandbagged. The guards at Buckingham Palace were in battledress. Policemen wore tin hats. There was hardly a taxi or a private car to be seen on the streets, rendering Cardale's ability to fill the tank of his thirsty V12 all the more mysterious. And the blackout seemed to plunge the city back in time, as Cardale warned him. 'It's more like 1740 than 1940 once night falls, old man. Beware pickpockets and footpads.'

During the week or so likely to elapse before any cable from Meridor arrived, Swan proposed to enjoy himself as best he could. Good food and fine wine were still to be had in the restaurants of the West End and a mood of desperate gaiety prevailed in Soho. He found diversion easily enough. The air-raid precautions seemed excessive to him. The war remained, in his own mind, just a rumour. He decided to test the mood of middle England and do his filial duty by visiting his parents over his first weekend back in Blighty. He fired off a letter telling them of his plan and travelled up to Leamington on Saturday.

He regretted going even before he arrived. The train was impossibly crowded, which his fellow travellers assured him was quite normal. Where taxis in London were scarce, in Leamington they were non-existent, obliging him to walk to his parents' house. He had never been there before and covered twice the actual distance thanks to a series of wrong turnings. Nor was meat rationing the only reason for the absence of a fatted calf when he reached the oversized mock-Tudor dwelling, set in half an acre of heavily treed garden, to which his father had retired after more than forty years in Africa. The move had evidently done nothing to improve his temperament. Always irascible, he had become in old age splutteringly choleric. The sight of his eldest son was as a red rag to a bull.

'I didn't fix you up with a job in Antwerp so that you could use it as an excuse to dodge the column, Eldritch. Your brother's in the Army, which is where you should be, goddammit, doing your bit for King and country. What the hell do you mean by still being in civvies? There's a war on. Hadn't you noticed?'

The storm eventually died, thanks to Swan's mother, a well-practised domestic appeaser. Swan himself was far from sure he wanted to do any appeasing. Verhoest's attempt to blackmail Meridor had led to revelations about Swan senior's activities while working for the East African Railways and Harbours Administration that sat ill with his self-righteous outpourings. A few judicious hints on the subject when the two were eventually left alone together ensured no further broadsides came Swan's way. A sullen truce prevailed, during which his father contented himself with complaints about Chamberlain's war leadership and the scandalous difficulty of hiring decent domestic staff in England compared with Tanganyika. When Swan left the following morning, his mother waved tearfully to him from the front gate, while his father scowled at him from the driveway behind her. If he had known he would never see either of them again, he might have gone back and crafted a tenderer farewell. But he did not know. How could he?

Next day was his first in the gallery. Little more was required of him than to mind the shop during Cardale's frequent absences. The knowledge of the art world he had picked up from Meridor would have been an advantage if there had been many customers to impress with it, but they were few and far between. He looked the part, according to Cardale: that was all that really mattered.

The direness of the current trading climate drove them to an early lunch at L'Escargot in Soho, where it was possible to imagine for a pleasant couple of hours that there was no war under way in the world. Cardale disclosed he was a widower who had also lost a daughter, though he had a young grandson to remember her by. 'I rattle round a too-big-by-bloody-half house in Richmond with the nipper, his nanny and a grumpy cook. It's not exactly how I imagined it would turn out.' The daughter, it emerged, had died in childbirth. The father of her child went unmentioned. He was evidently not on the scene. Swan felt genuinely sorry for Cardale, though he was aware that the second bottle of Pomerol might have contributed to the sentiment.

He also became aware, late in the proceedings, that Cardale was gently pumping him for information about Meridor's Picassos. When were they bought? Which dealer were they bought from? How much had they cost? Swan could not help. The pictures had all been acquired before his appointment as Meridor's secretary. It was Cardale's turn to be vague when Swan asked what Meridor had bought from *him*. 'Second-division Impressionists, as I recall, old man. He probably sold them all on at a healthy profit. Shrewd fellow, your boss.'

Cardale had plans for the afternoon that did not involve returning to the gallery. Swan volunteered to open up for a couple of hours solo. It promised to be an undemanding stint.

And so it was, until the arrival of a customer whose manner and appearance were not those of the average St James's gallery browser. He was a lean, sleek-haired, sallow-skinned fellow in a pale suit and two-toned shoes, with a heavy five o'clock shadow. Swan liked the look of him not at all.

'Can I help you, sir?'

The man broke off from ogling a bathtime-in-the-harem piece of Victorian kitsch and treated Swan to a hostile glare. 'Where's Cardale?' he growled.

'Out at present, sir.'

'I'll bet. Well, give him a message when he crawls back, will you? Tell him patience is on ration like everything else and he's had as much from us as he's going to get.'

'I beg your pardon?'

'You heard. Tell him.' The man levelled a stubby forefinger at Swan. 'Got that?'

'Very well. Who shall I say the message is from?'

The man smirked. 'He'll know.'

Swan felt strangely unsurprised by this turn of events. No one, in his experience, was ever as wealthy or as honourable as they cared

59

to imply. Meridor; Cardale; his own father: they all had feet of clay. But maybe his father was right about one thing. Maybe he should follow his brother's example and join the Army. War service was an escape route of sorts.

He assumed it would be the following day before he had the chance to pass on the message to Cardale and gauge his reaction to it. As it was, however, he saw Cardale much sooner than that.

He had locked up and was en route to Piccadilly, with the half-formed intention of kicking off his evening with a cocktail at the Ritz, when he saw Cardale bearing down on him along St James's Street, clutching a newspaper in his hand.

'There you are, Swan.' He was breathless and clearly agitated about something. He looked, indeed, like a man who had just received a great shock. 'I . . . I was on my way to see you.'

'I'm sorry. I thought you said you weren't coming back this afternoon.'

'I wasn't intending to. But—' He broke off and grasped Swan's elbow. 'You obviously haven't heard.' He flapped the newspaper. It was that day's *Evening Standard*, folded open at an inside page. 'Awful. Perfectly bloody awful.'

'What is?'

'This, man. Here.' Cardale stabbed at a side-column headline. 'See?' And Swan saw.

Belgian liner *Uitlander* torpedoed in mid-Atlantic
– no survivors

1976

NINE

Eldritch's idea of telling me everything I needed to know hadn't amounted to a lot by the time we reached London the following Monday. His spell as Isaac Meridor's secretary had ended with Meridor's flight from Antwerp in the face of the Nazi menace in May 1940. Eldritch had been diverted to London with the most precious part of Meridor's art collection, his Picassos, to be lodged with the dealer Geoffrey Cardale for safekeeping. As a precaution against the U-boat threat to transatlantic shipping this had proved all too prescient. The liner carrying Meridor had gone down, with the loss of everyone aboard. That had left Eldritch thanking his lucky stars and working as Cardale's assistant while he decided what to do next.

I had little doubt there was much more he could have told me about the circumstances surrounding these events, but he was a hard man to extract information from. He gave only what he wanted to give. Already, on the train ride up from Paignton, I'd begun to question the wisdom of accepting his offer. My mother, originally inclined to give him the benefit of the doubt, had reacted with dismay to my announcement that I was accompanying him to London. 'If he insists on stirring up the past, you should let him get on with it, Stephen. I don't want you getting into any trouble on his account. There's your career to consider. And London's a dangerous place these days. Only last week the IRA tried to bomb another Tube train. They killed the poor driver, you know.'

I did know. The IRA had been targeting London more and more of late. But nursemaiding Eldritch in return for a cut of the reward he stood to gain if he could prove the Brownlow Picassos had been stolen from the Meridor estate had sounded to me worth the remote risk of being blown up: at worst a waste of time, at best an exciting and lucrative proposition. More attractively still, it delayed my return to that career of mine Mum was so worried about but from which I badly needed an extended break. What can I say? I was young then, too young to let wisdom in on the act. Eldritch was leading me on. I knew that. But sooner or later he'd have to tell me the truth.

The first surprise he had for me was undeniably pleasant: the destination he named when we climbed into a taxi at Paddington station. He announced it with the relish of someone who'd waited a long time to be able to roll the sound around his tongue. 'The Ritz.'

'Are you out of your mind?' I demanded of him as the cab started away. 'Twisk's never going to pay us to stay somewhere as swanky as that.'

'Oh, but he is. In fact, I'm assuming he already has. I made it a condition of agreeing to do what his client was asking. Insist on the best when someone else is paying. It's always been a motto of mine.' He smiled. 'Besides, it's handy for the Royal Academy.'

Eldritch entered the Ritz with the air of one returning to his natural domain after a lengthy absence. As promised, Twisk had booked us in for the week, with the rooms paid for in advance. I must have had a look of incredulity plastered on my face going up in the lift, because Eldritch said to me as we stepped out, 'I didn't mention this before because I didn't want it to sway your decision.'

The quip was a sign of the change that had crept over him since that evening at the Redcliffe. He'd recovered some confidence. He'd realized it wasn't all over for him quite yet. The old fox was sniffing the breeze and wondering if his legs and lungs would support him for one last run in the open air with the sun on his back.

But the change only went so far. It was left to me to tip the porter.

I didn't dally over unpacking, but still Eldritch was back downstairs ahead of me, sitting by the entrance to the Palm Court, happily watching the smartly dressed couples and quartets arriving for tea.

'I used to dream about this hotel quite often while I was in the Portlaoise Hilton,' he said, rising to meet me. 'The tiny crustless sandwiches; the strawberries; the mirrors; the chandeliers; the champagne: the opulence.' He shook his head. 'I've missed a lot of opulence these past thirty-six years.'

'Maybe you should have kept your hands off Meridor's Picassos, then,' I said, keen to prevent his balloon of nostalgia inflating still further.

He smiled. 'That wasn't my mistake, Stephen. But it is why we're here. So, let's go and see those famous Picassos, shall we?'

The Brownlow Collection was doing healthy business at the Royal Academy. There were in fact too many visitors for proper viewing of the paintings. This didn't bother Eldritch unduly. He had no wish to peer and pose and cock his head in front of the late multimillionaire's sumptuous array of art in general. He was interested in one room only, to which we threaded our way through the goggling ruck.

There were eighteen Picassos in all: nudes twisted out of shape; portraits with dismantled features; still lifes in which nothing was still; collage-like assemblies of disparate objects; colourful explosions of form and figure. They spanned a period of about twenty-five years, from 1907 through to the early thirties. I recognized some of them from reproductions I'd seen. There could be no doubt they were a prime selection.

Eldritch went slowly round, scrutinizing each one in turn, often having to wait while someone else moved out of his way. I stood by the door after a brief circuit, wondering what exactly he was looking for. The attendant, a silver-haired, flush-faced fellow who looked to have put on a couple of stone since being measured for his uniform, was slumped in a chair next to me. He stifled a yawn at frequent intervals. Eventually, I took pity on him.

'Picasso not your thing?' I murmured.

'You said it, sir,' he replied in a gravelly undertone. 'I mean, what was he getting at? Give me Constable any day.'

'Time hangs heavy, I imagine, sitting here for hours on end.'

'Oh, they move us around a bit. And you never know. Someone might try to grab one of the pictures and leg it. Then I'd have to earn my money.'

'But it hasn't happened yet?'

'No, sir. Though we do have a young woman who comes in just about every morning as soon as we open and makes a bee-line for this room. She likes to see the pictures before there's anyone else in, so she tells me. Pleasant girl. But cracked as my coronation mug. She reckons as she's the rightful owner of this lot. Or her family are. I forget exactly. Anyhow, I wouldn't be altogether surprised if she tried to steal one.'

'Take it back, you mean. If she's telling the truth.'

'Exactly, sir. *If*. Either way, it'd be no hardship to have to rugby-tackle her.' He chuckled. 'I should be so lucky.'

It was a snap decision of mine not to tell Eldritch about the persistent young woman. He was holding things back. Most things that mattered, I strongly suspected. Now I'd been donated my own secret, to share as and when I judged appropriate. The girl had to be related to Meridor. That was obvious. Maybe, if I could engineer a meeting with her, in Eldritch's absence, I'd be able to find out more than he currently wanted me to know. Best of all, it paid him back for keeping me in the dark.

'They're Meridor's all right,' said Eldritch as we left the Picasso room. 'No question about it.'

'Are you going to tell me now how you went about stealing them?'

'There's more to learn first. Let's take a look at the catalogue.'

We each perused a copy of the catalogue in the gift shop. The official version of the Picassos' provenance was what he wanted to check. I watched him squinting at the page on the opposite side of the stack from me, flimsy old glasses perched on his nose. What we both read was that Jay Brownlow had acquired the paintings '*in the years immediately after the Second World War through dealers in Paris and Geneva*'. The dealers weren't named. It was thin stuff. We went out on to the front steps, where Eldritch delivered his verdict in a conspiratorial whisper.

'Brownlow bought the pictures from Geoffrey Cardale. I don't doubt that for a moment. These dealers in Paris and Geneva the catalogue mentions would have been intermediaries, nothing more. It was crucial Cardale's name shouldn't appear on any documents.'

'Because it was Cardale you delivered the pictures to on Meridor's behalf.'

'Exactly.'

'But surely there was plenty to prove they belonged to Meridor. Before and therefore after the war.'

'Ah, that's where Cardale was undeniably clever.'

'In what way?'

'It's a complicated story, Stephen.' He looked at his watch. 'And it's going to have to wait a little longer.'

'Why?'

'Because I'd like to call in at the Cardale Gallery before it closes. It's time to find out who minds the shop there these days.'

It looked no different from several other galleries in St James's. A couple of Rodinesque figurines and a murky oil painting of a stag being set upon by hounds occupied the window. The external paintwork was maroon, with *G. Cardale Fine Art* proclaimed in gold lettering. Eldritch glanced up at the higher floors for a recollective moment, then said, 'I suppose we should be grateful it's still here,' and led the way in.

The interior would have benefited from better lighting – or cleaner pictures. Heavy-framed Napoleonic sea battles and

Georgian hunting scenes that might once have sparkled but did so no longer dominated the display. Pop Art had made no inroads here.

As the jangling of the bell died away, a figure emerged from a room to the rear: a thick-set man of about forty, dressed in a tweed jacket, striped shirt, cravat and corduroy trousers that appeared to have been chosen for their match with the maroon frontage. He had the flushed, fleshy, floppy-haired look of a sporty public schoolboy sliding into sedentary middle age.

'Can I help you?' he asked, genially enough.

'Mr Cardale?' Eldritch countered.

'Yes. That's me.'

'But not, I'd guess, Mr G. Cardale.'

'No, no. He was my grandfather. Long gone, I'm afraid. I'm Simon Cardale.'

'Some nice stuff you have here,' I said in a sudden moment of sympathy for the fellow.

'Thanks. Looking for anything in particular?'

'We've just come from the Royal Academy,' said Eldritch, cutting off any answer I might have given. 'The Brownlow Collection. You've seen it?'

'Yes. I took a look last week. Ravishing. Quite ravishing.'

'But we can't all afford . . . Picasso.' Eldritch looked intently at him. 'Can we?'

'No.' Cardale seemed unruffled by the question. 'Indeed not.'

'Which prompted me to think of a painter I used to admire who's rather fallen out of fashion.'

'Oh yes? Who might that be?'

'Desmond Quilligan.'

It required no wishful thinking to detect a shocked response in Cardale. He winced and let out a gasp he immediately tried to camouflage with a spluttering cough. 'Quilligan, you say?'

'That's right.'

'I don't think I know the name.'

'Really? You surprise me. There was an exhibition of his work here once. That's why I called round. It seemed the obvious place to start.'

'When was this exhibition?'

'Oh, about . . . forty years ago.'

'*Forty years?*' Cardale looked relieved: the long lapse of time let him off the hook. 'That's way before my time, I'm afraid.'

'But not your grandfather's.'

'Obviously not.'

'And he's sadly no longer with us.'

'Correct.' Cardale frowned at Eldritch. 'He died twelve years ago.'

'Did you take over the gallery from him?'

'More or less. Look, what—'

'Your father never ran it, then?'

'No.' The frown tightened. 'He never did.'

'And your grandfather never mentioned the Quilligan exhibition?'

'No. Why should he? Amongst the scores of others he held in his time. Would something have made it particularly memorable?'

'I liked his work.' Eldritch smiled blandly. 'That's all.'

'Then you should have bought one of his paintings.'

'You're right. I should have done. But maybe it's still not too late.'

'Maybe not. I wish you luck in tracking one down. Meanwhile, I'd rather like to close up, gentlemen.' He forced out a smile. 'So, unless there's anything here I can interest you in . . .'

It was growing dark when we left the gallery. Eldritch stopped at the corner of the street and gazed back at it through the chill, gathering dusk.

'What are you looking at?' I asked.

'My ghost, I suppose. My former self. The man who briefly lived here thirty-six years ago.'

'Thirty-six isn't quite forty,' I pointed out. Nostalgic reveries were no use to me – or him, I sensed. 'What was this exhibition you were talking about?'

'I made that up, to see how young Cardale reacted. There was no exhibition, as far as I know.'

'So, who *is* Desmond Quilligan?'

'Yes. It's time you were told, isn't it?' He pulled his shoulders back, offsetting his habitual stoop for a moment. 'I'll explain over a drink – or two – in the Ritz bar.'

1940

TEN

It is a Saturday afternoon in June. Richmond basks in sleepy sunshine, the air thick with warmth, pollen-moted, summer-scented. Eldritch Swan, dressed in sports jacket and light trousers, a linen tie loosened at his neck, ubiquitous fedora tilted back on his head, emerges from the railway station and turns left, towards the centre of town.

The streets are quiet, the shops, those that are open, thinly patronized. Something in the busy step and preoccupied expressions of passers-by hints that all is not as tranquil as it appears. The reason is carried in the minds of every one of them. There is a war on. England is threatened by imminent invasion. Churchill has replaced Chamberlain as Prime Minister. The British Expeditionary Force has escaped from Dunkirk by the skin of its teeth. Belgium and the Netherlands have been overrun. France has surrendered. Italy has allied itself with Germany. Everywhere the news is grim.

Eldritch Swan is not immune to the national mood. He looks carefree enough, striding along, one hand in his trouser pocket, the other raising a cigarette to his lips at intervals. He has recovered from the shock of the sinking of the *Uitlander*, a minor loss, in the general reckoning, among so many major disasters, but he is genuinely worried about Marie-Louise, and the other servants at Zonnestralen, now that Antwerp is under German occupation, and pessimistic about England's chances of holding out alone. He knows he is lucky to be alive and free. But he also knows such luck is provisional. He has resolved, in his own way and time, to do his bit for the war effort. But he has no intention of giving his father the satisfaction of being informed of this. He proposes to embark on the performance of his patriotic duty with as little fanfare as possible.

He crosses into George Street and heads on towards the river. His destination is Geoffrey Cardale's house. It is the first time he has been invited there and he thinks it may be the last. Cardale, he suspects, has decided to close the gallery for the duration. Business has been so slack during the seven weeks that Swan has been working there that the decision would hardly be a surprise. It would, indeed, be more in the way of a surrender to harsh reality. As to the flat above, Swan has no wish to move out, but understands he may have to. His parting payment from Meridor is still largely untouched. Perhaps, when all is said and done, the time has come to move on. Though where to, in the present volatile state of things, he cannot hazard a guess.

Cherrygarth was a Victorian villa with an enviable location in Queen's Road, near the top of Richmond Hill. Cream-rendered, with nut-brown tiling, mullioned windows and a double-gabled front, it was set well back behind high walls and an imposingly gated and pillared entrance. The art business had done well by Geoffrey Cardale.

A squat, set-faced woman answered the door. The cook-housekeeper, Swan assumed. She had clearly been primed to expect him. 'Mr Cardale's in the garden,' she said. 'I'll take you round.'

Swan was sure he could have found his own way, but he fell in behind her as she waddled out through a trellised barrier of honeysuckle to the rear of the house.

A large shrub-bordered lawn merged at its farther reaches with an orchard, carpeted like snow with fallen blossom. At the edge of the orchard a wicker table and a couple of matching chairs had been set down. Cardale sat in one of them, dressed in baggy shades of white and a panama hat. At his feet a flaxen-haired boy of three or four kitted out in dungarees and a check shirt was engaged with his teddy bear in a game that involved crawling around the legs of the table and growling. Cardale raised a hand as Swan approached.

'Glad you could make it, old man,' he called.

'Shall I take Master Simon inside?' asked the housekeeper.

'Good idea, Mrs P. I'll see you later, squirt.' Cardale ruffled the boy's hair. 'Say hello to Mr Swan before you go.'

Master Simon scrambled up, bear held protectively behind him, and stared frowningly at Swan. 'Hello,' he said.

'Good afternoon, young man,' Swan responded.

The stare was held for a silent moment longer, then Mrs P grasped Simon by the bearless hand and led him off, back towards the house. Swan watched them cover half the lawn before turning back to Cardale.

'Does he take after his mother, sir?'

'Oh yes. I see Susan in him all the time.' Cardale waved to the vacant chair. 'Sit down.' Swan sat. 'Drink?' A jug of murky liquid and four glasses stood on the table. Cardale sloshed out half a glass for Swan. 'Barley water, I'm afraid. But we can pep it up a bit.' From behind his chair he hoisted a bottle of Plymouth gin. Sunlight sparkled in the clear liquid as he added a generous amount to Swan's barley water and some more to his own as well. 'Cheers.'

'Cheers.' Swan took a reviving gulp and gazed about him. 'Lovely place you have here, sir.'

'Not bad, is it? A haven in times of trouble. Far too big for me, of course, but it holds a lot of memories, good *and* bad.' Cardale smiled reminiscently. 'More good than bad on balance, I'm glad to say.'

They sipped their drinks. Swan lit a cigarette. A dove cooed in the eaves of the house. A bee buzzed lazily past. The summer afternoon held its trance.

'Curious why I asked you down here, old man?' Cardale asked.

Swan smiled. 'A little.'

'Well, I thought we ought to have a quiet word . . . about your plans . . . for the future.'

'I haven't looked very far ahead.'

'Taken any steps to enlist?'

'Yes. There's a chap I knew at Oxford who has a desk job at the War Office. I bumped into him the other day. He's promised to try and wangle me a junior commission on the basis of a couple of terms I did with the OTC. But it could take a while. The Army's been at sixes and sevens since Dunkirk. I might get the regular call-up before he finds anything for me. I'm not the only one he's helping out, apparently.'

'I dare say not.'

'So . . .'

'You could still do a few things for me . . . in the short term?'

'I'd be happy to. But, let's face it, sir, the gallery's—'

'Dead on its feet. I know, I know. I probably ought to bow to the inevitable and shut up shop till the war's over.'

'Probably, yes.'

A wordless minute or so slowly passed. Then Cardale said, 'Whatever happens, you can be sure normality will resume one day. It's the lesson of history. Empires rise and fall. Wars come and go. But there's always business to be done. It's what makes the world go round.'

'It's a reassuring thought.'

'It is, isn't it?' Cardale topped up their glasses with gin. Already the afternoon was beginning to blur at the edges. 'Remember that ugly customer who turned up at the gallery the day we heard about poor old Meridor?'

'Yes.' It had actually been the day after before Swan had passed on the man's threatening message. Cardale had received it with apparent equanimity, perhaps because the news of Meridor had put the issue – whatever the issue *was* – into its proper perspective. At all events, Swan had not seen the man again.

'Fact is, I owed the people he works for rather a lot of money. When Susan died, I . . . went through a rough patch. I did a few stupid things. The stupidest of all was going into partnership with a fellow who turned out to be a crook. He stole some paintings from me, leaving me seriously in debt to various clients. The worst thing about debts, of course, is that they mount if you don't pay them off, and since last autumn the art trade's been at a standstill, so my financial problems . . . rather multiplied.'

'Sorry to hear that, sir.' Swan was also puzzled as to *why* he was hearing it. Surely Cardale was not planning to ask him for a handout.

'I've been able to pay off my principal creditor, a necessity if I was to avoid grievous bodily harm, by persuading my bank to extend me a substantial loan, secured against the only asset I could offer up in the circumstances.'

'This house?'

'No, no. Mortgaged to the hilt long since, I'm afraid.'

'The gallery?'

'Leased, old man. I don't have the freehold.'

'What, then?'

Cardale took a deep swallow of gin and barley water, then set the glass carefully down on the table. 'Meridor's Picassos.'

Swan stared at him in amazement. 'The *Picassos*?'

'Yes.' Cardale smiled nervously. 'Since last year's New York retrospective, prices for his work have gone up and up. I hardly like to tell you how much Meridor's collection is worth. But it certainly got me off the hook.'

The drowsy effects of the gin had vanished completely. Swan was transfixed. 'But . . . they don't belong to you.'

'True. But the bank doesn't know that. They're deposited in my name.'

'I have your receipt for them.'

'Also true. But Meridor's widow doesn't, does she? And I suspect the original proofs of purchase went down with the *Uitlander*. Besides, I thought it probable she didn't know he put the Picassos off with you at Dover. My plan was to come to some agreement with you over the receipt in due course. To persuade you that your obligations to your employer . . . ended with his death.'

'That *was* your plan?'

'It's been overtaken by events, unfortunately. A letter's reached me from Meridor's lawyer in New York. His client apprised him of his intentions before leaving Antwerp. He wants me to confirm I have the Picassos. He's also asking if I know where you are. He considers it odd, apparently, that you haven't been in touch with Mrs Meridor to offer your condolences at her sad loss.'

Silence. The two men looked at each other. The afternoon was as somnolent and sultry as before. But they now inhabited a different place.

'Shall I tell you what I think, old man?' Cardale resumed. 'I think you've been playing your own waiting game. Waiting to see what the Meridors would do, if anything. Did they know about the Picassos? Did they know you were still alive? You've been asking yourself those questions and considering what your smartest move would be if the answers were no . . . and no.'

'Nonsense. You're judging me by your own standards.'

'I am indeed. And I don't think I'm misjudging you. Because my standards *are* your standards. Meridor wouldn't have hired you otherwise. Let's put our cards on the table. If Meridor was alive it would be a different matter. I for one would never try to defraud him. I'm sure you wouldn't either. But he isn't alive. And that presents us with an opportunity we really shouldn't miss.'

'What opportunity? Meridor's lawyer knows what he intended to do with the Picassos. You'll never get away with pretending he changed his mind. If the lawyer ever checks, which he will, he'll find a record of my leaving the ship with them at Dover.'

'Yes. He will. But when? When will he do that, Swan?'

'As soon as he can. As soon as—'

'The war ends. Exactly. That's the span of our opportunity. The duration of hostilities. They won't be coming to claim their property until it's safe to do so. Besides, I've written back to the lawyer assuring him I have the Picassos and there's nothing to worry about.'

'Then what the devil are we discussing? I really don't—'

'Listen to me, Swan.' Cardale stared him down for a second. Then: 'It's really very simple. What do Meridor's widow and daughter know about art? Nothing, I assume. It's certainly what he said to me on one occasion. "My family have no appreciation whatsoever of the paintings I collect, Cardale." His very words. Would you agree?'

'Well . . .'

'*Would you?*'

Swan shrugged. 'Yes. Mrs Meridor is a simple woman. And Esther is . . . charming but frivolous.'

'Exactly. So, neither would have been any the wiser had Meridor chosen to impress his friends and business associates in Antwerp with *fake* Picassos, would they?'

'Fake?'

'Copies. Pseudo-Picassos. Clever simulacra of the real thing.'

'You're suggesting . . .'

'We commission forgeries of the whole set and return those forgeries to the Meridors, who, with luck, will never notice the difference. It's no great matter if they do, though, because in that event we simply throw up our hands in horror and express astonishment at our late friend's duplicity. Meanwhile the real Picassos are acquired by buyers willing to pay what they're worth. In point of fact, I already have a buyer in mind who'd be happy to pay rather more than they're worth. The transaction would be handled by various discreet intermediaries to ensure it could never be traced back to us. Such arrangements can be made, take my word for it. You and I would split the proceeds fifty-fifty. I confidently predict we'd both be wealthy men.'

Swan leant across the table and lowered his voice. 'How wealthy?'

'The bank agreed a conservative valuation of three hundred and seventy-five thousand pounds. They'd fetch half a million on the open market for certain. More, if Picasso's stock continues to rise as it has recently. He's stuck in France. If we're really lucky, he'll fall foul of the Nazi authorities and get himself executed. Artists are worth much more when they're dead. So, you see, the sky's the limit.'

Swan sat back and absorbed the scale of the prize at stake. He took a last draw on his cigarette and stubbed it out, then lit another. 'Half a million pounds,' he said quietly.

'At least.'

'A quarter of a million each.'

'As I said, old man: strictly fifty-fifty.'

'What about the forger?'

'He's good, believe me. Quite good enough.'

'I meant how much will we have to pay him?'

'I'll look after his recompense.'

'Really?' Cardale was becoming altogether too reasonable. 'Why would you do that?'

'We won't be offering him money. It wouldn't do any good. He's above such things. But I have something he wants. That's my contribution. Yours is to go and fetch him.'

'Fetch him from where?'

'Ireland. His name's Desmond Quilligan. He had, presumably still has, artistic aspirations of his own. But the truth is that his talent lies in mimicry. He's a brilliant copyist, quite brilliant. I've seen him work. There's no question he can do this. Unfortunately, he fancies himself as some kind of Irish patriot. He fought in the Easter Rising when he was just a youth and he's still a member of the IRA. Currently interned by the Free State government. Apparently, de Valéra doesn't want his old chums in the movement endangering the country's neutral status.'

'If Quilligan's in prison, how—'

'Interned, not imprisoned, Swan. Important difference. He can get out any time he signs a pledge renouncing violence. That's what you have to persuade him to do. Then bring him here and we'll set him to work.'

'How the devil am I supposed to persuade him to abandon the cause if he's the dedicated Irish patriot you say he is?'

'By offering him something – possibly the only thing – he values more highly than an independent united Ireland.'

'And what might that be?'

'His son.' Cardale gazed past Swan towards the house. 'Desmond Quilligan is Simon's father.'

1976

ELEVEN

Now I knew why Eldritch had gone to Ireland in 1940: to recruit the forger whose help he and Geoffrey Cardale had needed to pull off their lucrative art fraud. Only Cardale had been able to profit from that fraud in the end, of course. Eldritch's return from Ireland had been delayed by the small matter of thirty-six years. Though as to precisely why, he was still not saying.

'I'm tired,' he complained as he polished off his second large Scotch in the Ritz bar. 'I'm not used to leading such an eventful life. I'll order some supper on room service. You can . . . enjoy the evening without me.'

Eldritch's fatigue sounded to me like an excuse for not disclosing a single fact more than he wanted to. I didn't bother to argue. It was all coming out, little by little. I just had to be patient. Meanwhile, I had a secret of my own to console me.

I considered contacting one or other of my old business friends who were based in London to suggest meeting later that evening. But I thought better of it. There'd have been too much explaining to do. So, I contented myself with dinner at an Italian restaurant in the Haymarket and a film afterwards at the cinema opposite.

It was gone eleven when I returned to the Ritz. It was raining by then and the hotel doorman was assisting some dowager into a taxi, umbrella protectively hoisted. From the other side of the street, where I stopped in surprise, it was possible to be deceived by the damp, jostling shadows of cars and passers-by. But I wasn't. I didn't have the slightest doubt that the raincoated figure climbing the steps behind the doorman and slipping quietly into the hotel was Eldritch.

It was reassuring, in one sense, to know I couldn't rely on anything he said. It made holding out on him a whole lot easier, to the point where it almost seemed like a necessary act of self-defence. I still had to make it to the Royal Academy without him knowing where I was going, or why, of course. But, in the event, my plans for doing so were never tested. I emerged from the bath next morning to find a note had been slipped under my door. *Stephen: I have to go out for a few hours. Meet me in the Red Lion, Duke of York Street, at noon. E.* Somehow, without even trying to, he'd wrongfooted me.

I felt ridiculously furtive as I entered the Royal Academy a few minutes after its doors opened for the day. The galleries were largely empty, staff heavily outnumbering paying public. I headed straight for the Picasso room. The attendant I'd spoken to the day before wasn't there. He'd been replaced by a stern-looking woman with her hair in a bun. Approachability wasn't her forte. I gave her a nod that went unreciprocated and started a slow wander round.

I was at the first corner, contemplating Picasso's ingenious re-arrangement of the physical features of a horse and rider, such that it wasn't possible to say which of them was actually in the saddle, when I heard a sigh from behind me that I knew instinctively hadn't emanated from the attendant.

I turned to see a young woman in jeans, trainers and a short light mac sitting on the buttoned-leather ottoman in the centre of the room, a satchel looped loosely over her arm. She sighed again as she gazed around at the paintings, apparently oblivious to my presence. She had long, dark, almost black hair, tied back in a ponytail, and large, dark, soulful eyes. I'd have said she was about thirty. She'd have attracted my attention even if the room had been crowded. There was something fragile as well as beautiful about her. Or perhaps the fragility *was* her beauty. Nothing in her looks was out of the ordinary. Yet that she was out of the ordinary was immediately apparent.

I walked slowly over and sat down a foot or so away from her. She cast me a fleeting glance. I sensed dismissiveness. Perhaps she thought I was some kind of art gallery pick-up merchant. I chanced my arm. 'I'm told you come here often.'

A second, less fleeting glance. 'I'm not interested,' she said, as if I'd made a sales pitch for a new brand of lipstick. Her voice was low and firm, American-accented.

'You should be.'

'For God's sake.' She grasped the strap of her satchel, stood up and made to walk away.

'You're related to Isaac Meridor, aren't you?'

That stopped her. She looked round. 'What's it to you?'

'Was he your grandfather?'

She coloured slightly. 'Yes.'

'Eldritch Swan is my uncle. Want to talk to me now?'

We had the tea-room virtually to ourselves. She'd taken off the mac by the time I got back from the counter with our coffees, revealing a collarless white shirt and a blue quilted waistcoat. Her make-up was minimal. There were no rings or bracelets. She seemed to be engaged in an attempt to look much plainer than she really was. She begged a light for a cigarette and emptied two sugar sachets into her coffee, her wide-eyed gaze fixed on me throughout.

'I'm Rachel Banner,' she announced. 'My mother married a New Yorker. I've lived in the city most of my life. I work at the UN. I'm on unpaid leave at the moment, trying to resolve a few personal problems. Most of them come back to those paintings we were just looking at. And therefore your uncle.' Her tone was candid yet challenging, pitched somewhere between confession and accusation. It was clear she didn't believe in letting herself – or anyone else – off lightly. 'What's your story?'

'Stephen Swan. Career in the oil business currently on hold while I help my uncle make up for his past transgressions.'

'Oh yeah?'

'A lawyer acting for an anonymous client has asked Eldritch to find proof that Brownlow's Picassos were stolen from your family. I've been assuming that client was your mother, their rightful owner. But something in your expression tells me that may not be the case.'

'It absolutely isn't. My mother's done her level best to forget the Picassos since her lawsuit against the Brownlow estate failed.'

'I see.'

'That's more than I do, Stephen. Where's your uncle been all these years? I reckoned he must be dead.'

'He's been in prison.'

'Honest?' She smiled. 'Well, that's something, I guess. What did he do? Murder someone?'

'I don't exactly know. But he's just got out, after thirty-six years.'

'Well, that's almost as long as he deserved to serve, for cheating my mother out of her inheritance. But, does that mean he never got any of the proceeds?'

'It does.'

'Better and better.'

'Listen, Miss Banner, I—'

'Call me Rachel.'

'OK. Rachel. You ought to know I had no idea about any of this until my uncle was released from prison. Like you, I thought he was dead. That's what my father always told me.'

'It figures. He was probably ashamed of him.'

'Yes. He probably was.'

'You should be too.'

'Would it help if I said I was?'

'No. Nothing would help. Except restitution.'

'Well, maybe if we could—'

'Do you know how much they're worth? All told, I mean. Those eighteen paintings.'

'Millions, I imagine.'

'Yeah. That's right. Millions, whether its dollars or pounds. And you're telling me your uncle is trying to *prove* he and Cardale stole them from my family? Why doesn't he just own up? Then we could

86

reclaim them and he could go back where he belongs: prison.'

'It isn't as simple as that.'

'No. It never is, is it?' For the first time since we'd started talking, she looked away, drawing exasperatedly on her cigarette.

'Eldritch was arrested long before the Picassos were copied, Rachel. Technically, he didn't steal them. Geoffrey Cardale did that all on his own.'

'I know Cardale stole them. Every member of my family knows that. And we tried to prove it as soon as we found out. We employed a small army of well-paid investigators to prove it. Without success.'

'None of them knew what Eldritch knows.'

'I can't argue with that.' She stubbed out her cigarette and faced me again. 'This . . . anonymous party . . . is offering some kind of a reward if Eldritch finds proof that will stand up in court, I suppose?'

'Yes.'

'Of course. It had to be about money. How much? No.' She raised a hand. 'Don't tell me. I really don't want to know. I don't think I could bear to. Do you know why I've come here almost every morning since I flew in? Let me tell you. So you understand. When my grandfather died, Mom and Grandma were suddenly hard up. All those paintings, those other paintings that were valuable in their own right, plus all the diamonds he was carrying, all his portable wealth, was at the bottom of the ocean. Within days, Germany invaded Belgium, cutting off access to his bank accounts. As a Jew, his savings were forfeit. There was nothing left. Except the Picassos, of course. Mom and Grandma just had to scrape by until the war ended. Then they could sell the Picassos. Well, they got them back in 1945 right enough. And they tried to sell them. Only trouble was, they turned out to be fakes. Good ones, it's true. Good enough to deceive anyone who wasn't an expert. But fakes nonetheless. Cardale said he was horrified. He had no idea. Grandma believed him. She burnt them in disgust. The whole lot. They were destroyed before I was born. I never saw them. I never saw the real ones either until recently. Now I like to take every opportunity to look at them, to sit in front of them, to imagine how life would have been if Cardale hadn't defrauded us.'

'How would it have been?'

'Different, that's for sure. Better, I can't help thinking. For starters, my mother would never have married my father. He offered her security, which she badly needed after the Picasso safety net collapsed under her and Grandma. But it wasn't worth it. He had his own business, which wasn't anything like as stable and profitable as he'd pretended. It went bust. He hit the bottle. Then he started hitting Mom. And me. And my kid brother, Joey. Mom divorced him in the end. But the end was a long time coming. Then Joey went off to Vietnam. He came through without a scratch. Not a scratch you could see, that is. But inside . . . there were plenty. He lives with Grandma now.'

'Your grandmother's still alive?'

'Yeah. She'll be ninety this year. Pretty fit, if mentally fuzzy. She went back to her old home in Antwerp after Mom got married. That's where Joey is now. He said he couldn't settle in the States after the Army had finished with him. I don't blame him. A lot of the time, I don't like it there much myself.'

'When did you realize the Picassos had been stolen from you?'

'When the Brownlow Collection went on view for the first time, at the Met three years ago. All eighteen of them together. All acquired post-war. It was too big a coincidence. Mom knew then Cardale had shafted us. She'd always assumed her father had believed the paintings to be genuine – otherwise why would he have gone to such lengths to save them? – and that he must have been cheated by the dealer who'd sold them to him in the first place. Three years ago, she realized they really had been genuine and that Cardale was the one who'd done the cheating. But he was dead by then. His grandson denied all knowledge. And the Brownlow estate stonewalled her. She spent a lot of money on lawyers and got nothing for it. Now she says she wishes she'd never found out. I guess she's right. It probably would have been better for us to have gone on in ignorance. It wasn't bliss. Take my word for it. But it beat turning over and over in your mind the things you could do and the changes you could make . . . with all those millions.'

'Maybe you should stop coming here, Rachel. It doesn't sound as if it's . . . good for you.'

'That's what my friends tell me. Forget it. Give it up. Put it behind you. Write it off. Move on. Well, I tried, but it just didn't work. So then I decided to attack the problem head on. I fixed myself up with a year off from the UN and came to Europe to check the Brownlow estate's version of how he'd acquired the Picassos. It's what our lawyers were supposed to have done, but I reckoned, if I double-checked everything, I'd find what they'd missed: the crucial connection to Cardale I needed to clinch our claim.'

'But you never found it?'

'No. The story was the same in Paris and Geneva and the other cities I moved on to, chasing leads. The dealer Brownlow had used was dead or retired or had bought the picture from another dealer who was dead or retired – or untraceable. Memories had failed. Documentation was missing. No one knew anything – or was prepared to admit it if they did. It was a maze without a centre. Eventually, I gave up. Since then, I've been staying here in London with an old college friend who works at the American Embassy, putting off as long as I can the day when I have to admit defeat and go home.'

'Well, maybe you don't have to admit defeat now.'

'Thanks to good old Uncle Eldritch and the anonymous money-bags who's signed him up?'

'Something like that.'

'Go on, then.' Her half-smile was wholly sceptical. 'Tell me he's homing in on proof positive that Cardale stole the Picassos.'

'It's early days.'

'Not for me.'

'Do you know who the forger was that Cardale used?'

'No. Do you?'

'Yes. Hiring him was as far as Eldritch got before he was arrested. His name's Desmond Quilligan.'

'Still alive?'

'I don't know. But I mean to find out. And it's something, isn't it? Something more than you've uncovered.'

She paused to put another cigarette in her mouth. I leant across the table to light it without waiting to be asked. For a second, we were so close I could feel her breath fanning my fingers. She went on looking at me, searching my face for some clue that she could trust me, which I sensed, for all her prickliness, she wanted to, very much. Then she leant back and took a long drag. She blew the smoke out slowly into the air above us. 'OK. That is something. Anyhow, it might be. And I want in on it. Naturally. Can I meet Eldritch?'

'Of course. Let me set it up with him.'

'When?'

'Tomorrow?'

'OK. Do you live in London?'

'No. We've come up from Devon.'

'Where are you staying?'

'The Ritz.' I winced as I said it. I knew Eldritch's choice of hotel would confirm all her prejudices about him. The arch of her eyebrows declared as much. But she said nothing. 'I'll need your phone number.'

She took a biro out of her satchel and wrote the number on one of the empty sugar sachets. 'You will call, won't you, Stephen?'

'It's a promise.'

'Promises have never amounted to much in my experience.'

'You must have been given them by the wrong people.'

'Yeah.' She gave a melancholy little nod. 'I guess I must.'

We parted in the courtyard at the front of the building. Rachel looked pensive, almost apprehensive. 'What's wrong?' I asked.

'Do you really not know what Eldritch served time for?'

'He won't say. He claims it was a condition of his release that he shouldn't discuss it. He went to Ireland in June 1940 to hire Quilligan and never made it back to London. That's all I can tell you.'

'How much will he be paid if he finds what we need to reclaim the Picassos?'

'You said you didn't want to know.'

'I've changed my mind.'

'Fifty thousand pounds.'

Her eyes widened. 'As much as that?'

'Someone obviously badly wants him to succeed.'

'Who?'

'I don't know.'

'Does Eldritch know?'

'I don't think so.'

'But you're not sure?'

'He's a hard man to read.'

'I'll bet he is. Tell me, Stephen, are you worried by how many sides there are to this you don't understand?'

'Do you think I should be?'

'Maybe.' She looked intently at me. 'Maybe we both should be.' Then, quite suddenly, she turned and walked smartly away across the courtyard.

'I'll call you later,' I shouted after her.

She raised a hand in acknowledgement. But she didn't stop, or even glance back at me, as she strode through the gateway into Piccadilly.

TWELVE

The Red Lion was still quiet at noon, the lunchtime crush at least half an hour away. The pub was close enough to Ryder Street for me to imagine Eldritch had been a frequent customer during his seven weeks of gallery-minding back in 1940. The cramped interior didn't look as if it had changed in a hundred years, let alone thirty-six. Catching my reflection in a mirror, which was difficult to avoid given how many of them there were, I seemed to see Eldritch's younger face, hair slicked, mouth curled, gazing ironically back at me.

Then the old man with the stoop and the furrowed skin and the antique suit that Eldritch had become walked in behind me. And only the irony remained, a ghost in his wary gaze.

He ordered his habitual Scotch and joined me by the window. 'Been having fun?' he asked, coughing as he lit one of his Sobranies.

'I took another look at the Picassos,' I said, uncertain how soon I should tell him about Rachel Banner. 'What have you been up to?'

'I went to the General Register Office. It's not called that any more and they've moved it from Somerset House. But I tracked down what I wanted in the end.'

'They've been gone from Somerset House for a few years now. I could have told you that if you'd said where you were going.'

He smiled. 'Indulge me, Stephen. There are still a few things I can do on my own. And I expect you were glad to be rid of me for a morning. Meet any nice girls at the Royal Academy?'

I must have looked at least half as shocked as I felt. 'Sorry?' I spluttered through a mouthful of beer.

'I used to find art galleries were excellent for picking up pretty girls. They tended to be of a ... sensuous disposition.' He chuckled. 'Intelligent too, of course, which could be a mixed blessing.'

'What were you looking for at Somerset House?' I asked, eager to change the subject.

'St Catherine's House. Remember? They've moved. As you could have told me.' He seemed highly amused, which I had to hope was because he thought me embarrassed rather than guilty. 'Well, I wanted to see what they had on Desmond Quilligan.'

'Was there anything?'

'Yes. I suspected he'd never have gone back to Ireland. He needed to be close to his son. And the IRA would have regarded him as a renegade for renouncing the armed struggle. So, he stayed in London. At all events he died in London. Twenty years ago, aged fifty-seven. Alcoholic poisoning. What a way to go, hey? But it does mean we have a last address for him. I suggest we have a spot of lunch here, then go and see if he's still remembered there.'

I probably should have reported my encounter with Rachel to Eldritch over lunch. But something held me back. It was inconceivable on a practical level that he'd managed to spy on me *and* burrow through old death certificates in the course of the morning, but I couldn't rid myself of the feeling that somehow he had. And it wasn't a pleasant feeling. It wasn't pleasant at all.

Desmond Quilligan's address at the time of his death in 1956 was a bay-fronted pebble-dashed semi in Dollis Hill, located halfway along a street full of bay-fronted pebble-dashed semis. The Irish patriot had bowed out in inner suburban obscurity. Eldritch rang the doorbell and, getting no immediate response, rang again. The chances that anyone would be at home in the middle of a Tuesday afternoon had never been better than fifty-fifty, of course. He squinted through the frosted oval of glass set in the door at eye-level and grunted negatively.

At that moment, a car pulled on to the farther side of the shared driveway serving the pair of garages that separated one set of semis from another. A plump, frizzy-haired woman in some kind of medical uniform clambered out, shopping bags in hand. I smiled across at her.

'Looking for Brenda Duthie?' she called.

'Has she lived here long?' I called back.

'Brenda? Goodness, yes. Since before the war, I think.'

'Then, yes, we are looking for her. Do you think she'll be back soon?'

The neighbour reckoned Brenda would be back before too long. We settled to wait. Eldritch sat on the low front wall, with his back to the privet hedge, while I walked up and down the pavement. Time inched by. The afternoon grew grey and cool. Eldritch coughed his way through a couple of cigarettes. Suddenly, I felt exhausted by the effort of holding out on him.

'I met Meridor's granddaughter at the Royal Academy this morning,' I announced, stopping in front of him.

He looked wintrily up at me. His gaze narrowed suspiciously. 'Who?'

'Meridor's granddaughter. Her name's Rachel Banner. None of her family is Twisk's client, Eldritch. She has no idea who might be. She's been trying to—'

'You told her about Twisk?'

'I told her what we're doing and why.'

He jumped up, the effort seeming to wind him so badly he had to grasp the gatepost beside him for support. He coughed raspingly, then found the breath to give me his opinion of my behaviour. 'You idiot. What in God's name did you think you were doing? You might have . . . might have endangered everything.'

'What's there to endanger? I'm trying to make progress. She gave me a lot of valuable information.'

'Not half as valuable as what you gave her in return, no doubt.

How did she just happen to be at the Royal Academy at the same time as you?'

'She goes there to look at the Picassos, to dream of how much better life would have been for her – and for her brother and her mother *and* her grandmother, Meridor's widow, who's still alive, you might be interested to know – if you and Cardale hadn't cheated them out of their inheritance.'

'You had no right to discuss my affairs with her.'

'They're my affairs too. I'm not going to lie to anyone, certainly not her, on your account.'

'You should have guarded your tongue until you'd consulted me.'

'Well, I'm consulting you now. She expects you to meet her tomorrow. I expect you to meet her too.'

'I won't be—'

'Good afternoon,' a voice cut in.

I whirled round to see a small, slightly built woman of seventy or so, dressed in raincoat and headscarf, a string-bag full of groceries in one hand, a handbag in the other, frowning at us in puzzlement. Despite the frown, a smile seemed also to be present on her face. She had chipmunk cheeks and laughter lines aplenty round her green-grey eyes. Grey hair curled out from beneath a headscarf.

'If you've something to argue about,' she continued, 'could I ask you to do it somewhere other than my front gate?'

I was on the point of apologizing, but Eldritch got in first, stepping forward and doffing his hat to her. 'Mrs Duthie?' He was all smooth gentility now and had spotted the band of gold on her ring finger much sooner than I'd have done. 'Please excuse us. It was more of a misunderstanding than an argument. My name's Swan – Eldritch Swan – and this is my nephew, Stephen Swan.' He was evidently betting Quilligan had never mentioned him to Mrs Duthie, whose expression suggested he was betting right. 'We're looking for someone I knew a long time ago. I gathered he lived here. Desmond Quilligan.'

'You knew Desmond?'

'As I say. A long time ago.'

'Were you friends?'

'Briefly. In Ireland. Before the war.'

'Well, Mr Swan, I'm sorry to say Desmond passed away. It must be twenty years he's been gone. My goodness,' – a thought had struck her, apparently a poignant one – 'how time flies.'

'Indeed.' Eldritch looked suitably solemn. 'And more and more of one's acquaintances fall by the wayside as it does so.'

'Yes. Dear, dear. That's only too true.' She sighed. 'Have you come far?'

'From Devon.'

'Come in for a cup of tea, then. It'll be nice to talk about Desmond again. Such a nice man.'

Indoors was a spotless repository of Art Deco furniture, ornaments and bric-à-brac. Brenda Duthie threaded a full auto-biography into her tea-making routine, revealing that early widowhood had prompted her to take in lodgers in the late forties, of whom Desmond Quilligan was the one to have stayed by far the longest. 'Such a charmer. And so helpful around the house. Leslie adored him.' (Leslie, her son, was now, she proudly informed us, a Woolwich Building Society branch manager.) 'But Desmond's heart was never as light as he'd lead you to believe. There was an abiding sadness in him, Mr Swan, as perhaps you know.'

'That must have come later,' said Eldritch, glancing a warning at me to let him vary his tactics as he saw fit. 'He didn't seem to have a care in the world when I knew him. Did he paint this?'

Eldritch nodded to a picture over the mantelpiece. We were in the sitting-room, where cups of tea and slices of Battenberg cake were being doled out. The picture was a large and plainly framed oil, depicting Mrs Duthie's house in precise and finely limned detail. Dollis Hill had surely never looked so beautiful, though whether this reflected the artist's fondness for the area or for the woman who'd taken him in was hard to tell.

'Oh yes,' said Mrs Duthie. 'That's one of Desmond's. The only one I have to remember him by.'

'Was his death unexpected?' I asked between sips of tea.

'To be honest, no. He, er, drank more and more, I'm afraid. He was no trouble when he was drunk. I'll say that for him. But . . .'

'It was always a weakness of his,' said Eldritch, toying with his Battenberg.

'Was it now? Well, I'm not surprised. I'd have turned him out if he'd been anyone else. The empty vodka bottles . . .' She shook her head at the recollection of the embarrassment disposing of so many bottles had obviously caused her. 'Such a shame. In the end, he used the drink as a way out.'

'A way out of what?' I asked.

'He had a son he hardly saw. I know that pained him. The boy lived with his grandfather in . . . Richmond, I think. The mother was dead. Desmond mourned her greatly, and there were other things, back in Ireland, that he dwelt on but never spoke of. Perhaps you know what they might have been, Mr Swan.'

'He'd been in the IRA as a young man,' said Eldritch. 'That could have been at the root of it.'

'Very likely,' said Mrs Duthie. 'Ireland's always loaded down its sons with tragedy.'

'Apart from the painting,' said Eldritch, 'do you have anything else of his?' This was the crux. We were there in search of clues. Brenda Duthie's reflections on the tragic course of Irish history were no help in that.

'Oh no. He had very little, to be honest. Just a wardrobe of clothes and . . . the paintings, of course. I let him use the attic as a studio. He built a staircase and installed a skylight to work by. A craftsman as well as an artist, he was. Oh, I think his travelling bag might still be up there.'

'Would it be putting you to a lot of bother if we took a look in the attic?' Eldritch asked solicitously. 'I'd like to . . . see where he worked.'

'Well, if you don't mind climbing two flights of stairs, Mr Swan . . .'

*

Eldritch did not mind, breathless though he was by the time we reached the attic. The room had been used to store unwanted odds and ends since Quilligan's death. Trunks, boxes, old suitcases, broken-backed chairs and shadeless table lamps had colonized his studio space. His easel remained, though, propped against the chimney-breast, and several cardboard boxes amongst the jumble had words in the Russian alphabet printed on them. He'd evidently drunk himself to death on the genuine article.

Eldritch panted his way across to the easel. Something had caught his eye: a small black-and-white photograph attached to the top of the vertical bar. I followed him.

The photograph was of a young fair-haired boy. Rust from the staple that held it in place had leeched over one corner. There were a few flecks of paint on it as well. The boy was smiling. He looked to be no more than three or four.

'That's his son,' said Mrs Duthie from behind us.

'I can see the resemblance,' said Eldritch. 'Did you ever meet the boy?'

'No. He never came here. And he wasn't at the funeral. Willesden Cemetery. Just about this time of year, it would have been. But colder; much colder. Now, where's that travelling bag?'

A few minutes of rooting around ended in the bag being hauled into the centre of the room. It was made of leather, frayed by age and use, with brass fastenings crisscrossed by the scratches of many journeyings. Mrs Duthie opened it up to reveal a yellowing pile of old magazines. They were editions from the Forties and Fifties of *Apollo*, the art monthly.

'I'd forgotten these were here,' she said. 'I really should get rid of them.'

'Did he paint a lot?' asked Eldritch, casting an uninterested glance at the magazines.

'When he wasn't drinking, yes. I often used to bring him a cup of tea when he was working up here. He seemed at peace when he had a brush in his hand. I remember—' She broke off, taken aback, it appeared, by the force of a particular memory. 'Good Lord. I'd forgotten that. Your name, Mr Swan.'

'What about it?'

'Well, the last time I saw him up here, a few weeks before he died, the picture he was working on . . . was of a man . . . standing by a lake, I think . . . Actually, I'm not sure about the lake. But there was certainly a swan flying past behind him. I remember Desmond asked me what I thought of it. I asked him what it was called. His paintings often had strange titles. The one in the sitting-room for instance. It's called *Low Tide*, though of course we're miles from the sea here. Anyway, that last painting was called *Three Swans*. But there was only one swan in the picture. He laughed when I pointed that out. But he never explained it. I wasn't surprised. He was never one for explaining himself, as you probably know, Mr Swan.'

'Indeed not,' said Eldritch thoughtfully. 'What happened to the painting, Mrs Duthie?'

'It went with the rest. His sister let me keep just the one.'

'His sister?'

'She took all his other paintings and personal belongings. Well, she was his next of kin. She said there was a brother as well, but I saw nothing of him except at the funeral.'

'His name was Ardal,' said Eldritch, his words coming slowly as he too sifted through his memories. 'And the sister was called Isolde. Ardal and Isolde Quilligan.'

'I believe you're right. Though she introduced herself to me by her married name, of course.'

'Do you have any way of contacting her?'

'She may have given me her address. In fact, I believe she did. In case I needed to forward post that came for Desmond after his death. Not that any did, as I recall. It'll be downstairs if you want it.'

Understandably enough, given the lapse of twenty years, Brenda Duthie had forgotten Isolde Quilligan's married name. While she laboured her way through her address book in search of it, we waited in the sitting-room.

'It could just be a coincidence,' I said. 'The title of his last painting.'

Eldritch cast me a scornful glance. 'Neither of us believes that.'

'But what does it mean?'

'Without seeing it, I can't say. He might have intended a reference to the superstition, I suppose.'

'What superstition?'

'Three swans seen flying together portend a death.'

'You're joking.'

'I'm not asking you to believe it. The question is did—'

'Here it is,' called Mrs Duthie from the hall, where the address book lived next to the telephone. 'I've found it.' She appeared in the doorway, holding the book open at the place. 'I've written *Desmond's sister* under the name. She's called Mrs Linley.'

'Linley?' Eldritch was left open-mouthed with surprise. 'That can't be right.'

'Oh, but it is, Mr Swan,' Mrs Duthie assured him. 'I remember now. Isolde Linley. She lives in Hampshire. Well, she did twenty y—'

'Did you meet her husband?'

'I don't think so.' Mrs Duthie pondered for a moment. 'No. I didn't. He wasn't at the funeral. And she came here on her own.'

'Do you know him, Eldritch?' I asked, though it was as plain as day to me that he did – and that the revelation of his marriage to Desmond Quilligan's sister was mightily disturbing.

'Oh yes,' said Eldritch, in what was barely more than a murmur. 'I know him.'

1940

THIRTEEN

Sunlight streams through the barred windows of the visiting hut at the Curragh internment camp, striping the bare, planked interior with shadows. Eldritch Swan sits on one side of a long table, topped with a wire-mesh barrier, that divides the room. His legs are crossed and he is tapping his knee with his forefinger to distract himself from his powerful desire for a cigarette. The warder who admitted him seemed to take some pleasure in telling him smoking was prohibited. It is Swan's impression that more or less everything is prohibited in this grim complex of tin-roofed wooden huts. He is drawn to contemplate, as he waits, the sheer horror of confinement in such a place. He could not bear it. He feels sure of that. It would crush him.

A door opens at the end of the room on the other side of the table. Swan sees a man enter, followed by a warder. The man is tall and broadly built, though clearly emaciated. There is not a spare ounce of flesh on him. As a result, his big-boned jaw is even more prominent than it might otherwise be and his eyes are set deep in their sockets. He has crew-cut fair hair, a deep scar across one cheek and a notch in one ear. He is wearing a buttonless green shirt and coarse-fibred trousers. His boots, Swan observes, are laced with string. But from his posture alone it is apparent that he is not crushed. He is in prison. But he is not in despair.

The warder closes the door behind him. 'You can sit down, Quilligan,' he says. 'One touch on the wire and we'll have you out of here and into solitary for a fortnight. Is that clear enough for you?'

Quilligan nods and sits down in the chair opposite Swan. Quite suddenly, the sunlight is extinguished by a cloud neither of them can see. The shadows dissolve.

'I beg your pardon,' said Quilligan, noticing Swan's nose twitch. 'They only allow us one shower a week. And we're in the middle of the week.'

'What did you do to end up here?' Swan asked, for want of any subtler opening gambit.

'I stayed true to my principles, Mr Swan. That's quite enough to put you behind bars in a country with a traitor for Taoiseach.'

'I know nothing about Irish politics.'

'That's the privilege of your race. I sometimes wish I knew nothing of them either.'

'Well, why don't you put them behind you, then?'

'How would I do that?'

'I'm here to discuss your son.'

'You're Cardale's errand-boy. Do I have that right?'

'I'm authorized to speak on his behalf.'

Quilligan smiled. 'I have it right, then.'

'Mr Cardale tells me you're a gifted artist.'

'That depends on your point of view. The last spell I did in solitary was for being found in possession of a charcoal portrait of Gerry Boland, our revered Minister of Justice. They didn't think it was sufficiently flattering. But, like I told them, an artist must remain true to his calling.'

'Mr Cardale wants you to lay down the rifle and take up the brush, Mr Quilligan. He wants you to follow the path of peace.'

'And he'll meet me on it, will he?'

'Wouldn't you like to see your son?'

Quilligan's right arm shot out. The warder started forward. Quilligan froze, his fist clenched. Then he bowed his head and lowered his arm. 'Watch yourself,' said the warder, stepping back, his key-chain jangling to rest.

'I don't know what Cardale's told you about me, Mr Swan,' Quilligan said quietly. 'I'll do you the favour of supposing he's misled you. It'd be unlike him not to. There was a time when I thought I could put the cares of my homeland behind me and make a name for myself in the world as a painter. I went to London. I impressed a few people. I tasted a modicum of success. It was sweet, but cloying. Then I met Susan Cardale. That such a man should have such a daughter is a mystery beyond my fathoming. She was altogether lovely. I adored her. And, wonder of wonders, she adored me. I would have died for her. That she should die for me – for our child – is a grief that will never heal. Cardale, to do him the small amount of justice he's owed, must mourn her as well, I know. But to use some weaselly lawyer to steal my son from me, to have me branded in an English court as such an unfit father on account of my patriotism – my *Irish* patriotism – that I wasn't to be permitted any contact with him . . .' He sat back in the chair and stared hard though the wire at Swan. 'I'll never forgive him.'

'Never's a long time.'

'A day's a long time in here.'

'Leave, then. See your son.'

'Cardale will allow me to do that?'

'Yes.'

'Why? What's softened his flinty heart?'

'Perhaps he thinks Simon, as he grows older, should know his father.'

'And perhaps you think I'm a credulous idiot.'

'He'll allow you to see Simon as often and for as long as you like. All you have to do in return is go to London and . . . paint a few pictures for him.'

'A few pictures?' Quilligan chuckled mirthlessly. 'I suppose you know what that means better than I do.'

'I'm just delivering a message.'

'He must be sorely pressed to resort to this.'

'I couldn't say.'

'Oh, I think you could. If you wanted to.'

'I have a document with me signed by Cardale. It commits him to waiving the order he obtained against you after his daughter's death. Would you like to see it?'

'My friend here would intervene before I had a chance to read it, Mr Swan. Keep it in your pocket.'

'Would you be allowed to look at a photograph?'

'What's the subject?'

'Simon. Taken recently.'

Quilligan seemed suddenly close to tears. He raised his hand to his face and took a deep breath, then turned towards the warder. 'Mr Swan has a snapshot of my son, Mr Grogan. I know you're a father yourself. May I take a look at it?'

Grogan walked over to a position behind Quilligan and nodded to Swan. 'You can go ahead and show him, sir.'

Swan took out his wallet and removed the photograph. He laid it on the table close to the wire. Quilligan leant forward and stared long and hard at it.

'Put it away now, sir,' said Grogan when half a minute or so had passed. 'Or you'll be upsetting him.'

Swan replaced the photograph in his wallet and put it back in his pocket. Grogan retreated to the door.

'Thank you,' murmured Quilligan.

'Why did you come back to Ireland, Mr Quilligan?' Swan asked.

'Susan was dead. I wasn't allowed to see Simon. I was no use to anyone in London, least of all myself. Here I could . . . serve the cause.'

'The cause hasn't served you very well in return, as far as I can see.'

'But, as you said yourself, you know nothing of Irish politics.'

'Mr Cardale's making you a generous offer.'

'I doubt that.'

'Doubt away. It's still the best offer you're going to get.'

'He expects me to renounce everything I've believed in and fought for since 1916.'

'He's not interested in the undertakings you need to give to extricate yourself from this place. Only in . . . what follows.'

'Time's nearly up,' said Grogan.

'What's it to be, Mr Quilligan?'

Quilligan sighed heavily. 'Take your document to my brother Ardal. He's a solicitor in Dublin. He has an office in Parnell Square. If I hear from him that it's legally watertight, I'll sign myself out of here and go to London with you. Is that good enough for you?'

It was more than good enough for Swan. He left the camp heartily relieved that he had done what was required of him and, with any luck, would never have to return there. The three-mile walk into the nearest town provided him with a badly needed breath of fresh air. Even a long wait at the station for a train to Dublin, and the agonizing slowness of the train when it eventually arrived, did not dent his spirits. All he had to do now was have Ardal Quilligan vet the document drawn up by Cardale's solicitor, which he was confident would bear any amount of scrutiny, then sit back and wait for Desmond Quilligan to arrange his release.

So far, Swan's journey to Ireland had been arduous and disagreeable. The so-called express from Euston to Holyhead had taken thirteen hours, most of them at night, with the windows blacked out. The ferry to Dun Laoghaire had been appallingly overcrowded even before seasickness had added its horrors to the voyage. And visiting the Curragh was an experience he would gladly have spared himself. But happier days lay ahead. He had booked himself into the Shelbourne, Dublin's finest hotel, and was looking forward to living without the blackout, food rationing and the nerve-nibbling threat of aerial bombardment as a prelude to full-scale invasion. The longer it took the authorities to acknowledge Quilligan's renunciation of the armed struggle and set him free, the longer Swan could enjoy the material advantages of neutrality – at Cardale's expense.

The train reached Kingsbridge station in Dublin late that muggy afternoon. Swan knew better than to hope for a taxi. There was petrol rationing in Ireland as in England. The buses were as jampacked as their London equivalents. He was minded to walk to the

Shelbourne, with a soothing bath and a fine dinner in prospect to reward him for the effort.

But his walk never took him further than the station exit, where a pair of burly, brown-suited men with narrow gazes and unyielding expressions closed in on him. One flourished a warrant card.

'Eldritch Swan?'

'Yes. What—'

'Garda Síochána Special Branch. We'd like you to come with us, please.'

'What the devil for?'

'Because you're under arrest, Mr Swan,' the other man growled. 'And if you want to reach the Castle with your skull intact, I suggest you quit blustering and do exactly what we say. There's a car waiting. Let's go, shall we?'

Thus was it fated that Eldritch Swan should spend his first night on Irish soil not between the crisply pressed linen sheets of the Shelbourne Hotel but in the dingy confines of Dublin Castle. He had told Quilligan he knew nothing of Irish politics, but he knew enough of Irish history to be well aware that his destination had been the bastion of British colonial rule until 1922. The police car that sped him along the Liffey quays and in through an arched gateway to the Castle's lower courtyard was taking him to a place riddled with bad memories and old grudges. It was odds on that one or other of the policemen he met there would relish the chance to give an arrogant Brit a taste of his own medicine. Standing on his rights, whatever they were in Irish law, was therefore unwise. He had been an unwilling visitor to police stations before, but such experiences, he suspected, would aid him little in the minefield of national sensibilities he was now entering.

Two uniformed constables marched him into a flagstoned basement room, furnished with a table and three chairs. He was deposited in one of them. The constables' glowering expressions deterred him from saying a word. The two Special Branch officers entered the room a few minutes later at a conspicuous saunter, smoking cigarettes. The shorter of the two pulled the vacant chairs into position on the opposite side of the table from Swan and sat down.

He was a lumpy-faced fellow with small eyes, yellow buck-teeth and a crooked grin. His colleague, a smarter dressed, handsomer man altogether, chisel-jawed and unsmiling, leant on the back of the other chair and looked levelly at Swan.

'Empty your pockets,' he said, with calm insistence.

Swan obeyed. Pen, handkerchief, cigarette case, wallet, passport and the envelope containing Cardale's document ended up on the table in front of him.

'I'm Inspector Moynihan, Mr Swan; Special Branch. This is Sergeant MacSweeney.'

'Grand evening for a chat, Mr Swan,' said MacSweeney, whose grin threatened to become a permanent feature.

'Can I ask what this is about?' Swan ventured.

Pointedly ignoring the question, Moynihan picked up his passport and flicked through its pages, pausing at the one bearing the most recent stamps. 'I see you entered the United Kingdom on the first of May. Where had you travelled from?'

'Antwerp.'

'I mean where did your journey begin?'

'Antwerp.'

'Sure about that, sir?' put in MacSweeney.

'Yes.'

'It wouldn't have been Germany, then?'

'No, it wouldn't.'

'Do you know who Sean Russell is, Mr Swan?' Moynihan asked.

'No.' MacSweeney sniggered at that.

'Chief of Staff of the IRA. Currently to be found comfortably accommodated in Berlin, discussing who knows what with the Führer. Something endangering this country's neutral status, perhaps. Coincidentally, he entered Germany just around the time you left . . . Antwerp.'

'This is ridiculous,' said Swan, reminding himself not to raise his voice. 'I know nothing about the IRA.'

'But you've just been to visit one of their trusted foot soldiers in the Curragh: Desmond Quilligan. We picked him up after the Magazine Fort raid last December. A ruthless man. A stick-at-nought character if ever I met one. What did you want with him?'

'Quilligan fathered a son while he was in England a few years ago. The mother died in childbirth. Her father secured custody of the boy and took out an order banning Quilligan from contact with him. Recently, the old man's softened his attitude. He sent me here to persuade Quilligan to leave the IRA, come back with me to London and help raise his son.'

'Do you seriously expect us to believe that?'

'It's the truth.' Swan opened the envelope and held out the document for them to see. 'Look.'

Moynihan craned forward and looked. He read for a moment, then nodded. 'What do you think, MacSweeney?'

'I think it's the biggest load of shite I ever heard, sir.'

'I'm inclined to agree. You can put your document away, Mr Swan.'

'But—'

Moynihan cut him off with a slap of his palm on the table top. 'Let's be clear. We want to know why you went to see Quilligan, what you were doing before you left Antwerp, whose orders you're following and what those orders require you to do next. We don't want fairy tales about love children in London and doting grand-fathers with hearts melting like butter left in the sun. Do you understand?'

'I'm telling you the truth.'

'We're not stupid, Mr Swan. It'd be a grievous mistake on your part to think we are.'

'I'm a British citizen. I demand you notify the embassy of my detention and the charge I'm being held on.'

Moynihan sighed and sat down. He gazed almost pityingly across at Swan. 'Your government doesn't have an embassy here, merely a humble legation. Pretending you don't know that is a nice touch, I must say. As for charges, under the Emergency Powers Act we can hold you indefinitely without charge. Indefinitely means as long as we like: as long as it takes for you to start telling us what we need to know. So, why delay? Why force us to resort to unpleasant methods of persuasion? You look like a reasonable man. Save yourself a lot of trouble. Believe me, you'd do well to.'

'This is outrageous.'

'No. This is good advice. Give us what we want.'

'I've told you everything.'

'Not yet. But you will.'

'That's a promise,' said MacSweeney.

FOURTEEN

When he woke and saw that it was light beyond the small, high, barred window of his cell, Swan felt faintly surprised he had slept so soundly. He should by rights have tossed and turned on the thin palliasse that was all he had been supplied with in the way of bedding. Certainly there was plenty for him to worry about. So far, no one had laid a hand on him, but Sergeant MacSweeney was clearly itching to try fists instead of mere threats of violence to extract the information they believed Swan possessed.

He would have revealed the true nature of Cardale's interest in Quilligan if he had thought it would do him any good. But there was no persuading MacSweeney or his impassive superior, Inspector Moynihan, that he was anything other than some kind of intermediary between German military intelligence and the IRA. His interrogation had lasted many hours, though exactly how many he could not have said. Nor could he recall any details of the interrogation beyond a repetitious exchange of accusation and denial. He suspected the fact that he was British had won him a few reluctant favours, but his pleas for them to ask Cardale to corroborate his story had fallen on deaf ears. And he was far from confident that the warder at the Curragh who had sat in on his visit to Quilligan would support his account of their discussion. All in all, his situation was grim and likely to become grimmer yet. But beyond cursing his folly and misfortune, there did not seem to be anything he could do about it.

An exchange he had had with Moynihan at some late stage in his questioning lingered sourly in Swan's memory. 'Are you sure this act you quoted applies to foreigners, Inspector?' he had asked.

'Oh yes, Mr Swan, I'm sure,' Moynihan has replied. 'While the emergency lasts, by which I mean the war, we can do pretty much what we like. As we will, with you, tomorrow.'

Swan doubted the literal truth of that. At some point, they would realize he was not what they thought and let him go. The problem was how many teeth he had to lose in the process, how many ribs he had to have broken. They had let him sleep on the knowledge that his interrogation, when it resumed, would take a harsher turn. He looked at the red bite marks on his arms that suggested he had shared his bed with at least one flea and pondered the likelihood that he would leave Dublin Castle with much worse wounds to remember it by.

His watch having been taken from him, he had only the haziest idea of what time it was. Eventually, a constable delivered his breakfast: stale bread and stewed tea. Swan asked him the time and was rewarded with an unhelpful answer the constable appeared to consider the height of wit. 'Don't worry about it, sir. We'll organize all your appointments for the day.'

Swan fell to wondering how Moynihan and MacSweeney would be breakfasting, while he sat on his bed, soaking the bread in the tea until it was soft enough to chew. Moynihan he imagined in some well-to-do house in the suburbs, adoring wife and rosy-cheeked children gathered round him at the table while he sipped fresh coffee, smoked a cigarette and checked the letters page in the *Irish Times* for expressions of dissident sentiment. MacSweeney, by contrast, he saw in a cramped tenement, forking down a fry-up prepared by a slattern to whom he might or might not be married.

At length, the witty constable returned with a colleague. They escorted Swan down the long, dimly lit corridor that led back to the room where he had been questioned the night before. He braced himself as best he could for the rigours of what lay ahead.

He was still doing so when they walked straight past the room and headed upstairs. Swan glimpsed sunlit cobbles in the courtyard beyond unbarred windows. They reached an office noisily full of other constables, where a uniformed sergeant presented him with a tray bearing his confiscated belongings and asked him to sign a receipt for them.

'What's going on?' Swan belatedly asked.

'You're free to go, sir,' the sergeant replied. 'Have you got everything you came with?'

'It looks like it.'

'Then we needn't detain you a moment longer.'

'Where's Moynihan? And MacSweeney?'

'The comings and goings of Special Branch aren't vouchsafed to the likes of me, sir. Do you want to leave a message for them?'

Swan made no reply as he loaded his pockets. The turn of events had left him lost for words.

'I thought not,' said the sergeant.

Swan walked out into the courtyard and sniffed the sweet morning air. Sheer incredulity allowed little room for relief. He was guided by an instinct to quit the Castle before they changed their minds about releasing him. Tie looped unfastened around his neck, shoelaces bunched in his hand, he headed for the gate he had been driven in through the previous afternoon.

As Swan strode across the yard, a man emerged from the deep shadow cast by the battlemented tower next to the Castle chapel and called out: 'Hold up.' Swan stopped and turned to look at him. He was short and dapperly dressed, with a distinctive cock-of-the-walk strut to him that stirred a memory.

The memory became disbelieving recognition when the man took off his hat to show his face – smooth-cheeked and rounded beneath slicked dark hair, a sardonic smile dancing around the lips.

'Linley? Miles Linley?'

'The very same.' They advanced to meet each other. 'I've been waiting for you.'

114

'You're a sight for sore eyes and no mistake,' said Swan as they shook hands. 'I can hardly believe it.'

'Nor me. A real turn-up for the books, eh, Cygnet?'

Cygnet was a nickname Linley had conferred on Swan at Ardingly, where Swan had fagged for the debonair young man Miles Bosworth Linley already was at seventeen and seemed still to be eighteen years later. 'What are you doing here?'

'Coming to your rescue. I'm with the British Legation. Anglo-Irish trade links are supposed to be my province, but when Special Branch contacted us this morning for info on a suspicious globe-trotting Brit who'd been out to the Curragh to visit one of the IRA hard men they have penned there, and his name happened to be the same as my uniquely monikered fag of times gone by, Eldritch Swan, I naturally took an interest. Luckily for you.' Linley grinned. 'Consider this an overdue reward for cleaning my rugger boots so assiduously all those years ago.'

'How did you persuade them to let me go?'

'By vouching for you, you clot. By assuring Moynihan's boss, who enjoys a regular round of golf with *my* boss, that your explanation for visiting Quilligan, quixotically implausible as it may have seemed, was entirely consonant with your character and that a less likely German spy than you would be hard to find. Friends in high places, Cygnet. They're invaluable, even when you don't know you've got them.'

'Good Lord, Linley, I can't thank you enough.' Swan shook the other man's hand a second time to make his point. 'I thought things were going to take an ugly turn today, let me tell you.'

'Rough stuff, you mean? I expect they held off until they could establish what we knew about you. Which was nothing, of course. Except that you're not working for the Germans.' Linley's face took on a look of mock solemnity. 'You aren't, are you?' Before Swan could reply, he went on: 'Just joking. You look pretty bloody awful, I have to say. I take it the accommodation here is seriously sub-par. Did you book into a hotel before all this blew up?'

'The Shelbourne.'

'Excellent choice. And it's only a short walk from here. What say you soak in the bath there and spruce yourself up, then meet me for lunch? Jammet's, in Nassau Street, at one. A little *cuisine française* at the legation's expense to help you forget your disagreeable tangle with the forces of law and disorder. We can chat about old times and you can tell me what you're really up to in Dublin.'

Linley was right: it was only a short walk through the shopping streets of central Dublin to the Shelbourne Hotel. But geography was no measure of transition in this case. From the forbidding purlieus of the Castle, Swan passed at once into a different realm. The shop windows of Grafton Street were filled with all the luxuries he had learnt to forgo in London. No barrage balloons floated overhead. And St Stephen's Green, which the hotel over-looked, was a riot of colourful flower-beds: no vegetable plots despoiled the parks of Dublin. He was in a place apart, where there might be an emergency, but there was still no war.

The comforts of the Shelbourne rapidly restored his equilibrium. He had always been able to rely on his own resilience. It was, he knew from long experience, one of his more abiding characteristics. Two hours after his hangdog arrival, he exited into the warm lunchtime air at a self-confident amble, in a clean shirt and pressed suit, bathed, buffed and shaved, revived and ready to face the world.

Linley was already waiting for him at a prime window table when Swan reached Jammet's. A bottle of champagne was on ice to celebrate their reunion. There had been many worse seniors to fag for at Ardingly than Miles Linley, several out-and-out sadists among them. Thus Swan was not just enormously grateful for being rescued from the clutches of Special Branch, he was also delighted to have discovered an Englishman in Dublin he could happily spend a few evenings (not to mention lunchtimes) with during his stay in the city.

The champagne and starters were seen off during an exchange of summarized autobiographies covering their adult years. There were

Oxford experiences to compare, though Swan was careful to say nothing about how his university career had ended. After that, their life stories diverged. The Diplomatic Service seemed, when Swan came to think about it, an obvious avenue for Linley to follow, with his natural charm, easy manner, cosmopolitan air and undertow of cynicism. Swan did his best to make his own tale of wandering from one unorthodox but well-paid job to another sound like the pursuit of a true vocation, though whether Linley was convinced was an open question.

'Cardale's a generous employer,' Swan explained as their roast mallard main courses arrived and a toothsome Saint-Émilion was opened. 'So, I didn't quibble when he asked me to make overtures to Quilligan on his behalf. An all-expenses trip to Dublin sounded like a welcome break from London, to be honest; more of a holiday than anything else.'

'A lot of people think that,' said Linley as he nodded to the sommelier in approval of the wine. 'And with good reason. Éire's must be the only tourist association in Europe that's still in business. We get a good few journalists over from Britain to research pieces condemning the Irish for staying neutral, but I notice they never fail to fill their boots while they're here. The GNR's had to lay on extra trains from Belfast to cope with the shoppers. Make sure you take a few pairs of silk stockings back with you, by the way. They'll win you a lot of favours with the ladies. I suppose I should be glad to be here myself.'

'Aren't you?'

'Not exactly. It's unreal, isn't it? A make-believe refuge from the war. It'll come to their doorsteps soon enough if we can't hold Herr Hitler at bay for them. Meanwhile, we dips have to watch our step. And we advise visitors from the mainland to do the same. I have to say, Cygnet, it was naïve of you to think you could just stroll into the Curragh for a chinwag with Quilligan without attracting some unwelcome attention. De Valéra's scared stiff the IRA will try to attack the North using weapons and expertise supplied by Germany. It's a fair bet that's why their chief of staff has gone to Berlin. So, Dev has to do everything he can to keep the lid on them. Hence internment for the duration. And hence Special Branch keeping a careful eye on any contact they have with the outside world.'

'But you've been able to persuade them my visit was entirely innocent?'

'I've been able to persuade them to give you the benefit of the doubt. But Moynihan won't have liked being told to release you. He'll probably be monitoring your movements from now on. I certainly wouldn't recommend calling in at the German Legation for tea and cakes.'

'It's not at the top of my list.'

'Glad to hear it. What is?'

'Well, I have to see Quilligan's brother. He's a solicitor. I need him to agree that the document Cardale's solicitor drew up is legally watertight. After that, it's just a question of waiting for Quilligan to sign himself out of the Curragh.'

'Then you take him back to London?'

'Post-haste.'

'Excellent. Better still, it's a perfect match with the argument in your favour I put to Superintendent Hegarty. An IRA member willing to give up the struggle, especially one with Quilligan's reputation, is a moral victory for the government. It might encourage others to follow his example. They should actually welcome your intervention.'

'What is his reputation?'

'As bloodthirsty as most of his kind. But he's a survivor of the Easter Rising, which gives him the status of a folk hero. And they tell me he's a gifted artist into the bargain. He's supposed to have sacrificed a promising career with palette and brush in England to resume the quest for Irish unity. I take it the death of Cardale's daughter might have had something to do with that decision?'

'You take it correctly.'

'Thought as much.' Linley paused to savour a succulent forkful of mallard.

'The Irish authorities will be pleased to see the back of Desmond Quilligan. You'll be doing them a favour.'

'Not as big as the one you've done me.'

'Not at all. Easing pressure points in Anglo-Irish relations is my job. But . . . one good turn does deserve another, doesn't it?'

'Absolutely. If there's anything I can do . . .'

'There might be, Cygnet, yes. There very well might be.' Linley took a sip of wine and beamed at Swan. 'I'll let you know.'

1976

FIFTEEN

The morning was cold but dry. Eldritch and I sat muffled up on one of the benches lining the main avenue across Green Park, Eldritch coughing and puffing his way through a succession of Sobranies while I made a show of reading a newspaper. He hadn't forgiven me for alerting Rachel Banner to his existence and promising her she could meet him, but, as he'd tartly informed me over breakfast, he wasn't about to let me mismanage a second encounter with her. Accordingly, he was waiting for her in the park along with me. We were where I'd told her we'd be at the time I'd told her we'd be there. But, as yet, she wasn't.

'I see Smith's rejected the latest deal,' I said, in a feeble effort at distraction.

'Who?' growled Eldritch.

'Ian Smith. The Rhodesian Prime Minister. I'd have thought you'd take a keen interest in African affairs, since you were born there.'

'I was born in the past. You won't find that in a world atlas.'

'Still, I expect you'd go along with Smith. Keep the blacks in their place. That sort of thing.'

He cast me a wary glance. 'Are you trying to provoke me, boy?'

'I told you not to call me boy.'

'No. It was "son" you objected to.'

'Well, you can—'

'*Excuse the interruption.*'

I recognized Rachel's voice at once. I looked round and saw her standing behind us on the grass, a few yards away. She was dressed as she'd been the day before. She looked cold, her face pale, her shoulders hunched. I heard Eldritch let out a sigh. Then he stood up and turned to face her.

'Miss Banner,' he said simply, discarding his cigarette and grinding out the butt. 'I'm Eldritch Swan.'

'I know who you are.' She stared at him for a moment, then smiled at me. 'Hi, Stephen.'

'Hello, Rachel,' I said. 'Come and sit down.'

She took a few steps towards us. But that was all. 'You ruined my mother's life, Mr Swan,' she declared flatly.

'I ruined my own in the process,' Eldritch responded. 'If that's any consolation.'

'It's some. But not a whole lot. You knew Mom when she was a young woman. She liked you. She told me so. She thought you liked her. Did you?'

'Yes.'

'But still you tried to cheat her. How does that work? Please tell me. I'd really like to know.'

'You know how it works. There's no mystery. I saw a chance of making myself rich. I took it.'

'And to hell with the consequences for my mother?'

'I'm afraid I put her out of my mind.'

'Has Stephen told you what happened to her?'

'Yes. I'm sorry, Miss Banner. Truly I am. But if there's one piece of advice I can give you, it's—'

'Advice? From you? I don't believe it.'

'You don't have to. You don't even have to hear it if you don't want to.'

'No. Go on. This should be . . . memorable.'

'Look,' I said, fearful that Eldritch had resolved to sabotage the meeting before it had properly begun, 'why don't we—'

'No, Stephen,' said Rachel. 'Let him give me his advice.' She was breathing heavily. 'I can hardly wait.'

'It's simple enough,' said Eldritch. 'Blaming your mistakes and misfortunes on other people is as futile as it's fallacious. I cheated your mother, yes. More correctly, I enabled someone else to cheat her. But as for all the things that went wrong later in her life, and in yours and your brother's, loading responsibility for them on to me is . . . unworthy of the sort of woman Stephen tells me you are.'

Rachel stepped closer still and looked Eldritch in the eye. 'You have a fucking nerve.'

'You know what I've said is true. Whether you admit it or not is up to you.'

'I'm sorry, Stephen,' – she looked round at me – 'I don't think this is going to work.'

For the moment, I couldn't help agreeing with her. I stood up. 'For God's sake, Eldritch, show a bit of humility.'

'Not something I've ever been good at, I'm afraid, Stephen. I thought it might come with age, but—'

'You both be sure to have a nice day,' cut in Rachel. With that she swung on her heel and started to walk away.

'Hold on,' I said, running after her.

I was nearly at her shoulder when Eldritch shouted, '*Miss Banner.*'

She stopped and turned round. To my surprise, I saw her eyes were red and tearful. 'Yes? What else do you have to say to me?'

'Stephen said you wanted to be involved in our attempt to prove Geoffrey Cardale stole your Picassos. I can't believe you don't. Whether you think I'm . . . cruel and contemptible . . . is really beside the point. So, please sit down. Hear me out.'

'More advice for me, Mr Swan?'

'No. A proposition.'

'It had better be good.' She walked slowly back to the bench and sat down. As I sat down beside her, she took out a cigarette. I lit it for her. She dried her eyes with the heel of her free hand and gazed past me across the park. She didn't so much as glance at Eldritch. 'Go ahead.' I silently echoed the sentiment she'd just expressed. This had better be good. I was well past being surprised that he'd given me no inkling what his proposition might be.

'Desmond Quilligan, the man who painted the fake Picassos

125

your grandmother destroyed, drank himself to death twenty years ago. We visited his old landlady, Mrs Duthie, yesterday. She gave us his sister's address in Hampshire. It seems Isolde Quilligan married an old schoolfriend of mine, Miles Linley. In 1940, he was working at the British Legation in Dublin. He knew I was trying to lure Quilligan to London, but not why. Not the real reason, anyway. Did Isolde know? I can't be sure. Maybe Quilligan told her later. In which case Linley also knows. How they came to marry is anyone's guess. They didn't know one another as far as I was aware. Clearly something changed after I was locked up. Probably lots of things. What I can say is this. Knowing Linley as I do, if he found out, he probably sought to capitalize on his discovery.'

'How?' asked Rachel.

'Perhaps by blackmailing Cardale.'

'If that's true, he and his wife aren't going to help us prove a damn thing.'

'Indeed not. *If* it's true. We need to find out. We also need to see a painting of Quilligan's which Isolde took away with her after his death. It's called *Three Swans*. It's the last thing he ever painted. And since his death was essentially self-inflicted, it might represent a form of suicide note.'

'Addressed to you?'

'Perhaps. Three swans seen flying together portend a death. So goes the superstition. But according to Mrs Duthie there was only one swan in the picture. It seems to be some kind of riddle.'

'Is this all you've got?'

'Yes. But we'll get more if we play our cards right. I can't be seen by Isolde or her husband. Especially her husband. With any luck, they don't know I'm out. And I'd like to keep it that way. They wouldn't speak to me under any circumstances. But you two might be able to extract some valuable information from them if you catch them on the hop, perhaps even get to see *Three Swans*. You need false names and a cover story. The names I'll leave to you. The story is that you're interested in the artistic career of Desmond Quilligan and you've been told they have most of his pictures: could you take a look at them?'

126

'What if they slam the door in our faces?' I put in.

'Then we'll know they're party to the fraud. But if you get past the door and convince them you're genuine Quilligan enthusiasts, there's no telling what you might learn. It'd be useful if you could establish whether Quilligan's brother, Ardal, is alive, for instance, and, if so, where he lives. He's another who may be in on it.'

'How current is the information you got from Quilligan's land-lady?' asked Rachel.

'It's twenty years out of date,' I answered.

'Then, they could have moved. Or died. This could all be a waste of time.'

'The frequency of your visits to the Royal Academy suggests time is something you have on your hands, Miss Banner,' said Eldritch. 'I'm suggesting how to put a little of it to good use.'

'Don't let him get to you,' I said, staring at Eldritch to let him know I wasn't on his side in this.

'I won't,' she said. 'I guess it makes sense. Follow every lead, however tenuous.'

'Exactly,' said Eldritch. 'So, unless you have something less tenuous . . .'

She nodded. 'I'll go. Stephen?'

'Gladly.' I wasn't exaggerating. A trip to Hampshire with Rachel was an enticing prospect. Whether Eldritch knew how enticing I couldn't have guessed. The reason he'd given for staying behind was sound enough. But that didn't have to be the only reason. Face value wasn't a coinage he generally dealt in.

'Do you have a car, Miss Banner?'

'I can borrow one.'

'How soon?'

'Probably right away.'

'In that case, what are you waiting for?'

We walked to the phone boxes by the entrance to Green Park Tube station. Rachel went into one to call her friend, Marilyn, owner of the car she was hoping to borrow. I stood by the park railings with Eldritch. Tube passengers, tourists and passers-by jostled amidst the noise and fumes of the Piccadilly traffic.

'Why didn't you tell me what you had in mind, Eldritch?' I shouted to him above the ferment.

'Because I didn't know whether she'd turn out to be someone we could safely collaborate with.'

'I'd already told you she was.'

'I reckoned you might be biased.' Before I could rise to that, he went on: 'Tread carefully with the Linleys, Stephen. Don't even hint you're related to me, or that you know anything about me.'

'I thought you and Linley were friends.'

'So did I, before—' He broke off. 'Ah. Here she is.'

Rachel had emerged from the phone box. She hurried across to where we were standing. 'Marilyn's fine about us using her car,' she announced. 'We just have to go collect it.'

'I'll leave you to it, then,' said Eldritch. 'Good luck.'

'What are your plans for the day, Mr Swan?' Rachel asked him.

'I'm an old man,' came his deadpan reply. 'I need my rest.'

We watched him walk away, slowly threading a path through the crowds in the Ritz arcade, a stooped and solitary figure from another age.

The same thought, it transpired, had occurred to Rachel as it had to me. 'What's he up to, Stephen?'

'I don't know. Perhaps he really does need a rest.'

'Could be, I suppose, after that performance he just put on.'

'I'm sorry. I had no idea he was going to be so . . . unashamed.'

'It's OK. I get the feeling I passed some kind of test.'

'You shouldn't have had to.'

'We all have to.' I turned to look at her, surprised by her tone. She sounded almost grateful to Eldritch for putting her through the mill. 'Sooner or later.'

Marilyn's car was parked near her flat in Islington. We began the Tube journey out there in silence. Only after the mass exit at King's Cross did Rachel suddenly turn to me and ask, 'What do you know about these people we're going to see, Stephen?'

'About Isolde Linley? Nothing. But her husband's not such a blank. He and Eldritch were at school together. Ardingly. Eldritch was his fag.'

'His *what*?'

'In public-school parlance, a younger boy who runs errands and does chores for an older boy.'

'Oh, I thought . . . Never mind. So, Linley's a few years older than Eldritch?'

'Four or five, at a guess. But he might look better on it in well-heeled retirement from the Diplomatic Service. Hatchwell Hall doesn't sound like a hovel to me.'

'And he was at the British Legation in Dublin when Eldritch was put away, right?'

'Right.'

'So, he must know *why* he was put away.'

'Probably. But we can't ask him. We have to stay incognito.'

'Yeah. But is that to protect us? Or Eldritch?'

'You don't trust him, do you?'

'Absolutely not.' She turned to look at me for emphasis. 'And neither should you.'

Marilyn's flat was the basement of a large semi-detached house in Barnsbury Square. I had little chance to gain much impression as Rachel swept me in. A postcard, addressed to her, with a foreign stamp on it, was lying on the mat. 'From Joey,' she said, scanning the message. 'He often writes me.' She plonked the card on the hall table, by a vase of lilies, and went to collect the car key.

The picture Joey had chosen was of Antwerp Cathedral. I turned the card over, wondering what he'd said. To my dismay, the writing was so minute and spidery I'd have needed a magnifying glass to decipher it. The message ran to about thirty lines.

A sudden silence told me Rachel was watching what I was doing. I turned. She was frowning at me from a doorway down the hall. 'Sorry,' I said sheepishly, laying the card back down. 'I shouldn't have pried.'

'It's all one sentence,' she said as she came towards me.

'Really?'

'You won't find a full stop or a comma anywhere. His cards are always like that.'

'Can you read them?'

'Oh yes. It's easy with practice. And I get plenty of practice. Sometimes I wish I didn't get so much. And sometimes . . .' She patted the card gently with the tips of her fingers. Her gaze lost its focus. Contemplation of her family's misfortunes was compressed into a silent second. This was her sad, wounded side showing itself. But she wasn't about to indulge the mood. 'Poor Joey,' she sighed. Then she tossed her head back and dangled the car key in front of me. Her smile was a touch rueful. But it was a smile nonetheless. 'Let's go.'

SIXTEEN

The drive down to Hampshire in Marilyn's Mini had, in retrospect, an improbably light-hearted, carefree quality to it. The thrill of the chase had taken us over. In my case, it was also the thrill of Rachel's company. Her beauty was heightened by her vibrancy. I couldn't have failed to be attracted to her. There was just so much life bubbling within her. Of course, I already had good reason to believe she was a creature of moods, but I wanted her current mood – laughing, teasing, bewitching – to last for ever. We talked about her work at the UN and mine in the oil industry. We tried to outdo each other with suggestions for improbable pseudonyms. The miles vanished. And several hours with them.

Hatchwell Hall stood in affluently farmed countryside between Basingstoke and Alton. I'd said it didn't sound like a hovel, but I hadn't quite expected the sweeping lawns, exuberant topiary and large red-brick William and Mary mansion that came into view as we crested a gentle fold of land a few miles south of the village where we'd stopped for a pub lunch. It was a house from another century, set amidst fields and coverts its original occupants would have noticed little change in. It was the dream of rural ease and order, preened and pointed in the early spring sunshine.

'Jesus,' said Rachel. And that pretty much said it all.

Hatchwell Hall's wrought-iron entrance gates stood open to

visitors. Rachel drove slowly through and up the curving gravel drive. Several cars were parked in front of the house. Most were at least twice the size of Marilyn's.

We stopped and got out. The air was aloofly cool, the quietude almost tangible.

'All this on a government pension,' mused Rachel.

'Inherited wealth?' I suggested. 'Or extorted?'

'Let's try and find out.'

We walked to the half-glazed front door and pulled at the bell. It clanged antiquely in the hallway, which, we could see, ran the depth of the house. There was a glimpse of rear garden beyond a farther door. Floral-patterned rugs and an oak staircase filled the middle ground.

A plump, aproned housekeeper answered the bell. 'Good afternoon,' she said quizzically, in a local accent. 'What can I do for you?'

'Is Mrs Linley at home?' Rachel asked.

'*Lady* Linley is, yes. But she's busy with her charity group. Was she expecting you?'

'Not exactly. We really called on the off chance. I'm not over here for long. It'd be so great if she could spare just a few minutes.'

'It's about her brother,' I put in. 'Desmond Quilligan.'

The housekeeper looked even more quizzical at that. 'You'd best come in for a moment. I'll see if she can have a word with you.'

We stepped inside and she bustled off, leaving us to the ticking of a longcase clock and the company of several paintings that clearly weren't the work of Desmond Quilligan.

'What's with the *Lady* Linley?' Rachel whispered to me.

'It means her husband's a knight of the realm.'

'She's done well for herself, hasn't she?'

'That's marriage to a public servant for you.'

'These people need bringing down.' I sensed she was talking more to herself now than to me. 'They truly do.'

It wasn't long before the lady of the house joined us. Isolde Linley appeared from one of the reception rooms to our left. A broad-belted green plaid dress and a string of pearls helped her look exactly what her title suggested she was: a privileged woman entering comfortable old age with the means and the wish to present herself as elegantly as she could. High cheekbones, sparkling blue eyes and a lingering trace of red in her hair added several natural advantages. She might have looked radiant if she'd smiled. But she wasn't smiling. Nor did I have the impression she was about to.

'I'm sorry,' she said, her original Irish accent overlaid with Home Counties English. 'I'm in the middle of a meeting. What is this about?'

'We're sorry too, Lady Linley,' said Rachel. 'To interrupt, I mean. We should have written ahead, but I have to fly back to the States in a few days and— Oh, I guess we should introduce ourselves. I'm Liz Spelling.'

'Peter Fordham,' I put in. (The names actually belonged to two people I'd worked with in Houston.)

'What exactly do you want?'

'I'm helping Liz with her thesis,' I replied. 'She's researching the later lives of Irish men and women who fought in the Easter Rising.'

'That's right,' said Rachel. 'People like your brother, Desmond. He's particularly interesting because he finished up in London and, of course, he had an artisitic strand to his life, didn't he? Now, his old landlady, Mrs Duthie, who gave us your address, mentioned you took all his paintings after he died and we—'

'You've spoken to Mrs Duthie?'

'We certainly did. And she was as helpful as she could be, but—'

'She had no right to discuss my brother with you. He's been dead twenty years and I'd have hoped he could be left to rest in peace.'

'We're not trying to sully his memory in any way, Lady Linley. I'm engaged in serious historical research. I thought you might be pleased to discuss his life and what the Rising meant to him.'

'Well, you thought—' The heavy closure of a door somewhere to the right drew Isolde's attention at once. She stepped back and looked along a passage that was out of our sight. 'Miles,' she called.

'What is it?' came the gruff, bellowed response.

'Can you help me with these visitors, please?'

'Visitors?' We heard approaching footsteps. 'I thought you had your charity ladies here.'

'I do. And I'd like to get back to them.'

Sir Miles Linley emerged into the hall, breathing heavily. He was ruddy-faced and white-haired, with an almost feminine softness to his chin that sat oddly with his brusque tone and impatient expression. He was dressed for gardening, in stout shoes, brown corduroys, check shirt and green padded waistcoat. 'Good afternoon,' he said, frowning suspiciously at Rachel and me.

'I'm Liz Spelling, Sir Miles,' said Rachel politely. 'This is my friend, Peter Fordham. We—'

'They've been asking me about Desmond,' Isolde cut across her. 'For some kind of research project.'

'My thesis, actually,' said Rachel.

'Which university?' snapped Sir Miles.

'Yale.' I was impressed. We hadn't settled on one as far as I knew. But I was also worried. If Sir Miles started nit-picking, our cover story might come apart at the seams. 'I'm particularly interested in Desmond Quilligan's paintings, which—'

'Can you deal with them, Miles?' asked Isolde. 'I really don't have the time. My meeting . . .'

'Yes, yes, my dear. You go. Leave this to me.' There was a hint of dismissal behind his husbandly smile.

'Thank you.' She glanced fleetingly at us. 'Goodbye.' The farewell was cool and final. She walked briskly away, closing the door she'd emerged from earlier firmly behind her.

'What's the subject of your thesis, Miss Spelling?' Sir Miles asked as soon as his wife was gone.

Rachel trotted out her rehearsed answer about the Easter Rising and the loose end in Desmond Quilligan's biography of his artisitic career. Sir Miles look unimpressed throughout, though not, it seemed to me, unconvinced. When Rachel mentioned Brenda

Duthie, he darkened thunderously. But no storm broke.

'You've had a wasted journey, I'm afraid,' he said when she'd finished, though I had the impression the statement had been prepared before she even started. 'My wife's done her level best to forget her brother and, frankly, so have I. You've chosen a strange time to research the lives of the IRA's original members, I must say, when their successors are blowing up pubs, restaurants and trains and assassinating innocent people all over Northern Ireland *and* Britain in pursuance of their blood-soaked agenda. At least Desmond Quilligan saw the error of his ways in the end and abandoned the cause. The kindest thing I can say about him is nothing at all.'

'Why did he abandon the cause, exactly?' I enquired disingenuously.

'Yeah, he's the only Easter Rising veteran who signed himself out of wartime internment,' said Rachel. 'I'd like to get to the bottom of that.'

'There's nothing I can tell you about the workings of his conscience,' came Sir Miles' tight-lipped reply. 'Now, if you—'

'How did you and Lady Linley first meet?' I asked, relishing the sense I had that we were beginning to get under his skin.

'Is that really any of your business?'

'No,' said Rachel, forestalling any sarcastic answer I might have come up with. 'It isn't. And we absolutely respect you and your wife's right to privacy, Sir Miles. I wouldn't want to press either of you to discuss issues you'd rather not.'

'I'm glad to hear it.' Sir Miles looked faintly mollified.

'It was actually primarily in the hope of seeing some of Desmond Quilligan's paintings that we came here.'

'As I said, you've had a wasted journey. My wife sold her brother's paintings years ago.'

'All of them?' He must have caught the incredulity in my voice.

'Yes. Every last damn one of them. Second-rate stuff they were, anyway. We didn't get much for them. Virtually had to give them away.'

'Didn't Lady Linley want to keep at least one or two as a memento of her brother?'

'Obviously not, young man. Otherwise she would have done. I didn't force her to dispose of them, though I can't say I was sorry she did. Some people are best forgotten. Desmond Quilligan was such a man. That's my last word on the matter. I'm sure your ... thesis ... will be an excellent piece of work, Miss Spelling. We won't expect a mention in the acknowledgements. Now, if you don't mind, I have roses to prune.'

He'd already herded us halfway to the front door. Now he opened it and stood back, inviting us to leave. Our time was up. Rachel rolled her eyes at me and headed out.

'How long ago were you knighted, Sir Miles?' I asked as I passed him.

'In 1968. When I retired.'

I paused on the threshold. 'Retired from what?'

'The Diplomatic Service.'

'A well-deserved award, I'm sure. Did you have any sensitive postings in your time?'

'One or two.'

'Ever get sent to Ireland?'

'Yes.' His eyes narrowed.

'Ah. That'll be how you and Lady Linley met, then. You might as well have said.' I smiled at him. 'An interesting choice of wife for a career diplomat: the sister of an IRA terrorist.'

'Is the Mini yours?' he asked Rachel, looking straight past me. Why he should suppose it was hers rather than mine was unclear. Perhaps he thought a Mini no car for a man.

'Yes,' she replied.

'Take the drive slowly, would you? I don't want gravel kicked up on to the lawn. It plays havoc with the mower. And the first cut of the season's due any day.'

'I'll go carefully.'

'You do that.' His gaze switched back to me. 'Good afternoon to you both.'

*

136

We pulled into a gateway half a mile or so along the road, from where we could look back at Hatchwell Hall. Rachel said nothing as she smoked a cigarette and stared towards the distant house. Eventually, I broke the silence.

'What do you think?'

'I think he's a pompous sonofabitch and she's got what she always wanted – and what she deserves.'

'You didn't like them, then?'

'*Sir* Miles and *Lady* Linley? No. Was I meant to?'

'We forgot to ask about Ardal.'

'They wouldn't have told us anything if we had – certainly not how to contact him. They were about as forthcoming as a pair of clams.'

'Do you believe they've sold all the paintings?'

'No.'

'Why not?'

'Because saying they have was the quickest and easiest way to get rid of us. I wouldn't be surprised if *Sir* Miles was already on the phone to Yale, checking up on me. Actually, I hope he is. I want him to worry. It'll be good for him.'

'We didn't come here to put the wind up Sir Miles.'

'No. But it's better than nothing.'

I wasn't sure Eldritch would agree with Rachel about that. From his point of view, we had nothing to show for our visit: no lead on Ardal; no sight of the paintings; no progress on any front. It didn't feel quite so bad to me, though I couldn't have explained why exactly. Perhaps it was that the Linleys' defensive reaction to our enquiries was a form of proof in itself. We were on to something.

Rachel offered to drop me at the Ritz when we made it back into central London through a grey, traffic-snarled dusk, but I opted to travel with her all the way to Islington, confessing I was in no hurry to face Eldritch with our news. She took pity on me, as I'd hoped she would, and suggested I have supper at the flat. I didn't need any persuading, as must have been obvious to her. She left a note for

Marilyn saying we'd be back for dinner and we walked round to their local for a drink. To my surprise, the Linleys' stonewalling hadn't dented Rachel's optimism in the slightest. She seemed, indeed, in a mood to celebrate.

'Thanks for everything, Stephen,' she said, chinking her glass against mine as we settled at a table.

'What have I done to deserve this?' I asked, genuinely puzzled.

'I've made more progress in constructing a case against the Brownlow estate in the past thirty-six hours than I have in thirty-six months. That's down to you.'

'We can't prove anything against the Linleys, Rachel,' I cautioned her. 'Not a thing.'

'No. But we know who they are, don't we? Simon Cardale won't have bargained for that. It means we can put more pressure on him. I've met him a couple of times and he's always been . . . nervily defensive. Next time, his defences might not hold.'

'When will next time be?'

'The sooner the better, I reckon.'

'I'll see what Eldritch says.'

'OK. But I'm not about to let slip whatever advantage we have. You can tell Uncle Eldritch that from me.'

'Maybe I won't have to.'

'Maybe not.' She lit a cigarette and smiled when I accepted the offer of one. 'Marilyn hates me smoking in the flat. I have to come here to puff away over my' – she raised her eyebrows in preparation for her attempt at an English accent – '*half a bitter*.' We both laughed at her effort. Then she frowned at me mock-solemnly. 'Listen, Stephen. I'd better come clean with you. Marilyn, like all my friends, thinks I'm crazy to be plugging on with the Brownlow case. So, don't mention where we've been or why, will you? My story is you're some good-looking guy I picked up in the Royal Academy. We've been to Stonehenge for the day.'

'*Stonehenge?*'

'It popped into my head when I was on the phone to her.'

'And did we enjoy ourselves?'

'Well, I did. What about you?'

*

Marilyn Liebermann was a much closer approximation to the all-American girl than Rachel, with blonde flick-ups, a big pink-lipped smile and a generous figure. She expanded the supper menu to accommodate three without difficulty and was mercifully incurious about the wonders of Stonehenge. I had the impression she was delighted her friend had finally done something as conventional as bringing a man back for a meal. In fact, it was a relief to chat idly about music, politics and our varied life stories, to be reminded there was a world beyond the mystery Eldritch had lured me into. And there was no reason I couldn't return to that world whenever I chose. Unless Rachel Banner was a reason.

I'd rather hoped I could avoid Eldritch until the morning. It was more than late enough when I reached the Ritz for him to be asleep, although whether sleeping was something he did much of I wasn't entirely sure. In the event my uncertainty on the point was only reinforced – and my choice in the matter effectively removed – by the note he'd slipped under my door.

'Come and see me when you get in, whatever the time. I'll be waiting up. We have much to discuss. E.'

1940

SEVENTEEN

It is a sunny morning of beguiling warmth in Dublin. Eldritch Swan ambles north along O'Connell Street, smoking a cigarette and savouring the sweetness of the contrast with yesterday morning, which he began in a cell at Dublin Castle. He is in ample time for his appointment with Ardal Quilligan and confident their meeting will go well. He realizes, however, that he cannot afford to take anything for granted. Trams and buses are filling and emptying in orderly fashion at their stands beneath Nelson's Pillar, the admiral watching them benignly from his stony perch. The city is going about its business at a calm and leisurely pace. But it has not always been thus. Swan is passing the General Post Office and there are bullet holes in the columns of its façade to remind him that in 1916 this was a scene of pitched battle. Glancing up at the building, he imagines Desmond Quilligan, rifle in hand, staring out defiantly from one of its windows twenty-four years earlier. The past and the future hold many surprises. And the wise man, as Swan fancies himself to be, must be prepared for them.

But some contingencies are simply too improbable, not to say incredible, to be prepared for. Never in his wildest imaginings would Swan suppose that twenty-six years from now he will be standing in the dinner queue at Portlaoise Prison when the inmate behind him whispers in his ear, 'The IRA have blown up your Nelson's Pillar in Dublin, Swanny. What d'you think of that, then?'

*

Ardal Quilligan was as tall as his brother, but narrower of build and humbler of bearing. Sleek-haired and bespectacled, neatly moustached and trimly dressed, he had acquired a palpable air of reticence and caution along with his legal training. He sat at his desk in a small, book-lined office overlooking Rotunda Gardens, carefully studying the document Swan had handed him, while Swan himself watched the smoke from his cigarette curl and spiral in the sunlight that streamed through the open window behind him. The hoof-clop and wheel-rumble of a horse and cart passing by in the square merged briefly with the clacking of typewriter keys in the next room. Then Quilligan laid the document down in front of him and plucked off his wire-framed glasses. His lengthy perusal was at an end.

'This undertaking has the effect of granting my brother un-fettered access to his son,' he said, enunciating his words slowly and precisely. 'You understand that, I assume.'

'I do. As does Mr Cardale.'

'It commits my brother to nothing in return.'

'Mr Cardale will ask him to perform a small . . . artistic service . . . as an expression of his . . . appreciation.'

'What service might that be?'

'It would be agreed between them. I'm not privy to the details.'

'But my brother already has some idea of what it might be?'

'He seemed to have, yes.'

'And is willing to perform it?'

'Apparently so.'

'Signing himself out of internment is no small matter, Mr Swan. It involves renouncing principles he's held dear all his life. He'll become a pariah to the men he's served and suffered with.'

'But he'll know his son. And his son will know him.'

'Indeed.'

'And wouldn't you welcome such a renunciation, Mr Quilligan? I'd imagine it must cause you some . . . professional embarrassment . . . to have a brother in prison.'

Quilligan coloured at that. Swan had ventured on to sensitive

144

territory. The lawyer cleared his throat. 'Internment is not imprisonment, Mr Swan. It's a . . . political matter.'

'It looked and smelt and felt like imprisonment to me.'

'Possibly, but—' Quilligan broke off and took a calming drag on his cigarette, studying Swan as he exhaled. Then he slid the document across the desk to him. 'We digress. And I've no wish to detain you. The undertaking is entirely satisfactory in form and content. I'll visit my brother and tell him so.'

'When will you go?'

'Tomorrow.'

'And how long before . . .'

'I'm not sure. I have no experience of such procedures. The Department of Justice isn't exactly noted for its administrative alacrity. A week at least, I should say. More likely two. Possibly longer. I'll keep you apprised, naturally. Where are you staying?'

'The Shelbourne.'

'Your wait will be a comfortable one, then.' A smile hovered warily beneath the moustache. 'A nice holiday from the war for you.'

'So people keep telling me.'

Quilligan swung round in his chair and crossed his legs. He ran a hand down over his knee. He seemed nervous, unsure of himself. 'About the boy, Mr Swan. My nephew. You've met him?'

'Yes. And I took a snapshot for your brother to see. Would you like to see it yourself?'

'Thank you, yes. That's . . . kind of you.'

Swan took the photograph out of his wallet and passed it over. 'He's a bright lad.'

'Is he, though?' Quilligan put his glasses back on and studied the child's face. 'He'll be breaking a few hearts when he's grown to manhood, I should reckon. Just like his father.' He sighed and handed the photograph back. 'My sister worries for him, Mr Swan. I know she'd like to see this and ask you about him. We've neither of us children of our own, you see. And our only nephew, little Simon, is being raised to be a perfect English gentleman. It saddens me, of course, but Isolde takes it harder. Women do, don't they?'

'If you want me to talk to her . . .'

'I was hoping you might agree to. We have a house in Ballsbridge. Well, it's the house we were born in, actually. Desmond too. Would you come to tea on Saturday?'

'I'd be happy to.'

'Let me just . . .' Quilligan took out a pocket diary and frowningly consulted it. 'Ah, no, I can't do Saturday, now I come to look. What about Sunday?'

'I have no plans at all for the weekend, Mr Quilligan.'

'We'll say Sunday, then. Would four o'clock suit?'

'Certainly.'

'Perfect.' Quilligan withdrew a small pencil from the spine of the diary and made a note of the engagement, then carefully replaced the pencil and put the diary back in his pocket. Every move he made, it seemed to Swan, and by inference every word he spoke, was closely considered. He was altogether a close man. 'One other thing, Mr Swan . . .'

'Yes?'

'Lord knows my brother has had his troubles. Many, you might feel, have been of his own making, though I could debate that, given the bitter and frequent intrusions history has made into the lives of Irishmen of our generation. But however grim his present situation may seem to you, there are in reality worse things he could be by far than an IRA internee. I wouldn't want to bear any responsibility for him yet becoming one of those worse things. The scale of the concession Mr Cardale is offering worries me, I can't deny it. And I shall tell Desmond so. You ought to be aware of that.'

'He may tell you to mind your own business.' Swan smiled coolly at the lawyer.

'He may indeed.' Quilligan sighed. To Swan's surprise, he did not appear to have taken the slightest umbrage. Perhaps he had already concluded that his brother would reject his advice. Perhaps his brother had always done so. 'I'll be able to let you know how he responds on Sunday.' He whipped off his glasses and stood up. 'Can I tell Isolde you'll definitely be coming?'

'Yes.' Swan rose. 'You can.' They shook hands. 'I'll look forward to it.'

'So will we, Mr Swan.'

A suspicion that had grown on Swan during his walk to Ardal Quilligan's office hardened into a certainty on the way back. He loitered by the bus stops outside the GPO, as if contemplating a journey to the suburbs. So did the scruffily suited chain-smoker he had noticed dogging his footsteps earlier. The man moved on when he did, only to stop again when Swan paused to admire the view from O'Connell Bridge. Linley had predicted Moynihan would set a tail on him and here he was, large as life. Swan wondered if Moynihan had instructed the man to make himself conspicuous. If so, the reason was clear. Swan had been freed. But he had not been forgotten. And he was not to be allowed to think otherwise.

Over coffee and an idle perusal of the *Irish Times* at Bewley's in Grafton Street, Swan came to the conclusion that his best response to Moynihan's tactic was to pretend he was unaware of it. He was, after all, an innocent man. Tailing him would only substantiate his story. He would affect a lordly indifference.

The consequence was that he was no longer sure whether he was being followed or not when he reached the Shelbourne. And the matter was briefly blotted from his mind by the surprise of seeing Miles Linley emerging from the hotel as he approached.

'Looking for me?' Swan called.

'Cygnet, old fellow.' Linley clapped him on the shoulder as they met. 'No. I've just been settling a VIP in at your very own home from home. But bumping into you is undeniably opportune. Can you spare me a few minutes?'

'I think I could probably squeeze you into my hectic itinerary.'

'Excellent. Let's step over to the green.'

St Stephen's Green was a haven of summery ease, with assorted Dubliners feeding the ducks or lounging on benches, relishing the warmth of the sun. Linley set off on an ambling circuit of the ornamental lake and Swan fell in beside him.

'Who's the VIP, then?' he asked, mildly curious as to the mystery man's identity.

'I shouldn't really say. I wouldn't want word to get round.'

'You're the only person I know in the entire city.'

'Really? We'll have to put that right. One of my many onerous responsibilities is organizing the legation cricket team. We have a match on Saturday and, as usual, I'm struggling to raise an eleven. Fancy a game? I could lend you some whites.'

'Well, I . . .'

'You were quite the budding Hobbs at school, as I recall.'

'That's not how I recall it.'

'Be that as it may . . .'

'All right, all right. I'll turn out on Saturday.'

'Capital. You'll enjoy it. And you'll meet a few people, some of them perfectly decent sorts.'

'You haven't told me who the VIP is yet, Linley. Don't think you've put me off the scent.'

Linley laughed. 'Perish the thought.' He glanced over his shoulder. 'But careless talk, etcetera, etcetera. There's an ugly customer bringing up our rear who looks uncommonly like a none too subtle Special Branch surveillance officer.'

'He's been following me all morning.'

'Really? Hold on here.'

Linley spun on his heel and strode towards the man in the shabby suit, who stopped in his tracks. Linley reached him in half a dozen strides. There was a murmured conversation. Shabby suit's expression moved from poker face to something suggestive of a sudden onset of biliousness. He scowled briefly in Swan's direction, then turned and plodded away, back the way they had come.

'What did you say to him?' Swan asked as Linley rejoined him.

'I said following a member of the British Legation during a hush-hush ministerial visit to Dublin was a serious breach of diplomatic protocol and would he kindly bugger off? He'll be back on your tail sooner or later, I don't doubt, but for a while at least you'll be left in peace.'

Swan smiled. 'Thanks a lot. That's another favour I owe you. So, the VIP's a government minister, is he?'

'Malcolm MacDonald. Son of Ramsay. Currently Minister of Health. But in his previous incarnation as Dominions Secretary he's supposed to have hit if off with de Valéra. He's been sent over to have yet another shot at persuading Dev to bring Éire into the war. A complete and utter waste of time and effort in my opinion, but we must show willing. So my boss tells me, anyway. Now, I'm glad you feel even deeper in my debt, Cygnet, because there's a little something I'm hoping you might agree to do for me.'

'What is it?'

'A matter of extreme delicacy.' Linley grinned. 'That's what it is.'

EIGHTEEN

They left the ornamental lake behind and struck out along the perimeter path round the park. Linley pitched his voice at a confidential mid-point between normal speech and a whisper. The 'little something' he was hoping Swan would do for him evidently merited greater secrecy then the comings and goings of the Minister of Health.

'I'm in love, old fellow. That's the long and the short of it. But the path of true love, etcetera, etcetera. She's Antrobus's secretary. He's number two at the legation. She's also married, which is the bugger of it. Husband in the Navy. I needn't tell you what it would do for my career prospects if I was discovered to be cuckolding a serving naval officer. But the fact of the matter is that we adore each other. We want to spend time together. But it's damnably tricky. She shares digs with a couple of other secretaries. I lodge with my boss in Donnybrook. We can't be seen out on the town. What we need is . . .'

'A love nest?'

'Exactly. That's *exactly* what we need. Somewhere we can—'

'No need to spell it out, Linley. I catch your drift. Tell me, you and . . .'

'Celia.'

'Right. You and Celia. Do you see a long-term future with her? Or is it just that you can't keep your hands off her?'

'We can't keep our hands off *each other*, since you ask. Anyway, I don't know about the future. A divorce could be messy. I can't look too far ahead with a war on. It's complicated. What isn't complicated is that we can't go on like this. Something's got to give.'

'Cold baths could be the answer.'

Linley shot Swan a daggered look. 'I don't think you're taking this seriously, Cygnet.'

'All right. What can I do to help?'

'I thought you'd never ask. An opportunity's come up. Furnished rooms to let. Just round the corner from here, as a matter of fact. Close enough to the legation, but not *too* close. If I rent them there's always the risk word will get back. But if someone else rents them . . . and lends me the key . . .'

'Someone you can trust who isn't in the diplomatic community would suit, I suppose.'

'He would. Perfectly.'

'We'd better take a look at this opportunity, then, hadn't we?'

They left the park and walked back past the Shelbourne round into Merrion Street. On the other side of the road was an imposing terrace of Georgian town houses, not all of them in imposing condition, facing the spectacular baroque dome of what Linley told Swan had originally been the Royal College of Science. They paused to look in through the colonnaded entrance. A fountain was playing in the courtyard. An Irish tricolour was fluttering next to the dome. A couple of studious-looking young men were walking up the steps beneath it. And a policeman was standing guard over the approach to the northern wing of the complex.

'Government Buildings, they call it now,' said Linley. 'Though University College still have the use of part of it. Dev's probably lurking in there even as we speak, pondering just how resounding a no to deliver to MacDonald. The RCS was the last public building we gave the Irish before independence. God knows what slum they'd be housing their Taoiseach in but for the gift of some decent British architecture. But never mind that. Walk a little further with me and direct your gaze across the street.'

151

They moved on to the corner of Government Buildings. The Georgian terrace ended opposite them, where it met the railinged greenery of Merrion Square.

'The Duke of Wellington was born over there, at number twenty-four,' Linley continued. 'The house had a better class of resident then. Now it's all dentists and solicitors and servants' agencies. But that means plenty of toing and froing, which is just the kind of camouflage I've been looking for. The widow Kilfeather, who lives at number twenty-eight, also owns number thirty-one.' It was the door of number thirty-one, adorned, like its neighbours, with decorative columns, architrave and fanlight, that they were standing opposite. 'A surveyor has the basement and ground floor. A chiropodist has the next two floors. The top floor, however, is currently vacant. And furnished for a private tenant.'

'Sounds perfect.'

'It does, doesn't it?'

'But why do I want it?'

'Let's walk on while I answer that question.'

They crossed an alley leading to the rear of Government Buildings and headed north, with further Georgian terraces flanking Merrion Square to their right and a sweeping lawn backing on to a large mansion to their left. 'Leinster House,' Linley explained. 'Seat of the Dáil.' High railings barred access and another policeman was in evidence at the gate. Neutrality, it appeared, required a deal of protection. 'You could attend one of their debates if you have a spare afternoon and a taste for windy rhetoric.'

'I'll bear it in mind.'

'Of course, as an elocutionist, you might take a professional interest in the deputies' varying methods of delivery.'

'Elocutionist? What the devil are you talking about?'

'I thought you might tell Mrs Kilfeather that's what you did for a living. It would account for you having visitors from time to time: strangers seen on the stairs by other tenants. But invent something else if elocution doesn't sit well with you.'

'You've gone into this very carefully, haven't you?'

'Well, Cygnet, in my experience, Burns had it all wrong. It's actually the *worst* laid schemes of mice and men that gang aft a-gley.'

'When do you want me to broach my interest in the accommodation?'

'ASAP. I have the address of the agent. As long as you don't haggle – and since I'm picking up the bill there's no need to – Mrs K will welcome you with open arms, I'm sure. A well-spoken, smartly turned-out chap such as yourself is just what she's looking for. She'll probably insist on a minimum of three months, with one of them paid for in advance. So, all you have to do is smile, write out the cheque and pocket the keys.'

'You realize I'm not going to be in Dublin for three months, Linley. Not even for one.'

'Don't worry about that. Once you've set things up, there'll be no problem. Simply send a regular cheque to the agent and I'll keep you recompensed. If you're worried about it, I'll pay you a lump sum.'

Swan glanced back towards the house where he was shortly to become an absentee tenant. 'I hope Celia's worth all this.'

'Oh, she is.' Linley chuckled. 'I can assure you of that.'

The agent was as helpful as might have been expected, given Swan's stated willingness to pay the rent demanded. A telephone call cleared the way for an afternoon appointment with Mrs Kilfeather. Swan spruced himself up, made sure he was on time and decided to refrain from smoking to cement a favourable impression.

As it transpired, Mrs Kilfeather was not a lady of censorious disposition. A big-bosomed, bun-haired woman of sixty or so, she greeted Swan with briskly businesslike amiability. He had been unable to devise a plausible alternative to Linley's suggested occupation, but Mrs Kilfeather remarked only, 'There are plenty round here who could profit from elocution lessons,' before inviting him to view the top-floor flat at number 31.

It comprised a sitting-room, bedroom, bathroom and kitchen, the sitting-room and bedroom facing Government Buildings, the bathroom and kitchen looking out over the rear gardens and courtyards of neighbouring properties. The furnishings were homely if scarcely stylish and some were in less than pristine condition. Flock wallpaper and framed hunting scenes did not conform to Swan's idea of a sympathetic domestic environment, but his requirements were hardly relevant and he suspected Linley and the seductive Celia would not be troubled by the odd frayed lampshade. The mattress of the double bed responded with well-sprung firmness to his prod, with the barest hint of a squeak. That, he felt sure, they would appreciate.

'I'll take it,' he announced, when the tour of inspection was complete.

'You know I'm insisting on monthly terms, Mr Swan?' Mrs Kilfeather responded.

'Yes, yes. That'll be fine.'

'The previous tenant paid weekly, but he left without so much as a day's notice, so I thought it best to revise the arrangement.'

'I quite understand.'

'If you get any post for the man, throw it away. He left no forwarding address. Henchy was his name.'

'Sounds an inconsiderate fellow.'

'You have that right, Mr Swan. But I can see you're a gentleman, unlike Mr Henchy. So, welcome to Merrion Street.'

'Thank you kindly. I'm sure I'll be . . . very comfortable here.'

Linley was already waiting for him when Swan strolled into the Horseshoe Bar at the Shelbourne shortly after six o'clock that evening. He was looking surprisingly nervous, as if fearful that Swan had somehow botched the negotiations with Mrs Kilfeather. But his face lifted when Swan deposited the keys to the flat on the table next to his whisky and soda.

'Well played, Cygnet,' he said, smiling wolfishly. 'Consider all debts discharged.'

'Glad to have been able to help, Linley. We Old Ardinians must stick together.'

'Absolutely.' Linley pocketed the keys. 'So, no problems?'

'None at all.'

'Splendid. Thanks again. Now, I'm afraid you're going to have to excuse me. Much as I'd prefer to stay here chatting with you, I have to skedaddle. I'm one of those deputed to dine with the minister this evening. I must dash home and put on my best bib and tucker.'

'How did the talks go?'

'No idea. Badly, I expect. Or well. It depends on your point of view.' Linley finished his drink and rose, a touch wearily. 'Steer clear of politics, old fellow. That's my advice. I'll see you on Saturday.' He played an airy cover drive with an imaginary cricket bat and clicked his tongue appreciatively. 'It'll be fun, I promise.' Then he gave Swan a farewell clap on the shoulder and hurried out.

Swan took himself off to the cinema to fill his evening. The Irish censor had clearly been at work on the newsreel – the war was nowhere to be seen or mentioned – and the B picture had either been extensively cut or very badly made (he could not decide which), but *Rebecca* was apparently considered harmless and was enjoyed to full weepy effect by the women in the audience. Swan found its depiction of unfettered international travel depressing and its melodrama overwrought. He left before the end, conceding to himself, there being no one else to concede it to, that there really was no romance in his soul. He suspected there was little in Linley's either and could only hope the same was true of Celia. Otherwise, he feared, heartbreak and disappointment lay in wait for her.

1976

NINETEEN

I'd expected the 'much' Eldritch's note had said we needed to discuss to include more details of his long-ago dealings in Dublin with Miles, now Sir Miles, Linley. All he told me on that front, however, was that he'd returned the favour of being sprung from detention in Dublin Castle by renting a flat for Linley's use in carrying on a surreptitious affair with a married secretary at the British Legation. The exact nature of Linley's eventual betrayal of him he still wouldn't disclose. But he seemed gratified that I'd disliked the decorated former diplomat and his haughty wife.

'I've never thought of them as a pair before. But, now that I consider it, they seem curiously well matched.'

Wrapped in a Ritz bathrobe, whisky glass in one hand and cigarette in the other, he regarded me with weary tolerance across the sumptuous wastes of his extravagantly appointed room, surroundings which somehow made him seem older and frailer and more tenuously connected to the present day than ever.

'I can't say I'm surprised you drew a blank with them, Stephen. It was worth a try, if only so you and Miss Banner could get the measure of them, but Linley spent his entire working life guarding secrets and he's not likely to change now. As for his wife, she's obviously more of a schemer than I gave her credit for. I think you're wrong on one point, though. I believe them about the paintings. Of course they sold them. They didn't want any reminders of Desmond Quilligan around the house. It might have made their children inconveniently curious about their late uncle.'

'How do you know they have children?' I challenged him.

'*Who's Who*. It occurred to me Linley might have greased his way into its pages. Well, so it proved. He gives the knighthood prominent mention, naturally. The son and daughter squeak in at the end. They're not named, but they are there. As is his sainted wife, of course. He married her in 1945, just before leaving Ireland for a posting in Portugal.'

'We saw no sign of the children.'

'Probably already fled the nest. Anyway, they're not important, other than to remind us that Sir Miles and Lady Linley have a family as well as a social position to protect. They'll do whatever they think they need to do to serve that end.'

'Then, what do we try next?'

'The weak link. Simon Cardale. My bet would be that the Linleys will have been in touch with him following your visit, warning him to be on his guard. But he doesn't have quite their strength of mind, does he? That was obvious when we met him. And it was even more obvious when I met him again today.'

'You went back to the gallery?'

'Yes. Just to stir the pot. I asked him if he'd had the chance to look through his grandfather's old files for a record of the Quilligan exhibition.'

'But there was no exhibition. You made it up.'

'Indeed. But Cardale doesn't know that. And it was clear to me he *had* been looking. Without success, naturally. He's a bad liar. And a worse dissembler. His reaction told me how it was. He must have severed all links with Quilligan long before Quilligan died, probably at his grandfather's insistence. Now, far too late, he regrets doing that. And a man with regrets is a man with weaknesses. Which we can exploit.'

'How?'

'Simon Cardale had no hand in the original fraud. He was just a child. So, he has less to lose than the others if the truth comes out. I'm not sure he even inherited much money from his grandfather.

The gallery doesn't look very prosperous and nor does he. I suggest we try shock tactics on him.'

'Meaning?'

'Take Miss Banner to see him. Ask him to deny to her face that his grandfather cheated her family and that his natural father, Desmond Quilligan, helped him do it. I don't think he'll be able to. In which case . . . we'll have him.'

I phoned Rachel early the following morning – too early, to judge by her groggy response. But Eldritch's proposal jolted her into wakefulness. She was all for it, as I'd expected she would be. It was more or less what she'd proposed herself. She joined us at the Ritz in time for a late breakfast and was so excited at the prospect of challenging Cardale that she forgot to be sarcastic about the luxuriousness of our surroundings.

'How sure are you he'll crack?' she demanded of Eldritch.

'I think there's a good chance, Miss Banner. That's all I can say.'

'Will you stop calling me Miss Banner? It's freaking me out. My name's Rachel.'

'Very well, Rachel. You'll have an advantage over us. You won't have to pretend you're someone else. I suggest you admit visiting the Linleys yesterday using a pseudonym, but we'll say the name Stephen used was genuine and he's your . . . English boyfriend. I'm his uncle, who happens to know a little about Quilligan's artistic career. I'm the reason you met: I suspected Quilligan was responsible for forging the Picassos and contacted you to tell you so, then introduced you to each other.'

'You're the reason we met anyway, Eldritch,' I pointed out.

He smiled at me. 'So I am.'

'All right,' said Rachel. 'Sounds good. Any reason why we don't go straight round there?'

Eldritch glanced at his watch. 'He might not open until ten. Have another cup of coffee. Then we'll go. There's no hurry.'

'How can you be so god-damn patient?'

'A fringe benefit of long-term imprisonment, I dare say. It teaches you the art of waiting if it teaches you nothing else.'

Twenty minutes later, we arrived at the gallery. My first thought was that Cardale opened even later than Eldritch had anticipated. There were no lights twinkling in the gloomy interior. Then I spotted the handwritten sign taped inside the door. ALL ENQUIRIES NEXT DOOR AT BEAUCHAMP FINE ART. Instantly, I feared the worst. And so did Rachel.

'He knew we were coming.'

'It's possible,' conceded Eldritch. 'But I doubt it. Let's do as the sign says.'

The proprietor of Beauchamp Fine Art was a suaver, more self-assured version of Cardale himself. 'Simon rang me this morning,' he explained. 'He's gone down with flu. But if there's anything you're interested in, I can let you in for a look.'

'We really need to speak to Mr Cardale,' said Eldritch.

'Well, you could phone him at home, I suppose. I can give you his number.'

'Home is still Cherrygarth, Queen's Road, Richmond, is it?'

'Yes. It is.'

'I see.' Eldritch gazed past the man into the shadowier recesses of the gallery, where his mind's eye did indeed seem to see something: the past, perhaps, when Cherrygarth was the home of another Cardale and Eldritch was his willing assistant.

'We'll take that number, Mr Beauchamp,' said Rachel. 'Thanks a lot.'

We retreated to an espresso bar in the Piccadilly Arcade to debate our next move. Rachel advocated heading straight for Richmond in the hope of bearding Cardale in his lair. I agreed. Eventually, after smoking his way thoughtfully through a Sobranie, so did Eldritch.

'He may not be there, but we can't phone to find out in case he takes himself off somewhere else. It's certainly worth a try. But you'll have to go without me. I have to stay here.'

'Why?' Rachel and I asked almost as one.

'I have an appointment with Twisk. He stipulated at the outset that I had to report progress to him on a regular basis. Our first meeting's scheduled for noon.'

'You never mentioned this before,' I pointed out, though that was hardly news. Eldritch clearly wasn't in the habit of confiding in anyone.

'I'm sorry, Stephen. It slipped my mind.' But Eldritch's mind let nothing slip. Rachel and I both knew that.

'We could wait until this afternoon to go to Richmond,' she suggested – mischievously, it seemed to me, since I knew she was itching to go straight away.

'Delay strikes me as a bad idea, Rachel. No, I think you should simply go without me. I'd probably only slow you down anyway.'

'In that case,' I said, 'you'd better tell us exactly what you're hoping we'll get out of Cardale.'

'That's simple,' he replied, lighting another cigarette in a flurry of coughs. 'As much as you can.'

Part of me was glad Eldritch wasn't coming. It meant I had Rachel to myself. Another part of me was suspicious. What game was he playing? There always seemed to be another, beyond the one I thought I knew the rules to.

Rachel, it turned out, felt much as I did. 'I'd be lying if I said I was sorry your uncle stayed behind, Stephen,' she said as we boarded the Richmond train at Waterloo. 'Cooperating with him makes sense, I know, but to me he's still one of the bastards who cheated my family. I reckon this'll work better with just the two of us.'

'I prefer it that way myself.'

'You don't know how good it is to hear you say that. I've been waging war on my own too long – a war no one believes I can win.'

'We may be able to surprise them.'

'It's not just that. It's all the . . . sacrifices . . . I've had to make along the way.' She looked out through the grimy window and fiddled with a cigarette. The whistle blew amidst a final slamming of doors. I struck a match. Our hands bumped together with the jolt of the train as she lit up. I was startled to see tears in her eyes.

'Sorry,' she said, shaking her head, as if annoyed by her own emotional fragility. Her mood was less confident, less sweeping, than the day before. It made me want to protect her, to shield her from the consequences of her stubborn pursuit of the truth. She sighed. 'I've kinda got used to it being a hopeless cause. And to fighting it alone.'

'You're not alone any more.'

She leant forward and kissed me – a wet and clumsy kiss thanks to the yawing of the train as it crossed the points. We both laughed. 'Bless you, Stephen,' she said.

It was cold and grey in Richmond, the famous view of the Thames from Richmond Hill blurred and dulled by wintry light. Eldritch had come here in high summer. I imagined a cloudless sky, cooing doves and horse chestnuts heavy with leaf. I also imagined profound quietude, thanks to wartime petrol rationing. Thirty-six years later, the traffic was thick and noisy, lorries rumbling to and fro along Queen's Road, serving what sounded like a big building project in the middle distance. Cherrygarth's setting was no longer a tranquil one.

It was a substantial Victorian residence set in its own grounds, behind a high wall and wrought-iron gates. The postman came out through them as we approached, wheeling his bike, and gave us a cheerier greeting than I reckoned the householder was likely to.

'Do you know if Mr Cardale's in?' Rachel asked him.

'Might be. Somebody's got a bonfire going out the back. I can tell you that.'

Smoke was drifting round and over the gables of the house to prove his point. We closed the gate behind him and moved towards the front door. 'So much for flu,' Rachel muttered.

'Maybe he has a gardener.'

'Or incriminating evidence to burn. Let's check out back before we try the bell.'

A flagstoned path led round through a screen of trellis to the rear garden. A lank-grassed lawn stretched away in front of us towards an orchard, at the edge of which smoke was billowing up from an incinerator. Simon Cardale, dressed in Barbour, sweater, corduroys and gumboots, was feeding handfuls of paper into the flames. Behind him, on a rickety old wicker table, stood a cardboard box, with a pile of paper beside it. There were two more boxes on the ground next to the table and a couple of others, clearly empty, lying on their sides near by.

'What did I tell you?' said Rachel.

Cardale seemed oblivious to our presence, tamping the contents of the incinerator with a rake between loads as we approached across the lawn. I called out to him. '*Mr Cardale.*' He looked up, his jaw sagging as he saw us. His face was flushed, perhaps not just from the heat of the blaze. I noticed a half-empty whisky bottle and a tumbler on the table behind him.

'*Cardale and I struck the deal over gin and barley water in his garden out at Richmond.*' So Eldritch had told me. Now, here we were, Rachel and I, confronting Cardale's grandson in the same place, but in a different time and season, haunted by all that had been set in motion that summer afternoon long ago.

'What the hell are you doing here?' Simon Cardale shouted at us, his voice faintly slurred. 'This is private property.' Then he recognized us – each of us in turn. 'You're the two who showed up at Hatchwell Hall yesterday, aren't you?'

'You remember me, then, Simon?' Rachel asked, challenging him with her familiarity.

'*Miss* Banner. And *you.*' He glared at me. 'I suppose I should have known you were in it together. Where's the old man?'

'My uncle isn't with us today,' I said. 'My name's Peter Fordham, Mr Cardale. I'm helping Rachel to—'

'I know what you're helping her to do.'

'Thanks to Peter and his uncle, I've found out who forged the Picassos, Simon,' said Rachel. 'Desmond Quilligan. Your very own father.'

'Quilligan was no father to me.'

'Are you going to deny he was the forger your grandfather hired?'

'I don't have to deny anything.'

'Does he get a mention in those papers you're burning?'

165

'Did good old Uncle Miles tell you to destroy any of your grandfather's papers you still had?' I put in. 'Our visit obviously had a bigger effect than we thought if you had to close the gallery to get straight on with it. He whistles and you do his bidding. Is that how it works?'

'You know nothing about it. Either of you. I've had a bellyful of questions and orders. You people and your wretched lawyers. *Sir* Miles Linley treating me like the under-gardener's assistant. My grandfather. My father. The bloody Picassos. I've had it up to here with the whole damn lot.'

'But why the fire, Simon?' Rachel persisted, stepping closer to the incinerator. 'What do you have to burn so urgently?'

'None of your bloody business.'

'Something tells me it's very much my business. Let me see those papers.'

She walked boldly past him, defying him to stop her. For a second, it seemed he wasn't even going to try. Then something snapped inside him, intent flared in his eyes. He swept the rake into the air and turned towards Rachel. With her gaze fixed on the prize of the pile of papers on the table, she didn't realize what was about to happen. But I did.

My charge took him off balance and I grabbed the rake as he fell. His shoulder struck the edge of the table, which toppled with him. Rachel cried out and jumped back in alarm. The papers, the empty box, the whisky bottle and tumbler all crashed down, the bottle catching Cardale on the brow as he hit the ground. He grunted and lay where he was.

'Oh my God,' Rachel gasped, her hand to her mouth.

'It's all right,' I said, tossing the rake away across the lawn. 'It's all right.' I moved between her and Cardale.

'What . . . what was he going to do?'

'Something stupid. Something very stupid.'

She clasped my hand. 'Is he . . . OK?'

As if in answer, Cardale moaned and looked up at us, blinking in shock. There was blood above his right eye, where the bottle had struck him. The bottle itself lay close to his face, the contents leaking out into the grass. He gazed blearily at it, then back up at us. 'Oh shit,' he mumbled. He touched the wound on his brow and winced. 'Sorry. I . . . I didn't mean to . . .'

'It looked to me like you meant it,' I said, stepping cautiously towards him.

He closed his eyes and slowly shook his head. He seemed as shocked by what he'd nearly done as Rachel was. And all the rage had left him. 'It's not worth any of this,' he murmured.

'Amen to that,' said Rachel, so softly I'm not sure he heard her.

He reopened his eyes and struggled to focus on us. 'What do you want from me?' he asked resignedly.

'What I've wanted all along,' Rachel replied. 'The truth.'

TWENTY

The kitchen at Cherrygarth, like the house itself, was scaled to serve the large family that Geoffrey Cardale, when he originally bought it, may have imagined would one day fill the place. Somehow that had never happened and now his grandson was the sole occupant. Simon Cardale was sitting with us at the wide table that filled one end of the room, looking absurdly childlike with his tousled mop of hair and the Rupert Bear slippers he'd swapped his gumboots for. He had a strip of plaster on his brow and a mug of coffee in his hand, both supplied by Rachel, who'd recognized in the man who'd just tried to attack her with a rake someone who was actually even more vulnerable than she was and had taken pity on him as a result.

The chaos of unwashed dishes in the sink and the fact that the sink in question, along with the stove and all the other fittings, appeared several decades old, reinforced the impression that Cardale was a man whose need for mothering – or nannying, in his mother's lifelong absence – hadn't ended with childhood. He knew as much himself, as his shamefaced glances around made clear. The gallery was a front. This was where the reality of his life was laid bare.

'Thank God you stopped me,' he said, slurping his coffee. 'I was ... het up. I wasn't ... myself.' He rubbed his eyes. 'You're right *and* wrong about those papers.' We'd brought the unemptied boxes into the kitchen with us. They stood on the floor by the table.

'Linley told me to destroy everything of Grandfather's I still had. But there's nothing about the Picassos – or Desmond Quilligan – in any of those documents. Bills of sale; catalogues; bank statements; business correspondence: it's all worthless stuff. I knew that. I've checked through it several times over the years. Linley wouldn't listen. "Burn the whole damn lot." His words on the phone to me last night. He'd guessed who you really were, Miss Banner, and the fact that you knew about Desmond scared him. I've never heard fear in his voice before. You know what? It was a good thing to hear. He deserves to be scared.

'There's something I ought to explain before we go any further. I don't know how much Grandfather made out of the Picasso fraud. The bank statements certainly won't tell you. He had a numbered account in Switzerland where all his illicit income was squirrelled away. I think there were other scams, you see. I think he was always up to something, though the Picassos were obviously his biggest killing. The thing is, though, I haven't got any of the money. Not a penny. Indirectly, I've benefited from it, of course, if you can call Charterhouse and a leg-up in the art world benefits, which I grant you most people would. And then there's Linley's investment in the gallery. I've made a few bad buys over the years. More than a few. He's helped me out. The money he's used to help me out? I'm not kidding myself. He had a share of the Picasso proceeds. There's not a doubt of it in my mind. He blackmailed Grandfather, using information Isolde got out of Desmond. Grandfather never said as much, of course. But then he never breathed a word to me about any of it.'

'How did you find out, then?' asked Rachel.

'Ardal told me, after Grandfather died. He said it was time I knew.'

'And how come you didn't inherit what was left of the money?'

Cardale cracked a rueful smile. 'Grandfather remarried late in life, Miss Banner. He spent most of his time in Montreux towards the end. My Swiss stepmother inherited everything except this house and the business. How much that amounted to . . . I have no idea. Swiss lawyers and accountants take Trappist vows. And she's married again herself since then. I don't even get a Christmas card from her now. If you want to chase her for what's rightfully yours, good luck.'

'You admit it is rightfully mine, then?'

'What would be the point of denying it? Desmond Quilligan painted the fake Picassos Grandfather delivered to your family in 1945. Grandfather kept the real ones and sold them to Brownlow. That's what Ardal told me twelve years ago and I realized at once it was true. I used to tell the other boys at Charterhouse my father was a fighter pilot slain in the Battle of Britain, his Spitfire blown out of a blue sky over Norfolk in the summer of 1940. Sometimes, I even used to believe it myself. And why not? I didn't want to admit or acknowledge the fact that my mother fell in love with an Irish terrorist, as we'd now call him. Or a Fenian rebel, Grandfather's preferred description. Desmond Quilligan. The man I was forced to meet and be polite to. My father. As soon as I was free to, I shut him out of my life. I couldn't do it completely. The Linleys kept in touch with Grandfather. *Aunt* Isolde and *Uncle* Miles. And Isolde always reminded me of Desmond. But I did my level best to forget that the man slowly drinking himself to death in Dollis Hill was my flesh and blood. I was glad when I heard he'd finally succeeded. I was relieved.

'The question remained, though: why had Grandfather let him near me in the first place? Why had he been so . . . understanding? Well, Ardal gave me the answer eventually. Because it was the quid pro quo for Desmond forging the Picassos. He wasn't in it for the money. He just wanted to know me, to be . . . some kind of father to me. And I wouldn't let him. I was too priggish and snobbish and self-centred to accept what he tried to offer me. It turns out he wasn't a bad man. He had principles, unlike my grandfather. And he had love to give. But I wouldn't accept it. I remember the last time I saw him. December, 1955. I was helping out in the gallery after my first term at Oxford. Learning the ropes, as Grandfather put it. It was late afternoon, a week or so before Christmas, just beginning to get dark. I looked out of the window and there he was, on the other side of the street, staring in at me. He was drunk and shabbily dressed, a wreck of the man he'd once been. I could have waved for him to come in, or gone out to speak to him. Instead I just . . . turned my back. And when I next looked . . . he was gone.'

'Isolde took all his paintings from the house in Dollis Hill,' I said. 'Did you ever see them?'

'No. She didn't mention them and I didn't ask. I didn't want to know anything about him, in life or in death. I didn't even go to his funeral, though I could have done, easily enough. Ardal made sure I knew where and when it was to be.'

'Sir Miles says they sold the paintings.'

'So I gather.'

'Do you believe him?'

'Oh yes. He'd have wanted to be rid of them.'

'We're particularly interested in one called *Three Swans*.'

'I can't help you. Ardal might have it, I suppose.'

'You mean Isolde gave him some of the pictures before selling the rest?' queried Rachel.

'Gave, no. Ardal bought them. Several, I believe. Anonymously. At auction.'

'Bought them?'

'So he told me. Confidentially. I wasn't to mention it to his sister or Linley under any circumstances.'

'Why not?'

'They'd take it amiss. Though you might ask why he'd care how they'd take it since he sees nothing of them. Maybe . . .' He frowned. 'What's so interesting about *Three Swans*?'

'It's the last picture he ever painted, according to his landlady,' I replied. 'We think there might be a . . . message in it.'

'A *message*?'

'Where does Ardal live?' Rachel asked, as keen as I was to deflect a question that might oblige us to explain Eldritch's part in all this.

'Majorca. He has an apartment in Palma. Bought it years ago and retired there after winding up his law practice. Nothing grand, so he tells me. The sun's good for his arthritis. In case you're wondering, he got nothing out of the Picasso fraud.'

171

'Are you sure about that?'

'As sure as I can be. You see, when he came and told me all about it twelve years ago, he advised me to go to the police and tell them what Grandfather had done. He repeated the advice when he heard about your mother's suit against the Brownlow estate. "Get if off your conscience, Simon," he said. "Put the record straight."'

'Why didn't you?'

'Because of Linley's stake in the gallery. Because I was afraid I'd be dragged down with him. Because it was easier and safer to do as he told me.'

'Plus you didn't want your old school chums getting to know who your father really was and what he did.'

'That's right.' He looked directly at Rachel. 'I didn't want anyone to know. I was ashamed of my father. And my grandfather.'

'The police would have been powerless to act anyway without proof,' I pointed out. 'Did you have any?'

'*I* didn't, no.'

'It would still have helped our case,' said Rachel.

'Hold on.' I'd spotted, as she apparently hadn't, the revealing emphasis in Cardale's answer. '*You* had no proof. But did someone else?'

Cardale sighed. 'Ardal claimed he had incontrovertible evidence that the Picassos were forged by his brother during the Second World War, scuppering Grandfather's story that Isaac Meridor bought the fakes himself.'

Rachel glanced across at me, a smile playing around her lips. This was more like it. This was what we needed. 'What kind of evidence?' she asked.

'He wouldn't tell me. He simply said that, as and when I was ready to make a clean breast of it, he'd supply the material that would render any denials by Linley futile. He didn't seem to doubt I'd be ready sooner or later. It was just a question of time.'

'He could have come forward himself,' said Rachel.

Another sigh. 'He said it had to be my decision, as Desmond's son. He's away from it all, on his Mediterranean island. I'm the one who'd have to face the flak. He encouraged me to do it, but he wasn't going to force me.'

'This "material" he has . . .'

'I honestly don't know what it is. But I'm sure he still has it.'

'Could it be the *Three Swans*?' Rachel was asking herself the question as much as anyone else.

'I don't see how,' said Cardale.

Nor did I. But it hardly mattered what the material was, so long as it was still in Ardal Quilligan's possession. 'Are you willing to go to the authorities with whatever Ardal has?' I asked.

Cardale bowed his head and slapped the back of his neck a couple of times, nerving himself to take a long-overdue decision. Then he looked up at us and said, 'Yes. I'll do it. I've had enough. Linley can go hang. The Brownlow estate can . . . carry the loss. You win, Miss Banner. I'm throwing in the towel.'

'Thank you,' Rachel said coolly, with more satisfaction – and probably disbelief – than gratitude.

'We can't do anything without the evidence,' I cautioned.

'I'd better phone Ardal, then,' said Cardale, shaking his head in surprise that the time his uncle had predicted would come . . . had come at last. 'Before I change my mind.'

Cardale led us through to a drawing-room, furnished and decorated, like the kitchen, in the style of an earlier age. There were newspapers and books scattered around and enough paintings stacked against one wall to suggest the room was used as an over-flow for the gallery. There was a deep hollow in the cushion of a leather armchair facing the television, a whisky bottle and tumbler standing ready on a small table beside the chair. The air was frowsty, the light thick.

Cardale hoisted a telephone off the floor, plonked it on the table and slumped down in the chair. The tangled cable put up some resistance when he raised the receiver to his ear. He nodded to the French windows as he dialled.

'Would you mind waiting outside? I'd like to be alone when I speak to him.'

'Why?' Rachel asked, frowning suspiciously.

'I don't know. I'd just be . . . happier.'

'Maybe I'd be happier sitting in on the conversation.'

'I'm not trying to trick you. I simply—' He broke off, his attention switching to the person on the end of the line. 'Hello?' he shouted. 'Hello?' Then the connection improved. 'Ardal? It's Simon . . . Yes, I know . . . Yes . . . Just hold on.' He looked back at us, covering the mouthpiece of the receiver with his hand. 'Please, Miss Banner.' He nodded at the French windows.

'Come on,' I said, sensing somehow that it really would be better to leave him to it. 'Let's do as he asks.'

It was obvious Rachel had misgivings. As we stood on the flag-stoned patio, watching the dumb show through the glass, she stared intently at Cardale, twirling her fingers round the top button of her raincoat as she watched him. Much was riding on this one telephone call and it was possible, though I didn't believe it for a moment, that our host had deceived us about its purpose.

'Don't worry,' I said, resting my hand on Rachel's arm. 'It's going to be all right.'

'I guess so. I guess I . . . just can't quite believe it. All the lawyers; all the letters; all the journeys: and this is how it ends.'

'It's not over yet.'

'No.' She turned to look at me. 'But we're close, aren't we?'

Ten minutes must have passed, during which Rachel smoked two cigarettes and paced up and down the patio, before Cardale, the receiver now cradled against his chest, waved us back into the sitting-room.

'He wants to speak to you, Miss Banner,' he said, offering her the phone.

'Really?'

'Yes. Go ahead.'

She cast me a wide-eyed glance, then moved to the table and took the phone. 'Hello? . . . Yes. I'm Rachel Banner.'

Cardale rose from the chair and stepped across to the French windows, where I was standing. He rubbed his eyes. 'It's as good as done, Fordham.' He didn't seem to notice my tardy reaction to the use of my fictitious surname. 'You'll soon have what you want.'

'Better late than never.' I didn't intend to let him off lightly.

'You're right, of course. I shouldn't have tried to cover it up. The truth is I'm relieved it's all going to come out. I may end up losing the gallery, I suppose. Maybe even this house. But whatever happens, however bad the fallout . . . I'll be free. I realize now how much that counts for.' A cloud had visibly lifted from his expression, a burden from his shoulders. It seemed we really had done him a favour.

'You won't tell me what the material is?' I heard Rachel ask. There was a pause as Ardal Quilligan replied. Then she said, 'All right. Tomorrow . . . Yes. I understand . . . Yes . . . Goodbye. And . . . thank you.' She put the phone down and nodded to herself, settling something in her mind.

'What did he say?' I prompted.

She looked at me. 'He'll call the gallery tomorrow afternoon to make arrangements to deliver the material.' She shrugged. 'We have to wait a little longer.'

'But not much longer?'

'No.' She shook her head. There was still a measure of disbelief to conquer. 'He confirmed what he has will clinch it for us. And he's willing to hand it over. I think it really is going to be all right.'

TWENTY-ONE

Rachel and I were both buoyed up by the exhilaration of what we'd achieved when we left Cherrygarth. We treated ourselves to a celebratory late lunch at an Italian restaurant. The second bottle of wine was probably unwise, though at the time it seemed the perfect fuel for our foretaste of triumph, a triumph which encompassed much that went unstated. A grey afternoon in Richmond, through which we laughed and ate and drank. The occasion felt magical, though it wouldn't have looked so to any observer. The magic was all in our eyes and minds.

Telling Eldritch what had happened should have been a relishable prospect, given his implied scepticism about my ability to handle matters properly. As it was, I didn't really want to see him and thereby break the spell that had somehow been cast over Rachel and me. Clearly, however, he had to be told. So, back to the Ritz we went, only to be informed that he wasn't there, though he had left a message for me. *'There has been a development which I need to deal with. But there is something else we need to address later. Be in your room at ten tonight. E.'*

'What the hell does that mean?' Rachel asked, leaning over my shoulder to read the note as we stood in the foyer.

'I've no idea.'

'Does he always issue instructions like that? "Be in your room at ten."' She laughed. And so did I.

'It seems to be his style.'

'Looks like you have an empty evening ahead of you – until ten.'

'Want to help me fill it – starting with champagne in the bar?'

'Are we still celebrating?'

'Definitely.'

'Then, lead on.'

Drunk on each other as much as the champagne, we moved from the bar to my room. Before either of us, I think, quite knew what was happening, we were making love amidst warm lamplight and sultry shadows. We'd met only two days before, but I felt as if we'd known each other much longer. There was nothing hurried or impetuous about what we did. Beyond the tenderness lay a trust we were both surprised by in the other, beyond the passion a glimpse of a future sweeter and fuller than any we'd previously anticipated. We laughed a lot, I remember. It was the laughter of discovery and disbelief.

The phone rang while we lay together afterwards, sharing a cigarette. I answered only because I thought it might be Eldritch. If he was back, I wanted to stop him coming to the room. But it was actually my mother, calling to see how I was. Rachel had to stifle a giggle as she rested her head on my shoulder, listening while I proffered bland answers to questions about what Eldritch and I were doing and how comfortable the Ritz was.

'Will I ever get to meet her?' Rachel asked after I'd rung off.

'I hope so.'

'And will she like me?'

'Oh yes.'

'How can you be so sure?'

I kissed her. 'Because nobody could fail to.'

'Plenty have.'

'They must be fools, then. And my mother's no fool.'

Nor, of course, was my uncle. Neither of us wanted him to know we'd become lovers. So, much as I wanted Rachel to stay, she had to leave. We showered and dressed and I walked her to Green Park Tube station. She blew a kiss to me as she vanished down the escalator to the Victoria line and I walked back to the Ritz feeling as if there was only air beneath my feet.

I left a message for Eldritch at reception and went into the bar for more champagne. The last thing I wanted to be now was sober.

Eldritch found me there half an hour later and, as far as I could judge, believed my euphoria was solely due to the success of our trip to Richmond. 'You've done well,' he said, sounding as much as if he meant it as he was ever likely to.

'This means we've won,' I pointed out, too stridently, it seemed, for his taste.

'It means we've a chance of winning,' he corrected me. 'We need to see the material first.'

'Ardal's promised to hand it over.'

'But when?'

'Soon.'

'It needs to be.' He lowered his voice and raised a cautioning hand. 'Linley isn't going to sit idly by, Stephen. Obviously, we'll have to hope Cardale can keep his mouth shut. But there are other things to worry about. Brenda Duthie rang me late this afternoon. That's why I wasn't here when you returned. She's been burgled.'

'*Burgled?*'

'She came home from shopping to find her back door had been forced open and every drawer in the house emptied, the contents strewn around. But some money she keeps in the kitchen was still there and her late husband's gold hunter hadn't been taken either. Theft clearly wasn't the motive.'

'So . . . was anything taken?'

'The painting Quilligan gave her and the photograph of Simon Cardale as a child he had stapled to his easel.'

'Nothing else?'

'Not as far as she can tell, though it's too much of a mess to be absolutely certain. She's very upset, particularly about the painting. They left the frame and the stretcher behind, presumably for ease of carriage. She blames us for this happening and she's right to, of course. For every action there's a reaction.'

'What do you think they were looking for?'

'Anything connected to Quilligan. Linley's behind this, Stephen. You can be sure about that.'

'You're not seriously suggesting he broke into the house?'

'Not personally, no. Of course not. But he may have resources he can call upon.'

'What resources?'

'Government personnel.' Eldritch lowered his voice still further. 'The intelligence services.'

'You can't be serious. Why should they want to help him?'

'There may be reasons.'

'Such as?'

Eldritch hesitated. He was either unable or unwilling to reveal what reasons there might be. 'Linley's a retired diplomat,' he said at last, in a tone that suggested he knew how weak his argument was. 'He might be owed a few favours for services rendered.'

'You'll have to do better than that. If you really have good cause to suspect MI5 are involved, now's the time to come out with it.' But he wasn't going to. I could tell that just by the tight set of his mouth and the evasive look in his eyes. The secret of what had really happened to him in Dublin couldn't be shared – with me or anyone else.

'The burglary happened, Stephen,' he said stubbornly. 'I'm not imagining it. Any more than Brenda Duthie is.'

'OK. It happened. I'm sorry for Mrs Duthie. But what are we supposed to do about it?'

'At the very least, we should be on our guard. We've poked a stick into an anthill, you and I. Stand still too long and we'll be badly bitten.'

'But we're not standing still. Ardal Quilligan will be in touch tomorrow to arrange delivery of the evidence we need.'

'Yes. But there are things we can usefully do sooner than that.'

'Like what?'

'I want to know who's put us up to this. And why.'

179

'Did you press Twisk to tell you?'

'Of course. Naturally, he refused. I explained I was bound to be circumspect in what I told him about progress in view of his client's anonymity. In fact, I was vague to the point of uselessness. It didn't seem to worry him. I imagine his fee is all that concerns him. There was certainly no budging him on the central issue. His client remains nameless. But I don't propose to leave it there.'

'What can you do?'

'It's more a question of what you can do.'

'Me?'

Eldritch leant towards me. 'While I was at Twisk's offices, I asked to use the lavatory,' he whispered. 'An advantage of old age is that such a request arouses not the least suspicion. I released the latches on the sash window while I was in there. The number of cobwebs on it suggests to me it's never opened. So, I doubt anyone ever checks the latches. An agile young man like yourself should be able to climb in without much difficulty. Then you can go into Twisk's office and take a look at the file he consulted during our discussion. And then . . . we'll know who his client is, won't we?' He smiled. 'Drink up. We have a busy night ahead of us.'

I might have put up more resistance to Eldritch's proposal if I'd been sober, or if the evening hadn't left me giddy with wish-fulfilment. The fact remained, though, that he'd engineered us a chance to put a name to the mystery man – or woman – who was pulling our strings. To hear Eldritch tell it, the risks were minimal. There was no way I could refuse to make the attempt.

We set off for Holborn on foot at half past midnight. There were still a few knots of drunken revellers in Shaftesbury Avenue, but all was quiet by the time we reached Hatton Garden. The diamond merchants were doubtless burglar-alarmed to the hilt, but Eldritch assured me the same wasn't true of F. J. Twisk, solicitor and commissioner of oaths.

His offices comprised the extended rear of an architect's practice in Ely Place, accessed by a door off the alley running through to Hatton Garden, just along from the Old Mitre pub. A six-foot wall blanked off a light-well, into which, according to Eldritch, the lavatory window looked. The light-well was currently consumed in darkness, of course, but Eldritch had brought a torch. We'd come equipped. And it was true: there was no sign of an alarm box.

'Twisk's client chose him because of his proximity to the diamond district,' said Eldritch, as we took a slow walk along Hatton Garden after completing our reconnaissance. 'They evidently thought it more important to send a message to me than question the security of Twisk's premises. That misjudgement's handed us a golden opportunity.'

'Of getting ourselves arrested, you mean?'

'That isn't going to happen. I'll be there to make sure the coast's clear when you come back out.'

'And if it isn't?'

'We wait until it is. It's very simple, Stephen. I'd do it myself if I was thirty years y—' He pulled up sharply and looked at the sign above the shuttered frontage of yet another diamond merchant: L. BURG & SONS. 'Well, well, they're still going, then.'

I allowed him twenty seconds for silent reminiscence, then said, 'Are we going to do this or not, Eldritch?'

Eldritch nodded. 'You're right. Let's get on.'

Ely Court was as empty and quiet and shadow-shrouded as it had been during our first walk along it. There was no reason to hesitate now and my nerves couldn't have borne any further delay. Eldritch gave me a leg-up, an effort that started him coughing, hard though he tried to stifle it. It wasn't the best of starts, but I was already scrambling over the wall, aware that it was too late to turn back. I flashed the torch into the void on the other side and gauged the drop to the flagstones below, then lowered myself as far down as I could before letting go. I made a safe landing. Eldritch was still battling his cough in the alley as I shone the torch at the building and spotted the frosted glass of the lavatory window. I moved towards it.

The sash put up so much resistance that I thought at first it must

181

have been relatched. Then, quite suddenly, it gave, in a squeal of wood and a shower of paint fragments. I stood listening for a moment, but heard only silence. Eldritch had stopped coughing. I clambered up on to the sill and in through the window.

I switched on the torch and followed the route Eldritch had plotted for me earlier: out of the lavatory, along the passage past the door into the alley and the receptionist's room, then up half a flight of stairs to Twisk's office.

There was the filing cabinet, in the corner of the room behind Twisk's desk. I made straight for it and pulled open the third drawer down, as instructed. I didn't know what file title I was looking for until the answer gleamed back at me in the torch beam. SWAN. I lifted the file out, laid it on the desk and flicked it open.

1940

TWENTY-TWO

The summer holds in Dublin. It is an idyllically mellow, caressingly zephyred Saturday afternoon in late June. Gentle applause from the smattering of spectators around the pavilion in Trinity College Park greets the emergence on to the field of the British Legation's cricket XI. They are still somewhat lethargically taking up their positions when still gentler applause marks the arrival of the Royal Dublin Society XI's opening batsmen. Play is about to commence.

The scene appears so quintessentially English that Eldritch Swan, despatched to patrol the third-man boundary, is moved to remind himself that he is actually in Ireland – an independent, neutral Ireland at that. It is, as Miles Linley has recently reminded him, a looking-glass world of distorted reflections. Swan does not expect to enjoy himself over-much, despite Linley's assurances that he will. But he has, quite literally, nothing better to do.

His team mates are a mix of career diplomats and super-numeraries, such as himself, drafted in on account of their supposed cricketing competence and vaguely British affiliations. The captain, a natty little fellow with a parade-ground voice called Grigg-Mathers, clearly views the supernumeraries as regrettable necessities and directs them much as he would native troops in a colonial regiment under his command. Third man, or some other un-glamorous posting, will be, Swan is certain, his lot for the duration of the innings. But since there are many worse places to be in the world as it is currently ordered, he is not about to complain.

Neither the batting nor the bowling scaled any heights as the RDS team progressed uneventfully to a score of 168 for 7. It should have been 168 for 8 according to Grigg-Mathers' assessment of a skyer Swan had failed to reach. 'Are you with us, Cygnet?' Linley had called from the slip cordon. 'Barely' would have been the truthful answer.

But the arrival of the RDS number 9 seized Swan's attention as nothing else had. He was Ardal Quilligan, lean as life, his spectacles flashing in the sun beneath the peak of a cap worn at the most conventional of angles, as he meticulously took guard. He edged his first ball to second slip, where Linley promptly dropped it. Grigg-Mathers scowled and Swan wondered whether it was clumsiness or surprise at the batsman's identity that accounted for the lapse.

The tea interval gave Swan a chance to pursue the point. To Grigg-Mathers' chagrin, Quilligan had knocked up a useful twenty-odd and the RDS had totalled 207.

'Only just seen the blighter's name in the scorebook,' Linley explained, emerging from the pavilion, sandwich in hand, as Swan reached it after his journey from the far boundary. 'I'd wait and see how he wants to play it if I were you. There could be something to be said for your not appearing to know each other.'

That was evidently also Quilligan's view of the matter. He did no more than twitch his eyebrows at Swan when they glimpsed each other in the press by the tea table. And Swan was soon distracted by overhearing one of the ladies responsible for the lavish spread ask 'Celia' to check the urn.

Celia was a strawberry blonde with a good figure and a ready smile, though to Swan's eye there was nothing startling about her. He was disappointed. Linley's infatuation with the girl had led him to expect someone altogether more spectacular. But he was also relieved that he did not have to feel jealous. Celia was no Aphrodite. And, from Swan's point of view, she was all the better for it.

*

Sir John Maffey, the United Kingdom Representative in Éire, as neutral a job title as the politicians either side of the Irish Sea had been able to agree upon, arrived during tea to see how his team was faring. A tall, handsome man in his mid-seventies, with the weathered look and light linen suit of someone who had served his country in many hotter spots than Dublin, chatted courteously with the opposition and effortlessly charmed the tea ladies. Eventually, his eye alighted upon Swan, whom Linley introduced as an old school friend who happened to be in the city on business.

'Good of you to turn out, Mr Swan,' said Maffey. 'Occasions like this are excellent for Anglo-Irish relations.'

'Glad to be able to help, Sir John.'

'Linley keeping you entertained?'

'Entertained but not necessarily enlightened.' Swan enjoyed the start Linley gave at that.

'Really? On what particular subject do you lack enlightenment?'

'I'm staying at the Shelbourne. I shared the lift yesterday with Malcolm MacDonald, the Minister of Health.' (This was true enough. Swan had heard the concierge address MacDonald by name and had chanced his arm during their brief journey together by claiming to recognize him from a photograph in the *Sunday Pictorial*. MacDonald, whose appearance was in reality wholly unmemorable, had seemed flattered by this, though not flattered enough to reveal why he was really in Dublin.) 'He told me he'd come over to look at Irish hospitals, which struck me as so unlikely I asked Linley what he was really up to. But my old chum simply wouldn't let on. You can take it from me, Sir John, Linley's discretion is indefatigable.'

Maffey laughed. 'I'm delighted to hear it.'

'I explained to Swan that we don't know any more than he does,' said Linley, looking by now more than a little relieved.

'Exactly. London keeps us firmly in the dark, Mr Swan. Now, what about that total the RDS put up? Think you can knock the runs off?'

'Don't pull any more stunts like that,' Linley growled when Maffey had left them to it. 'I told you MacDonald's mission was hush-hush.'

'But I did meet him in the lift.'

'Well, kindly pretend you didn't.'

'How is his mission going?'

'It's gone. He left this morning. And that's definitely my last word on the subject.'

It was his last word on any subject for a while, since Grigg-Mathers called them into the pavilion at that moment to be informed of the batting order. Despite not bowling, Swan was to go in at number 7. Linley meanwhile was allotted number 3. He bustled off to pad up.

The innings commenced shortly afterwards. Swan waited until a wicket had fallen and Linley had gone in to bat before wandering into the pavilion kitchenette and striking up a conversation with the legation secretaries, Celia among them, who were doing the washing-up. He made clear his connection with Linley, but Celia gave no hint that she knew who he was. She was either well practised in the art of amorous subterfuge or unaware that the flat in Merrion Street had been rented in his name. Swan's knowledge of Linley inclined him to the latter conclusion.

The Legation XI continued to lose wickets, while Linley held up one end. Grigg-Mathers hit a stylish fifty, but was undone by the left-arm wrist spin of none other than Ardal Quilligan. 'The damn fellow's bowling chinamen,' he complained upon returning to the pavilion, as if accusing him of cheating. But whatever Quilligan was bowling, it was too much for the next man in, who fell first ball.

'For God's sake try to bat better than you fielded,' Grigg-Mathers muttered to Swan in parting advice. The score was 128 for 5, the light perfect and the occasion ideal, in Swan's estimation as he strode out to bat, for a match-winning contribution from his good self. He had become increasingly irked by the captain's sarcasm, the failure to use him as a bowler and his lowly placing at number 7. He could recall regularly hoisting sixes into the chestnut trees during house matches on the Green at Ardingly and reckoned something along the same lines would do the trick here. He had always been a murderer of spin bowling.

Linley had a more cautious approach in mind when they met in the middle. 'Don't try tonking him, Cygnet. I'll take most of the bowling and we'll see this through.'

There were only two balls left in the over. Swan dutifully blocked them, studying Quilligan's action carefully and noting the amount of turn he was extracting from the pitch. He reckoned he could handle him with some ease. Linley did not seem eager to give him the chance, however. He hit a couple of twos off the innocuous medium-pacer at the other end and tried for a single off the last ball to keep the strike, but Swan sent him back. He had to dive to make his ground in the end and looked none too pleased.

Swan allowed himself one more sighter against Quilligan, then drove the next ball sweetly to the extra cover boundary, holding the pose so that anyone who had a mind to could admire the stroke properly. A spectator picked the ball up after it had crossed the rope and proved strangely reluctant to return it. The fielder had to walk right up to him before he handed it over. As he did so, Swan recognized him and cursed under his breath. It was Sergeant MacSweeney. And Swan did not suppose the man was given to taking strolls in Trinity College Park on Saturday afternoons.

He was still thinking about MacSweeney when the next delivery came floating down. Perhaps, if he had been concentrating, he would have spotted the googly. As it was, he played an airy drive, the ball spun away instead of in and neatly removed his off bail.

Linley did not shout 'What did I tell you?' from the other end of the pitch. His disgusted expression meant there was really no need to. Swan walked off to face the imprecations of Grigg-Mathers, watching MacSweeney marching round the boundary towards the pavilion as he went. They met, as MacSweeney was clearly determined they should, at the pavilion gate.

'Bad luck, sir,' he said, grinning broadly as he blocked Swan's path.

'Excuse me,' said Swan levelly. 'You're in my way.'

'Am I, though? Well, I can't guarantee that won't happen again while you're in Dublin, if you know what I mean.'

'Watch out,' said the number 8 batsman, who by now MacSweeney was also obstructing.

'Sorry, I'm sure.' MacSweeney took an exaggerated step to one side. 'Be seeing you, Mr Swan.' He touched his hat and headed on round the boundary.

The Legation XI were eventually all out for 171, losing the match by 36 runs, with Ardal Quilligan collecting seven wickets. Linley was last man out, still a few runs short of his fifty. Grigg-Mathers lapsed into geniality as soon as the cares of captaincy were lifted from his shoulders and astonished Swan by asking if he was available for their next match the following Saturday. Swan prevaricated. Linley urged him to agree. 'You weren't the only one Quilligan was too much for, Cygnet. Don't worry about it. Coming to drown your sorrows?'

The venue for sorrow-drowning was a nearby bar, to which both teams adjourned, with few exceptions, though Ardal Quilligan was one. 'More noted for his googly than his gregariousness, our Ardal,' explained Brendan, the affable RDS wicketkeeper, while urging Swan on in his efforts to develop a taste for Guinness. 'That four of yours off him was a lovely shot. He'd say as much himself if he was here.'

'I did the collecting of that,' said Joe, his equally affable team mate. 'And some fellow was so impressed he didn't seem to want to give the ball back.'

'He was a policeman,' said Swan impulsively. Then, seeing the surprised looks he had drawn in response, he added, 'Our paths crossed recently in the line of work.' (There was, after all, no reason why Joe and Brendan should doubt he was a member of the legation staff.)

'What would the Garda be doing spectating at one of our matches?' queried Brendan.

Swan shrugged. 'I've no idea.'

'Maybe he was looking for Heider,' suggested Joe, laughing at his own wit, wasted as it was on Swan. 'I expect the Garda reckon a German spy would very likely disguise himself as a cricketer.'

Brendan chortled at the remark and Swan felt obliged to join in as if he knew all about Heider. He tackled Linley on the subject when they met each other heading for the Gents.

'I don't know any more about Heider than the average reader of the *Irish Times*,' Linley declared as they lined up at the urinal. 'The Army spotted a Heinkel flying low over the County Meath countryside a few weeks back and found a radio transmitter attached to a parachute in the area. Conclusion: the Germans had dropped a spy who'd lost track of his radio after landing. About ten days ago the police raided a house here in Dublin where they suspected the spy was being sheltered by a former Blueshirt – the Irish equivalent of Mosley's Blackshirts. They arrested the house-holder, but Heider – the cleaning woman knew his name, would you believe – managed to give them the slip. He's still on the run. I imagine the authorities think he's trying to establish links with the IRA.'

'Making them even twitchier than usual about visits by foreigners to IRA internees at the Curragh?'

'Somewhat, yes.'

'So, in a sense, MacSweeney *was* looking for Heider.'

'But in the wrong place, naturally.' They crossed to the wash-hand basin. 'You've nothing to worry about, Cygnet. Just don't talk to any strange Germans. That's my advice. Sound as ever, I think you'll agree.'

The evening grew blurrily uproarious. Swan began to think he really was developing a taste for Guinness. Linley slipped away. Swan suspected he knew where he was going and who was waiting for him there. He wished him well. When he came to leave himself, he was well past worrying about police surveillance. They could follow him or not, as they pleased. They would learn nothing, because there was nothing for them to learn.

TWENTY-THREE

The Quilligan residence in Ballsbridge was a handsome bay-fronted red-brick house adorned with decorative plasterwork and wide, railinged steps up to an arched porch. Stained-glass panels around the front door depicted songbirds and seasonal scenes of sowing and harvest. Swan, but lately recovered from a hangover best described as stout, assumed the door would be answered by a maid or someone of the sort, and was surprised when it was actually opened by a woman who was quite clearly Isolde Quilligan.

She was wearing a demurely long-sleeved, round-necked, pleated dress, although its purplish colour somehow suggested reined-in fervour. She was thirty or so, young but no longer girlish, with shortish red hair and an ivory-pale, placid face on which calm contemplativeness seemed more fitting than a smile, as the modesty of the smile she offered him went some way to confirm.

'Mr Swan,' she said. 'Do come in.'

'Thank you.' He stepped into a wide hallway where a marble Nubian slave-girl supported a miniature fernery next to a hatstand. Swan shook Miss Quilligan's cool, soft hand and hung his fedora among the assorted straws and felts. He was already aware that his hostess was the sort of woman to whom he was strongly attracted, confounding his expectations of the spin-bowling solicitor's sister. More confounding still, he had the strange sense that Miss Quilligan was also aware of this.

'Ardal's told me all about your encounter on the cricket field yesterday, Mr Swan. I'd have come along if I'd known you'd be there, though, to be honest, I don't share my brother's passion for the game.'

'Strictly between us, Miss Quilligan, neither do I.'

She laughed gently. 'It'll be our secret. Do come into the drawing-room.'

He followed her into a large room with a bay overlooking the garden. The fireplace was monumental, the cornicing and rosetting ornate, but midsummer sunlight and pastel-hued carpet and furniture kept Victorian glumness at bay. Ardal Quilligan, looking scarcely less formal in his weekend attire than his office kit, advanced to greet Swan with a smile. They shook hands.

'Well played yesterday, Mr Quilligan,' Swan said. 'Exceptional bowling.'

'You must call him Ardal, Mr Swan,' said Miss Quilligan. 'And you must call me Isolde. I do hate all the misters and misses and madams of what passes for respectable society.'

'Very well . . . Isolde. Then you must call me Eldritch.'

'An unusual name.'

'I've tried to live up to it.'

'I'm sure you have. Now, sit down while I see to the tea. You might have fared better on another day, Eldritch. Edna deserts us on Sundays and Wednesdays and we have to fend for ourselves. Ardal tells me my scones aren't a patch on hers.'

'I tell her nothing of the kind,' her brother protested.

'He doesn't tell me in words, of course,' she explained as she left.

Ardal waved Swan into a chair and sat down opposite him. A cooling breeze, scented with blossom, drifted in through the open bay window. 'Well . . . Eldritch, our business . . . can be swiftly concluded. I visited Desmond on Friday and told him Cardale's signature on the document his solicitor supplied gives him exactly what he wants. He instructed me to inform the authorities that he wishes to sign himself out of internment as soon as possible. I've already set the ball rolling. Now it's just a question of time.'

'You told me you intended to warn him against accepting Cardale's offer.'

'Which I did.' Ardal smiled weakly. 'As you correctly predicted, he ignored me.' He spread his palms. 'Well, there it is. I am not my brother's keeper, merely his . . . adviser.'

'Have you any idea how long it'll be before he's released?'

'A week to ten days, at least. As I explained . . .'

'I should try to enjoy my holiday from the war?'

'Well, yes, you should. More cricket, perhaps?'

'Not if you're in the opposing team, Ardal. You spin the ball like a top.'

'Large hands and long fingers.' Ardal held them up for inspection. 'A trick of nature. No real skill at all. Whereas you looked to me to be a skilful batsman who's simply short of practice.'

'I have an even better excuse for getting out so cheaply, actually. There was a Special Branch policeman called MacSweeney watching my every move. Knowing you're under surveillance hinders concentration.'

'I see.' Ardal looked undismayed by the news, not to say unsurprised. 'Is this because of your visit to Desmond?'

Swan nodded. 'They hauled me in for questioning as soon as I got back to Dublin. They appeared to think I might be a German spy.'

'Oh dear. I'm afraid they rather see Germans spies everywhere at present.'

'I gather there's a real one on the loose.'

'Apparently so. Let's hope they catch him soon. Then they'll stop breathing down your neck.' Ardal clasped his hands together and leant forward in his chair. 'I know how you feel, Eldritch. I've been the object of Special Branch attention myself over the years. It's the price of having a brother in the IRA.'

'Has it made life difficult for you?'

'Occasionally very difficult. But I've never resented Desmond on that account. It's impossible to resent someone who's following his patriotic conscience, however extreme the actions it drives him to.

I've rather envied him, to be honest: his dedication; his sincerity. I suppose that's why I'm saddened by the thought of him abandoning the cause.'

'Whereas I rejoice in it,' said Isolde as she wheeled a tea trolley into the room. 'I barely remember the Easter Rising, but Father's horror at Desmond joining the rebels was something I grew up with. They were never reconciled. And the Civil War taught me the perniciousness of following your conscience regardless of the consequences. Women understand better than men that the true foundation of liberty is compromise.'

'I fear I've let you in for a lecture I've heard my sister deliver more than once, Eldritch,' said Ardal with a smile.

'You're preaching to the converted, Isolde,' said Swan. 'Compromise is my dearest principle.'

'I can't tell you how glad I am to hear that,' said Isolde. 'You may enjoy my scones after all.'

Tea was a far more relaxed and congenial occasion than Swan had anticipated. After cooing over the snapshot of young Simon Cardale, Isolde fetched the family photograph album and showed him how closely the boy resembled his father at the same age. There they all were in faded portraits and informal poses: Desmond, Ardal and Isolde as children with their parents – a portly father and a plump mother – beaming at the camera in the very same drawing-room, or assembled at picnics and bathing parties in years gone by. Isolde was clearly pinning her hopes for some kind of future for the family on establishing links with her nephew. 'Otherwise, what is there?' she declaimed. 'Ardal and I fossilizing in this house while Simon passes his childhood in England deprived of a father as well as a mother.'

'You could always marry someone, Issie,' said Ardal, smiling mischievously, 'if the lack of a next generation weighs so heavily on your mind.'

'But marry *who*, pray? I see no obvious candidates among the available manhood of Dublin.'

'Your standards are too high.'

'They're as low as I can bear them to be. And I might point out that marriage is open to you too.'

'But any woman I brought into this house would have to compete with you, Issie, causing me to fear for her sanity.'

A well-aimed serviette landed squarely on Ardal's face as his reward for that. To Swan's surprise, he laughed quite genuinely at his own discomfiture, even when he discovered a blob of plum jam on his shirt after removing the serviette. He excused himself to wash it off, leaving Swan to assure Isolde the apology she offered for the incident was unnecessary.

'Perhaps so, Eldritch,' she said. 'But I do need to thank you for the service you're doing this family. Whatever ill will there is between Desmond and Geoffrey Cardale needs to be set aside. Susan Cardale can't be brought back from the dead. But her son can be brought into our lives.'

'You know Cardale expects Desmond to do something for him in return for this?'

'Of course.'

'Are you worried what it might be?'

'Is it worse than breaking into the house of a so-called traitor in the middle of the night and shooting him in front of his wife and children?'

There, again, was the hint of fervour. Swan was impressed by her. She knew her own mind and, he suspected, the minds of others. 'No. It's nothing like that.'

'Then I'm not worried.'

'Of course, to see your nephew, you might need to go to England.'

'That would be no hardship.' Indeed, her tone implied, it might be just the excuse she needed to leave Ireland.

'Most people would say you're better off here,' her brother pointed out, dabbing at his shirt with his handkerchief as he strolled back into the room. 'And you may be forced to agree, when Germany starts bombing London.'

'You think they will?' Swan looked up at him.

'I'm sure of it.'

'A little danger might serve as a useful reminder that we're actually alive,' said Isolde. 'I've had cause to doubt it since this . . . emergency . . . began. Neutrality's turned out to be a synonym for sterility.'

'Perhaps Churchill will be able to talk de Valéra into joining the war,' suggested Swan, curious to see whether they were aware that such efforts were actually being made.

'There's not the remotest chance of that,' said Ardal, picking up his teacup and carrying it to the window, where he gazed out into the afternoon sunlight.

'Why not?'

'Firstly because no one's ever talked Dev into anything. And secondly—'

'Because the Taoiseach thinks Germany will win the war,' Isolde cut in. 'The high moral stance of our leader amounts to ensuring that he doesn't put Hitler's nose out of joint.'

'Well, he's right, isn't he?' mused Ardal. 'Germany will win.'

'I wish we hadn't started discussing the war,' said Isolde. 'It only depresses me.' She sighed. 'Would you like to see the garden, Eldritch? It's looking lovely just now.'

Ardal did not join the expedition into the garden, during which Swan did his level best to enthuse over the flower borders and the wisteria-draped pergola and the trio of elegantly candled horse chestnuts, until Isolde eventually took pity on him as they completed a second circuit of the lawn.

'You have no interest in any of this, do you, Eldritch?'

'Well . . .' He smiled. 'No.'

'I quite understand. It's actually quite pathetic. I shouldn't be filling my days with pruning and planting. I'm old before my time.'

'I wouldn't say that.'

'Only because you're too much of a gentleman.'

'Not an accusation often levelled at me, I must tell you.'

'Really? You surprise me.'

'But do I disappoint you? That's the question.' Swan took out his cigarette case. 'Smoke?'

Isolde shook her head. 'I'd better not. Ardal doesn't like me to. But don't let me stop you.'

Swan lit up. His first puff of smoke drifted between them in the sweet, laden air. Isolde's eyes were shaded from him. Yet he knew they were on him, searching, testing, pondering. To Ardal, watching from the drawing-room, if he was watching, the tension of the moment, the sudden concentration of possibilities, would have been wholly unapparent.

'What would you stop me doing, Isolde?'

'Nothing . . . that I can imagine.'

Swan took a long draw on his cigarette. The tension stretched. But it did not break. 'You mentioned Edna's other day off was Wednesday.'

'So I did.'

'I wouldn't like to think of you . . . alone here all day . . . with time hanging heavy on your hands.'

'It's how it'll be for me, I'm afraid.'

'Oh, I don't think so.' He blew a couple of smoke rings into the air and watched them gradually distort and dissolve. 'I have the distinct feeling this Wednesday will be very different for you.'

1976

TWENTY-FOUR

'You did *what*?'

Rachel stared at me in amazement as I told her about my late-night antics. I had some difficulty myself, in the cool grey light of morning, believing I'd gone through with Eldritch's plan to raid Twisk's office. We were sitting in the kitchen of the flat in Islington, with Marilyn long departed, breakfasting late and more frugally yet also more happily than I could have done at the Ritz. I'd slept poorly, nerves frayed by wondering whether Rachel would regret what had happened between us. The risks I'd run at Eldritch's say-so had taken their toll as well. My heart was at ease now, though. It was too soon to put a portentous name like love to the feelings Rachel and I had aroused in each other. But they were good feelings. There was no doubt about that.

'If you'd been caught, Eldritch would have left you to carry the can. You realize that, Stephen, don't you?'

'Technically, I wasn't committing a crime. I didn't break in. I just climbed.'

'OK. You got away with it, I'm glad to say. Now, are you going to tell me who Twisk's client is?'

'I can't.'

'Why not?'

'Because Twisk doesn't know himself. All the file contained was correspondence with the Belgian solicitor who hired him, acting on behalf of an anonymous client. We're back where we started.'

'Except that we know who the Belgian solicitor is?'

'His name's Oudermans. He has a practice in Antwerp.'

'*Antwerp?*'

'It occurred to me Eldritch could have been right all along. Maybe a member of your family really did hire him. Not your mother, of course. But . . . your brother?'

'Joey would never do that. It's far too . . . practical. Besides, he has no money of his own.'

'Your grandmother, then?'

'She wouldn't do something like that without telling Mom. I'm not sure she's mentally up to it, anyway. No. It has to be someone else.'

'But who?'

'I guess we'll have to ask Oudermans that, won't we?'

'You think we should go to Antwerp?'

'I think we have to. Just as soon as we've collected whatever it is Ardal Quilligan means to deliver to us. Ever been to Antwerp, Stephen?'

'No. Rotterdam would be the closest. Are they similar?'

'Antwerp's nicer, trust me.'

'I never doubted it would be. You weren't with me in Rotterdam.'

She pointed her finger at me and narrowed her gaze. 'Don't try to smooth-talk me.'

I smiled. 'Why not?'

She smiled too. 'Because you're too good at it.'

We went out to Hampstead and walked on the Heath. Time vanished as we strolled together, arm in arm. I felt absurdly contented, sitting with her on Parliament Hill, gazing down at the city, or into her eyes, always waiting, as they seemed to be, to meet mine.

'Is this going to work, Rachel?' I asked at some point.

'You don't mean whatever we fix up with Ardal Quilligan, do you?'

'No.'

'The answer's the same anyway. I hope so. I truly hope so.'

I kissed her. 'So do I.'

'Did I mention Marilyn's going away this weekend?'

'No.' I smiled. 'You didn't.'

'So don't try anything, OK?'

'As if I would.'

'That from a man who fits seduction and cat burglary all into one night.'

'I've given up cat burglary.'

'To concentrate on your other specialty?'

'If you think I should.'

Now she kissed me. 'I'll let you know.'

Eldritch, it turned out, agreed with Rachel: we'd have to go to Antwerp if we were to find out who was manipulating us. He showed us the temporary passport it had taken him most of the day to obtain when we met him back at the Ritz that afternoon. I sensed he knew, or at least suspected, that Rachel and I had become lovers. But nothing was said, not least because we had urgent business to attend to. We walked round together to Ryder Street, reaching the gallery, as agreed, at four o'clock.

There were no customers for Cardale to hurry on their way. He flipped the sign in the window round to CLOSED, locked the door and ushered us into a poky office at the rear.

'Ardal phoned about half an hour ago,' he reported. 'He wants you to call him back.'

'OK,' said Rachel. 'Give me the number.'

'Not you, Miss Banner. It's Fordham he wants to speak to.'

'Why?' asked Eldritch.

'He gave no reason. But he was emphatic on the point.'

'It's no problem,' I said, though I was as puzzled as Eldritch. 'I'll make the call.'

Cardale dialled the number and handed me the phone. 'Be careful,' said Eldritch as I took it.

It was several seconds before the ring tone cut in, enough time for Rachel to give me an encouraging smile, which I was sure didn't escape Eldritch's attention. Then Ardal Quilligan answered, so quickly he must have been sitting by the phone. His voice was hoarse, his Irish accent no more than a weak inflection. And he wasted no time on preliminaries. 'Is that Peter Fordham?'

'Yes.'

'You're sure about that, are you? You're sure your name's Fordham? Not . . . Swan?'

I didn't know what to say. And my failure to say anything was probably the answer he was looking for.

'As soon as Simon described your uncle to me, I guessed who he was. I suppose they were bound to let him out eventually. He once mentioned to me he had a brother. So, you'll be the brother's son, helping out old Uncle Eldritch. Maybe you find enquiring into his tangled past exciting. I must warn you, though: excitement can very soon turn to deadly danger. I'm sure Eldritch would agree with me on that. Is he there now?'

'Yes,' I replied cautiously.

'Good. Listen to me very carefully, Mr Swan. And don't interrupt. I have the proof Miss Banner needs to win her case and I'm willing to give it to her. But I'm not coming to England. That would be foolhardy.'

'Why?'

'*Didn't I tell you not to interrupt?*' His tone had suddenly sharpened. There was a brief silence. Then he continued, reverting to his gentle half-whisper. 'I don't trust my brother-in-law and I'm sure Eldritch doesn't either. So, we'll do this very carefully and outside Sir Miles Linley's bailiwick. I'll leave here tomorrow. We'll meet in Ostend on Sunday. You, Simon and Miss Banner will travel on the noon ferry from Dover. Don't bring Eldritch with you. I don't want this complicated by our . . . personal differences. When you arrive, go to the Hotel Hesperis.' He spelt out the name before continuing. 'It's on the Albert Promenade. I've reserved rooms for you. I'll contact you there. Is all that clear?'

'Yes.'

'Good. Until Sunday, then.' And, with that, he hung up.

*

Cardale gave no impression that his uncle had told him who *my* uncle really was. Perhaps Ardal was worried the knowledge might throw him into a panic, when what we all needed was for him at least to remain calm until this was settled. He certainly seemed calm, unfazed by the need to travel to Ostend and unshifting in his conviction that he was doing the right thing. He volunteered to drive us to Dover and we agreed to meet at the gallery on Sunday morning.

I saved a full account of what Ardal had said until the three of us had left the gallery and settled round a table at the espresso bar in the Piccadilly Arcade.

'So, Ardal's rumbled us, has he?' was Eldritch's straight-faced reaction. 'I wondered if he might.'

'Looks like you'll have to leave this to us,' said Rachel, sounding as happy about the prospect as I secretly was myself.

'Hardly,' said Eldritch. 'I'll be in Ostend on Sunday. I wouldn't miss it for the world.'

'You can't be. If Ardal sees you, he might call the whole thing off. We can't risk that.'

'Rachel's right, Eldritch,' I said.

'I'm going to have to become accustomed to you two joining forces against me, am I?' He looked at us with his narrow, inscrutable gaze.

'You know she's right,' I insisted.

He sighed. 'I won't be travelling with you, obviously. I'll go tomorrow, alone. I'll phone and let you know where I'm staying. Then, when you've laid hands on whatever it is Quilligan has and packed Cardale off back here, we'll meet and proceed to Antwerp. Don't worry. Quilligan won't spot me. I'm no keener to renew our acquaintance than he is.'

'What's the big problem between you and him?' asked Rachel.

Another sigh. 'When we've wrapped this up, Rachel, I'll tell you everything you want to know. Meanwhile, ask yourself this: why, out of all the Channel ports he could have chosen, did Quilligan opt for the one closest to Antwerp?'

'I don't know. Do you?'

'No. But it makes you think, doesn't it? At any rate, it makes me think. You'll be spending most of Sunday with Cardale. Pump him for information about his uncle. See if you can find out whether Quilligan's spent any time in Belgium recently.'

It was clear to me now what Eldritch suspected. But it was a suspicion that made no sense. 'Ardal Quilligan can't be our mystery man,' I said. 'Why would he hire us to search for proof he already has?'

'Because he wants someone to do his dirty work for him. If I'm right, he'll make it a condition of surrendering the proof that you deny you got it from him.'

'Well, I'll be happy to oblige him,' said Rachel. 'If that's all it takes to get it.'

'Of course. But remember: when your eyes are fixed on the prize, you don't see the ground crumbling beneath your feet. Who is Quilligan afraid of?'

'Linley,' I replied.

'Exactly. And we should be afraid of him too.'

'There's nothing he can do to stop us,' said Rachel.

Eldritch looked across at her as he took a thoughtful drag on his cigarette. 'Let's hope you're right,' he said softly.

Rachel was having none of Eldritch's caution. 'An old man who thinks a lot but not as sharply as he used to' was her summing-up over a champagne cocktail in the Ritz bar. Eldritch had gone up to his room, claiming he was tired and needed a rest. This seemed to confirm Rachel's view of him, which I half suspected was his intention. But my half-suspicions counted for very little compared with the intoxicating pleasure of Rachel's company.

We dined by candlelight at a French restaurant in Soho, then headed out to Islington. I didn't expect to be returning to the Ritz that night and Rachel clearly didn't want me to, even though neither of us came out and said as much. We were still, to some degree, feeling our way.

The flat was in darkness. Marilyn had gone. We'd have the place to ourselves until we left for Ostend and the prospect was a delicious one. Then, as we descended the basement steps, Rachel noticed something: a neat circular hole cut in one of the window-panes close to the latch. I knew at once what it meant.

The flat had been given the same treatment as Brenda Duthie's house. Every drawer had been turned out, their contents scattered across the floor. Rachel began to cry as she stared at the chaos in her room, her confidence drained in an instant. 'Linley's on to us,' she mumbled miserably. I did my best to comfort her, but the truth was undeniable. He *was* on to us. As Eldritch had foreseen.

I made some coffee. We drank it in the kitchen, where there were the fewest signs of disturbance. The caffeine, and several cigarettes, along with a large shot of Southern Comfort, restored Rachel's equilibrium. She dried her eyes. More accurately, I dried them. Her stubbornness began to win out. 'Whatever they were looking for, they won't have found it. There's nothing here they can use against me. All Linley's accomplished by resorting to this is to piss me off, which I'll make sure he regrets when my lawyers drag him into court.'

'That's the spirit,' I said, kissing her softly.

'Will you help me put everything back where it belongs?'

'Of course.'

'How are you on window repairs?'

'Fair to middling.'

'I want it so that Marilyn doesn't notice anything's happened when she comes back Sunday night.'

'Aren't you going to phone the police?'

'What for? We know who did this. But they won't be able to touch him, will they? No. This was designed to intimidate me. And it isn't going to work.'

The clear-up didn't take too long. Rachel was more or less certain by the end of it that nothing had been taken, which meant they really had found nothing to use against her – whoever *they* were. Eldritch's suggestion that the Secret Service were staging break-ins on Linley's orders still struck me as far-fetched, but the fact remained that the break-ins had happened. Was there a dimension to this Eldritch wasn't telling us about? In my own mind, I was convinced there was, but I was no closer to finding out what it might be.

I covered the hole in the window with cardboard, pending a proper repair in the morning, and took a turn round the square in case anyone was keeping watch on the flat. I saw no one except a man walking his dog who was clearly a local resident. His cheery 'Good evening' served somehow to propel the Secret Service theory further into the realms of improbability. A shady private investigator acting solo was nearer the mark. He was long gone, I reckoned. And he wouldn't be coming back.

'Once I've got the proof, I'll phone my mom and have her come to Antwerp,' Rachel said as we lay together in bed. 'I want the family to be united when we reopen the case. I want us to win together. All we have to do now is get from now to then. Thank God I've got you to help me, Stephen. A pointless break-in isn't going to stop us, is it? Nothing is. We're going to nail this. We really are.'

TWENTY-FIVE

Eldritch was in Ostend by the time we returned to the Ritz the following afternoon. He phoned at six, as promised, to report he'd booked into the Hotel du Parc. He gave me the address and telephone number and a final, predictable piece of advice. 'Be careful tomorrow, Stephen. Be very careful. There's a great deal riding on this.'

I needed no reminding of that, which was probably why I decided in the end not to tell him about the break-in. I took Rachel off to a West End musical for much the same reason. We needed distraction. We needed a reminder that a real if superficial world was whirling on its way while we prepared for our rendezvous in Belgium. It worked. We left the theatre light-hearted and un-worried, as lovers should be, happy to let tomorrow take care of itself.

Only to be brought up short by the placard at the nearest news-stand: 85 INJURED IN OLYMPIA BLAST. The front page of the *Evening Standard* was devoted to a report that a bomb hidden in a bin had exploded at the Ideal Home Exhibition earlier in the day. It was undoubtedly the work of the IRA. Irish history, it seemed, was determined to dog all our footsteps.

'Mom worries about me getting caught up in something like that,' said Rachel as we stared bleakly at the headlines. 'I guess she'd be pleased to know I'm leaving London tomorrow.'

'You'll soon be able to leave for good.'

She looked at me, her eyes in shadow. 'If I want to.'

We walked on then in silence. I prayed that what she wanted and what I wanted would turn out to be the same; and that our journey to Belgium would free us to discover that it was.

Simon Cardale's bullishness was undented when we met him at the gallery on a chill, grey morning, surrounded by the silence of a St James's Sunday. Linley had phoned him, asking if we'd been in touch again, but he'd stonewalled successfully, at least to hear him tell it. He didn't turn a hair at Eldritch's absence and news of the break-in didn't worry him, because, naturally, we didn't mention it. His mood was still that of a man enjoying the sensation of having a long-carried burden lifted from his shoulders – a mood we wanted to last.

The drive down to Kent in his big Volvo estate was a rerun in reverse of the journey Eldritch had taken from Dover with Cardale's grandfather thirty-six years earlier. I said nothing of that, of course, instead probing gently for information about Ardal Quilligan. Cardale couldn't tell me much. He had no reason to think his uncle had spent any time in Antwerp, but he couldn't rule it out either. 'I don't see or speak to him from one year's end to another. He generally keeps himself to himself.'

It was only as the ferry was easing away from the dock at Dover that Rachel admitted she usually suffered from seasickness on such crossings. The swell that was running didn't suggest this trip was going to be any different and the only antidote was to stay on deck in the fresh air, which became numbingly cold as soon as we left the harbour. Brief trips below to warm up were essential, during which I checked that all was well with Cardale. And so it was. Quietly installed in one of the lounges with his pipe and an Anthony Trollope novel, he looked preposterously contented.

It was late afternoon when we docked at Ostend. Seaside resorts need sunshine to look their best, a commodity this one currently lacked, along with people and warmth.

We left the ferry terminal and walked round the largely deserted promenade to the Hotel Hesperis, a modern medium-rise balconied block that looked out over a stretch of empty sand at a greyly heaving North Sea.

Our rooms were ready for us. My impression was that numerous other rooms were ready as well. We asked if there was a message for us. There wasn't. Cardale asked if a Mr Quilligan had checked in. He hadn't, though there was a reservation in his name. The receptionist then asked us if we were the people who'd phoned earlier, enquiring about Mr Quilligan. We weren't, of course.

Nor was Eldritch. I called him as soon as Rachel and I made it to our room. 'Do you think I'm a fool?' he snapped. 'Of course I didn't.'

'No one else knows Quilligan's coming here,' I pointed out.

'Wrong, boy. Somebody else does know.'

I was too perturbed to complain about him reverting to calling me *boy*. He was right, anyway. Somebody knew. But how? 'Cardale must have let something slip when he spoke to Linley,' I said. 'What do we do?'

'Sit tight and wait for Quilligan. It's all we *can* do.'

Not quite, in my assessment. I marched round to Cardale's room and demanded to know what he'd told Linley.

'Nothing, Fordham. Not a thing. I swear it. Maybe the call was from some friend of Ardal's in Majorca who knows he's due here.'

I conceded this was possible, partly to keep Cardale calm. I felt far from calm myself. I went back to our room and found Rachel standing out on the balcony, despite the chill wind that was blowing. She was smoking a cigarette and gazing down at the darkening beach. She didn't give Cardale's theory much more credence than I did. But the fact remained that neither of us could come up with a better explanation. We just had to hope he was right.

Several hours slowly and uneventfully passed. There was no word from Quilligan. He hadn't said when he'd contact us, of course, but the later he left it the nervier the waiting grew. Eldritch was holed up in one hotel and we in another, watching the clock and wondering when, or if, we'd hear something.

Eventually, we went down to the hotel restaurant with Cardale for a meal. There were few other diners and we were in no state to concentrate on food and drink. Conversation was faltering and aimless. Cardale embarked on an account that never seemed to reach any kind of conclusion about how he'd been called out recently to value a vast hoard of paintings at a country house in Norfolk. If the story had a point, it was lost on me. And his confident assertion that his uncle would be in touch soon didn't make much impact either.

'What if he isn't?' asked Rachel.

'But he will be, Miss Banner,' Cardale blithely insisted. 'He wouldn't have brought us all this way just to stand us up.'

It was hard to disagree with him about that. But the fact remained that we still hadn't heard from Quilligan – and nor had the front desk – when I phoned Eldritch at eleven o'clock.

'Do you think he's got cold feet?' I asked.

'Either that or he's playing safe and waiting until morning,' Eldritch replied. 'Which is exactly what we'll have to do.'

'There's something you ought to know,' I said then, Rachel and I having agreed we couldn't delay telling him about the break-in any longer.

I'd expected him to be alarmed, or angry with me for not telling him sooner. But his reaction was undismayed, not to say muted, as if he'd already assumed something of the kind was bound to have occurred. 'Linley's pulling out all the stops,' he said. 'The only question that really matters is whether we can move faster than he can anticipate. And the answer brings us back to Ardal Quilligan.' I heard him sigh. Then he surprised me by asking, 'What's the Hotel Hesperis like, Stephen?'

'Modern. Comfortable. Why?'

'The Hotel du Parc was modern and comfortable forty years ago. I stopped here for the night on my way to Antwerp to take up my post as Isaac Meridor's secretary. I wasn't sure I wanted to be stuck in Belgium, working for a Jewish diamond merchant, beholden to my father for fixing me up with the job in the first place. I seriously considered not going through with it. But I was short of money *and*

212

options. So, I carried on to Antwerp. In retrospect, I wish I hadn't. Whatever I'd have done instead couldn't have ended worse. I wasn't to know, of course. You only recognize turning-points in life when you look back at them.'

'What are you trying to say, Eldritch?'

'Only this: if you want to leave now – *you*, I mean, not Rachel, or me, or Cardale – if you want to clear out and leave us to it, I wouldn't blame you. In fact, I'd probably give you credit for being sensible.'

'What do you take me for? I'm not going to do that.'

'I know.'

'Then—'

'Try to get some sleep, Stephen. That's my final piece of advice.' And he hung up, leaving me wondering, not for the first time, what went on in that old man's mind.

I woke late the following morning, grey light and the whisper of the sea filtering into the room to rouse me. Rachel was still sleeping soundly when I went to take a shower. I stood under the hot jets of water, helpless to resist as the frustration and uncertainty of the previous night reassembled themselves in my mind. Where was Ardal Quilligan? Why hadn't he contacted us? And how much longer did we have to wait?

Rachel was awake when I came out of the bathroom. She'd opened the curtains to the dull Belgian day and ordered breakfast. 'I want you to know something,' she said as I bent to kiss her. 'This would be a whole lot harder to bear on my own.' It was almost as if she'd guessed what Eldritch had said to me. 'Oh, and there's something else as well.'

'What's that?'

'I think you're very sexy with wet hair.'

I laughed and kissed her again, then ambled to the window. Instantly, I locked eyes with a man leaning against the railings down on the promenade. He was tall and rangy, dressed in jeans and a leather jacket. He had dark, tightly cropped hair, a raw-boned face and a fixed, intent gaze.

Then I heard the doorbell buzz behind me. I looked over my shoulder at Rachel. 'They're quick with the breakfast here,' she said. 'Can you get that, Stephen?'

'Sure.' I took a glance out of the window as I turned away from it. The man was walking off along the promenade now, lighting a cigarette. Had he been watching our window? I couldn't be sure. Yet I sensed he had. I sensed it very powerfully.

The bell buzzed again as I neared the door. 'Hold on,' I called.

'They obviously don't want our croissants to get cold,' said Rachel. 'I like that.'

I flicked off the safety chain and opened the door. My smile of greeting for the waiter with the breakfast trolley froze, then faded. Three men, two of them uniformed police officers, were standing in the corridor.

'Mr Swan?' said the one not in uniform. He was thin, balding and narrow-faced, dressed in a suit and raincoat. He was holding out some kind of warrant card for me to see. 'Police. My name is Leysen. Miss Banner, she is with you?'

'What's going on?'

'Miss Banner?'

'Yes. She's here. What—'

'We need to speak to her. And to you.'

'What the hell's this all about?' demanded Rachel, tightening her bathrobe round her waist as she joined me at the door.

'We talk inside, please.' With that, and no indication that our permission was being sought, Leysen advanced into the room. One of the policemen stayed outside. The other strode in at Leysen's shoulder and closed the door behind him.

'What's happened?' asked Rachel. It was the right question. Clearly something *had* happened. And clearly it was nothing good.

'You're Stephen Swan and Rachel Banner?'

'Yes,' we replied in unison.

'You know Mr Ardal Quilligan?'

'Yes,' I began. 'That is—'

'We were due to meet him here yesterday,' Rachel cut in. 'He didn't show.'

214

'You and . . . Simon Cardale?'

'That's right,' I replied. 'The three of us came here to meet Quilligan.'

'But Mr Quilligan never arrived?'

'I just said that,' Rachel responded.

Leysen pursed his lips, pausing for a moment to take note of her tetchiness. 'Mr Quilligan was found dead in his car in the hotel's underground car park early this morning,' he said, with quiet emphasis.

'*What?*'

'We think he died some time last night.'

'*How?*'

'His throat was cut.'

'Oh God.' Rachel reeled as if struck. If I hadn't grabbed her, I think she'd have fallen to the floor. 'Oh dear God.' She rested her head against my shoulder.

'Your meeting with Mr Quilligan,' Leysen went on: 'what was it about?'

'He had something for us,' I replied, my mind struggling to assimilate the reality of what had happened and all its many consequences and implications.

'What was the something?'

'We don't know . . . exactly. It's . . . complicated.'

'Do you recognize this?'

He must have been holding the transparent plastic bag at his side the whole time. Only now did I notice it, though, as he held it up for us to see. There was a wooden-handled knife inside. The blade was about six inches long and was caked with blood.

'Oh Christ,' murmured Rachel. 'The knife.'

I looked down at her. 'What is it?'

'There's one just like that in the kitchen at the flat.'

'One just like . . . or the same one?'

'The same. It has to be. I've often used it. My fingerprints will probably be on the handle. The break-in, Stephen. Don't you see?'

And I did. Much as I didn't want to.

'*Do you recognize this?*' Leysen repeated.

1940

TWENTY-SIX

Sunlight slides across them as the half-closed curtains stir in the breeze from the open window. Swan gently withdraws from Isolde as their breathing slows. She falls away from him, rolling on to her hip, her eyes closed. He bends over her, stroking her shoulder, then running his fingers through her hair, flame-red where his ruffling of it catches the light. She opens her eyes and watches him slide down on to the bed beside her. She smiles and so does he. But neither speaks. Loving words would sound false, if not absurd.

Isolde rolls on to her back and lets out a long, slow breath. Somewhere below them a clock begins to strike. It is five o'clock this hot Wednesday afternoon in Dublin. The practicalities of life and the precautions necessary in the leading of it intrude upon the small, secret world they have shared these past few hours. Swan swings his legs to the floor and stands up. He stumbles slightly as he does so and Isolde chuckles. He turns to face her.

'Has this afternoon taken a lot out of you, Eldritch?' she asks, waiting for him to look her in the eye.

He smiles. 'Rather more than I expected, certainly. You're a very . . . demanding woman.'

'And you're just the man a demanding woman needs.'

'I'm glad to have been of service.'

'We must do this again . . . some time.'

'So we must.' He stoops over her where she lies and kisses her nipples, then her wide, smiling mouth. 'Some time very soon.'

Eldritch Swan walked away from the Quilligan house half an hour later, reflecting upon the difficulties of arranging another afternoon of sexual abandon with Isolde any sooner than the following week, disappointingly distant though that currently seemed. She had spoken of persuading Edna to take a half-day off in addition to her usual allowance, but if Ardal learnt of it he might grow suspicious, a risk Swan could not run given how vital Ardal's help was in securing his brother's release from the Curragh. Isolde could come to the Shelbourne, of course, but was concerned that many ladies of her acquaintance took tea at the hotel on a regular basis. It was all a damnable pity in Swan's estimation, and, he did not doubt, in Isolde's also, but he consoled himself with the thought that delay is perhaps the most potent of all aphrodisiacs.

Isolde's perfume, the softness of her skin and the taste of her lips still filled his mind as he entered the Shelbourne Hotel and went to the desk for his key. There, to his slight surprise, a letter was waiting for him, delivered by hand. He read it on his way up in the lift.

Dublin, Wednesday

Dear Mr Swan,
I am the former tenant of the top-floor flat at 31 Merrion Street. I believe there is a matter of mutual interest which we need to discuss. You will find me in the front snug at O'Connor's Bar in Lower Baggott Street at seven o'clock this evening.
    Your humble servant,
    Lorcan P. Henchy MA

Swan could not for the life of him imagine what interest he could share with a man who incorporated a middle initial and an academic qualification in his signature. In ordinary circumstances, he would have ignored the invitation. But his arrangement with

Linley meant the circumstances were far from ordinary and Henchy had succeeded in arousing his curiosity as well as his suspicion. He debated what to do while soaking in the bath and had made up his mind by the time he towelled himself dry.

It was well gone seven o'clock, though still short of 7.30, when Swan entered O'Connor's Bar. Trade was brisk, generating thick clouds of smoke and blather. The door to the snug was closed and the frosted glass that partitioned it off meant he could not see into it. 'Is there anyone in the snug?' he asked the barman as he paid for his whiskey.

'There is, sir,' came the tight-lipped reply.

'Lorcan Henchy?'

The barman smiled. 'The very same. You know him, do you?'

'You could say so.'

'I'm guessing he backed nothing but losers at Leopardstown races this afternoon. That'll explain his stand-offishness. You might tell him that if all our customers drank as slowly as him, we'd have to close down.'

'I'll do that.'

Henchy looked up from a rapt perusal of the *Irish Times* as Swan stepped into the snug. He was a short, round, ruddy-faced man of fifty or so, bald-headed but extravagantly bearded. He was wearing a frayed tweed suit, a shirt that looked as if it had missed the iron and a grubby yellow silk cravat. A three-quarters-full pint of Guinness stood on the table in front of him. He studied Swan over the rims of his half-moon spectacles and nodded at the door.

'Close that, would you?' he said in a gruff voice.

Swan eased the door shut behind him. 'Lorcan Henchy?'

'The very same. You're Swan, I take it?'

'I am.'

'Have a seat, why don't you?'

Swan sat down and played for time by lighting a cigarette. 'I got your message.'

'And you came to meet me. I'm obliged to you, sir.'

'This is only a short step from the Shelbourne. You're not putting me to any great inconvenience.'

'No, indeed.'

'How did you know where to find me?'

'Oh, I got your name and hotel from a fellow at Mrs Kilfeather's agent's who owed me a favour. I was a little surprised, of course, upon enquiring, to learn you were still staying there, when you have the use of my cosy old flat just around the corner. But no doubt there's a perfectly simple explanation for that.'

'Why should it concern you, Mr Henchy?'

'And why should you consent to be summoned here by a complete stranger? Good questions both, Mr Swan. Shall we take turns at answering them?' He took a swig of Guinness.

'I asked first.'

'So you did. Very well, then. It concerns me because I never wanted to move out and it's doubly galling, having been prevailed upon to do so, to find my successor so tardy at taking up residence. I've been keeping an eye on the old place, you see, and having words in appropriate ears. You are an absentee tenant, Mr Swan. A terribly well-spoken one, of course, as befits an . . . elocutionist, is it? Your fees must be formidable if you can run to a suite at the Shelbourne and rooms in Merrion Street for which you evidently have no pressing need.'

Swan's instincts were divided. He was minded to stand up and walk out without another word. He did not care to be cross-questioned by a man like Henchy, especially when the cross-questioning was so well reasoned. But the temptation to stay was stronger. He backed himself to learn more from their exchanges than Henchy was likely to. 'My affairs are my own, Mr Henchy. I don't like people prying into them.'

'On that principle we're agreed. I don't like having to do it myself.'

'Then why are you?'

'Because we must all shift for ourselves in the current . . . emergency.' He grinned knowingly.

222

'What did you mean by being prevailed upon to move out?'

'Do you not know what I meant?'

'I wouldn't ask if I did.'

'That's not necessarily so. I find more and more people I encounter these days feign ignorance – or knowledge – of a great many issues.'

'I see you have your paper open at the crossword page. And you appear to have solved most of the clues. You obviously enjoy puzzles. I confess I don't. They bore me. So, if you'll excuse me . . .' Swan started up from his chair.

'Bear with me a moment longer, sir.' Henchy raised his hands appeasingly. 'I crave your indulgence.'

Swan stood still for a few theatrical seconds of deliberation, then sat down again. 'A moment, then.'

'Thank you. I'm obliged. I'll take you at your word, Mr Swan. I'll assume you really are unaware of the circumstances of my sudden departure from thirty-one Merrion Street. Well, this was the way of it. I had my arm twisted, actually as well as meta-phorically, in point of fact. I was persuaded that my health would benefit from a move. Likewise my bank account. For the latter I'm naturally grateful. As, incidentally, are the bookmakers of Leopardstown.'

'I don't understand, Mr Henchy. Who persuaded you?'

'They didn't favour me with their visiting cards. All I can say is that they were . . . fellow countrymen of yours.'

'You're saying they were English?'

'Either that or first-class impressionists.'

'Why would they want you out of your flat?'

'A question I've pondered long and hard.'

'With what result?'

'I believe I have the answer. And I'm doing you the honour of supposing that you don't. I hardly think you'd have put your name to this enterprise if you understood its real purpose. That would be . . . foolhardy in the extreme. No, no. You've been talked into this, I have no doubt. You've been presented with some . . . innocent explanation . . . by a friend of yours at the British Legation, perhaps. Or perhaps, like me, you've been . . . bought off, if you'll pardon the phrase. The particulars hardly matter. The point to be grasped, Mr Swan, is that you've been deceived.'

'I don't think so.'

'Perhaps not. But you will, when you reflect on our discussion.' That, Swan was beginning to suspect, might well be true. There was something horribly credible about what Henchy was saying.

'So, you want to warn me I've been misled in some way, do you?'

'I fear you overestimate my generosity of spirit. No. What I want is to recruit you as a means of communication with those who are behind this: your friends, or friends of friends, at the British Legation. I want them to understand that my price has risen dramatically now that I've seen through their scheme. By a factor of ten, to be precise. A thousand pounds, by Friday. Those are my . . . revised terms.' He grinned disarmingly.

'You're crazy.' And Swan genuinely hoped he was.

'Not crazy, sir, though I'll own to desperate. Take a look at this.' Henchy pulled his wallet from his pocket and slipped something out of it, which he held out for Swan to see.

It was a head-and-shoulders snapshot of a young curly-haired girl. She was standing in front of a cottage doorway, smiling prettily, her head cocked shyly to one side.

'My daughter Moira. I left fatherhood late and still managed to make a poor fist of it. She lives with her mother down in Cork. Suffice to say I've been an even worse husband than I have a father. But redemption presents itself in the strangest of guises. Moira's a bright girl. There's something about her that needs . . . bringing on. I want her to have a good education. She might make more of it than I have. She could hardly make less. This is my best and very possibly only chance of doing right by her. You understand, Mr Swan? Perhaps you have children of your own.'

'I've no children.'

'Then you'll have to take my word for the way they tug at your heart.'

'I'm sure it's laudable you should want to help her.'

'So you'll . . . convey my terms?'

Swan was caught now on the horns of a dilemma. If he agreed, he implicitly admitted that Henchy's reading of his situation was correct. If he refused, he would be left wondering whether Linley had lied to him, with no pretext for challenging him on the point. 'Why don't you just go to the legation and convey them yourself?'

'Because once I'd walked in and said my piece, I might never walk out again.'

'This is all nonsense.'

'Is it? Are you sure of that, sir? There's an easy way for you to find out.'

'By acting as your messenger-boy?'

'If you wish to call it that. I think your friends might thank you for carrying this particular message. I know what their game is. And they wouldn't want me hawking that information on the open market.'

'And what, in your contention, is their . . . game?'

Henchy sat back in his chair, folded his arms and regarded Swan levelly. 'If you don't know, I'd—' The snug door suddenly opened. Henchy glanced up scowlingly at the newcomer, who promptly withdrew, closing the door behind him. 'I'd be doing you no kindness to tell you,' Henchy resumed. 'And it's hardly to be spoken of in such surroundings.'

'Supposing you were . . . persuaded . . . to leave your flat by . . . what should I call them, British agents? . . . how would they know you weren't bluffing when you claim to have deduced what their . . . sinister motive . . . was?'

'A reasonable question. Give them this name.' Henchy unfolded his newspaper and turned to another page, which he slid round for Swan to see, tapping with his forefinger at the side-column headline **Garda search for Heider continues**.

'Heider? The German spy?'

'That's certainly what the *Irish Times* calls him. A German spy. And if you believe everything you read in the papers, I suppose that's what he must be.'

'What are you getting at?'

'The truth. As they'll understand when you mention Heider. I'm not bluffing. I want my thousand pounds. I think they'll agree it's a fair price. I'll collect it from you. No one else.'

'Now, hold on just a—'

'You have more to lose than anyone if this gets out, Mr Swan. I'm actually doing you a favour. But I'm prepared to pay you a ten per cent handling fee nevertheless, in recognition of the inconvenience you'll be put to. It's generous of me in the circumstances. But as those who know me will tell you, I am a generous man.'

A hundred pounds. Wherever Swan turned, people seemed determined to offer him money. And he often had to do surprisingly little to earn it. 'Very well. I make no guarantees, Mr Henchy. But, as it happens, I do know someone at the British Legation. I'll tell him what you've said.'

'Thank you. I'll telephone you at the Shelbourne at seven o'clock tomorrow evening for news of his response.'

'Since you know where I'm staying, perhaps I should know where you're to be found.'

'I think not. Just be in your room at the Shelbourne when I call.' He pulled out his watch and peered at it. 'Well, well. Is that the time? I must be on my way.' He took a deep swallow of Guinness and stood up, wedging his tightly rolled *Irish Times* in his jacket pocket. 'It's been a pleasure, Mr Swan. I predict we'll soon be glad we met like this, two gentlemen thrown together in a world we barely comprehend but whose rules we must abide by whether we like it or not. Yes indeed. I'm sure of it. A happy outcome and an early one. That'll suit the pair of us, I'm thinking.' He smiled and offered Swan his hand, as if an eminently satisfactory business arrangement had been concluded between them, which, as far as Swan could tell, it had been from Henchy's point of view.

Swan reached up and shook his hand. 'You should know I don't necessarily believe a single word you've said to me, Mr Henchy.'

'Oh, I'm well aware of that. But your scepticism won't last long, I can assure you.' He moved past Swan to the section of the bar serving the snug and called to the barman. 'Another whiskey for my friend here when he wants one, Jim.' There was a jingle of coin on wood. 'And whatever you're having yourself.' Then he clapped Swan on the shoulder and lumbered out.

Swan drained his glass, stood up and stepped across to the bar to claim his refill. He was sure of very little at that moment. But his need of another whiskey was definite.

TWENTY-SEVEN

Miles Linley arrived at O'Connor's Bar less than an hour after Swan's telephone call had interrupted supper at his lodgings in Donnybrook. He entered the snug, which Swan had had to himself since Henchy's departure, with the flustered air and evasive expression of a man uncertain just how serious the problem was that confronted him. But his uncertainty was not destined to be prolonged.

'What's this all about, Cygnet?' he asked with forced joviality. 'You sounded a touch overwrought on the blower.'

'Do you know Lorcan Henchy, Linley?'

'Never heard of him.'

'He's the previous tenant of the flat I'm renting for you.'

'Really? Well, no reason I should have, then.'

'He was here earlier.'

'Was he? What of it?'

'He reckons I've been duped.'

'Duped? What are you on about?'

'It's simple enough. Deceived. Lied to. Taken for a ride. By you.'

'This is preposterous. I don't know what nonsense this fellow's been feeding you, but—'

'Save it. Just tell me, here and now, to my face: is it true Henchy was bribed and threatened into moving out?'

'Of course not.'

'Only he claims he was, you see. And he also claims he's found out why, which somehow I don't think has anything to do with you and Celia. Because that grubby little secret wouldn't be worth a thousand pounds, now would it?'

'A thousand pounds?'

'The price of Henchy's silence.'

'The fellow's mad.'

'Mad or not, he wants an answer within twenty-four hours.'

'Look, there must have been some—'

'Misunderstanding? I should say. But before you utter any more denials you might later regret, consider this. Henchy proposes to deal with you through me. He won't negotiate with you direct. And he seems confident you don't know where he's been living since he left Merrion Street. So, either you tell me the truth or you dare him to do his worst. You'll be a better judge than I am of whether you can afford to do that. To help you assess the risk, I'd better give you a name he asked me to mention.' Swan lowered his voice. 'Heider.'

Linley sighed and rubbed his eyes. 'Damn it all to hell,' he murmured.

'Is that an admission you've been lying to me?'

'No. I . . .' Linley turned away, as if unable to face Swan. 'Yes. But I had to. It was a matter of . . .'

'A matter of what?'

Linley polished off the remainder of his whiskey in a single swallow. 'We can't talk here. I can explain everything. But . . .' He managed to look back at Swan. 'We'd better step outside.'

'I'm sorry, Cygnet,' Linley began, as he led the way towards St Stephen's Green. 'It's true. I'm not having an affair with Celia. I needed someone unconnected with the legation to rent the flat and you providentially presented yourself as a candidate, so I . . . spun you a yarn I thought you'd fall for. No harm would have been done if Henchy hadn't crawled back out of the woodwork. You wouldn't have suffered by the deception. It was . . . a white lie.'

'So you were trying to spare my feelings in some way, were you?'

'Not exactly. It's, er . . . a delicate business.'

'How delicate?'

'Very. Sensitive, perhaps I should say. It's a matter of ... national security. And naturally ... I'm not referring to the nation we find ourselves in at the moment.'

Reaching the corner of St Stephen's Green, they crossed over to the entrance to the park. The keeper was locking the gate in preparation for closure, so they headed south along the pavement, next to the railings. The light still held and the air was warm. Their voices were hushed in the silence of the summer evening. Swan was holding his anger in check, awaiting the moment when he would know whether the lies Linley had told him could in any way be justified.

'What I'm about to say mustn't go any further, Cygnet. I'm deadly serious. These are state secrets. I'm breaking the Official Secrets Act just by discussing them with you. But if we're to stop Henchy making trouble, I can't very well keep you in the dark about the sort of trouble that might be. I must have your assurance you won't breathe a word of this to anyone else.'

'You are going to tell me the truth this time, aren't you, Linley?'

Linley cast him a rueful sidelong glance. 'I appear to have no alternative.'

'Then you can rest assured I'll keep it to myself.'

'Good.'

Linley warmed up for his explanation with a swig from a hip flask, which he then offered to Swan. The taste of fine cognac came as a pleasant surprise, though perhaps it should not have. Linley had never been one to stint himself.

'This is how it is. De Valéra knows that if Germany overruns England, as he believes they will, Éire, neutral or not, won't be far behind. So, he's planning ahead, considering what kind of accommodation he can come to with Hitler. Is he to be a Pétain or a de Gaulle or something in between? And can he somehow achieve Irish unification in exchange for an acceptance of German overlordship? We think this so-called spy the Germans parachuted in, Heider, may be more in the way of a negotiator, you see, proposing a deal acceptable to both Dev and his former friends in the IRA.

The failure of the police to capture Heider in that recent house raid had a put-up look about it to us, as if they didn't really want to catch him at all. The pressing question is: what does Heider have to offer? Guarantees of Irish unity and autonomy in exchange for opening a back door for a German invasion of England? It's possible. And it's very worrying. You don't need me to tell you how narrow the thread is the old country's hanging by at the moment. It could be all up for us if Dev strikes terms with Berlin.

'What does this have to do with thirty-one Merrion Street? Well, it's quite simple, really. The flat overlooks the entrance to Government Buildings, where Dev has his office. It enables us to monitor all comings and goings. It means we know who calls on him and for how long. The identity of those visitors and the duration of their visits may provide clues to his intentions. Early warning is what London requires above all else. It may become necessary to launch a pre-emptive invasion of Éire from the North if it appears Dev is willing and likely to stab us in the back. I was charged with finding a suitable spot from which to carry out such surveillance. Henchy's flat was one of several that fitted the bill. Enquiries suggested he'd be the tenant most easily induced to move out – an impecunious solitary with no visible means of support; someone unlikely to cause us any problems.'

'You got that rather dramatically wrong.'

Linley sighed heavily. 'So it appears.' They had turned the corner now and were traversing the southern side of the Green. 'Anyway, winkling Henchy out of the flat was one thing. I was also required to arrange a tenancy that couldn't be traced to the British Legation. I needn't spell out for you how disastrous it would be if the Irish found out what we're doing. I was still wrestling with how to accomplish that when I heard you'd been picked up by Special Branch.'

'And you calculated you could turn my gratitude for being bailed out to your advantage?'

'It's not as bad as you make it sound. I was doing my patriotic duty. I just didn't tell you that you were doing yours.'

Patriotic duty. It was an argument Swan could not easily defeat.

If the situation was as critical as Linley had described, it was impossible to condemn him for what he had done. 'You might have levelled with me,' Swan nevertheless complained. 'I'd hardly have refused to help out with so much riding on it.'

'For God's sake, Cygnet, it was a top-secret assignment. I had no authorization to let someone like you in on it.'

'What do you mean – someone like me?'

'A civilian who'd come over from England to visit an IRA internee. A man Irish Special Branch are highly suspicious of. Frankly, you're the last person we'd want to involve.'

'But you *are* involving me.'

'Because I have to. If Henchy's found out what we're up to and reports it to the authorities, our goose is cooked. He has to be stopped.'

'Pay him, then.'

'And then what? Blackmailers always come back for more. No. It's not as simple as stuffing Henchy's mouth with gold, I'm afraid.'

'I doubt he would come back for more. This is all about his daughter, actually.'

'What daughter?'

'She lives with her mother in Cork. He showed me her photograph. He's quite sentimental about her and wants to see she has a good education.'

'My heart bleeds.' Linley pulled up and rounded on Swan. Now he was the one, it seemed, who was suppressing anger. 'Listen to me, Cygnet. This is not some kind of operetta. This is the survival of our country. Henchy and his daughter in Cork can go to blazes for all I care. When MacDonald came over last week he as good as offered Dev the North on a plate if Dev would only bring Éire into the war. We're that desperate.'

'How does Craigavon feel about that?' It struck Swan as inconceivable, in point of fact, that Northern Ireland's notoriously intransigent Prime Minister should have consented to such a proposal. And he was right.

'Craigavon doesn't know anything about it. If he did, he'd be spitting blood. You see? There are people far more important than you we haven't . . . levelled with.'

'How did de Valéra respond when MacDonald offered him what he's always wanted?'

'He said he'd think about it. And he's still thinking. A great deal hinges on the eventual answer. Which way will he jump? The surveillance operation may give us a clue. Hence its vital importance.'

'All right, all right. You've made your point. I can see you had little alternative but to string me along.'

'So, my apology's been accepted, has it?'

'Yes. Of course.' They shook hands then, like the two English gentlemen they wished to be thought, and walked on round the Green.

'When did Henchy say he'd contact you?' Linley asked.

'Seven o'clock tomorrow evening.'

'Very well. I'll alert my boss tonight. He'll confer with *his* bosses in London tomorrow. You and I had better meet at six so that I can tell you what to say to Henchy.' He fell silent for a moment, then said musingly, 'A thousand pounds. Well, well, well. The fellow has more nerve than I gave him credit for. It's a dismal insight into human nature, even so. If he was a loyal Irishman, he'd have gone straight to the authorities. Instead, he seizes an opportunity to enrich himself.'

Now hardly seemed the moment to mention the share Swan had been promised of Henchy's pay-off. Instead he asked mildly, 'Do you intend to ask me to deliver the money to Henchy?'

'If we decide to pay up, yes. You're not going to object, are you?'

'No, no. As you say, we all have to do our bit. And Henchy's insistent on dealing only with me. But what about Moynihan's mob? It could get sticky if they were on my tail when I meet him.'

'I've seen no sign of them this evening.'

'Nor me. They seem to have laid off today.' That was only partly true. In fact, Swan had gone to some lengths to lose the fellow he had believed to be following him earlier by a hazardous last-minute race for a train leaving Westland Row station. He had got off at the

233

next stop and walked from there to the Quilligan house. Naturally, he had no intention of recounting any of that to Linley. 'I fear they won't lay off for good, though.'

'There are various reliable techniques for shedding unwanted company in emergencies. I'll run over some of them if you like.'

'I think you'd better.'

Linley laughed for the first time that evening. 'We're making quite the undercover operative of you, aren't we, Cygnet?'

'Apparently so.'

'It's on my conscience that I've placed you in an invidious position. It had to be done, but I don't want you to think I did it without a qualm. As the new tenant at thirty-one Merrion Street, you'd find yourself in hot water with the authorities if they discovered what the flat was being used for. We'd have a full-scale diplomatic incident on our hands, but you'd certainly have grave difficulties of your own. Deportation would be the least of it, I should say.'

'That thought had already occurred to me.'

'I'm relieved to hear it.' Linley shot Swan a knowing grin. 'For a moment, I was beginning to believe you were doing all this just for King and country.'

1976

TWENTY-EIGHT

The picture-postcard charms of Bruges were nowhere apparent at the Palace of Justice. Rachel and I were driven there in separate cars, our last words exchanged before we knew it in our room at the Hesperis. I was left in a windowless holding cell while they questioned Rachel. Shock and confusion were no friends to clear thinking. I knew what they'd said had happened and how bad it looked for us, but how much I should reveal when my turn came I couldn't decide, not least because I had no way of knowing what Rachel had already revealed.

I assumed they'd brought in Cardale as well, though I hadn't seen him as we were bustled out of the hotel. As for Eldritch, had Rachel mentioned him? Did he even know where we were? There again, I was clueless. In the end, all I could trust was my own instinct. Rachel would tell them the truth, but not quite the whole truth. She'd leave Eldritch out of it. And since Cardale didn't know the old man had travelled to Ostend in the first place, he'd be in the clear – to help us as best he could, or was willing to. Thirty-six years in prison had doubtless left him with a well-founded dread of the police. Whatever he did for us he'd do at arm's length.

Sir Miles Linley had arranged Ardal Quilligan's murder. I didn't have a doubt of that, dismissive though I'd been earlier of Eldritch's claim that he was behind the break-ins. The choice of murder weapon clinched it, designed as it was to frame Rachel. The proof Quilligan had brought with him that his brother had forged the Picassos was gone now. That too I didn't doubt. And without it, all we could aim for was our own exoneration. Victory of the sort that had briefly been within reach was now unattainable.

But there had to be more driving Linley than fear of being caught up in a costly lawsuit. Murder – of his own brother-in-law – was too extreme a response. That more would explain everything, I felt certain. But what it might be Eldritch had kept to himself and the Belgian police weren't going to be fobbed off with vague accusations. They'd need evidence. And the only evidence they had so far suggested Rachel Banner had killed Ardal Quilligan – with or without my assistance.

The interview room featured utilitarian furniture, blank grey walls and a barred window through which the medieval spires and belfries of Bruges could be distantly glimpsed. Leysen had handed over to a predatorily tall, stooped, grey-bearded man who introduced himself as Herman Bequaert, *onderzoeksrechter* – judge of investigation – for our cases, as he explained in fluent English. He was accompanied by a clerk and a uniformed officer was also in attendance, presumably in case I cut up rough. The truth was, though, that I felt as weak as a kitten. My hands were shaking, my heart palpitating. Two hours of solitude – as the clock on the wall revealed it had been – had left me with little grasp of anything except the seriousness of the situation. I wondered how close Rachel actually was to me within the starkly functional architecture of the building. I wished I could see her, or speak to her. I wished we could explain *together* how this had come about. But they wouldn't allow that, I knew. We'd be kept rigorously apart, so that our separate accounts could be compared and contrasted.

I stumbled out a request to be allowed a phone call to a lawyer, ignorant though I was of whether I had any such right in Belgian law. Bequaert surprised me by the affability of his response. Would I choose the same one as Rachel – Oudermans of Antwerp? Yes, of course. Who else was there to turn to? Well, Oudermans had been contacted. Someone was on their way. But Bruges was a ninety-kilometre drive from Antwerp. Besides, he explained, our legal representative wasn't entitled to sit in on the interviews. So . . .

'How do you know the firm of Oudermans, Mr Swan?' Instantly, I was on treacherous ground. How had Rachel answered that question? I said she'd mentioned them in some context I couldn't recall. 'Were you and Miss Banner together the whole time you were in Ostend?' This was my chance to distance myself from her, I realized: to assert that there'd been an opportunity for her to go down to the car park on her own and kill Quilligan. It wasn't a chance I had any intention of taking.

But Bequaert didn't drop the subject. 'Mr Cardale says you visited him in his room last evening and Miss Banner wasn't with you.' Well, that was undeniable. But I'd only been there a few minutes. Still, it disproved my claim that Rachel and I hadn't parted, even briefly. Already, the interview was going badly.

The break-in in London during which the murder weapon had supposedly been stolen: naturally, we'd reported it to the police, hadn't we? No, we hadn't. And would Rachel's flatmate be able to confirm such a break-in had actually taken place? No, she wouldn't. Bequaert looked at me wearily. I knew what he was thinking. Was this the best I could do? Did I seriously think this was good enough? No, I didn't. But at least I didn't have to say as much.

We came to the forgery story. That, his expression implied, was all it was: a *story*. The only luggage in Quilligan's car was an overnight bag. It contained nothing remotely relevant. 'Of course not,' I said. 'They stole it after killing him.'

'And *they* are?' enquired Bequaert. I didn't hold back, any more than I guessed Rachel had. Linley, Linley, Linley. It was all down to him. 'Sir Miles Linley,' Bequaert carefully specified. 'Retired diplomat. A man with . . . an impeccable reputation. Ardal Quilligan's brother-in-law. He is the murderer? And the burglar?'

'Not exactly. He must have . . . hired people to steal the knife and kill Quilligan.' It sounded hollow even to me.

Back to the break-in – the *alleged* break-in: could Rachel have turned the flat over herself to convince me it had taken place? The carrot was being dangled in front of my nose again. Say yes. Say she could have skipped out of the hotel room while I was asleep, met Quilligan in the car park by secret prior arrangement and then . . . cut his throat.

'Why would she do such a thing?'

'You tell me, Mr Swan. You tell me.'

'I can't. Because she didn't.'

He was unconvinced. That was obvious. But a contradiction he never directly referred to clearly bothered him. If Ardal Quilligan had brought the much mooted proof to Ostend, where was it now? And why would Rachel want to kill him? Had I seen blood on her clothes? There'd have been a lot of it. 'Arterial spray carries a long way,' Bequaert emphasized in his perfectly enunciated, painstaking English. I assured him I hadn't. If he didn't believe me, what had become of those blood-stained clothes? They must have searched our room thoroughly.

We were going in circles by now. Rachel's fingerprints were on the knife. Mine weren't. I could sell her down the river if I wanted to save myself. It's what Bequaert was implicitly urging me to do. Eventually, he realized I wasn't going to. Then, and only then, he played his trump card. There was a record of two telephone calls from our room to the Hotel du Parc. Who did we know who was staying there? The game was up. They were bound to have checked already and learnt another Swan had booked into the Parc.

'My uncle, Eldritch Swan.' *Sorry, Eldritch*, I silently apologized to him. *I have no choice.*

'Your uncle accompanied you to Ostend?'

'No. He went ahead.'

'Why?'

'He, er . . . didn't want Simon Cardale to feel . . . outnumbered.' What kind of an answer was that? It was pitiful.

'Mr Cardale was surprised when he learnt from us that your name is Stephen Swan. We knew because that was the name the hotel took from your passport. But he thought you were called Peter Fordham. Why the alias?'

'My uncle and . . . Sir Miles Linley . . . were at school together.

240

They . . . fell out . . . years ago. We didn't want Cardale to . . . make the connection.'

'Where is your uncle now?'

'Isn't he at the Hotel du Parc?' Obviously he wasn't, which gave me some small cheer to offset the prevailing bleakness.

'He checked out this morning, shortly after you and Miss Banner were detained. A porter at the Hesperis told Inspecteur Leysen later that an elderly Englishman had asked him why there were police in the hotel. The porter told him about the body in the car park. Of course, he did not know who the dead man was.' No. But Eldritch knew. Right away. 'So, where is he?'

'I don't know.'

'Where do you *think* he is?'

I shrugged. 'Travelling back to England?'

'Not staying here to help you and Miss Banner?'

'How could he do that?'

'By speaking to us, perhaps. By telling us the truth.'

'That hasn't done me much good.'

Silence fell. The ticking of the clock became audible. Bequaert said something to the clerk in Dutch, then stood up. 'Take some more time to think, Mr Swan,' he said, sighing. Then he walked out.

As far as I could judge, in the absence of my confiscated wrist-watch, the second stay in the cell was even longer than my first. The thinking Bequaert wanted me to do didn't lead where he'd have hoped. The truth, incredible though it might seem, was all he was going to get from me. I had nothing else to offer. I tried to fix Rachel's face in my mind, to draw some comfort from knowing we weren't far apart, even though we couldn't see or speak to each other. And I willed her to do the same.

When they next came for me, I thought I'd be taken back to the interview room. Instead, I was shown into a smaller room, where a man who was surely too showily dressed to be a detective was wait-ing for me, smoking a cigarette and sipping a cup of coffee. His suit was gigantically lapelled and gaudily herringboned, paired with a zigzag-patterned tie. He had shoulder-length dark hair and a round, boyish face. He jumped up from his chair as I entered and shook me vigorously by the hand, smiling broadly.

'Pleased to meet you, Mr Swan. I'm Bart van Briel. From Oudermans. We're getting you out of here.'

'You are?'

'One or two pesky conditions. They're keeping your passport, for instance. They have no legal right to, but if you don't agree they won't release you, so I said you'd be willing. It's . . . better than the alternative, I reckon.'

'What about Rachel?'

'Ah, no. Miss Banner they're holding. At least overnight. Nothing I can do there.'

'I'm not leaving without her.'

'You must.' He lowered his voice, though the policeman on the door wasn't far enough away to miss even a whisper. 'You'll be more use to Miss Banner on the outside. I'll explain when we're on the road.'

'The road to where?'

'Antwerp, of course.'

Van Briel whisked me through the formalities of my release, most of them conducted in Dutch. All my possessions except my passport were returned to me. One thing made very clear to me in English was that I wasn't to leave Belgium. I kept asking to see Rachel before I left but that was firmly ruled out. It was van Briel who finally shut me up on the point. 'Miss Banner's already been transferred to the local prison on the other side of—'

'*Prison?*'

'It's not as bad as it sounds. She'll actually be more comfortable than she would be staying here. But if you fuck about like this any more, the *onderzoeksrechter* might change his mind and send you there as well. He's not like a judge in England. He's in charge of the whole investigation. So, please, can we just get the hell out?'

He loaded me into his Porsche and we headed for the autoroute.

242

The loud, fast-moving world was a shock after so many hours of confinement that had felt like days in the living of them. Dusk was falling and I wondered what sort of an evening, and a night to follow, Rachel would have, in a prison cell.

Van Briel seemed to read my thoughts. 'She'll be OK, Mr Swan. Detainees who haven't been charged yet get treated well, I assure you.'

'And where are you taking me?' I asked.

'My place in Antwerp.' Van Briel grinned. 'They had to have an address for you before they'd let you go. Without a passport, you couldn't stay in a hotel anyway. I've got a form for you to carry in case you're stopped and asked for identification. We don't want you charged with vagrancy while you're still a murder suspect.' Another grin. 'That would look kind of bad.'

'You think they might release Rachel tomorrow?'

'No chance. They've got the evidence to charge her with murder any time they like. But they can hold her for five days before she has to go before the *raadkamer* for a decision on whether to charge her or not.'

'But you said—'

'You weren't thinking straight, Mr Swan, so I said what I reckoned you wanted to hear.'

'I want to hear the truth.'

'So do I.'

'What the hell's that supposed to mean?'

'It means my boss sent me to do the best I could for you and Miss Banner. He chose me because I cut corners and get results.' A horn blare and a torrent of Dutch obscenities, aimed at a driver who'd just had the temerity to pull out in front of us, provided an instant demonstration of van Briel's attitude to life in general and quite possibly the law in particular. 'This is where we are, right? Ardal Quilligan dead.' He made a slashing gesture across his throat with his forefinger. 'Murder weapon belongs to Miss Banner and has her fingerprints on it. But not yours. Which is why you're in this car and she's back there. Plus your uncle's missing. And Mr Cardale—'

'Yes. What about Cardale?'

243

'Not my client. Not my business. My understanding is they let him go earlier, *with* his passport. So, probably headed back to London. Your uncle too, maybe?'

'I don't know.'

'Tell me what you do know. Everything. The whole lot.' He chuckled. 'Well, as much as you can, anyway. My boss told me about our anonymous client, Mr Swan. Not who he is, but what he wants from your uncle. So, I'm in the picture on all that. But last night? Different story. You need to explain to me what happened. Beginning to end. OK?'

I sighed. 'OK.'

TWENTY-NINE

It was dark by the time we reached Antwerp. The city was a form-less presence beyond the lights of the autoroute. I was tired and depressed. I couldn't help feeling I'd deserted Rachel, even though, according to van Briel, she'd been relieved to hear they were going to let me go. She was counting on me to retrieve the situation, of course. I knew that. I only hoped I could.

Our destination, though I was unaware of it, was Zurenborg, the turn-of-the-century residential district famous for its architectural riches, where Isaac Meridor had chosen to live when he was up-and-coming, where he'd continued to live when he'd very much arrived, and where his widow and grandson were still to be found. I realized we were in the area when I glimpsed a road sign reading COGELS-OSYLEI and remembered Eldritch saying the Meridor res-idence, Zonnestralen, was in the Avenue Cogels-Osy.

'We're near Zonnestralen,' I said, breaking a silence that had glumly ruled since van Briel had given up interrogating me about the events of the previous night.

'Yes, Mr Swan, we are. In fact, here it is.'

He pulled over to the side of the street and I recognized the house at once from Eldritch's description: tall, high-windowed and balconied, with serpentine wrought ironwork and Art Nouveau styling. There were few lights showing and an air of neglect hung around it. Good times were just a memory lodged in the masonry.

'I live a couple of streets away,' said van Briel. 'My place looks very different, but that's Zurenborg. All kinds of houses. All kinds of people. I love it. I guess Mevrouw Meridor and her grandson must too.'

'Do you know them?'

'Never heard of them till my boss called me in this morning. Hey, maybe he chose me just because I live round here. Anyway, it's lucky for you. You won't have far to go when you visit.'

He was right, of course. I'd have to go and see Mrs Meridor and her grandson, Rachel's brother, Joey. I'd have to go and explain to them what had happened to Rachel – and why I was free, but she wasn't.

'Leave it till tomorrow, hey? I would if I was you. Now might not be good.'

'Do they know Rachel's been arrested?'

'*Ja*. They know. Leysen let her speak to them on the phone. I spoke to them also. Well, to her brother, anyhow.'

'How did he sound?'

'Vague. Like he wasn't taking it in. Maybe by tomorrow . . . he'll be easier to talk to.'

'Let's hope so.'

We drove almost literally round the corner to Velodroomstraat. Van Briel lived in a modestly proportioned but starkly uncompromising Art Deco town house wedged between grand if grubby Art Nouveau residences. He stowed the Porsche in the garage that occupied most of the ground floor and took me up to the living quarters, where starkness also prevailed, with black leather furniture and white marble tiling.

'This thing turns into a bed,' he said, pointing to a large couch. 'Sorry, but that's it.'

'Well, thanks for taking me in, anyway.'

'No problem. I'll put rent on the bill. My girlfriend will be round later. Do you like Indonesian food?'

'Never tried it.'

'You'll like hers, I guarantee. Now, do you want a beer? Or something stronger?'

'Something stronger.'

'Me too.'

Vodkas, with lots of ice but very little tonic, were van Briel's prescription for the occasion. He lit a cigarette and I gladly accepted his offer of one. I must have looked a mess, both physically and psychologically, as I slumped on his couch, vodka in one hand, cigarette in the other. But if he was regretting volunteering to put me up, he didn't say so.

'After another one of these,' he said, taking a deep swallow, 'a shower and a bowl of Lasiyah's babi pangang, you'll feel better, Mr Swan.'

'Please. Call me Stephen.'

'OK, Stephen. I'm Bart.'

'How do Rachel and I stand in law, Bart? You may as well spell out how bad it is.'

'Well, it is bad. But it could be worse. They don't have a motive for Miss Banner – Rachel – to kill Ardal Quilligan. Could be that's why they let you go. To see what you do. Lead them to your uncle, maybe, for starters. Do you know where's he gone?'

'Haven't a clue.'

'Then you don't have many options. That means I don't have many either. I'll go back to Brugge tomorrow. I'll visit Rachel. Make sure she's OK. I'll try to persuade Bequaert to let Rachel out, same conditions as you. But he won't and even if he did she could still be charged. So could you. You say Sir Miles Linley's behind it. But tell me, I need to know: can you prove that?'

'No.'

'Can your uncle?'

'I doubt it.'

'What about Simon Cardale?'

'He can't help us. Even if he wants to.'

'Is there anyone else who can?'

'Your firm's anonymous client, maybe.'

'OK. I'll talk to my boss about that. But client confidentiality is . . . hard to break.'

'Yeah? Well, something's got to break. That's for sure.'

247

'My job is to stop that being you or Rachel,' van Briel said, grabbing the vodka bottle and topping up my glass. 'And, lucky for you, I'm good at my job.'

Lasiyah's babi pangang failed to work the promised miracle. My dejection didn't lift. If anything, it deepened, as the reality of the situation seeped into my mind. Rachel was alone and frightened in a prison cell in Bruges, while I sat in Antwerp, washing down sweet-and-sour pork with Trappist beer. The contrast tasted bitter.

Lasiyah herself was a tiny, almond-eyed girl with lustrous waist-length hair and a watchful expression. She didn't speak more than a word or two of English and something in the way she looked at me implied she wasn't happy at having my company foisted on her.

Van Briel filled the conversational void with a personalized history of Zurenborg. It had been a toss-up, apparently, whether he became a lawyer or an architect. He'd often regretted choosing the law. Over the years, he'd talked his way inside many of the houses in the area, Zonnestralen sadly not among them, and he gloried in their diversity. He recommended particular examples I should take a look at, as if supposing I was likely to spend my time studying local architecture. He confirmed Cogels-Osylei had originally been Avenue Cogels-Osy, just as Velodroomstraat had once been Rue du Vélodrome. The street names had all been altered from French to Dutch after the War. Not much else had been altered, though. He'd proudly played a part in defeating a scheme hatched a few years back to demolish the houses and chuck up modern hotels and apartment buildings in their place. The memory of this, evidently still raw, led him off into a sarcastic monologue about the probity or otherwise of local politicians.

I'd long since ceased to pay much attention when a telephone call interrupted him. Lasiyah answered and looked as if she was baffled by what the caller said. She relayed it to van Briel in Dutch. He started with surprise. 'A man, asking for you,' he explained.

'But no one knows I'm here except the police.'

'You want me to speak to him?'

'No. It's all right.' I wondered, in the teeth of logic, if it could be Eldritch. I took the phone from Lasiyah. 'Hello?'

'Stephen Swan?' The voice was low and confident, the accent English.

'Yes. Who—'

'I'll meet you at Tramplein in ten minutes. Van Briel will tell you how to get there.'

'Who is this?'

'If you want to help Rachel Banner, be there. Alone.'

'Hold on. I—' Too late. The line was dead.

Van Briel advised me not to go. We didn't know who was behind Ardal's murder, but they were clearly ruthless. It was crazy to put myself at their mercy. If I insisted on going, he should accompany me. I sensed he relished the drama of the late-night summons, although Lasiyah looked far closer to terrified. None of it made any difference to me. 'I've got to go, Bart. And on my own, as instructed. This could be Rachel's best chance, maybe her only chance. I can't let her down.'

Tramplein was the square at the northern end of Cogels-Osylei, where it converged with two other streets and met one of the railway lines that bounded the district. The tramlines serving the route between Berchem and Centraal stations passed beneath the railway tracks through one of the wide arches of a low viaduct. At ten o'clock on a cold, damp Monday night, the tram stop was deserted, the square empty. One of the strange rules of urban life – that you can be alone, though surrounded by thousands of people – was eerily applicable.

But I wasn't quite alone. A figure detached itself from the deep shadow of one of the arches as I approached. His build and clothing told me he was the man I'd seen that morning in Ostend well before he'd moved far enough towards me for any lamplight to fall on his hard, lean features. He was smoking a cigarette, though both his hands were in his pockets. He removed one to take the cigarette from his mouth, then the other, which he held up, palm facing me, as if to reassure me he wasn't armed, though I was painfully aware it didn't actually prove that.

He nodded. 'Mr Swan.'

'Who are you?' I asked, coming to a halt about six feet from him.

'The name's Tate. Let's step back where we're less conspicuous, shall we?'

'Maybe I'm happier being conspicuous.'

'If I wanted to kill you, Mr Swan, I wouldn't phone beforehand. I'm here to talk and so, I assume, are you. Let's step back.'

He retreated into the shadow of the archway. I hesitated for a moment, then followed.

'Thanks,' he said. 'You want a cigarette?' He held out the pack.

I did want one. But I was determined not to take it from him. I shook my head. 'No. I'd rather have an explanation.'

'Can't help you there. Not a *complete* explanation, anyway.'

'Who do you work for?'

'Her Majesty the Queen, God bless her.'

'The Secret Service.'

'In simple terms, yes, though at the grey, deniable, off-balance-sheet end of the spectrum. The dirty end, if you know what I mean.'

'You kill people to order.'

'Only bad people, Mr Swan. Or good people doing bad things. The distinction's a little blurry.'

'Why Ardal Quilligan?'

'We've been remiss. We took our eye off the ball. And the Irish let us down. Not for the first time. Or the last, no doubt. Don't you sometimes wish Cromwell had finished the job? We'd have been spared three centuries of death and destruction if he had.'

'I don't know what you're talking about.'

'No. Probably not. Just as well, really. Otherwise, you'd be more of a threat than an asset. I suppose your uncle kept you in the dark because he knew it was safer for you that way. Good old Eldritch. What a trooper, eh?' He took a drag on his cigarette and tossed the butt away into the shadows.

He seemed intent on talking in riddles. But riddles were no use to me. 'Why did you kill Quilligan?'

'Because he foolishly phoned his sister yesterday and warned her he was about to hand over to you and Miss Banner proof that their brother forged the Picassos. And once that was proved, a lot of grubby secrets would have come into the open. How could Ardal have afforded to wind up his practice and retire to Majorca? How could Isolde and her husband have funded their Hampshire squiredom? Valid questions, with venal answers. They took their cut from what Geoffrey Cardale made out of the swindle is the sum of it. Which means Sir Miles and Lady Linley could be dragged into a reopened Banner/Brownlow lawsuit. We can't let that happen.'

'What does it matter to you?'

'Sir Miles gets triple-A protection. Not my decision. But it is my responsibility. Which, I admit, I should have paid more attention to. The break-ins were small beer. Precautionary, in essence. Trawling operations that yielded empty nets. Except the kitchen knife, of course. We like to have compromising material we can use if we need to. I just didn't expect the need to arise so soon in this case. That it did is down to the fact that we were unaware Ardal Quilligan possessed the proof he promised you, or a guilty conscience to go with it, until his phone call to Isolde.'

'Why does Linley merit such a high level of protection?'

'Because there's a danger that if he's backed into a corner over his involvement in the Cardale fraud, he might blab to the press about exactly what he was up to in Dublin thirty-six years ago. Public knowledge of certain . . . details . . . of his work there would do considerable, possibly irreparable, harm to Anglo-Irish relations. Our war with the IRA won't be won by allowing that to happen.'

'What are the details?' I knew he wouldn't tell me, of course, but I couldn't let the question go unasked. And his answer surprised me even so.

'I don't know. I'm neither trusted nor required to know. But your uncle knows. That's our problem. And yours. You see, we believe Eldritch planned to use the proof you were going to get from Quilligan to blackmail Linley into putting on the record what really led to his arrest and imprisonment in Ireland. The truth, the whole

251

truth and nothing but the disastrous, havoc-wreaking truth. That's what we have to prevent at all costs.'

'No problem, then. You've killed Quilligan and by now you've presumably destroyed what he had with him.'

'No. Actually, we haven't.'

'Why not?'

'Because he didn't have the proof. It wasn't there, Mr Swan. We searched him and every inch of his car. Nothing. And I've just had a report from Palma de Mallorca. There was nothing in his apartment either. Not that we expected there to be. He left Majorca with it. That's clear. What's not clear is what happened to it next.' Tate sighed in evident exasperation at the turn of events. 'Our best guess is in point of fact your best chance.'

'What's that supposed to mean?'

'The proof is missing. So is your uncle.'

'You think Eldritch has it?'

'Who else? He left England a day before you. What did he do with that twenty-four-hour start? Meet Quilligan before he got to Ostend, maybe. It's what we suspect. It's what we greatly fear. We know he hasn't gone back to England. There's an all ports alert out on him. But where *has* he gone? That's the question. He gave the police the slip in Ostend and he may be able to stay out of our reach. The oldest foxes are often the hardest to catch. We need help. *Your* help.'

'To do what?'

'Find him. And find the proof. Deliver that to us and we'll persuade the Belgian authorities to drop any charges they bring against Miss Banner – or you.'

Was Tate right? Did Eldritch have the proof? I'd sensed he was playing a deeper game all along and maybe forcing Linley to exonerate him was it, although somehow I doubted it. Not that it made much difference. If he had the proof, we could at least bargain ourselves out of trouble with it, even if we couldn't achieve what we'd been aiming for. Tate was certainly right on one point. This was our best chance.

'He's your uncle, Mr Swan. He trusts you. He's served time in prison and he wouldn't wish that experience on you, I'm sure. Nor would he refuse to do whatever he could to save you from it.'

'Probably not.'

'He'll contact you sooner or later. He's bound to. Or you'll contact him. Don't bother to deny you're in a position to do so. It may well be true, but I've no way of verifying it, so your denial would be irrelevant. Just get the proof. And then we'll call off the dogs.'

'As simple as that?'

'Sometimes things are simple.'

'And what's Eldritch supposed to do?'

'Whatever he wants.'

'Except clear his name.'

'He'll never get back those thirty-six years he spent in prison, Mr Swan. He should be grateful the Irish let him go. We made the mistake of supposing they never would. Don't let him make the mistake of throwing his freedom away for the sake of his good name.'

'What did the Irish think he'd done?'

'I told you: I don't know. And Eldritch obviously reckons you're better off not knowing either. My advice is to leave it like that. Persuade him to hand over the proof. Then you and Miss Banner can get out from under. I can't say fairer than that, now can I?'

A rumble had grown above us as he spoke, echoing around in the archway like rolls of thunder. A train was approaching. Tate didn't try to shout above the noise. He lit another cigarette as the train passed overhead. It was slow and heavy, a growling, squealing succession of trucks. He'd had time to smoke most of the cigarette before it was gone.

Then he said quietly, 'I take it you'll give it a go.'

THIRTY

Van Briel had waited up for me. I told him frankly what had happened and noticed in his response a marginal loss of confidence. Tangling with MI5, or MI6, or whatever outfit Tate represented, wasn't part of the assignment he'd taken on.

'My legal tricks aren't going to be much use to you in that world, Stephen.'

'Leave me to worry about Tate, Bart,' I said, surprising myself by how I was now the one sounding a reassuring note. 'You concentrate on helping Rachel.'

'OK. But what will you do? How will you find your uncle?'

'I don't know. Maybe *he'll* find *me*.'

'And if he doesn't?'

It was a question I didn't have an answer to. Tate had given me a card with a number on it that he said I should ring with news of Eldritch. His bet was that I stood a better chance of finding my uncle than he did. But I wasn't sure about that. It all depended on what Eldritch was really aiming to accomplish: *what* and *why*.

After van Briel had stumbled off to bed, I made a few hopeful phone calls. There was a possibility, I supposed, that Eldritch had made it back to England. But, if so, he hadn't returned to the Ritz. '*No, sir. We haven't seen your uncle since he checked out on Saturday.*' I considered asking my mother if she'd heard from him, but I didn't want her to start worrying about me. It seemed best to leave her unaware of the fix I was in. I tried Cardale's home

254

number, conscious that I ought to apologize in some way for throwing his life into turmoil and helping to set in motion the events that had led to his uncle's death. But all I got was the engaged tone, so consistently I began to suspect he'd taken the phone off the hook. Exasperation as much as desperation drove me to try another number, one I'd found scrawled on a piece of paper in my wallet.

'*You've reached the answerphone of Moira Henchy. Leave your name and number after the tone and I'll be sure to call you back.*'

'Miss Henchy, this is Stephen Swan. We spoke a couple of weeks ago. You wanted information about my uncle, Eldritch Swan. If you're still interested, there's a great deal I can tell you. I'm in Antwerp. Please call me as soon as you can on . . .'

I put the phone down after recording van Briel's number, switched off the light and lay back on the sofa-bed. I was drained and exhausted, but sleep felt a long way off. My thoughts raced on unavailingly in the silence and the darkness. I whispered words of comfort to someone who couldn't hear them and stared into the void.

Morning came with the surprising realization that I had slept after all, for several hours at least. Van Briel was in the kitchen, clad in a black dressing-gown, quaffing orange juice by the half-gallon while his coffee brewed to kick-start strength. He couldn't manage much more than grunts until the coffee was ready. Then he poured us a cup each and we sat down at the table.

'I'll go into the office, then to Brugge,' he announced. 'Any message for Rachel?'

'Tell her I'm doing everything I can.'

'Will do. This is the office address.' He handed me an Oudermans card. 'Call round there this afternoon. Let's say four o'clock. I'll leave a message for you about Rachel's . . . situation. Also my boss might want to talk to you about our anonymous client. No promises, but I'll ask. Now, there's a spare set of keys.' He pointed to where they hung on a hook by the door. 'You won't see much of Lasiyah. She's shy and . . . she doesn't know what to make of you.'

'Sorry.'

'Not your fault.' He slurped some coffee. 'While I'm gone . . .'

'Yes?'

'Watch your back, hey? You seem to be playing with some bad boys. I wouldn't—'

The ringing of the telephone interrupted him. He raised his eyebrows quizzically at me, then stood up and padded across to answer it. I looked at the clock. It was 7.45. Therefore 6.45 in Ireland. It was surely too early for Moira Henchy to return my call.

'*Hallo? . . . Wat zegt u? . . .* Hold on, please.' Van Briel held the phone towards me. 'For you, Stephen. Moira Henchy.'

He must have been able to read the surprise in my expression as I jumped up and took the phone from him. 'Hello?'

'Good morning, Stephen. I just got your message. So, you're in Antwerp, are you?'

'That's right. I—'

'I just dropped by my office to pick up a few things. I'm on my way to the airport.'

'Oh yes?'

'For a flight to Brussels. I heard about Ardal Quilligan's murder late last night. You know something about it, do you?'

'You could say so, yes.'

'I guess that's why you're in Belgium. So, what do you know about the people they have in custody? The Belgian police haven't revealed their names yet.'

'I'm one of them.' I heard her gasp at the other end of the line. 'Well, I *was*. They let me go yesterday. They're still holding my girlfriend, Rachel Banner.' It was strange to hear myself describe Rachel as that. But it was true, of course – a truth I was desperate to cling on to.

'Does Quilligan's murder have something to do with your uncle, Stephen?'

'Oh yes. Everything, really.'

'We should meet.'

'I agree.'

'The police are holding a press conference in Bruges this afternoon. I plan to attend. Could you meet me there?'

Pushing myself back under the noses of the police, not to mention encountering the media, sounded like a bad idea. And it sounded even worse to van Briel. When I said, 'Me, come to Bruges?' he flapped his hand frantically and mouthed, '*No, no, no.*' 'I can't do that,' I went on. He sighed with relief then and gave me a thumbs-up.

'Why not?'

'We should meet here, Moira. In Antwerp. It'll be worth the journey, I promise.'

She thought for a moment, before agreeing. 'All right. I was planning to stay overnight in Bruges. But we'll make it Antwerp instead. I'm not sure when I'll get in. Can I reach you on that number this evening – some time after six?'

'Yes,' I said decisively.

'I'll call you, then. You will be there, won't you?'

'Without fail.'

Van Briel didn't ask me much about Moira Henchy. I had the impression he'd decided the less he knew about what steps I was taking to find Eldritch the better. He showered and dressed and was gone within the hour, his Porsche growling away along the street. Within another hour, I'd set off for Zonnestralen.

Watery sunlight revealed the faded delicacy of the building, albeit obscured by layers of dust and grime. I stood before the paired front doors of numbers 84 and 86, wondering if anything at all had changed since Eldritch's time there. Soon enough, I noticed one thing that certainly had. A small brass plaque declared that someone called Wyckx now lived at 86. By implication, only 84 was still a Meridor preserve.

The bell was answered by a plump, round-faced woman of sixty or so, dressed in a floral housecoat. '*Bonjour, monsieur,*' she said, refracted light from the sunburst panel in the door imparting a gleam to her dark eyes that contrasted with the weariness of her features.

257

'Good morning. Is Joey Banner in? Or his grandmother, perhaps?'

She said nothing for a moment, but stared at me in growing amazement. '*Mon Dieu,*' she murmured.

'What's the matter?'

'You're Stephen Swan.'

'Yes. I am. How did you know?'

'You look like your uncle when he was your age.' She shook her head. 'So like him.'

'You knew Eldritch?'

'*Mais oui.* I knew him.'

'Can I come in?'

'*Oui, oui.* Come in.' She stepped back and I entered the light-filled hall. The door closed behind me just as a tram rattled by. The sound was instantly muffled, the present day shut out. I heard a clock ticking, saw heavy-framed family portraits hung between candelabra, smelt camphor and furniture polish, sensed all the years since Isaac Meridor had bought this house compressed into an unchanging moment. Zonnestralen was the end of its own rainbow.

'I believe my lawyer, Bart van Briel, spoke to Joey yesterday.'

'Yes. We have heard about Rachel.' She went on staring at me, as if deeply moved by my resemblance to Eldritch.

'Can I . . . see Joey?'

'Ah, no. He is out. He goes to the Zoo every morning.'

'The *Zoo*?'

She shrugged. 'He likes to be with the snakes.'

Pottering off to the zoo after being told your sister was under arrest for murder didn't strike me as even close to normal behaviour. The housekeeper must have seen how dismayed I was. But it wasn't her fault, of course. 'Is Mrs Meridor in?'

'Yes. She is in. She is always in. But . . .' She lowered her voice. 'Madame Meridor . . . is very old and . . . very confused.'

'She knows about Rachel?'

'We told her.' The *we* implied her role in the household went well beyond that of a servant. 'But she may have . . . forgotten.'

'Can I see her?'

258

'If you wish. This way, please.'

She led the way into a rear drawing-room. It was thickly curtained, stiflingly heated by a vast, hissing radiator and loaded with enough bric-à-brac to stock a market stall. There the lady of the house awaited me.

Isaac Meridor's widow was dressed as if she was still in mourning, layered in black and propped up in a brocaded armchair, dozing over a newspaper while a cup of coffee went cold on a table beside her. She was white-haired and hollow-featured, her skin paper-thin and deathly pale, bangles bunched at her wrists, fat-stoned rings trapped on her fingers by swollen knuckles.

The presence of a stranger roused her sharply but shallowly from her reverie. She said something in Dutch that included the name Marie-Louise. The housekeeper replied in French. Mrs Meridor cast a rheumy, unfocused glance at me, then spoke in heavily accented English. 'You are . . . Eldritch Swan's son?'

'Nephew,' I corrected her, to no obvious effect.

'You dare to come here? My husband . . . would not like this.'

'I'm here about your granddaughter. Rachel.'

'The girl? She keeps me awake with her crying. That is why I sleep in the day. That is why . . . I finish nothing.' She suddenly noticed her coffee and pointed a shaky forefinger at it. '*Koud*, Marie-Louise. *Koud*.' Then she looked back at me. 'My husband has Jean-Jacques to look after him. I have only this . . .' Words to describe Marie-Louise's inadequacy failed her. 'You cannot be here, *meneer*. It is . . . an insult.' She directed a volley of Dutch at Marie-Louise, or perhaps the figmental Jean-Jacques. Only her meaning was clear. I was to be shown out. I was to leave. I was *persona non grata* on account of the dreaded name Swan. There were some things she never forgot.

Marie-Louise rolled her eyes at me as we left. Closing the drawing-room door behind us, she signalled for silence with a finger across her lips. She walked down the hall to the front door and opened it, then closed it again, heavily enough to rattle the letterbox. As far as Mrs Meridor was to know, I'd gone. But I hadn't. And Marie-Louise clearly didn't want me to.

She opened the narrow door beneath the staircase and beckoned me to follow her down to the basement. I trod softly on the stone steps. We came to a large kitchen, with an equally large scullery beyond, where a washing machine was working away. Marie-Louise moved to the range and set about making coffee. I whispered, 'Yes,' when she asked me if I wanted some.

At that she smiled, transformingly, pleasure bursting through drudgery. 'She can't hear us now, Stephen.' My first name seemed to have come to her quite naturally. 'And she hasn't been down here for years and years.'

'She doesn't seem to have registered what's happened to Rachel.'

'*Non*. That is how she is. The past like crystal. The present . . . a fog. But Madame Banner, Rachel's mother, will be here soon. She will know what to do. I called her last night.'

'You? Not Joey?'

'He and his grandmother, they are a little alike. They . . . live somewhere else . . . in their minds.'

'Where does Joey live?'

'Vietnam, I think. That is where he got to like snakes.'

'Rachel didn't do what the police say she did. You understand that, don't you, Marie-Louise?'

'Of course. She wouldn't kill anyone. Certainly not poor Monsieur Quilligan.'

'You speak as if you knew him.'

'But I did. He has visited here several times. And he came again . . . on Sunday.'

'*Ardal Quilligan was here? On Sunday?*'

'Hush.' She looked up, listening anxiously. 'She will hear you if you shout.'

'Sorry.' The truth was I hadn't realized I was shouting. 'But what you said . . .'

'*Oui, Oui*. It is strange, I know. And I will tell you about it. First I must take madame her hot coffee for her to let go cold like the one before. Then we will talk.' She poured the coffee. 'Then we *must* talk.'

THIRTY-ONE

Marie-Louise began with questions about Eldritch, or *Eldrish*, as she pronounced his name. She'd believed, like the Meridor-Banner family, that he'd shared in Cardale's profit from his fraud and vanished to some sunny clime. When I told her he'd spent the past thirty-six years in an Irish prison, she was incredulous and transparently moved. 'Ireland? In prison? He would not like to be . . . locked in.'

'You knew him well?' I asked, though the answer was obvious.

'Oh yes. Very well. When I was young. And he was young.'

'How long have you worked here?'

'Since when I was fifteen.' She smiled. 'More than forty years. I stayed on through the War, when German officers lived here, and after, when nobody did for a while, except me and Bernard and Ilse, who are both dead now. Madame Meridor came back after Esther married. She had builders to fill in the wall between the two houses. Since then we have lived only on this side. Madame Meridor used to be a strong woman. It is disappointment, I think, that has . . . made her like she is. The Picasso fraud. The lawsuit. Joey's . . . condition. They have worn her down.'

She pressed me to tell her more about Eldritch. As much for her sake as his, I didn't dwell on the effects of age and imprisonment she'd no doubt have been dismayed by if she'd met him. It was clear she was in some way consoled to know he hadn't willingly stayed away so long, though whether he'd have returned if he'd been able to was quite another matter. They'd been more than mere colleagues in the Meridor household. That was obvious. But what it had amounted to, from Eldritch's point of view, was far from obvious. He hadn't mentioned her to me. And he hadn't contacted her since his release.

'Perhaps he thinks I am dead,' she said, with pitiful generosity.

I described our efforts to find proof that Desmond Quilligan had forged the Picassos. Marie-Louise was cheered to hear of them, proving as they did to her that Eldritch was trying to do the right thing by the family. I couldn't find it in myself to explain that he'd only embarked on the exercise in the hope of funding a comfortable dotage on the French Riviera. As for Ardal Quilligan, the discovery that his brother was the forger accounted to her mind for a great deal.

'He came here, not long after madame returned from New York. He offered to help her, with money, with . . . whatever she needed. I wasn't supposed to know, but I . . . listened to them talking together. He told her Cardale felt sorry for her. Cardale wouldn't admit stealing the Picassos, but he didn't want his old friend's widow to live poorly, so he sent Mr Quilligan, a lawyer, to . . . do things for her. There was a condition. Madame must never tell the rest of the family. She agreed. Well, of course she agreed. She needed help. The times were hard. Mr Quilligan came every few years to check on her, to . . . arrange matters for her. I don't know what, exactly. And madame couldn't tell you now even if she wanted to. So, she'll never know Mr Quilligan lied to her. He wasn't acting for Cardale, was he? He was acting for himself. He was the one with the guilty conscience. And that conscience is what got him killed, I suppose.'

'I'm afraid so.'

'He was a nice man. Polite. Considerate. He always asked me how I was.'

'And he came here on Sunday?'

'Yes. He was in the house when I came home from church at about midday. He left soon after. He'd been talking to Joey. It was the first time they'd met. I was surprised to see him. He was . . .

friendly as usual, but . . . flustered. In a hurry, I think. Worried . . . about something.'

'What had he and Joey been discussing?'

'Joey said Mr Quilligan was shocked by how bad madame was. She'd understood him during his last visit, some years ago. But now, of course . . . she didn't even recognize him. So, maybe he wanted to tell her something, but realized he couldn't. *Alors*, his visit was for nothing. Joey wouldn't have asked him many questions. It's not his way.'

'That's a pity.'

'Who killed Mr Quilligan, Stephen?'

'People who don't want the truth to get out.'

'Ah yes.' Marie-Louise nodded solemnly, as if this confirmed a lesson of her less than idyllic life. 'There are always such people.'

'It's possible Eldritch has the proof Quilligan was carrying.'

Her face lifted. 'You think so?'

'You knew him well. He can't leave Belgium. Where would he hide?'

'Here. Antwerp. It's the city he knows.'

'And where . . . in Antwerp?'

She chewed her lip for a moment, then said, 'He could be anywhere. If Eldritch wants to hide, he will be . . . difficult to find.'

'Difficult or not, I have to find him.'

She frowned thoughtfully. 'When did they release him from prison?'

'January.'

She nodded, satisfied on a point. 'It wasn't him, then.'

'What wasn't him?'

'Last autumn, October or November, someone broke into the other house: number eighty-six. The Wyckxes were away. They didn't find out until they came home. The burglar had forced open a window at the back. He hadn't taken anything, though. Nothing belonging to the Wyckxes, anyway. But there was soot in one of the grates.'

'Soot?'

'I think the burglar took something that was hidden in the chimney, Stephen. From before the Wyckxes' time.'

'Who were the previous occupants?'

'Professor Driessens. A bachelor. He died there.'

'And before him?'

'It was all one house.'

'Well, whoever it was, it can't have been Eldritch. What did the Wyckxes think?'

'That maybe the burglar was disturbed and just . . . went away. And the soot was . . . because of a bird.'

'I suppose that's possible.'

Marie-Louise shrugged. 'It makes them happy to believe it.'

'What could have been hidden in the chimney?'

Another, heavier shrug. 'Anything. Nothing. I—' Three loud thumps interrupted her. She looked up. 'Madame wants me. Perhaps she has spilt her coffee. Or seen another ghost. I will have to go.'

'I must go too.' I tore a corner off the front page of the newspaper that was lying on the kitchen table and scribbled down van Briel's address and phone number. 'Let me know if anything happens.'

'If I hear from Eldritch, you mean?'

'Anything. You can rely on me for help, Marie-Louise. OK?'

Her smile briefly reappeared. 'Thank you, Stephen.' As she slipped the piece of paper into her housecoat pocket, another three thumps echoed through the floor. She rolled her eyes and stood up. So did I.

'How long will Joey spend at the Zoo?'

'Hours. Perhaps all day.'

'With the snakes?'

She nodded. 'Always with the snakes.'

The tram to Centraal station was handy for the Zoo as well. The entrance was off the square in front of the grime-encrusted palace that was the station building. I grabbed a map after paying to go into the zoo and threaded my way through the school groups and wandering tourists to the reptile house.

It was dark, as all good reptiles prefer, and thinly populated with visitors, as doubtless they also prefer, happy to be outshone by bigger and more active creatures. The man who'd drawn up a camp chair in front of the python's glazed patch of simulated jungle looked young and American enough to be Joey Banner. He was dressed in faded denims, T-shirt and baseball boots, with a yellow bandana holding his greasy, shoulder-length hair out of his eyes. He seemed to be trying to outdo the python in an immobility contest. I had to tap him several times on the shoulder to get his attention.

He turned his narrow, melancholy face to look at me. The dim lighting gave him a sallow, wraithlike appearance. 'Yuh?' His voice was low and husky.

'Joey Banner?'

'So they tell me, man.'

'I'm Stephen Swan.'

He stood up slowly, revealing in the process that he was six inches taller than me. 'Stephen Swan,' he repeated.

'That's right. My lawyer, Bart van Briel, spoke to you yesterday. I'm the chap the police arrested along with Rachel.'

'But you got out.'

'They let me out.'

'Get out. Let out. According to my dictionary, they're the same thing.'

'Can we talk?'

'This is talking, man. Only kind I know.'

'Outside, I mean.'

'You don't like snakes?'

'I neither like them nor dislike them.'

He smiled. 'Good answer. That's just how they feel about you.'

'Can we?' I pointed to the exit.

'OK.' He carefully folded his chair and ambled out with it, blinking as we emerged into the daylight like a miner finishing a shift. 'Same old same old out here, right?'

'If you say so.'

'You want to grab a snack?'

'I don't mind.'

'Hamburgers this way.'

We descended a ramp and headed past the zebra enclosure. It was obvious Joey had no need of maps to find his way around. He pulled a notepad out of his jacket pocket and began studying it as we walked. I glimpsed sketches of snakes surrounded by jottings in the minuscule hand I'd already seen on one of his postcards to Rachel. He asked me nothing: how she was; how we'd got ourselves into so much trouble; how I'd known where to find him. I decided to fill him in on that point at least.

'Marie-Louise said you'd be here.'

'Guessed she must have.'

'I wanted to explain to you . . . what happened in Ostend.'

'Oh yeah?'

'Don't you want to know? Your sister might be facing a murder charge.'

'So your lawyer said. Good, is he?'

'He seems to be.'

'He'll be more help to her than I could be. And Mom hits town tomorrow, so between her and him . . . she'll have all the attention she needs.'

We reached the snack bar. Joey ordered himself a burger and a Coke. I followed suit. He didn't wait for me to pay and had plonked himself down at one of the tables out front, in the lee of a sorry-looking tree, by the time I caught up with him.

We had the area to ourselves. It was no weather for alfresco snacking. Joey didn't acknowledge my arrival. His attention was fixed on his burger, which he was munching methodically between slurps of Coke.

'Why do snakes appeal to you, Joey?' I heard myself ask.

'They won't bite you if you leave them alone.'

'Unlike humans?'

'You said it, man.'

'And why did you move to Antwerp?'

'Belgium isn't the US of A.'

'Did you have a bad time of it in Vietnam?'

266

'Do you know what I hate?' he countered. 'What I really fucking hate?'

'Tell me.'

'People who won't come straight out and ask what they want to know.'

'All right. What did Ardal Quilligan say to you when he called at Zonnestralen on Sunday?'

'The old Irishman? To me, zilch. It was Gran he wanted to talk to. But he was out of luck. Her tuner doesn't work any more. She's kinda between frequencies. Which isn't a bad place to be, let me tell you. Out there, all you get is . . . occasional bursts of static. No words. No . . . voices in your ear.'

'Rachel needs your help.'

'No one needs my help.'

'Didn't Quilligan say anything to you?'

'Hi and goodbye . . . was about it.'

'You do realize he's the man the police think Rachel murdered, don't you?'

'What's the point?'

Joey's detachment from worldly affairs had ceased to be pitiful and was verging now on the infuriating. 'The point of what?'

'Investigating one murder out of all those millions. It's a murderous century, man. People live. People die. I can't . . . get into it.' He swallowed the last of his burger, screwed the paper bag into a ball and pitched it into a nearby bin. 'Who's to say they really die anyway? Gran still sees my grandfather. Hell, sometimes I think I see him myself. Him and . . . quite a few others who are supposed to be buried someplace . . . a long way from here.'

Where was he now, in his head? Vietnam? I supposed so. And I stood to gain nothing by following him there. 'I think I'll leave you to it, Joey,' I said, getting up from my chair.

'OK, man.' He gazed at me with transparent indifference.

''Bye now.'

'Do me a favour?'

'Sorry?' I was genuinely surprised by the question.

'The lawyer. Van Briel. He visits Rache, right?'

267

'Yes.'

'Ask him to give her this.' He pulled a postcard out of his pocket and handed it to me. The picture was a nightscape of Antwerp, with the cathedral centre stage. He'd already addressed the card to Rachel in London. He'd even put a stamp on it. The message, naturally, was eye-strainingly microscopic. 'No sense mailing it now, I reckon. But I'd like her to get it.'

'I'll see what he can do.'

Joey raised his paper cup of Coke in salute. 'Thanks, man.'

THIRTY-TWO

Antwerp March 29 1976 Dear Sis You've asked me more than one time why I like to compose these messages to you in one sentence and I wonder if you've guessed it's because I have a mortal fear of full stops on account of all the rude interruptions I witnessed in Nam that pretty soon revealed themselves as sudden terminations and also because I neurotically suppose that if I don't pause for breath you won't either and that way we'll get to talk the only way I feel I can which is right out and right on for a dare even when there's nothing much to tell you which is pretty much all the time in my cotton-wooled exile of a life here and—

I gave up there and shoved the card back in my pocket. I reckoned I might spare Rachel this latest dose of her brother's self-obsessed ramblings. Good news was what she needed to hear and it was what I longed to be able to deliver. Instead, I was sitting in a bar on Antwerp's Grote Markt, gazing through the window at the Brabo fountain and the imperiously raised finger of the cathedral spire, persuading myself to order a coffee rather than another beer. I knew I was accomplishing nothing by lingering there, but I was unable for the moment to think of anything else I could do to extricate Rachel and me from the godawful mess Eldritch had landed us in.

*

I presented myself at Oudermans' offices on the dot of four o'clock. Punctuality was about the only thing I had going for me. They were on the third floor of an anonymous block south of the main shopping centre. The whole operation occupied a different century from Twisk's one-man band in London, with modern art, chrome-legged desks, golfball typewriters and fashion-plate secretaries.

Oudermans himself, it transpired, was awaiting my arrival. Any message from van Briel would reach me through him. I was kept waiting no more than a few minutes before being ushered into his spacious sanctum of neatly ordered papers and plush-carpeted quietude.

He was a small, spry, immaculately suited man in late middle age, thinning hair neatly trimmed, skin tanned, eyes sparkling behind gilt-framed spectacles. Discretion and precision seemed wound up in his every restrained gesture. To my surprise, his English was as sharp as his dress sense.

'A pleasure to meet you, Mr Swan. The circumstances are of course regrettable. We are here to help you make the best of them. The past thirty-six hours can't have been easy for you. May I offer you coffee? Or tea?'

'No, thanks.' I'd drunk two cups of coffee before leaving the bar and was glad of it now.

'I spoke to Meneer van Briel about twenty minutes ago. He apprised me of the current situation. You'll want to know what it is. Well, the Prosecutor's office still haven't charged Miss Banner with anything, but they have ample evidence to justify detaining her for several more days at least. That seems to be their intention. There was a press conference this afternoon. Inspector Leysen referred to several different lines of inquiry, which is promising. It suggests Judge Bequaert isn't convinced of Miss Banner's guilt. Or yours.'

'That's good.'

'To some degree, yes.' Oudermans studied me intently. 'Earlier, Meneer van Briel told me of your meeting last night with a man claiming to represent British Intelligence.'

'Yes. His name was Tate.'

'We will represent you and Miss Banner in this case, but I must emphasize we can have no dealings on your behalf; nor can we encourage you to have dealings, with such persons.'

'I wouldn't expect you to.'

'Our position in Belgian law is . . . delicate.'

'Has Bart – Mr van Briel – told the police a client of yours offered my uncle fifty thousand pounds to find the proof we were hoping to collect from Ardal Quilligan?'

'No. He wouldn't deny it if asked, of course, but they have no reason to ask him. And we are not required to volunteer such information.'

'Does your client know what's happened?'

'Yes. I told him myself.'

'Face to face?'

'By telephone.'

'Have you ever met him?'

Oudermans smiled, placidly but discouragingly. 'Without his approval, I can't answer such questions.'

'What's he going to do?'

'I don't know. He is . . . considering his situation.'

'Great. What about my situation? And Rachel's? Which he helped create.'

Oudermans took off his glasses, frowning at me thoughtfully as he did so. 'I assure you, Mr Swan,' he said eventually, 'that I made him aware of the conflict of interest we may face if you and/or Miss Banner are charged.'

'And?'

'That is the situation he is considering.'

'His identity could be crucial to this, Mr Oudermans.'

'I understand. But his identity, as you call it, is not, strictly speaking, known to me. I know his name, of course. But I've wondered recently whether that's his *real* name.'

'I need to know who he is.'

'Give him a little time, Mr Swan. He may agree to . . . reveal himself.'

271

'I don't know how much time I have. I could be arrested at any moment.'

'That is regrettably true.' Oudermans carefully replaced his glasses on his nose. 'Meanwhile there is ... another issue.'

'What?'

'Mr Quilligan's sister, Lady Linley, arrived in Ostend today to claim her brother's body. She met Inspecteur Leysen and spoke to Meneer van Briel. She wants to meet you, Mr Swan. The police won't allow her to see Miss Banner, so she ... demands to see you.'

'I don't mind meeting her.' That was an understatement. It would give me a chance to gauge how much she knew of her husband's activities. Had she really consented to her brother's murder? If not, I might be able to drive a wedge between her and Sir Miles. 'I've nothing to hide, Mr Oudermans.'

'Good. I suggest we invite her here. It is important we ... manage the encounter carefully. She may bring a lawyer of her own. I don't know.'

'Will she bring her husband?'

'As I understand it, Sir Miles has not accompanied her to Belgium.' No. Of course not. He couldn't afford to take the slightest risk that the Belgian police might believe our allegations against him. Oudermans' pursed half-smile let me see that he appreciated how his absence could be interpreted in just such a way. 'It will be important to let Lady Linley say and ask exactly what she wants, Mr Swan. Cooperate with her. Sympathize if you can. Then we may ... draw something out.'

'I'll be on my best behaviour.'

'Good. That brings us to Mr Simon Cardale.'

'You've heard from him?'

'No. We've tried to contact him on both of the numbers you supplied, without success. He left yesterday on the six p.m. ferry from Ostend to Dover. That is all we know.'

My hunch was that Cardale had been so distraught at his uncle's death he'd shut himself away with the phone off the hook. What he thought had really happened in Ostend I couldn't imagine. But his confidence must have been shattered. He was probably in fear of what Linley might do to him. Small wonder he'd gone to ground. 'We can ask Lady Linley where he is,' I suggested. 'Her response could be . . . illuminating.'

Oudermans nodded. 'Indeed. We must anticipate, of course, that she will in turn ask you where your uncle is.'

'I'm still looking for him.'

'If he contacts you . . .' Oudermans hesitated.

'Yes? If he does?'

'You will advise Meneer van Briel at once, won't you?'

'Of course.'

'Good.' Oudermans' expression gave no hint of the weight he placed on my assurances. The truth was that I had no idea what I'd do, or who I'd tell, if and when I found Eldritch. It all hinged on what I could least predict: Eldritch's own intentions. 'Now, I must advise you to proceed cautiously at all times, Mr Swan. The police regard you as a suspect in a murder inquiry. They may hope you will incriminate yourself. It's vital you avoid doing anything they could . . . misinterpret. You understand?'

I understood all right. The police wanted me to trip myself up. Oudermans wanted me to tread carefully. But Rachel needed me to do whatever it took to expose the truth. Walking away from Oudermans' offices along the streets of a city I didn't know, surrounded by strangers, I felt wholly unequal to the challenge. But it was a challenge I wouldn't dodge. Some kind of reckoning was approaching and I was determined to face it.

I wandered aimlessly round the diamond district west of Centraal station, backing a frail hunch that Eldritch would return to the area of the city he'd worked in. The idea that I'd simply see him there on the street was preposterous, of course, but it filled the hour or so I had to spare before I needed to head back to van Briel's place to await Moira Henchy's call. Naturally, there was no sign of Eldritch. And the bland façades of the diamond dealerships and brokerages were designed to ensure that the business conducted

273

within them was safe from prying eyes. As an outsider, I was permitted to pass by. That was all.

Van Briel returned home to find me sitting by the telephone, waiting for it to ring. He looked tired and a little defeated. He poured himself a large vodka and expressed surprise that I hadn't already helped myself to one. I gladly joined him.

'How's Rachel?' was my first question. And it was the one that mattered most.

'She has nerve, Stephen. You maybe know that already. Nerve . . . and spirit. But she's being tested. It's hard for her. They tell her nothing. And there's not much I can tell her either.'

'Except that I'm doing everything I can.'

'*Ja.* And she believes it. But . . .'

'What does it amount to? Well, Bart? What can I actually do to get her out of there?'

He studied me over the rim of his vodka glass. 'No progress, huh?'

'Not much. I met Mr Oudermans. He told me about Lady Linley. I gather I'll be meeting her soon.'

'Tomorrow. That'll be . . . difficult, I guess.'

'Not for me. I'll just tell her the truth.'

'Not always good enough, Stephen. They teach you that in law school.'

'We'll see.'

'We'll see something, for sure. But—' The telephone's strident ring interrupted him. He smiled. 'I guess that's probably for you.'

And it was.

Moira Henchy was waiting for me in the bar of the Plaza Hotel. She was dressed for business, in a black trouser suit, with a determinedly unfrilly blouse. She had a round, open face, framed by curly auburn hair, Celtically pale skin, a steady blue-eyed gaze and a stubborn set to her jaw. A female freelance journalist, it was clear, couldn't afford to be thought a pushover.

'When I heard about Ardal Quilligan's murder, I knew at once

Eldritch must be involved,' she said, as soon as the preliminaries of handshaking and drinks ordering were done with.

'Eldritch didn't kill him.'

'And I guess you're going to tell me Rachel Banner didn't either.'

'You're right there, Miss Henchy.'

'Call me, Moira, Stephen. We're on the same side, OK?'

'Are we?'

'You promised me information about Eldritch.'

'I'm here to trade, Moira. What you know about his activities in Dublin in 1940 for what I know about his activities since they let him out of prison.'

'When I spoke to you a fortnight ago, you claimed your mother and you hadn't heard from Eldritch.'

'I lied.'

'Why?'

'To protect him. But now I need to protect myself. And Rachel.'

'Right. Well, I can't say I'm surprised. People who have dealings with Eldritch Swan often end up in need of protection. They don't necessarily get it, of course. Take my father, for instance.'

'He knew Eldritch?'

'Their paths crossed. In Dublin. In 1940.'

'Tell me more.'

She lit a cigarette to cover a pause while our drinks were delivered. Then she smiled at me and said, 'This is a two-way street, Stephen. We're clear about that, aren't we? I trust you. You trust me.'

'We're clear.'

'I'll need to know everything.'

'So will I.'

'Fair enough.' She frowned, ordering her thoughts, wondering, I supposed, how much *everything* really meant. 'OK. Dublin: July 1940. My father: Lorcan Henchy. And your uncle: Eldritch Swan. Some of it I don't know. Most of it, maybe. But this is what I do know. For sure.'

1940

THIRTY-THREE

The weather has changed in Dublin. Rain is falling on St Stephen's Green, from clouds driven in on a keen westerly wind. Through the half-open window of his room at the Shelbourne Hotel, Eldritch Swan can hear the soughing of the trees and the hiss of the heavier bursts of rain. He lies on the bed, propped up on two pillows, smoking a cigarette and lethargically reading an Edgar Wallace novel he picked up earlier in the day for sixpence at a second-hand bookstall. At intervals, he glances at his watch, noting the progress of the hands towards seven o'clock. He wonders if Lorcan Henchy will actually ring on the stroke of the hour. He hopes so, for he cannot leave his room until Henchy's call comes through. Until it does, he must wait as patiently as he can.

He finishes one cigarette and lights another. He turns a few more pages. The rain grows heavier again. The hands of his watch move at their set and stately pace. And then . . .

'Hello?'

'Front desk here, Mr Swan. There's a Mr Henchy on the line for you. Shall I put him through?'

'Yes please.'

'Hold on, sir.'

A moment's silence was broken by a click. 'Hello?'

'Good evening, Mr Swan. Your humble servant Lorcan P.

Henchy here.' The confounded fellow sounded as if he had been drinking.

'Better luck at the races today, Mr Henchy?'

'A little, yes. It's kind of you to ask. And yourself? A successful day?'

'From your point of view, certainly.'

'Your friends are happy to accommodate me, are they?'

'Let's just say willing. On certain conditions.'

'Conditions? That's not a word I like the sound of.'

'They want you to leave Ireland, Mr Henchy. They want you . . . out of the way.'

'Do they now?'

'You can have your money, but not all at once. Five hundred pounds down, then a hundred at weekly intervals until the balance is paid, collectable by you in person from Martins Bank, Lombard Street, London.'

'Meaning I have to desert the golden city of my forefathers for the lair of our ancestral oppressor, on which Herr Hitler may soon be raining bombs, if I'm to be paid in full.'

'Those are their terms.'

'And if I reject them?'

'I can't answer for the consequences.'

'Can you not? Well, sir, I call you a famishing poor kind of negotiator.'

'What's your answer?'

Henchy fumed silently for a moment, then said, 'If you think I'm going to pay you ten per cent of a sum before I'm in possession of it . . .'

Quibbling over commission was a promising sign. Swan smiled to himself. 'I'll settle for seven and a half per cent.'

'Two and a half.'

'That's ridiculous.'

'I have to wait for a full settlement. You can take your share out of the initial payment. It's a generous offer.'

It was far from generous. But there was something undeniably attractive about removing the irritant that Henchy was from his life within twenty-four hours. Being paid anything at all into the bargain constituted a bonus. Largely for form's sake, however, Swan pushed for more. 'Five.'

And he got it. 'Very well, damn you.'

'We're agreed, then?'

'We are. Now, as to the arrangements for delivery of my four hundred and fifty . . .'

'Ah, that's the other condition, Mr Henchy.'

'What?'

'They want you on your way tomorrow night. Aboard the eight o'clock ferry from Dun Laoghaire to Holyhead.'

'They're in a tearing hurry to send me into exile, aren't they?'

'You're better placed to understand why than I am.'

'Am I so?'

'I'll be on the seven o'clock train from Westland Row to Dun Laoghaire, with a first-class ticket through to Euston in my pocket and a Gladstone bag containing a large amount of money in my hand. I suggest you get on at one of the intermediate stops. I'm to see you off on the ferry.'

'Make sure I'm gone, you mean.'

'If you like.'

'Well, I don't like.'

'Possibly not. But you'll do it anyway, won't you?'

The answer to that, as Swan reported to Linley in the Horseshoe Bar shortly afterwards, was a reluctant yes. Naturally, he left the details of his commission unreported, though Linley was so pleased he would probably not have complained.

'Dextrously managed, Cygnet. Congratulations. And many thanks on behalf of His Majesty's Government.'

'Do I get an MBE for this?'

'No. But you do get the evening's bar bill paid for you by the British Legation. I rather think this calls for champagne, don't you?'

*

281

Swan woke late the following morning, champagne in the bar having progressed to dinner at Jammet's and a foray to a dance-hall. Most other breakfasters had been and gone by the time he made it downstairs and he was consuming bacon and eggs, washed down with black coffee, in conditions of virtual solitude, when an unexpected face appeared at the entrance to the room: that of Ardal Quilligan.

'I have some news for you, Eldritch,' he announced, joining Swan at his table and accepting the offer of coffee. 'And I had to see a client in Fitzwilliam Square, so I thought I'd drop in on you on my way back to the office to deliver it in person.'

'Good news, I trust.'

'For you, certainly. A Mr Boyle from the Justice Department rang me first thing this morning, regarding Desmond's application for release from internment.'

'What did he have to say?'

'That he could see no reason why Desmond shouldn't be a free man by the end of next week.'

'Excellent. None of the foot-dragging you feared, then?'

'Apparently not. It—'

'Excuse me, Mr Swan,' one of the bellboys breathlessly inter-rupted. 'There's a phone call for you from a Miss Quilligan. Do you want to take it?'

Swan was momentarily lost for words. He looked across at Ardal, who frowned back at him. 'Well, well. Issie never mentioned she was intending to contact you.'

'I'd better go and see what she wants.'

'Yes. I suppose you had.'

Swan hurried into the foyer, part of him intrigued by Isolde's call, the other part annoyed by its timing. The concierge directed him to one of the phone booths to take it.

'Isolde?'

'Stephen,' she responded breathlessly. 'I'm so glad I caught you.'

'You caught Ardal as well.'

'Oh God. He's with you?'

'Waiting for me in the restaurant.'

'Damn, damn, damn. What did you say to him?'

'That I'd go and find out what you wanted.'

There was a lengthy pause, filled by a crackle of static. Then she said, 'You know what I want, Stephen.'

'Indeed. Would you like me to explain that to him?'

'Don't be cruel to me.'

'But I was. And it seemed to me you rather enjoyed it.'

'You are an evil man, Mr Swan. And a corrupting influence on well-bred young ladies.'

'So I should hope.'

'What are we to do?'

'Now? Or next Wednesday afternoon?'

'I rang because I want to see you. That's all. Just . . . be with you . . . for a while. I thought we could meet . . . in the National Gallery, perhaps.'

'This morning?'

'Unless you're busy.'

'No, no. Let's meet, by all means. I'll tell Ardal you were . . . concerned I might think Dublin an uncivilized city and rang to . . . offer your guidance to its artistic treasures.'

'Yes. He'll believe that of me. Why has he come to see you?'

'To give me news of Desmond. He should be out by the end of next week.'

'So soon?'

'Ardal will expect you to be pleased.'

'And I am. But . . . Never mind.' Swan knew what she was thinking, of course. He would have no reason to remain in Dublin once Desmond was free. He heard her sigh. 'The National Gallery, an hour from now?'

'It's a date.'

Ardal Quilligan seemed more amused than puzzled by Swan's account of his telephone conversation with Isolde. 'I'm afraid she thinks me rather a Philistine, Ardal. A dose of Hibernian art has been prescribed. And apparently I have no choice but to swallow it.'

'Quite right too.'

'She was delighted to hear Desmond will soon be free.'

'I suspect she'll follow him to London before long. She can't wait to get to know her nephew.'

'Will you go with her?'

'I can't readily leave my practice. But I'm sure . . . I can rely on you to entertain her.'

'Certainly.' Swan smiled obligingly. 'It'll be my pleasure.'

Aesthetic enlightenment was unforthcoming for Swan that morning in the thinly patronized, muddily lit rooms of the National Gallery. Nor did Isolde exert herself to bestow any upon him. They drifted from room to room, exchanging whispered remarks, whose contents would have scandalized anyone who heard them. But they took good care to ensure no one could. And the fleeting kisses they occasionally allowed themselves went unobserved.

They left and strolled around the flower-bedded park in the centre of Merrion Square. The weather was damp and cool, the day grey and muted. Isolde shared a cigarette with Swan and spoke, as Ardal had predicted, of visiting Desmond and her nephew in London as soon as possible.

'No doubt you'll be too busy to see me once you're back there,' she said, fishing for reassurance.

'That depends,' he teased her.

'On what, pray?'

'Whether you think you're likely to fall in with . . . the wrong crowd . . . for lack of guidance from a man of the world.'

'And if I were?'

'Then I should consider it a point of honour to . . . come to your rescue.'

'I may need rescuing quite often.'

'You may indeed.' He smiled at her. 'But I'm willing to accept the responsibility.'

They parted after lunch at a restaurant Isolde knew. Back at the

Shelbourne Swan prescribed for himself a doze and a session with the resident masseur in preparation for his tiresome duties of the evening. Shortly after six o'clock, he set off. He made his way across St Stephen's Green blithely unconcerned as to whether Special Branch were tailing him or not, for the simple reason that anyone following him was bound to do so on foot and would be left helpless by his departure on the other side of the park in a fast-moving car.

The driver was silent and expressionless. Linley, sitting next to him in the front seat, turned to greet Swan with a smile as they sped south along Harcourt Street.

'I think we happen to be going your way, Cygnet, so sit back and relax. Henchy's money is in there.' He pointed to the Gladstone bag on the floor behind the driver's seat.

'I can't help noticing we seem to be heading in the wrong direction. Westland Row is north.'

'A precautionary detour, nothing more. Willis knows what he's doing.'

'Lucky man.' Swan hoisted the bag up on to the seat beside him and opened it. Beneath a folded newspaper, he found the promised wad of banknotes. 'Rather like Lorcan P. Henchy.'

'It's not always the good and godly who are rewarded in this life, I'm afraid. Just put the wretched fellow on that boat and we can forget all about him. Then your work for the legation will be done. Well, apart from propping up our middle order batting, of course. You will turn out tomorrow, won't you?'

'Not if I'm stuck down at number seven and never allowed to bowl.'

'I'll see what I can do.'

'So I should hope. I'd be disappointed if my labours on your behalf went unrewarded.'

'Perish the thought, Cygnet. Perish the thought.'

The precautionary detour delivered Swan to Westland Row station in ample time for the seven o'clock train to Dun Laoghaire. 'See you later,' was Linley's parting cry as the car pulled away, a reference to their agreement to meet for a nightcap at the Shelbourne.

Swan went into the station lavatory, shut himself in a cubicle and transferred fifty pounds from the Gladstone bag to an envelope, which he put in his pocket. Then he strolled back out and boarded the waiting train.

The connection with the eight o'clock ferry meant it was three quarters full when it left and heavily loaded with luggage. Most of the passengers looked glum, the drizzly, overcast weather doing nothing for any voyager's spirits. Swan lit a cigarette and consoled himself with the thought that he at least would not be leaving dry land. The man opposite him pulled his hat well down over his eyes and fell instantly asleep. The train steamed lethargically on its way.

At each stop, Swan lowered the window and peered out to see if Henchy was on the platform. Finally, at Blackrock station, there he was, portmanteau in hand, threadbare Inverness overcoat draped around him. Swan held the door open for him and he clambered aboard, taking the seat next to the sleeper under the hat.

'I wondered if you'd make it,' Swan remarked.

'I wondered that myself about you,' said Henchy with an ironic smile. 'Got much luggage?'

'Just this.' Swan pointed to the Gladstone bag between his feet.

'I like to travel light myself.'

'Are you a good sailor?'

'As good as I am anything else.'

'Cigarette?'

'Why, thank you.'

Swan's striking of a match roused the sleeping man where no number of jolts, whistles and shouts had. He blinked and looked round at Henchy. 'Good Lord, where are we?'

'Just left Blackrock.'

'Then I've not missed Seapoint. That's lucky. I can't tell you how often I overrun.' He was pasty-faced and shabbily suited. An overworked clerk of some sort, Swan surmised, feeling sorry for him and also faintly scornful. Swan was confident he would never be reduced to such an existence.

The train had already begun to slow as it approached Seapoint station. The man gathered himself together. He appeared to have no luggage. Whatever work he did, he was at least taking none of it home. As the train came to a halt, he eased the door open and stepped out. Swan gazed past him at the calm grey expanse of Dublin Bay, stretching away beyond the sea wall next to the platform.

'Goodbye,' said the man, turning back to face them.

There was a loud crack. Swan jumped in surprise, thinking the man had broken something in the door as he slammed it shut. But the door, he suddenly realized, was still open. Henchy uttered a strange, gurgling cry and slumped down in his seat. There was blood on his coat and shirt, spreading like spilt wine. His face was contorted in pain and shock.

Swan looked from Henchy towards the door. The man had a revolver in his hand and was staring grimly at him. Swan saw the barrel of the gun move to point in his direction. There was no doubt in his mind what was about to happen.

But in that instant the train started forward with a lurch, swinging the door against the gunman just as he took aim. There was another loud crack, a ping as the bullet missed Swan and ricocheted off the luggage rack, a scream from behind him, a confusion of shouts. Swan grabbed the Gladstone bag and lashed out with it, striking the gunman in the face. The man toppled backwards. A whistle blew stridently. 'Watch out there,' someone bellowed. The train continued to move. And the gunman moved with it, his foot trapped between the step and the platform edge. The revolver was knocked from his grasp. He slipped further down into the gap and let out a shriek. There were more whistle blasts and cries of alarm.

Seeing his chance, Swan sprang out of the carriage. He moved to where the revolver had fallen and picked it up. Looking back, he saw the train continuing to drag the gunman along even as it began to slow. He was trapped somewhere around his thigh. His shrieks had become a yowl of agony. The guard was rushing towards him, along with several passengers who had just got off.

But Swan turned away. He opened the bag, dropped the revolver inside, clipped it shut and hurried towards the footbridge.

1976

THIRTY-FOUR

'I suppose the mystery of my father's death was one of the reasons I became a journalist,' said Moira Henchy. 'You always hope you can get to the bottom of a story, though you seldom do. I've prayed that one day I may get to the bottom of his. I can only remember him as this remote, awkward, shadowy figure, standing in the doorway of our cottage in Cork, or at the front gate, looking towards me. Never inside, never at home. Always . . . leaving.

'My mother told me he was dead, of course, but years passed before she admitted he'd been murdered. She didn't know – or want to know – why. It was the kind of scandalous end she'd expected of him. Probably related to unpaid gambling debts. I was determined to find out as much as I could, so I looked up the newspaper reports of how it had happened.

'At Seapoint railway station, south of Dublin, at about seven twenty on the evening of Friday the fifth of July, 1940, my father, Lorcan Parnell Henchy, was shot dead by a man leaning in through the doorway of the train he was on. Witnesses disagreed about whether the killer had just got off the train or was waiting for it to arrive. He tried to shoot another man, who was apparently travelling with my father, but missed. I'm certain that man was your uncle Eldritch Swan, who struck the killer with his bag, causing him to fall and become trapped between the platform edge and the train as it started moving. The main artery in his leg was severed before the train came to a halt and he bled to death at the scene. He was never identified.

'Eldritch had vanished by the time the police and ambulance arrived. No one had noticed him leave the station amidst the general confusion. The gun had also vanished. I assume he took it. He had good reason to be in fear of his life, after all.'

'How can you be sure it was him?' I asked, though I didn't for a moment doubt it.

'My chance to make further enquiries came when I moved to Dublin as a student. I checked the last address we had for my father: thirty-one Merrion Street. Mrs Kilfeather, the old lady who owned the house, told me he'd moved out of his flat a couple of weeks before his death. She also mentioned that the new tenant, an English elocution teacher called Eldritch Swan, had been arrested there the day after my father's murder. Oddly, she didn't know why. "But he must have been up to no good" was how she put it. I couldn't find anything in the papers about this man, Swan, but there was a court record of his trial later that month on charges under the Offences Against the State Act. It was held in camera and he was sentenced to life imprisonment. Now, that was altogether strange. The Offences Against the State Act was designed for use against the IRA. They always acknowledge their own. But they clearly knew nothing about Eldritch Swan. Neither did anyone else.

'I didn't have much to go on. In my father's pocket the police found a single ticket from Blackrock, the station before Seapoint, to Dun Laoghaire, but he had a large bag with him, containing most of his worldly possessions, including his passport, which suggested he was planning to go far further than Dun Laoghaire. England would be my guess, with or without Eldritch. Both men were supposed to be killed, but one got away, only to be arrested the following day. Why? What had they done? What did they know?

'I worked as a reporter for the local paper in Cork after university and it wasn't until I got a job in Dublin a few years later that I was able to go back into the case. I cajoled the Justice Department into telling me which prison Eldritch was being held in: Portlaoise. I applied for permission to visit him. It was refused.

I went to see the barrister listed as representing him at his trial. He'd retired and refused to speak to me. But his office suggested I contact the solicitor who'd brought the case to them: Ardal Quilligan. He wouldn't tell me anything either. He claimed the police had never divulged to him exactly what Eldritch was supposed to have done.

'Then my editor called me in and said he'd been officially warned off by the Justice Department. He wasn't best pleased, since he didn't have a clue what I'd been doing. I agreed to drop it. I didn't, of course, not completely. But there wasn't much more I could do anyway. I found out Ardal Quilligan's brother, Desmond, had been an IRA activist, but he'd renounced the struggle and been released from internment in July 1940. There it was: that month again. I tried to track Desmond down in London. But he was dead by then. It was all tied together somehow. I knew it was. I just couldn't see how.

'Eventually, earlier this year, Eldritch was released. I only found out after the event. It was as unpublicized as his original imprisonment. I couldn't establish where he'd gone. I was actually planning to call in on you and your mother in Paignton when I caught the news that Ardal Quilligan had been murdered in Ostend. I knew it had to be the break I was waiting for, although nothing the police said at this afternoon's press conference told me anything about Eldritch. I suppose I'm relying on you to do that, Stephen.'

I told her as much as I could then: about the Quilligans and the Cardales and the Linleys; the forgery, the lawsuit, my efforts, along with Eldritch and Rachel, to prove her family had been cheated – and how those efforts had ended in disaster. What I didn't mention was that if I found such proof now I'd help suppress it to win Rachel's freedom. Nor could I solve for Moira the mystery of why her father had been killed and Eldritch incarcerated thirty-six long years ago.

'Who can solve that mystery, Stephen?' she asked when I'd finished.

'Eldritch. And his old schoolmate, Sir Miles Linley.'

'Who was using the flat in Merrion Street as a love nest.'

'Supposedly. But that doesn't quite fit with Eldritch being arrested there, does it?'

'No. In fact, it sounds like a cover story.'

'Cover for what?'

'The secret I've been trying to gouge out of the solid stone wall they put up round this case thirty-six years ago.'

'And who are *they*?'

'Linley's Secret Service friends and their Irish equivalents. I have a few contacts in the Dublin Government. Someone in my line of work has to. I tapped them for information after I learnt Eldritch had been released. They made it clear to me – *very* clear – that I should leave the story alone. There was a, quote, "security" dimension to it, whatever that meant in the context of something that took place so long ago. Of course, the IRA haven't gone away in all those years. Quite the reverse. So, do they have something to do with it? I couldn't persuade anyone to do more than frown enigmatically at me and change the subject. The one thing – the only thing – I got was almost a throwaway remark. "They'd never have let him go while Dev was living."'

'When did de Valéra die?'

'Last August, two years after stepping down from the Presidency. And within months Eldritch was out.'

'Does that imply de Valéra would have blocked his release, or simply been offended by it?'

'I don't know. But it certainly implies he knew what Eldritch was in for and wasn't likely to have forgotten. Though, to be fair, Dev had a famously long memory and an old-school attitude to crime and punishment. Perhaps Eldritch is lucky he wasn't hanged. A good few IRA prisoners were executed during the Second World War at Dev's say-so.'

'Whatever Eldritch was up to in July 1940, Moira, I can guarantee he wasn't aiding and abetting the IRA.'

'No. Of course not. But he was up to something, wasn't he? Something big. Something it's still very dangerous to know the truth about.'

'Perhaps you should heed those warnings, then.'

'Perhaps you should too.'

'I can't.'

'No, well . . .' Moira stubbed out her cigarette forcefully. 'We have that in common, Stephen.' Then she lit another.

'Eldritch mentioned Linley was nursemaiding a government minister from London when they met in Dublin.'

Moira nodded. 'That would have been Malcolm MacDonald, sent over by Churchill to have a go at persuading Dev to take Éire into the war. He's supposed to have offered Irish unity in return, though how Northern Ireland was to be forced down that road never became clear, because, after a lot of humming and hawing, Dev rejected the offer. Maybe he regretted turning it down when the current Troubles broke out. More likely not, though. He wasn't a man prone to regrets.'

'Could that be the "something big"?'

'I don't see how. It's not a secret. And what Eldritch was caught up in definitely is – to this day. It seems to me you badly need to find him.'

'I know.'

'Any clues?'

'None, at the moment. I'm hoping he'll come to me.'

'Well, if he does, tell him I can get his story into the public domain – anonymously and lucratively. That must be what he wants: the truth, on the record. It's certainly what I want. And I think he owes my father that much.'

I doubted if Eldritch felt he owed the late Lorcan Henchy anything. Thirty-six years in prison didn't leave much room for moral niceties. I assured Moira I'd put her offer to him if I got the chance, but I had no real intention of doing so. If Eldritch had the proof Ardal Quilligan had been carrying, I needed to persuade him to let me hand it over to Tate and bury his doubtless highly marketable story in the process. It wasn't going to be easy, but it had to be done. *If* I got the chance.

*

I took another futile prowl round the diamond district before returning to van Briel's house. He wasn't there. I cut myself a sandwich and sat in the kitchen, glumly munching through it. I was weary with the effort of trying to devise a way out of the difficulties that confronted Rachel and me. And knowing the agonies of uncertainty she must be going through didn't make my thinking any clearer.

Van Briel seemed similarly at a loss when he got in. He'd taken Lasiyah out for dinner and a film and I sensed, in his tone and manner, a growing exasperation with my invasion of his life, maybe stoked by complaints from Lasiyah.

'I've pulled clients out of all sorts of trouble, Stephen, but trouble isn't a big enough word to describe your situation. You need to find that uncle of yours. You need to find him fast.'

'Any suggestions how I go about that?'

He seized his hair in both hands and tugged at it, then dolefully shook his head. 'Not one. Except . . .'

'What?'

'Get some sleep. Problems always look smaller in the morning.'

This one didn't. Anything but. And van Briel gave a poor impression of believing it did himself. 'I'm sorry, Stephen,' he said as we consumed a liquid breakfast. 'Today could be tough.' He looked at his watch. 'Mrs Banner flies in around now. I'll have to tell her how things are for Rachel. She'll probably want you to explain how you got her daughter in this mess. I would if I was her. Then there's Lady Linley. She won't be exactly happy either.'

'I'm not bothered about making Isolde Linley happy, Bart. I have as many questions for her as she has for me.'

'You see? This is what worries me. You've got to be . . . careful. She might bring a lawyer with her. You know, one almost as smart as me. Actually, the less you say, the better it'll be for you.' He sighed and rubbed his eyes. 'Look, this is how we'll play it, right? I'll go to the office. You wait here. I'll call you when I know how we're going to set up these meetings.'

296

'I don't like the sound of just sitting by the phone, waiting to be summoned.'

'Maybe not. But you have to—' Van Briel broke off, frowning at the bing-bong of the doorbell downstairs. 'It's too early for the postman. Hold on.' He went into the lounge and looked out of the window. '*Goddank*. It's not the police. I thought maybe . . . Leysen had come for you.'

'Who is it, then?' I asked, following him to the window.

'I don't know. I've never seen her before.'

But I had.

Marie-Louise was anxious and confused. She kept apologizing for calling at such an hour. It took a cup of van Briel's potent coffee, laced with brandy, to untangle her meaning. Joey, it appeared, had vamoosed.

'Madame Banner will be here soon. What do I say to her? I got up early because I heard him moving around. But he was already in the hall, with that army kitbag of his packed, ready to leave, when I went down. "I've hung around Antwerp long enough," he said. "Time I was rolling." What does that mean – *rolling*? "What about your mother?" I said. "Tell her I'll be back someday." *Some day? Mon Dieu!* She will say I should have stopped him. But I couldn't do anything. He gave me a hug, told me to . . . look after myself, then . . . he walked out.'

'Which way did he go?' asked van Briel.

'Towards Berchem station.'

'I guess that figures. More connections than Centraal. His destination could be . . . anywhere in Europe.' He shrugged. 'Or beyond.'

'How did he seem last night?' I asked.

'I did not see him. He came in very late. That is why I came, Stephen. I wanted to ask if you spoke to him yesterday. You said you were going to the Zoo . . . to try to find him.'

'I found him all right. But he didn't say anything of any consequence – certainly nothing about going away.' But at that moment I remembered he might have done – just not to me. I went to my coat and took out his postcard. This time, I would read it to the end.

Antwerp March 29 1976 Dear Sis You've asked me more than one time why I like to compose these messages to you in one sentence and I wonder if you've guessed it's because I have a mortal fear of full stops on account of all the rude interruptions I witnessed in Nam that pretty soon revealed themselves as sudden terminations and also because I neurotically suppose that if I don't pause for breath you won't either and that way we'll get to talk the only way I feel I can which is right out and right on for a dare even when there's nothing much to tell you which is pretty much all the time in my cotton-wooled exile of a life here and which I'd have staked all the little I have on being as true of yesterday as all the days before days before yesterday but actually isn't on account of a rare caller at our sunburst-paneled door who was a stranger to me but maybe isn't to you and a stranger with a mission to boot that he was set on with a kind of guttering candle desperation and for the sake of that desperation if nothing else because it reminded me so of other desperations I've witnessed or experienced and wished oh wished hadn't been futile but were I'll tell you that he said he'd left something you'd want over Cheng-Sheng in that place we've been to the namesake of in NJ before I light out for a while guaranteeing my next card will at long long last come from some place else though always with my love Bro

'What do you think all that's supposed to mean, Stephen?' asked van Briel, when the three of us had read it through.

'Eldritch doesn't have the proof. Ardal dropped it off somewhere along the way. He must have realized the danger he was in, so he put it in a safe place and asked Joey to tell Rachel where that was in the event of his death.'

'Why don't you go get it, then?'

I glared at him. 'Because I can't understand the message.'

'That's no problem.' He winked. 'I can.'

'How?'

'Local knowledge. "That place we've been to the namesake of in NJ" must be Hoboken, New Jersey, named after Hoboken, suburb of Antwerp.' Suddenly enthused, he grabbed the Antwerp phone book from amongst a stack of papers and began a search through its pages that ended in a whoop of triumph. 'Cheng-Sheng is a Chinese restaurant in Hoboken. Let's go.'

THIRTY-FIVE

Cheng-Shengs Chinees Restaurant was at the less prosperous end of Hoboken's main shopping street. It was several hours away from being open and there was no sign in the stark interior of Cheng-Sheng or any of his family and/or staff. Not that it was them van Briel and I were waiting for on the other side of the road in his far from inconspicuous Porsche. Joey had said '*over* Cheng-Sheng'. And there was indeed a flat above the restaurant, with a separate entrance. But there'd been no answer to our several stabs at the bell.

'They could be gone for the whole day,' groaned van Briel, lighting his umpteenth cigarette. 'Some people round here work.'

'What do you suggest? Go away and try again this evening? I can't do that.'

'Maybe you'll have to.'

'Not before I've spoken to the people in the restaurant. They'll know the name of the occupant, if nothing else.'

'We can't wait all morning.'

'Why not?'

Van Briel rubbed his chin thoughtfully. It sounded like sandpaper, thanks to his abrupt and unshaven departure from home. I was no better groomed myself. 'Look, Stephen, I have to contact the office. There's a phone box back along the street. I'll call them from there. I won't be long.'

Van Briel got out of the car and trudged away. I took out the postcard and studied it again, even though I already had the important part off by heart. There was no doubt we were in the right place, improbable as it seemed that Ardal Quilligan had known anyone living here.

Whoever they were, though, and however they were acquainted with him, they might be gone all week, let alone all day. And there was nothing, absolutely nothing, I could do about it.

Marie-Louise had promised not to mention the postcard to Rachel's mother when she arrived. The last thing we needed was Esther Banner following us to Hoboken. But we couldn't expect Marie-Louise to cover our backs indefinitely. Sooner rather than later, something had to give.

To judge by van Briel's expression when he returned to the car, it already had. 'Meneer Oudermans wants me to go in right away. Mrs Banner has arrived and expects me to arrange for her to visit Rachel. And, big surprise, she's asking if I know where Joey is. Also where you are. Plus, if we needed a plus, which we don't, a lawyer representing the Linleys has made contact.'

'You'd better go in, then. But I'm staying here.'

'Come on, Stephen. It'll look bad for both of us if I say I've lost you. Worse if I say what you're actually doing.'

'Go for the lesser evil, then. Claim I've given you the slip. Buy me some time.'

'How much time?'

'I don't know. A few hours, at least. I promise I'll phone in by this afternoon.'

Van Briel sighed. 'All right, all right. But a few hours only. OK?'

'OK.'

'What will you do if no one comes to the flat and Cheng-Sheng's can't help you?'

'I'll think of something.'

I already had thought of something, which it was best for van Briel to have no inkling of. After he left, I stationed myself in a café with a sight-line on the restaurant. Two coffees later, nothing had changed. It was time to go for broke.

Steely rain had begun to fall, which I reckoned was good for my purposes. It ensured no one was loitering in the service yard behind Cheng-Sheng when I arrived there a few minutes later. The restaurant's kitchen had been extended to the rear, with the flat above looking out over its asphalted roof. I wheeled one of three large lidded bins against the wall, clambered on to it and hauled myself up by the extractor flue, then crouched low as I crossed to the windows of the flat. A couple of whacks with the heel of my shoe punched a big enough hole in the glass of one for me to reach in and turn the handle.

As I climbed into the room, I was aware that I had no way of being sure my break-in had gone unobserved. Someone might already be phoning the police. Why this didn't worry me as much as it should have I can't explain, except that I wanted answers of some kind and I was determined to get them, whatever risks I ran in the process.

I was in a small and sparsely furnished bedroom. I stepped out on to the landing, from which stairs led down to the street door. There was a bathroom to my left, a tiny kitchen to my right and, beyond that, a lounge. The flat was clean but frowsty, stale cigarette smoke souring the air. There was little in the way of decoration. A couple of buff-enveloped letters were lying unopened on the work top in the kitchen. They were addressed to a P. Verhoest.

I walked into the lounge. The impression I already had of a solitary, unsociable male occupant was reinforced. The walls were bare, the three-piece suite cheap and shabby, the television at least a decade old.

Then, glancing behind me, I noticed a large rectangular object, all of seven feet high, covered with a sheet and propped up against the wall. It looked like it might be a painting. If so, it was the only one in the flat. And yet it was shrouded. I stood in front of it and lifted the sheet off.

It was *Three Swans*. I knew that at once from Brenda Duthie's description of Desmond Quilligan's last work of art. I knew it also from the fact that the man in the picture was clearly Eldritch, much younger than he now was and looking, as Marie-Louise had prepared me to expect, quite a lot like me, though with shorter hair and the addition of a pencil moustache. He was dressed in his trademark brown and gold pinstripe suit and fedora and was shown leaning against a stile set in a dry-stone wall, amidst high-summer countryside. He was in the act of lighting a cigarette, one hand holding the flaming match, the other the box he'd taken it from. Beyond the wall could be seen a stretch of calm blue water: part of a lake, above which a swan was shown, rising in flight, its take-off trail still visible on the lake's surface.

Brenda Duthie had seen only one swan. But there really were three: the bird, the man, and the emblem on the familiar green, red and yellow box of Swan Vesta matches Eldritch was holding between the forefinger and thumb of his left hand. I peered closer. Eldritch's portrait was life-size, which had enabled Quilligan to incorporate a real box of Swan Vestas in the picture: a tiny piece of collage work which wouldn't be apparent when viewed from any distance. But there was something odd about it, something very odd indeed, which detracted from the naturalistic effect. The match-box was hollow. The cardboard tray containing the matches them-selves was missing.

I stood up, retreated to the sofa and sat on its arm, staring at the painting, struggling to divine Quilligan's intention when he'd painted it. The title was a tease. '*Three swans seen flying together portend a death,*' Eldritch had said, citing a proverb I'd never previously heard. But only one swan was shown in flight. Back in 1956, when Quilligan had produced this, Eldritch had been in prison, all possibility of flight denied him. And whose death was portended? The artist's own? It had certainly followed soon enough. Or his brother's, which had followed Eldritch's eventual release?

Had the tray inside the matchbox always been missing? That was the more pressing issue. If not, who'd taken it out? Ardal? Or the mysterious Mr Verhoest? I cast around the room, wondering if I'd spot it lying somewhere. There was a box of matches in the grate next to the gas fire, but it was a Belgian brand, smaller than Swan Vestas. I headed for the kitchen.

*

A walking-stick crashed down on to the handrail of the banisters as I rushed out of the lounge, blocking my path. To my shock and bewilderment, I was face to face with a thin, stooping old man. He had white hair, watery blue eyes magnified by the cloudy lenses of a pair of black-framed glasses and a dusting of stubble on his tightly clenched jaw. He was dressed in a grubby raincoat, his shirt collar open beneath, revealing a scrawny, tracheotomy-scarred neck.

'*Waar ga u naartoe?*' he croaked.

Even if I'd understood his question, I couldn't have answered it in that moment. He was Verhoest. He had to be. This was his home. And I was an intruder. How he'd been able to enter without my hearing him I couldn't imagine. And how I was going to stop him phoning the police I couldn't imagine either.

Then, bizarrely, he began to laugh – a dry, rasping laugh. He swung the stick slowly through the air and prodded the rubber ferrule against my chest. 'You're Swan's nephew, aren't you? That's who you are. I know the look. The Eldritch Swan look. Quilligan told me you might come here. But breaking one of my windows to get in? He didn't tell me to expect that.'

'I'm sorry. I . . .'

'Tell me your name.'

'Stephen Swan.'

'I'm Pieter Verhoest.' He lowered the stick to the floor and leant heavily on it. 'Has Eldritch ever mentioned me to you?'

'No. I don't think so.'

'You'd remember if he had.'

'You . . . know him?'

'*Knew* him. A long time ago.'

'I . . . I'm sorry I . . . broke in. I . . .'

'Couldn't wait.'

'No. That's right. I couldn't.'

'You got Quilligan's message, then.'

'Yes.'

'And you've seen the painting.'

'Yes.'

'What does it mean, young Swan? What does the picture mean?'

'I don't know.'

'But Quilligan's dead because of it. You must know.'

'How much did Quilligan tell you?'

'How much did he tell *you*?' Verhoest smiled crookedly. He propped his stick against the wall, took off his raincoat and slung it over the banisters, then grabbed his stick again and limped slowly past me into the lounge. He slumped down in the armchair facing the painting and gazed across at it. 'Isaac Meridor didn't hang fake Picassos on the walls of Zonnestralen. They were the real thing. The exhibition that's on in London comes to Brussels later this year. I might go and see it for old times' sake. When Ardal Quilligan told me how his brother helped defraud Meridor's widow and daughter, I was pleased, though not as pleased as when I heard the old man had drowned. I'd have held his head under the waves to finish him if I'd had the chance.' He looked up at me. 'I owe Meridor's brood nothing. You understand?'

'No. I don't.'

'Sit down.' He pointed to the sofa. 'I have a story for you. About your uncle.'

I sat down on the sofa opposite him. I wanted to ask about the matchbox in the painting behind me, but I sensed it would be futile. There was an answer and he would give it to me. On his own terms. In his own time.

'Who do you blame when you realize you've wasted your life? Yourself? It's the last answer you're left with when the . . . comfort . . . the alternatives give you runs out. Eldritch and I are a lot alike. He's spent thirty-six years in prison. I've spent thirty-six years . . . growing old and poor and lonely. Maybe, if I'd never gone to the Congo, it would have been different. I was young and arrogant and . . . greedy. Of course I was. The colonial regime rewarded arrogance and greed. It was what it was for. Rubber. Copper. Gold. Diamonds. We took everything. Women when you wanted them, *how* you wanted them. Boys too. There were no limits, only rules.

'I saw my chance to get out and get rich when I found out about Meridor's diamond-smuggling racket. I traced it to its root: your grandfather, George Swan, over the border in Tanganyika. I put together all the evidence. Then I had a wealthy man at my mercy. I came back here on leave in the spring of 1940 and gave Meridor a simple choice: buy me off or go to gaol for defrauding the government.

'It was stupid of me to think it would be so easy. Meridor was ruthless. That's how he'd made his money. There was a third choice and he took it. He ordered Eldritch to hire some men to kill me. They picked me up the night before I was supposed to sail to New York on the *Uitlander*. But they didn't kill me. They kept me locked up in a shed at a farm outside the city for two days, then dropped me over the Dutch border and told me to stay away from Antwerp. They said they didn't like the idea of killing a fellow Belgian when the country was in danger. I reckoned I was the only Belgian who had his life saved by the threat of a German invasion. They invaded for real pretty soon anyway. I spent the war in Eindhoven, working in a light-bulb factory.

'When I came back here in 1945, the Government took me on again in my old job. So, I went back to the Congo. I didn't last long. I'd had malaria before, but this time it was much worse. I nearly died. I need dialysis now, twice a week. They sent me home in 1948 and gave me a job in the Antwerp tax office. I hated it. And I hated being short of money. So, I went to see Mevrouw Meridor. With Meridor dead, my information on the diamond smuggling was much less damaging, but I hoped his widow would pay me something to save his reputation. I gave her time to think it over. She sent Ardal Quilligan to see me. I had no idea then about his brother's part in the Picasso swindle. I thought he was just ... Mevrouw Meridor's man of business. We agreed a payment. It was more than I expected to get. It should have been enough to keep me going. But it wasn't.

'A man I'd worked with in the Congo persuaded me to invest in a cigarette factory he'd opened in Stanleyville. It was supposed to make us both rich. But he was killed and the factory was destroyed in the fighting after independence. I lost every centime. I've been lucky, but never with money. That's why I live in this ...

varkenshok. I contacted Quilligan. He told me there'd be no more money from Mevrouw Meridor. I was on my own.

'Then he came to see me last Sunday. He asked me to keep that painting safe until he came back for it. If he didn't, I was to keep it until you or Eldritch came. He paid me some money. Not much. I'm not sure he had much. He told me what his brother had done. He was in danger, he said. He wasn't frightened, though. He seemed . . . very calm, almost . . . contented. His only worry was the painting and how to hide it. He knew I'd agree. And he knew he could trust me. Eldritch had told him something about me, you see, something secret, just before he went to prison. Quilligan passed it on to me. But I already knew. One day, not long after the war, I recognized one of the men Meridor hired to kill me in a bar near the docks. I had nothing against him. I was grateful they hadn't killed me. We had a drink together. Quite a few drinks. Then he told me. They were paid not to kill me. By Eldritch. On top of the money from Meridor. Your uncle has a conscience. Maybe you didn't know. You know now. He saved my life twice, once accidentally, once deliberately. By stopping me sailing on the *Uitlander*. And by stopping that man and his friends from killing me. Pretty funny, isn't it?' He laughed his rattling laugh. 'I spent a long time thinking how good it would feel to stick a knife in Eldritch's guts. Then I found out I . . . owed him everything.' He laughed some more, then raised his stick, which he'd leant against the arm of the chair, and pointed it at the painting. 'Have you seen there's something missing, young Swan?'

'The inside of the matchbox.'

'*Ja.* That's right. The inside of the matchbox. Swan Vestas. Irish humour, I suppose. When I read in the paper yesterday that Quilligan had been murdered in Ostend some time Sunday night, I took a long, careful look at the painting. I saw the matchbox was real, with its ends painted over. I thought that was strange. So, I slit the paint with a knife and took out what was inside the box.'

'Not matches, I imagine.'

'Oh no. Not matches.'

'What, then?'

307

'Photographic negatives. Six of them. Cut from a strip.' He swung his stick to point at the bureau in the corner of the room. 'I had them developed. The prints are in there.'

I jumped up and strode over to the bureau. The flap was up and the key wasn't in the lock.

'You'll need this,' he said. I turned and he tossed the key over to me.

I unlocked the flap and lowered it. A yellow paper wallet with the word *Kodak* printed on it caught my eye at once. I flicked it open and slid out the photographs it contained.

THIRTY-SIX

There were six black-and-white photographs of a man I assumed was Desmond Quilligan, fair-haired, square-jawed and stocky, aged about forty, dressed in a paint-spattered boiler suit, looking more like a house painter than an artist, cigarette wedged jauntily in the corner of his mouth. He was sitting on a chair next to two easels, on one of which stood a Picasso I recognized from the exhibition at the Royal Academy – a Cubist portrait of a horse and rider – and on the other a half-finished copy of it. Quilligan had arranged the chair and easels on the patio outside the French windows of the drawing-room at Cherrygarth. And to clinch the when as well as the where, he was holding a folded newspaper at arm's length in front of him, with the title and date clearly visible. It was the *Daily Mail* of Wednesday, 23 October 1940.

'Is that what the Meridors need to win their case?' asked Verhoest.

I'd have needed to be a lawyer to answer his question with any confidence, but photographs of Desmond Quilligan apparently in the act of copying one of the Brownlow Picassos at Geoffrey Cardale's house in the autumn of 1940 would surely drive a coach and horses through the estate's defence. 'I think so, yes,' I murmured. Then I noticed something else. In two of the photographs, a figure could be seen inside the drawing-room looking out through the French windows: a boy of three or four, dressed in dungarees and a check shirt. Simon Cardale had obviously forgotten glimpsing this meticulous recording of a forgery, though no doubt if he saw the pictures, which I was obliged to ensure he never did, he'd have his memory jogged of that strange afternoon in his childhood when two men he was later to be told were his father and uncle had busied themselves with one of those many adult activities he was too young to comprehend. 'I think this would clinch it.'

'Except that you'd need the negatives to prove the photographs weren't faked.'

Verhoest was right, of course. The negatives were crucial. And they weren't in the wallet. I turned round and looked at him. 'Where are they?'

'In a safe place. I went to my bank this morning and deposited a small package. You can't be too careful, can you?'

'No. Very wise. So, could we . . . retrieve it?'

'*Ja*. Of course. *I* could. But we need to agree something first.'

'What?'

Verhoest sighed. 'How much they're worth.'

'I thought, since you owe Eldritch your life . . .'

'Ah, I do, young Swan. *Ja*. That is why I'm not selling the negatives to the Brownlow estate. But I need money, just like Eldritch. The need . . . sharpens . . . as you grow older. He will understand.'

'How much do you want?'

'A million francs.' He smiled. 'That's actually only about fifteen thousand pounds.'

'All right.' I'd get the money from somewhere. I had to.

'No argument?'

'Like you say. We have to have the negatives.'

'*Ja*. OK.' Verhoest grasped his stick and struggled to his feet. 'We agree?' He offered his hand.

'We agree.' I walked over and we sealed the agreement with a handshake.

He let me take the photographs with me. He could obtain extra prints any time he liked. That was why the negatives were really all that mattered. If I could deliver them to Tate, Rachel and I would be in the clear. Otherwise . . .

I boarded a tram heading for Groenplaats and tried to decide what exactly was the best move to make. I needed a million francs to pay Verhoest and secure storage for the negatives before I contacted Tate. Without my passport, I wasn't going to be able to persuade a bank to do anything for me. Clearly, I had to rely on Oudermans, even though he'd left me in no doubt of his disapproval of striking terms with the people responsible for Ardal Quilligan's death. He wouldn't stand in my way, though. I was confident of that.

The tram left Hoboken and trundled north. I took the photographs out of the wallet and leafed through them again. It was strange to see, in black and white, the physical reality of what I'd only till now been told about Desmond Quilligan, twenty years dead, but alive and happy and vigorous in these pictures I felt certain his brother had taken, posing proudly with the fruits of his very particular artistic gift one autumn afternoon – somehow I'd convinced myself it was the afternoon – thirty-six years in the past.

I knew I'd regret handing the negatives over to Tate for him to destroy them, but I had no alternative. Rachel was going to be charged with murdering Ardal unless I met Tate's demands. I might well be charged as her accomplice into the bargain. She wouldn't want me to surrender the proof she'd spent so long searching for. But what else could I do? The choice was between defeat and imprisonment, which, as Eldritch might have told me, was an easy choice to make.

But it didn't feel easy. Not anything like. The tram lumbered on through the grey streets of Antwerp, filling up steadily as it went. It crossed the autoroute van Briel had driven me in on two nights before and steadily closed on the centre. Oudermans' office was a short walk from Groenplaats. The debate with myself would soon be over.

Then I heard a voice in my ear. 'I'm getting off at the next stop, boy. What about you?'

I whirled round and there, leaning forward in the seat behind me, was Eldritch, the collar of my father's old raincoat drawn up almost high enough to touch the pulled-down brim of his fedora.

He gave me half a smile. 'Those pictures came out well, didn't they?'

I was too shocked even to speak until we'd got off the tram. Eldritch calmly lit a cigarette as the other disembarking passengers wandered away from the stop. We were in a quiet street, a busier one crossing it ahead of us. He looked around curiously, re-acquainting himself with the city he'd once known.

'Where the hell have you been?' I demanded at last.

'Eighty-six, Avenue Cogels-Osy. Or Cogels-Osylei, as they call it now. Antwerp's changed a lot since I was last here. They've built a motorway where there used to be a moat round the old city and—'

'Never mind all that. What do you mean – eighty-six Cogels-Osylei? That's next door to Zonnestralen.'

'Actually, it's the other half of Zonnestralen. The half I used to live in. And still have the key to. The Wyckxes are away. They go away a lot, apparently.'

'You've been hiding there?'

'There was nowhere else I could think of to go.'

'For God's sake, Eldritch, I've been going crazy.'

'I wouldn't have helped you by getting myself arrested. They might have sent me back to Ireland. I've just spent thirty-six years in prison, Stephen. What did you expect me to do but run?'

'All right, all right.' I glared at him in anger and astonishment. I couldn't argue with the truth of what he'd said. However much Rachel and I stood to lose, he stood to lose more. 'How did you find me?'

'Marie-Louise told me where you and van Briel had gone.'

'She knows you're using number eighty-six?'

'I followed her when she went shopping yesterday. It was quite a surprise for her when I tapped her on the shoulder.' He smiled. 'She dropped a whole bag of potatoes. We spent the first few minutes of our reunion picking them up. For a while she couldn't decide whether to kiss me or box me round the ears. Now I come to think about it, it's not the first time she's had that dilemma.'

'Still, you managed to persuade her to keep your secret.'

'I assured her it wouldn't be for long. And I can be very persuasive.'

'Did Joey rumble you? Is that why he cleared out?'

'No. The reasons were all his own.'

'And do you know who I've just been with?'

'Oh yes. I saw Verhoest arrive shortly after you broke in. I was surprised, yet somehow not surprised. You could say the same about the photographs. I followed you on to the tram and managed to bag the seat behind you. You weren't paying much attention to the people around you – any attention, really. That was careless. It meant someone other than me could have seen what you had.'

'Verhoest is hanging on to the negatives.'

Eldritch nodded. 'Naturally. How much does he want?'

'Fifteen thousand pounds.'

'Well, we can spare him that with fifty thousand coming our way.' His gaze narrowed. He'd caught something in my expression. 'Unless you're going to tell me it's not coming our way.'

I shrugged. 'I've had to do a deal.'

'Really? And what kind of a deal is that – exactly?'

We headed for the riverside as I related all that had happened since Sunday night. Eldritch asked only strictly practical questions, offering neither approval nor disapproval of the moves I'd made and the decisions I'd taken. He knew delivering the negatives to Tate amounted to surrender, albeit conditional. But he also knew, as a moment's reflection on his own life confirmed, that surrender was sometimes necessary.

The wharves of the Scheldt were lined with old open-sided storage sheds, with a railinged terrace above that led north round the river's gentle eastward curve. We walked slowly towards the city centre, the ancient buildings around the cathedral massed ahead, modern office and apartment blocks clumped on the opposite shore.

'I have no choice, Eldritch,' I said, beginning, at this stage, to repeat myself. 'Thanks to Ardal's foresight, we have this one chance to retrieve the situation. Otherwise, it's only a matter of time before Rachel's charged with murder. Me too, quite possibly. I have to give Tate what he wants.'

'And in the process let Linley get away with it. As usual.'

'You said yourself he has powerful friends. And you were right. Too powerful for us.'

'*Us* meaning you and Rachel?'

'She'll lose more by this than you will. She's been trying for years to prove Cardale cheated her family. Now I have that proof. But I have to give it up to save her.'

'Let's stop for a moment.' He was breathing heavily from the walk, though that didn't stop him lighting another cigarette as we sat down on one of the benches facing the river. A spasm of coughing shook him violently. I waited while it slowly subsided.

'You should give up smoking,' I said gently.

'Like I should give up resisting this cosy deal you've struck with Tate?'

'There's nothing cosy about it. And you know there's no alternative.'

'Do I?'

'I'm sorry. OK?'

'So you should be.'

'And so you should be too. This is as much your fault as mine. More, in fact. A lot more.'

He said nothing for the next minute or so, merely puffing at his cigarette and gazing out across the river. Then he said, 'It's just as well, I suppose, that old age and long-term imprisonment resign you to disappointment. This isn't the biggest one to have come my way. It's a lot of money to miss out on, of course.' He sighed. 'But I won't deny I'd have done the same as you. In the circumstances.'

'I know. But thanks for saying it. And I *am* sorry.'

'Of course. We both are. But I think I have cause to be sorrier. It was just along from here that I boarded the *Uitlander* thirty-six years ago. I was supposed to be quitting Europe, probably for good. In my own mind, the United States was where I was destined to be. The New World. The future.' He tossed the butt of his cigarette to the ground and crushed it. 'So much for that.'

'Why did you pay to have Verhoest's life spared?'

'Because I didn't think he deserved to die. And I didn't want his blood on my hands.'

'I'm having trouble adjusting to this idea of you as a man of principle.'

'No need. Principles have nothing to do with it. It comes down to personality. The kind of man you are. Meridor would have dismissed me on the spot if he'd found out about Verhoest, which I calculated he would eventually, of course. My plan was to have moved on by then to bigger and better things. Meridor had taste and cunning and judgement and a certain sort of wisdom. But he had no scruples. He'd have said I was a weak-willed fool and in many ways I think he'd have been right. I suppose he was rather like Linley. The strength of such men is their certainty. They never falter. They never hesitate. Those who do . . . become their victims.'

'What happened between you and Linley in Dublin?'

'Ah. The great secret you're helping Tate bury. Is that it, Stephen? You want to know what it's really all about?'

'I think I should know now, don't you?'

Eldritch lit another cigarette and took a long, deliberative draw on it, then slowly nodded. 'Yes. You probably should.'

1940

THIRTY-SEVEN

It is early on a dank Saturday morning in Terenure, a village on the southern fringe of Dublin, too early for the trams that link it with the city to be running or for more than a handful of people to be about.

There are no signs of life at Doyle's bar, hard by the crossroads in the centre of the village, nor would anyone expect there to be. Friday night is likely to have been a late one. The door of the general store and newsagent opposite is open, however. The proprietor is standing on the threshold, smoking a cigarette as he contemplates the day ahead.

An hour or so from now, he will take delivery of his stock of daily newspapers and shake his head with concern at the prominent reports of a murder at Seapoint railway station the previous evening. He will make no connection with the figure he barely notices making a sidelong exit from the residents' door of Doyle's bar and hurrying off along the street, a figure clad in a brown and gold pinstripe suit, fedora angled low over his eyes, a Gladstone bag clutched in his hand. No one will register or report the going of Eldritch Swan.

A night in Doyle's one and only guest-room had come cheap, which was ironic, in view of the fact that Swan could have afforded to pay handsomely for accommodation. He had arrived in Terenure on foot after an anxious march of several miles from Seapoint along

319

the lanes skirting Dublin to the south and had decided it was safer to put up there than to go any further. During the largely sleepless hours since, he had soberly assessed his situation and had concluded that he was a marked man. Linley had placed him in the path of an assassin. He was some kind of dupe, though in what, and *for* what, he could not fathom.

Flight was his obvious course of action and one to which he was instinctively drawn. But hard reasoning told him any attempt to board a ferry at Dun Laoghaire or a Dublin to Belfast train would merely be to invite arrest – or worse. He could hope to evade capture by heading west, perhaps, to Limerick or Galway or somewhere close to the Northern Irish border, but he suspected that would end badly. His major difficulty was that he did not know why he had been targeted or how far-reaching the conspiracy was in which he had become caught up. And turning himself into a fugitive would do nothing to assuage the rage he felt at what Linley had done to him.

In the end, he had decided that his best chance of survival lay in attack. Linley would expect him to run and to hide. Instead, he would attempt to find out exactly what game his treacherous old school friend was playing. He would head for the one place where the truth was surely to be found.

Where the road from Terenure crossed the Grand Canal, he turned east along the towpath. From Leeson Street Bridge he followed back lanes as far as possible, emerging on to Merrion Street just opposite the main gate of Government Buildings. All was quiet. It was still early – not yet eight o'clock – and a sleepy air prevailed. He walked smartly along to the door of number 28 and rang the bell.

Mrs Kilfeather looked surprised to see him, as well she might. 'What can I do for you at this hour, Mr Swan?'

'I'm sorry to be a nuisance.' He treated her to his most ingratiating smile. 'The fact of the matter is that I've locked myself out. I haven't been sleeping well and I decided to go for a walk before breakfast. Stupidly, I left my keys behind.'

'Insomnia is a curse,' said Mrs Kilfeather. 'My late husband suffered from it. I believe it may have shortened his life, God rest his soul.'

'It can certainly make one abominably forgetful. I wonder if I might impose upon you for the loan of your set of keys.'

'By all means.' She glanced frowningly at the Gladstone bag in Swan's hand, perhaps wondering why he should have taken luggage on his pre-breakfast stroll. 'I'll just fetch them.'

Swan stepped inside the porch while she bustled off, casting a wary glance behind him. There was no one anywhere near by, except a policeman guarding the door into the ministerial wing of Government Buildings further up the street. The morning was still and grey and quiet.

'Here you are, Mr Swan,' Mrs Kilfeather announced, returning with the keys.

'Thank you. I'm obliged. I'll drop them back to you later.'

How much later that might be he had no idea. He had, in truth, very little idea of what awaited him in the top-floor flat at number 31. It was a mystery. But it would not remain so for long.

He slipped quietly into the house he had entered only once before and started up the stairs. The surveyor's and chiropodist's offices were still unstaffed. Silence ruled and he trod lightly, keeping to the edges of the steps to minimize creaks. On the half-landing between the second and third floors, he paused to open the Gladstone bag and take out the revolver. He had already checked that the remaining chambers were loaded.

As Swan reached the top of the stairs, the policeman on the other side of the street broke out of his reverie at the sight of a familiar vehicle approaching from the direction of St Stephen's Green: a black, gleamingly polished limousine. He squared his shoulders, tugged down his uniform jacket and stepped towards the edge of the pavement.

Swan put the Gladstone bag down, tightened his grip on the

revolver and slid the second key on the ring Mrs Kilfeather had given him into the Yale lock of the door serving the flat.

He entered at a lunge, hardly knowing what he might see. The hallway was empty, the doors to the bedroom, bathroom and kitchen standing open. But the sitting-room door was closed. He strode forward and flung it open.

'*Damnation!*'

The voice had come from the window. A man who had been crouching by it looked round at Swan, his lean, hard, moustached face creased by a frown. He was dressed in dark trousers and a sweater. An armchair had been pulled close to the windowsill beneath the raised lower sash, its back partially blocking Swan's view.

Swan pointed the gun at the man and motioned for him to stand up. 'Who are you?' he demanded.

'Eldritch Swan,' the man blithely replied, rising slowly to his feet.

'I don't think so. You see, I'm Eldritch Swan.'

'Really?' The false Swan glanced through the window down into the street. The sound of a car engine was growing steadily louder. 'That tears it.'

'What are you doing here?' Swan moved to see round the chair and caught his breath. A rifle, with telescopic sight attached, was propped on the arm facing the window.

In his surprise he looked at it a second longer than he should have. Something hard and heavy struck the side of his head. He went down, hitting the floor with a thump that winded him. He saw the shards of a smashed vase lying beside him on the carpet and found himself gazing at them in puzzlement, unable for the moment to understand what had happened. Then his assailant stamped on his wrist, snatched the revolver from his fingers and threw it across the room. Swan heard it slide over the bare boards into the hallway.

The false Swan swung back towards the window. 'Bloody hell,' he cursed, throwing himself to his knees and clapping the rifle to his shoulder. Swan heard a car door slam down in the street, then another. The vehicle's engine was idling, the note setting off an audible vibration in one of the windowpanes.

He rolled on to his elbow and pushed himself up. The false Swan was about to fire. There could be no doubt of it. His head was cocked to the telescopic sight of the rifle, his left hand bracing the barrel, his right curled around the trigger-guard. Swan lashed out with his foot, catching the other man behind the knee. He grunted and toppled to one side, squeezing the trigger before he was ready. There was a loud bang, and a splintering of wood where the misdirected bullet hit the window frame. He recovered himself and turned as Swan tried to scramble to his feet.

Swan saw the rifle butt descending towards him as he rose. And then he saw no more.

He was roused by shouts from outside the flat and a hammering at the door. There were raised voices down in the street as well. He propped himself up on his elbows, his brain seeming to follow the movement several seconds late, accompanied by a pulse of pain. When he raised his hand to the source of the pain, somewhere above his right eyebrow, he winced and saw blood on his fingers. He turned on all fours and dragged himself to his feet by the arm of the chair.

'Open up! Garda Síochána!' The shouts from the landing were accompanied by the thuds of what sounded like body charges at the door. The false Swan was nowhere to be seen, but his rifle still lay on the chair. Swan stared woozily at it, aware that he needed to act fast to save himself, but unable to translate his thoughts into motion.

He heard pounding feet on the stairs and a medley of thickly accented exchanges. Then something different struck the door, something sharper and harder that hewed the wood as if it was a log: an axe.

He staggered into the hallway. The false Swan was gone. Swan was alone in the flat, though he would not remain so for long. A vertical split opened in one of the door panels as the axe hit it again. The noise was deafening and disabling. He glanced desperately around. The revolver was also gone. But there was a wooden chair standing outside the bathroom where there had not been one before – and above it an open loft hatch. A prepared escape route? He could only hope so. Another blow of the axe brought its blade clean through the panel. Swan fled along the hall.

He heard a shout, '*Got it!*', from behind him as he jumped on to the chair and thrust his arms through the hatch. He anchored himself by the elbows and levered himself up, feeling the chair topple beneath him as his trailing foot caught its back. He could see a square of light in the loft towards the rear of the roof. He lunged towards the nearest rafter.

But he never touched it. His ankles were grabbed and pulled with such force that he could not keep hold. He fell, hitting the toppled chair and several broad uniformed shoulders before he thumped to the floor.

A hand on the back of his head ground his face into the boards. Other hands grabbed his wrists and yanked his arms round behind him. '*Cuff him,*' someone ordered. There was a clink of metal. He was pulled on to his side. There were thickly booted feet all around him. Then a face, red and angry, close to his own.

'*Sprechen Sie Deutsch?*' the man rasped, spraying Swan with spittle.

'No. I'm English. For God's sake, I—'

'English? Jesus fucking Christ.' The face vanished. Then a boot struck Swan hard in the groin. He cried out. And another boot mashed into his lower back. 'A fucking Englishman trying to kill our Chief.'

'I haven't tried to kill anyone,' Swan gasped. 'You're letting the gunman get away. *Listen to me.*'

But no one was listening. They had their would-be assassin. And that was enough.

1976

THIRTY-EIGHT

'So,' I said, as Eldritch fell silent and stared out at the grey waters of the Scheldt through a drift of cigarette smoke, 'what you were locked up for was nothing less than trying to assassinate the Taoiseach.'

'Yes,' he replied reflectively. 'Though hardly anyone knew that. It was hushed up. And as you've discovered, it's still being hushed up. Small wonder, really. Anglo-Irish relations would take a real knock from the revelation that the British Government plotted to knock off the sainted Eamon de Valéra.'

'You think Churchill approved of the plot?'

'I don't know. Someone high up, for certain, though whether *that* high up . . .' He shrugged. 'Linley might be able to tell you, if he had a mind to.'

'You surely explained how he'd set you up?'

'Not at my trial, no. I . . . exercised my right to remain silent.'

'*Why?*'

'It's more complicated than you think. Linley was acting under orders, of course. He'd used me to gain access to the flat not to keep de Valéra under surveillance but to have him killed if he refused to take Éire into the war. As refuse he did. While you and Rachel were rubbing the Linleys up the wrong way in Hampshire last week, I went to the Public Record Office to check exactly when de Valéra turned down MacDonald's offer. The answer's in the Downing Street files: a testy note from the Taoiseach, dated the

327

fourth of July, 1940, stamped as received on the fifth, the day of Henchy's murder and the day before my arrest. It opens with the words "We are unable to accept the plan outlined". No room for doubt, then: an unambiguous rejection. Plan B was put into effect immediately: assassinate de Valéra – who obligingly entered his office every morning by the door opposite thirty-one Merrion Street – blame it on an unholy alliance of the Germans and the IRA, then sit back and wait for the new Taoiseach to be forced into the war by sheer strength of public feeling. And it would probably have worked.'

'But for you.'

'Yes. I saved de Valéra's life. And got precisely no thanks for it. I doubt he knew who to believe was responsible, though I'm sure he must have suspected London because of the timing – straight after delivery of his note. Whether he ever read the statement I made to Special Branch I can't say. In a sense, it's irrelevant. To maintain neutrality, it couldn't be admitted that either the British or the Germans had tried to assassinate him. No word of the incident could be allowed to get out. I was tried in camera, by a judge without a jury. Acquittal simply wasn't an option. I was going down. Luckily for me, the execution of a British citizen was considered too ... conspicuous. Luckily also, none of my fellow prisoners knew what I was supposed to have done. I was discreetly put away.'

'But why didn't you at least try to persuade the judge you weren't the gunman?'

'In the first place because he wouldn't have believed me. And in the second—'

'Excuse me, gentlemen.' A tall, thin, stooping old man of obviously African origin was standing by our bench. He was well-spoken and immaculately dressed, in an elegant dark overcoat, pinstripe trousers, patent-leather shoes and a black homburg. He held an ebony cane in his gloved hand, the silver head of which matched the gleam of his tie-pin. He touched his other hand to the brim of his hat and smiled down at us with every sign of neutral benevolence. 'May I join you?'

'There are plenty of other benches,' said Eldritch discouragingly.

'But none quite so close, I think, to where the SS *Uitlander* was moored prior to its last, ill-fated voyage.'

'What did you say?' Eldritch stared up at him.

'The *Uitlander*, Meneer Swan. We both remember it well.'

'Who are you?'

'Do you not know me?'

My eyes were fixed on Eldritch. His expression was a mixture of disbelief and amazement. Then he shook his head in wonderment. 'It can't be.'

'Yet it is.'

'J-J.'

The old man nodded and switched his gaze to me. 'You are Meneer Swan's nephew, I assume. Meneer Oudermans has told me about you – and your current predicament, of which I must confess to being the unwitting architect. I often stroll along this quay, although this morning's visit was somewhat more purposeful than usual. It occurred to me that of all the places in this city where I might find your uncle loitering, this was one of the likeliest. I am the hitherto anonymous client you have been pressing Meneer Oudermans to identify: Jean-Jacques Nimbala, former valet to the late Meneer Isaac Meridor.'

'But—'

'You drowned with Meridor,' said Eldritch, finishing my sentence for me.

'As you see, I did not.' Nimbala lowered himself stiffly on to the bench beside me. He held the cane upright in front of him, clasping the head with both hands. 'The *Uitlander* sank at night. The chaos and fear were dreadful but for most of the passengers and crew mercifully brief. The ship went down very fast. Meneer Meridor was beside me one moment and gone the next. By pure chance I found myself in the water close to a drifting lifeboat. I managed to climb aboard. I did not expect to survive, even so, but late the following day I was picked up by a Brazilian freighter. Fishing a half-dead negro out of the Atlantic was not something the captain considered important enough to report to anyone. My race confers certain advantages, one of which is invisibility. It also confers certain disadvantages. As soon as I had recovered my strength, I was put to work in the galley. The ship proceeded to Lisbon, then to Dakar and finally, after many weeks, to Rio de Janeiro. I spent the remainder of the war as a servant in the household of the vessel's owner. I stayed on afterwards in a more senior capacity and remained there until his death three years ago. Then I decided to return home – to the Congo. But I did not care for what I found there. So, I came back to Antwerp. This is my home now.'

'Why did you never contact the Meridors and tell them you were alive?' asked Eldritch.

'Mevrouw Meridor has always disliked me. I served her husband and her husband was dead. I was grateful to him for conferring on me the comforts of his position in life, but there were actions he took that I . . . disapproved of. So, I was content to let his family believe I had died with him. It freed me of an obligation I might otherwise have felt bound by. That is the somewhat shameful truth.'

'You both worked for Meridor,' I said, suddenly grasping the similarity. 'But you both disapproved of him.'

'To what do you refer, young man?' Nimbala asked, frowning curiously at me.

'Verhoest isn't dead either.'

'Really? That is . . . surprising.'

'Eldritch paid the men hired to kill him *not* to kill him.'

'Well, well.' Nimbala looked past me at Eldritch. 'What a singular man you are, Meneer Swan. Though not a fortunate one, alas.'

'Not so far.'

'You are nearly as old as I am. "Not so far" leaves little time for improvement.'

'I was hoping to make enough money to see me out in style by finding proof that Geoffrey Cardale stole Meridor's Picassos.'

'Have you made any progress?'

'Show him the photographs, Stephen.'

I took the wallet from my pocket and handed it to Nimbala. He examined each photograph in turn, smiling and nodding his head in satisfaction as he did so. 'These are . . . remarkable.'

'But useless,' said Eldritch. 'Except for keeping Stephen here and his girlfriend, Rachel Banner, out of a Belgian gaol.'

'Meneer Oudermans mentioned the deal you've tentatively struck. Such a pity. I had hoped . . .' Nimbala handed the wallet back to me. 'Never mind. It cannot be. Meneer Meridor would always value his granddaughter's welfare above his own good name. I could not have served him as long as I did without understanding that.' He sighed. 'Only a simpleton expects the affairs of men to be simple. You evidently dabbled in matters of greater moment in Ireland than mere fraud and forgery, Meneer Swan.'

'I'm afraid so.'

'And we are both old and realistic enough to know when we must . . . withdraw from the field.'

'Why were you bothered about the case, anyway? I thought you were free of any obligation to the family.'

'Not as completely as I'd supposed during my years in Brazil. Returning here brought me into close proximity with my memories of service to Meneer Meridor. Whatever else he may have been, a buyer of fake art he most certainly was not. I felt I had to do something to redeem his reputation. It seemed clear you had played a part in the swindle, yet it was equally clear you hadn't profited by it. Forgive me, but I thought I could rely on your . . . venality. I needed someone to act on my behalf if I was to preserve my anonymity, someone who was as certain as I was that Meneer Meridor's Picassos were genuine. In the circumstances, you were the perfect choice.'

'How kind of you to say so.'

'Where did you get the reward money?' I asked.

'From the chimney at Zonnestralen,' Eldritch answered for him.

Nimbala smiled. 'You are correct, Meneer Swan. I knew, as Mevrouw Meridor did not, where her husband had concealed a cache of diamonds prior to our departure for New York as a precaution against . . . mishaps on the voyage. I did not regard taking them as theft. I believe Meneer Meridor would have regarded my use of the money they fetched as a prudent investment. He would even have been pleased that I am able to dress more smartly these days. He placed a high value on appearance.'

'I'm sorry to have to be so blunt, Mr Nimbala,' I said, acutely aware that my priority was meeting Tate's demands, 'but I need fifteen thousand pounds to secure the negatives of these photographs and since, as you admit, Rachel and I are in this jam partly because of you . . .'

'I will pay. Gladly. In fact, I will pay the entire fifty thousand. Thanks to Meneer Meridor, I can comfortably afford to do so. And you have, after all, done what I asked.'

'But Meridor's reputation will remain sullied,' Eldritch pointed out.

'It cannot be helped. I've done as much as I can. And so have you. The money is in a suspense account under Oudermans' control. It can be drawn upon at any time I specify.'

'How about today?' I asked. 'At least for the fifteen. It can be in Belgian francs if that helps. He'll settle for a million.'

'And who is *he*?'

'Verhoest.'

Nimbala chuckled. 'That man keeps costing you money, Meneer Swan. Do you think it's well spent?'

'It's *your* money, J-J.'

'Technically, it's Meneer Meridor's. And he would definitely not approve.'

'But you'll do it anyway.'

'Yes.' Nimbala tapped his stick decisively on the ground. 'Of course.'

I called Verhoest from the nearest phone box and agreed to exchange the money for the negatives at two o'clock at the bank where he'd deposited them earlier. Nimbala then called Oudermans with instructions to make the cash available. Their agreement came, he reported, with a string attached, one I wasn't at all surprised by. Van Briel would deliver the money.

He looked disappointed when he saw me waiting for him alone outside the Banque Belgo-Congolaise in Arenbergstraat a quarter of an hour before my appointment with Verhoest. 'Where's our client?' he instantly demanded.

I was forced to tell him he was missing Eldritch as well as Nimbala. Neither of them had been keen to encounter Verhoest after so many years, so they'd taken themselves off like two men about town for lunch at a restaurant they remembered from former times. 'Verhoest would recognize him from the old days, which might complicate matters,' I explained. 'And we don't need any more complications, now do we?'

Disappointed though he was, van Briel was forced to concede the point. 'You're right, of course. We have Lady Linley coming to the office at four with a lawyer called Govaert. He has quite a reputation. We also have Mrs Banner sitting by the phone at Zonnestralen expecting us to call her with news of you. And the Irish journalist you met last night, Moira Henchy, has been in my ear as well, telling me things about your uncle and her dead father that make me wish I'd gone skiing this week. I feel like the kid with his thumb in the dyke. Are we going to get drowned, Stephen? Or does a million francs buy us a good bung?'

'Good enough.'

'Who is Verhoest?'

'Someone Ardal Quilligan left these with.' I handed him the wallet of photographs.

He sorted through them for a minute, then whistled his appreciation. 'Nice. Where are the negatives?'

'In a safe-deposit box in this bank.'

'So, we're here to buy them from Verhoest?'

'Exactly.'

'And what do you plan to do with them?'

'Put them in your office safe, then phone Tate and tell him we have what he wants.'

Van Briel nodded. 'OK. Good. Not really a bung, then.' He grinned. 'More a whole new dyke.'

THIRTY-NINE

Our business with Verhoest was concluded with anticlimactic ease. He arrived on time, looking dowdy and unremarkable in his grubby hat and raincoat, inspected van Briel's proffered wads of high-domination Belgian franc notes with a degree of satisfaction that fell far short of enthusiasm, then retired to the vault with one of the bank clerks to fetch the negatives.

'Do you think he has a whole boxload of secrets down there, Stephen?' van Briel mused as we waited.

'Maybe.'

'He's an old Congo hand. You can always tell them. There's a deadness in the eyes.'

'Is that right?'

'How does it feel to know what this is all about?'

'You reckon I do?'

'Oh yes. There's a change in you since yesterday. Then you were more like me. Now . . . you're more like him.'

The *him* was Verhoest, returned from the vault, the envelope containing the negatives in his hand. I checked them. Van Briel double-checked them. They matched the prints. There could be no mistake. Van Briel handed over the money and we left Verhoest to pay it into his account. 'Give my regards to your uncle if you see him' was his parting remark, which, it seemed to me, was about as effusive an expression of gratitude as he was capable of.

'Any similarity to him is temporary, Bart,' I proclaimed as

334

we stepped out into the street. 'Once this is over I'll revert to type.'

'We'd better get it over fast, then.'

'Amen to that.'

We walked the short distance to Oudermans' offices. Oudermans himself was waiting to greet me, his politeness stretched thin by professional disapproval. This solution to his clients' problems wasn't the kind to be found in a textbook of ideal case management. But if it worked . . . it worked. With the negatives stowed in the safe, I phoned the number Tate had given me.

The man who answered wasn't Tate, though he sounded English. His manner was brisk. 'Do you have the proof, Mr Swan?'

'Yes.'

'There can't be any room for doubt.'

'And there isn't any.'

'Sure?'

'Absolutely.'

'Good. You're in Antwerp?'

'Yes.'

'Very well. Mr Tate will meet you in the Centraal station buffet at four o'clock.'

Oudermans seemed almost relieved that I wouldn't be able to attend their meeting with Lady Linley and her lawyers. 'Call Govaert,' he instructed van Briel. 'Persuade him to postpone the meeting.'

'Until when?'

'It doesn't matter. If Mr Swan can reach an accommodation with Mr Tate this afternoon, I imagine the meeting will never take place.'

I made another call before leaving Oudermans'. After some delay, Eldritch came to the phone of the Metropole Hotel restaurant. He sounded subdued, almost mellow.

'I've secured the negatives,' I reported. 'And I'm to meet Tate at four.'

'You're doing well.'

'So far.'

'So good.'

'Exactly.'

'Meet me in the Angel – *Den Engel* – in the Grand Place – Grote Markt, I suppose I should say – at six o'clock. Then you can tell me the worst.'

I thought at the time that Eldritch had been giving rein to his natural pessimism with his last remark. As I sat in the smoky, bustling, cavernous buffet at Centraal station an hour later, though, it occurred to me that the best I could achieve was also the worst for Eldritch, at least in one respect that he might justifiably regard as crucial. Nimbala's pay-off would keep him in comfort for a good few years, but my surrender of the proof that Desmond Quilligan had forged the Picassos meant Sir Miles Linley would live on in unthreatened comfort himself. There was compensation. But there was no justice.

Tate materialized silently out of the prevailing fug as the hands on the clock above the counter registered four o'clock exactly.

'What have you got for me, Mr Swan?' he asked, gliding into the chair on the other side of my table.

'These.' I slid the wallet of photographs across to him.

He examined them carefully – and expressionlessly. Then he replaced them in the wallet. 'Very nice. Very . . . definitive.'

'That's what I thought.'

'Can I keep them?'

'Sure.'

'I'll need the negatives, of course.'

I laid Oudermans' card in front of him. 'They're in safe, legal custody.'

'Well, that's reassuring.'

'Isn't it?'

Tate took a drag on his cigarette, studying me dispassionately as he did so. Then he said, 'Here's what I'll do for you, Mr Swan. First thing tomorrow morning, a man will walk into Ostend police station and report that he witnessed Ardal Quilligan's murder. His description of the killer – male, middle-aged, built like a brick shit-house – will conclusively rule out you and Miss Banner. I can't be answerable for the speed and efficiency of the Prosecutor's Office, but I'm confident the police will have released Miss Banner before the day's out and informed you both that you're free to go.' He smiled tightly. 'How does that sound?'

'Acceptable.'

'I thought it might. Meanwhile, we'll confirm the present location of the negatives' – he picked up the card – 'and arrange a suitable time for their collection.'

'Fair enough.'

'How did you persuade your uncle to hand them over?'

'I didn't need to. They were with someone else.'

'I see.' Tate ruminated on that for a moment. 'There are just the six pictures, are there?'

'Yes.'

'Holding on to an extra few would be foolish, you know. In the extreme.'

'This is all there is. Sir Miles Linley can sleep soundly in his bed.'

'In that case, so can we all.' Tate pocketed the photographs and the card, then stood up and headed for the exit.

Den Engel, as I realized when I arrived, was the bar I'd killed time in the day before. It probably hadn't changed much since 1840, let alone 1940. Eldritch was sitting at a table towards the rear, smoking one of his Sobranies and sipping a local beer. He looked tired and thoughtful, which was no surprise, since he had plenty to be tired by and thoughtful about.

I told him the particulars of my deal with Tate, to which he reacted with a nod of acceptance and a murmured, 'That should do it.' Then he seemed to remember something. 'Oh, this is for you,' he said, reaching into his pocket.

It was a cheque from Nimbala for £5,000: my share of the reward. My instinctive reaction was to hand it back, but Eldritch grabbed my wrist and forced me to hear him out.

'Never refuse money unless there are strings attached, Stephen. That's a piece of wisdom that comes with age. Rachel isn't going to be best pleased when she finds out what you've bought her freedom with, even though you had no alternative. She'll need . . . perspective. You should take her away somewhere where she can get it. A long way away. Five thousand pounds' worth of away.'

'It's a nice idea.' And so it was. In that moment, after all we'd been through, it was richly tempting.

'Make it more than an idea.'

'She may turn me down.'

'I doubt that.' He let go of my wrist. And I didn't let go of the cheque.

'What will you do, Eldritch?'

'I plan to go away myself.'

'With anyone I know? Marie-Louise, perhaps?'

'We'll see.' He glanced past me, deflecting the question. 'It would have been satisfying to make Linley suffer for what he did to me. But I decided a long time ago that if I ever got out of prison I wasn't going to waste however many years I had left striving for vengeance. We played our hand and we lost. I wouldn't say we were defeated, though.'

'No?'

'I'm hoping you'll do something for me.'

'What?'

'J-J said I could stay at his apartment for a couple of nights. So, I don't have to go back to Zonnestralen. If I did, I'd have to meet Rachel's mother. Frankly, I can't face all the explanations and apologies I owe her. Could you . . . go and see her on my behalf?'

I could hardly refuse his request after trading away his chance of revenge. I nodded. 'All right.'

'Thanks.'

'Is this goodbye, Eldritch?'

'If everything goes according to plan, yes.' He stubbed out his cigarette. 'We've both got what we originally wanted, Stephen. Isn't that enough?'

'It doesn't feel like enough.'

'Then you should adjust your expectations.'

'Why didn't you speak up in your own defence at your trial?'

'Ah, that last unanswered question, eh?' Eldritch chuckled drily. 'I didn't think you'd leave it hanging.'

'Well?'

'Finish your beer and step outside with me. I need some air.'

Darkness had descended on the Grote Markt, its cobbles gleaming damply in the lamplight. Eldritch lit another cigarette and wandered across the square towards the Brabo Fountain, gazing up at its statue of a youth clutching an outsized severed hand, poised as if to throw it.

'Do you know the Brabo legend?' he asked.

'Inexplicably, I haven't found the time to follow the tourist trail round Antwerp,' I replied.

'Well, it goes like this. Shipping on the Scheldt in ancient days was at the mercy of the giant Antigonius, who used to tear off the right hands of captains who tried to dodge paying his toll and throw them into the river. Along comes a brave young Roman soldier, Silvius Brabo, supposedly a nephew of Julius Caesar. He challenges Antigonius to combat, outfights him, cuts off *his* hand and throws it into the river. Biter duly bit. Or maimer maimed. The name of the city is a corruption of *hand werpen* – to throw a hand.'

'Are you telling me this for a reason?'

'It's a legend, Stephen. A myth. That's the point. In real life, you can't outfight a giant. There's only one way to get the better of him.'

'And that is?'

'Hire a bigger giant.'

'What if there isn't one available?'

'Pay the toll.'

'Meaning?'

'You have to know when to resist and when to give in. Also *how* to resist. And *how* to give in.'

'Is that supposed to explain what happened at your trial?'

He nodded. 'Amongst other things. Then. Now. And in the future.'

339

1940

FORTY

It is a drizzly, clammy Wednesday morning in Dublin. The greyness of the day is somehow intensified by the atmosphere prevailing in the Taoiseach's office in Government Buildings. Éamon de Valéra sits at his desk, tight-lipped and frowning, the folds of flesh on his raw-boned face suggesting that this is a far from uncommon expression. His eyes gleam behind round, steel-framed glasses and are apparently fixed on the two men sitting at the table in the centre of the room. This cannot literally be true, however, since he is partially sighted to the point of blindness. But the literal truth has never been regarded by Éamon de Valéra as any kind of obstacle. He sees what he needs to see.

In this case, he sees, accurately enough, Frank Aiken, the Minister for Defence, and Gerald Boland, the Minister for Justice. They are contrasting figures – Aiken big, bluff and burly, militaristically moustached, dominant of bearing; Boland bland of face, slighter of build, melancholically undemonstrative. All three are veterans of the Easter Rising and, notionally at least, the staunchest of old comrades. But the collusions and compromises of the past twenty-four years have left their mark. Aiken, a former IRA Chief of Staff, believes Germany will win the war and advises de Valéra accordingly. Boland believes and advises the opposite. And de Valéra himself, who serves as Minister for External Affairs as well as Taoiseach, takes his own counsel.

'The fellow's English,' declares Aiken, referring to the man who has been in custody for the past four days on suspicion of attempting to assassinate the Taoiseach. 'Doesn't that just speak for itself?'

'There are Irishmen on both sides of this conflict and Englishmen too,' observes Boland. 'The Germans are quite devious enough to have calculated the benefit of recruiting a British citizen to carry out their plot.'

'You're falling over yourself to excuse Churchill, Gerry. Why not simply face the truth? He'd have had us all up against a wall in 1921 if he'd had his way. Now he's in charge what else should we have expected? It's all but a declaration of war.'

'There's no evidence the British government sent Swan here or told him what to do. He denies being the gunman anyway. It's possible the real culprit got away. He could have been German for all we know. Heider's still on the run, remember.'

'If Swan could be working for the Germans, as you suggest, then Heider could be working for the Brits. We can debate ifs and maybes from now till doomsday and it'll get us nowhere. Swan was at school with a member of staff at the British Legation, for God's sake. Doesn't that tell you all you need to know?'

'It seems to tell you all you need to know, Frank. That's clear. A little too clear for my liking.'

'If he'd got away with it, you'd have said he was Heider. That was the plan they cooked up in London and you're still falling for it. We're just lucky it miscarried.'

'I'm perhaps luckier than either of you,' de Valéra cuts in. 'But we've all—'

A knock at the door silenced him. It was scarcely more than a tap, though quite sufficient to be heard by a man whose ears were these days doing much of the work of his eyes. The door opened and a clerk stepped into the room. 'Inspector Moynihan,' he announced.

'Come in, Inspector,' said de Valéra, rising stiffly from his chair. 'We've been expecting you.'

Moynihan, a clean-cut, good-looking man, dressed rather more elegantly than the average Garda Síochána Special Branch officer, nodded to Aiken and Boland, who responded in kind, on his way to shake the Taoiseach's hand. The clerk withdrew, closing the door gently behind him.

'Mr Aiken and Mr Boland I'm sure you know,' said de Valéra, resuming his seat. 'Do we have a chair for the Inspector, Frank?'

A chair was swung into position by Aiken. There were further handshakes and a general settling. Moynihan cleared his throat.

'As you'll be aware, Inspector,' de Valéra resumed, 'the events of last Saturday morning are still unknown to the general public, as they are indeed to most members of my Cabinet. They must remain so, until or unless I decide otherwise. We speak here freely but in absolute confidence. You appreciate the extraordinary delicacy of the situation, I trust.'

'I do, sir, yes.'

'Good. Now, could you précis the results of the suspect's interrogation for us, please?'

'Certainly, sir.' Moynihan consulted his notebook. 'Eldritch Swan was born in Kenya in 1908. Educated Ardingly and Oxford. Sent down by his college for seducing the Master's daughter. Subsequent career patchy at best, shady at worst. Recently employed in an obscure, possibly illicit, capacity by a Jewish diamond merchant in Antwerp, more recently still by an art dealer in London. Alleged reason for presence in Dublin: to persuade Desmond Quilligan, an internee at the Curragh, to quit the IRA and resume his artistic career. Alleged reason for renting the flat at thirty-one Merrion Street: to oblige his old schoolfriend Miles Linley, an official at the British Legation, who wanted to use it for liaisons with a married woman who also works at the legation. Realized this was a fairy tale when contacted by the former tenant, Lorcan Henchy. Then told by Linley the true purpose of renting the flat was to use it for surveillance of this building. Agreed to bribe Henchy to leave the country. Henchy's subsequent murder, and his own narrow escape from death, alerted him to the falsehood of Linley's explanation. Proceeded to the flat last Saturday morning, discovered a would-be assassin on the premises and prevented him getting off a clean shot before being knocked unconscious and then arrested.'

'What does Linley say about this?' asked Boland.

'He denies Swan's claims in every particular, sir.'

'But Henchy was murdered right enough,' said Aiken.

'Yes, sir, he was. At Seapoint railway station, the evening before
. . . last Saturday's events. The killer died at the scene, of injuries
suffered when he fell under the train. We've been unable to identify
him. Swan matches the description we have of a man said to have
run off with the killer's gun. The gun itself is still missing. However,
a Gladstone bag containing four hundred and fifty pounds was
found outside the door of the flat at thirty-one Merrion Street.
And Swan was carrying fifty pounds in an envelope in his pocket
when he was arrested.'

'Any evidence there was another man in the flat when the rifle
was fired?' asked Boland.

'Nothing conclusive, sir. The rifle had evidently been wiped,
since there were no fingerprints. There was a skylight found open
in the attic, accessible from the flat, which would have permitted
escape across the roofs of neighbouring properties. But we have no
reports of any such . . . escape.'

'So,' said Aiken, 'Swan could have invented this other man in
order to exonerate himself.'

'Certainly he could, sir.'

'Just as he could have invented Linley's role in the affair in order
to implicate the British Government,' said Boland.

'Indeed, sir.'

'You've interrogated him exhaustively, Inspector?' asked de
Valéra.

'Yes, sir, we have.'

'Exhaustively and . . . energetically?'

'We haven't used kid gloves, if that's what you mean, sir. We've
employed . . . all necessary techniques.'

'Which would normally be expected to yield reliable results?'

'Yes, sir.'

'Then I have a simple question for you. Do you believe he's told
you the truth?'

Moynihan hesitated and licked his lips. Then he said, 'Yes, sir. I do.'

'I see.' De Valéra permitted himself a fraction of a smile, perhaps in appreciation of his own irony. 'Where's Quilligan now?'

'Still in the Curragh, sir. I should perhaps mention that his brother is acting as Swan's legal representative. Ardal Quilligan is a qualified solicitor.'

'What about Linley?'

'Going about his diplomatic business, sir, though under close observation.'

'Has he offered you anything more than a denial of involvement?'

Moynihan cleared his throat once more. 'Yes, sir. He's suggested it might . . . suit our purposes . . . if he persuaded Swan to withdraw his statement and offer no defence at his trial.'

Aiken groaned. 'Are we really going to give this wretch the benefit of a trial?'

'We are, Frank, yes,' said de Valéra. 'In camera, naturally. And limited by emergency regulations. But to return to Mr Linley's offer, Inspector. Does he seem confident he can prevail upon Swan to cooperate?'

'Exceptionally confident, sir.'

'I wonder why.'

'Bloody old-school ties, that's why,' grumbled Aiken.

'Thank you, Frank. And thank *you*, Inspector. I think you've given us all the information we need. Would you mind waiting outside while we . . . consider the situation?'

'Not at all, sir. Thank you, gentlemen.'

Aiken saw Moynihan to the door and closed it after him, then prowled discontentedly back to his chair, muttering under his breath.

'Recommendations?' de Valéra prompted.

'Send the British Legation packing,' growled Aiken. 'Warn Churchill he's answerable for the consequences of this attempt on your life.'

'Demand a formal response from the British, certainly,' said Boland. 'But don't break off diplomatic relations, and make it clear we regard German responsibility as equally likely.'

'Both courses of action have their advantages,' said de Valéra mildly. 'But I shall follow neither. It would be impossible for us to establish with any degree of certainty the level of government at which this plot was authorized. I've little doubt it was hatched in London rather than Berlin, as a direct response to my rejection of MacDonald's proposals, though whether as an attempt to intimidate me or actually kill me is hard to say. It has failed in any case. Swan is very possibly telling the truth, but it's a truth we can't afford to broadcast. Neutrality requires stoicism and forbearance on my part and on yours. Officially, last Saturday's events . . . did not take place.' There was another groan from Aiken. 'Is that clear?'

'Yes, Dev,' said Boland.

'Frank?'

'If you say so, Dev.'

'I do.' De Valéra gave a little half-smile. 'An assassination attempt is water off a duck's back to me anyway. There was a time when it was virtually a daily occurrence.' At that Aiken and Boland both obliged with a chuckle. 'I'm sorry for Mr Swan. He may have saved my life. But we must all make sacrifices. If Linley can persuade him to say nothing in court, we should proceed with a swift trial in camera under the Offences Against the State Act, the charge to be vaguely drawn with no reference to the Taoiseach being endangered. Can you arrange that, Gerry?'

'Yes, Dev.'

'What if Swan can't be persuaded to keep his mouth shut?' asked Aiken.

'Then he'll be tried *in absentia*. But he will be tried.'

'And what do we do about Linley?'

'Leave him where he is. He may prove useful to us now that he's been compromised.'

'What sort of sentence do you envisage for Swan?' asked Boland.

De Valéra sighed. 'Oh, life, of course. If we're to suppress this story, he must stay behind bars for good.'

'Why not just hang him and have done?' suggested Aiken.

'Because Swan alive in an Irish prison is a threat to those behind the plot. It's a sorry way to treat an innocent man, if he is innocent, but it can't be helped. See to it, Gerry, would you? Oh, and both of you . . .'

'What is it, Dev?' they asked in virtual unison.

'Remember not to mention the name of Eldritch Swan to me in future, would you? By "not", of course . . . I mean never.'

Later that day, Miles Linley was admitted to Eldritch Swan's cell in Dublin Castle. Swan raised himself gingerly from the hard bunk bed to greet his visitor. The ugly bruises visible on his face were more than matched by those elsewhere on his body. He was missing a couple of teeth and could only properly open one eye. The shirt and trousers he was wearing, and the laceless boots standing beside the bed, were of the kind issued to internees at the Curragh, as he was personally well placed to know.

'Hello, Cygnet,' said the dapperly clad Linley, keeping his distance, as far as he was able to in the narrow confines of the cell.

Swan slipped his feet into the boots and stood slowly up. He said nothing. His one-eyed glare conveyed all he wished or needed to. He took a step towards Linley.

'There are half a dozen constables just down the corridor, Cygnet. I can summon them at any moment if I need to. I'm assured they'll administer another beating with pleasure if you give them cause.'

'Do you think another would make any difference?' Swan croaked. He stretched out his hand, spreading his fingers as if to grasp Linley by the throat.

'You should listen to what I've come to say.'

'I've listened to you too often.'

'Smoke?' Linley took out his cigarette case, and held it open in front of him. Swan hesitated, then slid one of the cigarettes out and put it in his mouth. 'That's the ticket,' said Linley. He put the case away and struck a match.

'Nervous?' asked Swan, noticing the wavering of the flame. He grabbed Linley's wrist tightly. Linley flinched, but did not cry out. Then the cigarette was alight. Swan let go.

'I've read your—' Linley had to cough to banish the hoarseness from his voice. 'I've read your statement.'

'All old news for you.'

'It's put me in a difficult position.'

'Not half as difficult as mine.'

'I can't deny that.'

'But no doubt you're denying everything else.'

'I was following orders. I still am. I'm sorry I had to involve you. Though sorrier still that your . . . interference . . . caused events to miscarry.'

'Your orders required my murder, as well as Henchy's, in addition to de Valéra's assassination, did they?'

'I had no idea you were to be killed. You have my word.'

'And that's worth . . . what, exactly?'

'Listen to me, Cygnet. Listen carefully. Our attempt to engineer a change of leadership here in Dublin having failed, it's in no one's interests to make that failure a matter of public knowledge. De Valéra's policy of neutrality gags him on the issue. I've read your statement. But no one else will. You'll never get the chance to tell your story. I don't know what advice Ardal Quilligan's given you, but I've spoken to him more recently than you have. Also to his charming sister, Isolde. They understand very clearly that their brother won't be released if they disseminate any of your . . . wilder allegations. For your own sake as much as anyone else's, you must withdraw them.'

'Why the hell would I do that?'

'Because, if you think you have nothing to lose, you're wrong. They'll sentence you to life imprisonment, but I can arrange for you to be out as soon as the war's over.'

'How?'

'We'll need to do a fair amount of repair work on Anglo-Irish relations after the war. Your discreet transfer to a British prison – and subsequent release – will be part of the . . . healing process. Naturally, however, our intercession on your behalf depends on your silence at this sensitive stage. Plead not guilty, by all means, but offer no defence. Deny everything.

350

But explain nothing. That's what your country needs you to do.'

'What if *my country* loses the war?'

'Then obviously I can't help you. You might actually be better off in prison over here than marching to Hitler's tune in England. But God help us all in that event. I'm working on the assumption that we'll win. You should too.'

'The assumption I'm working on is that every word that comes out of your mouth is probably a lie.'

'I've nothing to gain by misleading you. I was told it was intended to ship you off to England last Friday after Henchy had been dealt with. I would never have gone along with it if I'd thought you were going to be killed.'

'No?'

'Of course not. What do you take me for?'

'Someone who does what he's told to do, whatever it is and whoever suffers as a result.'

'This is the best I can do for you, Cygnet. It's the best anyone can do for you.'

Swan said nothing, but went on staring hard at Linley. A minute or so silently passed. Then Swan took a last drag on his cigarette and threw it down at the foot of the door.

'Well, then?' Linley raised his eyebrows. 'Will you withdraw your statement?'

1976

FORTY-ONE

I hadn't been prepared for how strongly Esther Banner would resemble Rachel. Her hair was shorter and shot with grey and naturally there were more lines around her eyes and mouth, but the similarity in her bearing and gestures, quite apart from her looks, took me aback. She was even dressed similarly, in clothes that belied her age.

She was fretful and confused and more than a little angry that no one, not even her daughter's lawyer, had yet given her straight answers to straight questions about how and why Rachel had become a murder suspect. She was bound to take a leery view of the new boyfriend she'd never previously met or heard of, but whose uncle she *had* heard of, of course. I was aware I had a great deal of explaining to do. And so was she.

Marie-Louise hovered in the background, shooting me eloquent glances of caution and complicity, until Mrs Banner asked her to leave us alone. There was no sign of Mrs Meridor. An upward roll of Marie-Louise's eyes as she left the room seemed to indicate the old lady had taken to her bed, for which I couldn't blame her.

Mrs Banner asked surprisingly few questions as I recounted the events Rachel and I had become caught up in, but her gaze never left me. Nor did a frown – of scepticism, concentration, anxiety: I couldn't tell which – ever leave her. I claimed not to know why Sir Miles Linley merited special protection or why Eldritch had served thirty-six years in an Irish prison. And I said nothing about Jean-Jacques Nimbala. Those were revelations for another day. There were more than enough for her to cope with as it was.

What they amounted to in the end was that neither Rachel nor I would be charged with Ardal Quilligan's murder, but our freedom came at a price, one Rachel and her family would have to pay: clinching evidence that Desmond Quilligan had forged the Picassos would now never come their way; and I was responsible for putting it out of their reach.

'I had to do it, Mrs Banner,' I concluded defensively. 'There are forces the likes of you and I simply can't compete with.'

'Do you love my daughter, Stephen?' She was still looking hard at me. This, for her, was evidently the crucial issue. Not *what* I'd done, but *why*.

'Yes,' I replied, relieved to be able to state such an uncomplicated truth. 'I do.'

'I'm glad to hear that, because she'll need your love in the days and weeks and months ahead. I've given up on the case, but Rachel's never been able to let it go. What would we do with the money now, anyway? You can't buy back the past. So, don't apologize to me for the bargain you struck. Apologize to her.'

'I will, as soon as I get the chance.'

'And when will that be?'

'Tomorrow, I hope.'

'Maybe we'll have heard from Joey by then, as well.'

'I'm sure it won't be long before you do.'

'You can't be sure of anything with Joey.'

She stood up and walked over to a cabinet on which silver-framed photographs were arranged. She brought one back to show me. It was a picture of her as a young woman, sitting in the very chair she'd just left, with the same bookcase behind it. She was heavily made up, pearl ear-ringed and sleekly coiffed, wearing an elaborate dress decorated with lace flowers.

'That was taken on my twenty-first birthday, in 1939. I can hardly believe now I was that person. So much has happened to me since, so much I wish hadn't and quite a lot I wouldn't change for the world. Joey and Rachel, for instance. I want the best for them. I always have. I think that's why I started the case against the Brownlow estate. For their sakes. It was a mistake. I see that now. It's too closely connected with this house and my father and . . . all the things my children should be free of. When my mother dies, I'll sell up and that'll be the end of it. This isn't my home any more and I don't want it to be theirs.'

'Are you saying . . . you're actually pleased I disposed of the negatives?'

'What I'm saying is that Joey and Rachel have to put all that behind them. Maybe what's happened is a blessing in disguise. Although I'll only be able to believe that when the police let Rachel go and say she's no longer a suspect.'

'Well, they soon will.'

She took the photograph back to the cabinet and set it down, then turned to face me. 'Are you sure Rachel loves you as much as you love her, Stephen?'

'I believe she does, yes.'

'I've no doubt Mama would tell me, if she recovered her senses, that it would be madness to let my daughter have anything to do with a nephew of Eldritch Swan.'

'Eldritch isn't quite the unprincipled rogue you think. And I'm no more responsible for his behaviour than you are for your father's.'

The remark was out of my mouth before I'd measured the risk of antagonizing her. At first she didn't respond, but gazed down at the photographs, tilting one of them – a picture of Isaac Meridor, I guessed – the better to see it. Then she looked up and said, 'You're right, of course. Papa doted on me, but I know the wealth he used to buy the Picassos and the rest of his art collection wasn't reputably come by. He was a loving father, but a ruthless man. I'm glad in a way that I was cheated out of my inheritance. One day I hope Rachel will be too.'

'So do I.'

'Where is your uncle now, Stephen?'

'I don't exactly know.' And technically that was true, since I didn't have the address of Nimbala's apartment. 'But somewhere here in Antwerp.'

'You look a lot like him, you know. Like he was when I knew him, I mean. It's . . . unsettling.' She frowned thoughtfully at me. 'But if Rachel really is as stuck on you as you are on her . . . I suppose I could get used to it.'

We were interrupted shortly afterwards by Marie-Louise, who reported that Mrs Meridor was asking for her daughter. I took that as my cue to leave. While Esther headed upstairs, Marie-Louise saw me to the door. 'You have seen Eldritch?' she whispered, reinforcing my suspicion that Mrs Meridor would have forgotten her request by the time Esther reached her room, for the simple reason that she had never made it.

'Yes. I've seen him.'

'Where is he now?'

'Staying with a friend.'

'What friend?'

'He'll explain to you later. What I can tell you is that the police are going to release Rachel. Everything's going to be all right.'

'*Everything?*' She grasped my hand.

'Yes. I promise.' And with that I was smothered by a hug.

Making promises on Eldritch's behalf was reckless, of course, but my encounter with Esther Banner had left me in an optimistic mood. Rachel *was* going to be released, after all. Everything *was* going to be all right. Like Marie-Louise, I badly wanted to believe that. And I could see no reason not to.

A surprise was waiting for me at van Briel's house, however. Isolde Linley hadn't taken our cancelled meeting for an answer and wasn't going to let me avoid her any longer. I heard her voice as I climbed the stairs to the lounge and then I saw van Briel waiting for me at the top with a grimace on his face that expressed everything he wasn't free to say.

She was wearing an elegantly cut black dress that made her appear out of time as well as place amidst van Briel's modernistic furnishings. But remoteness from her normal milieu hadn't dented her determination or her confidence. 'My lawyer advised me against coming here, Mr Swan,' she said, staring at me coolly and rolling the name *Swan* around her tongue as if to emphasize that it wasn't the name I'd been going by when we'd last met. 'And your lawyer' – she twitched an eyebrow in van Briel's direction – 'is clearly put out by my visit. Well, I'm sorry for that. But I hope you'll agree you and I need to discuss my brother's death.'

'I've explained to Lady Linley that this isn't a good idea, Stephen,' said van Briel.

'It's OK, Bart. I'm happy to talk to her.'

'Maybe we should—'

'No, no. Really.' I smiled at him, though how reassuring he found my insouciance I couldn't tell. 'Why don't you leave us to it?'

He looked torn between his professional obligation to me and a keen desire to be somewhere else. It was Isolde who eventually resolved the conflict for him. 'Neither of us wants to put you in an invidious position, Mr van Briel. You can't be blamed for what we say to each other while you're not here.'

Van Briel puffed out his cheeks, gave me a second longer to reconsider, which I didn't, then surrendered. 'OK. I'll . . . take a walk.' He touched me on the shoulder as he passed and murmured, 'Good luck.'

We said nothing until the front door had closed behind him. The silence was so complete I could hear his short-paced footsteps on the pavement outside. 'Well?' said Isolde as they faded away.

'Well, what? You must know what happened. And why.'

'You and Miss Banner deny killing Ardal. But someone killed him. And the knife they used belonged to Miss Banner.'

'It belongs to her flatmate, actually. It was stolen from their basement flat in London last Friday.'

'So you say.'

'What do you really want from me, Lady Linley? If you

genuinely believe I had a hand in your brother's murder, you shouldn't feel safe at the moment, alone here with me, a kitchen full of sharp knives just a few strides away. But you don't look worried. You don't look worried at all. Why is that?'

'I want you to tell me what happened, Mr Swan. That's all.'

Suddenly, I understood. She wasn't there to accuse or berate me. She didn't believe Rachel had killed Ardal. She didn't know what to believe. 'Does Sir Miles know you're here?'

'We can leave my husband out of this.'

'I don't think we can, I'm afraid. He's responsible for Ardal's death.'

She glared at me. 'That's a monstrous suggestion.'

'It is, isn't it? But it happens to be true. I don't know if he explicitly approved the murder. Probably not. Probably this man Tate I've been dealing with took the decision. But responsible? Yes, I think we can fairly say Sir Miles is that all right. Ardal phoned you the day he died, didn't he, to warn you he was going to deliver proof to us that your brother Desmond forged the Meridors' Picassos? You told your husband about the call. He told Tate. And Tate took the action he deemed necessary to stop the proof reaching us.'

Her indignation had turned to dismay. 'How do you know Ardal phoned me?'

'Tate told me. And how could he know, unless Sir Miles told him?'

'Who is this . . . Tate . . . you keep referring to?'

'Ask Sir Miles. He can explain how these things work. If he wants to.'

Her self-control was faltering. She began fiddling with her wedding ring and looked past me, focusing, it seemed, on someone and somewhere else. She was breathing more rapidly, but also more shallowly. I wasn't sure what she'd expected to hear from me, but I was in no mood to hold back.

I told her everything then: about the photographs Ardal had taken at Cherrygarth in October 1940; how Desmond had concealed them in one of the paintings she'd auctioned off; about the lengths Ardal had gone to to obtain the painting and preserve its secret; where he'd been – and where he'd ended up – on the day of his death; and how I'd been forced to do a deal with Tate to hand the photographs over in return for Rachel's freedom. I told her. And she listened. To every word.

I poured myself a stiff drink when I'd finished. She said nothing, except a hoarse and belated 'Thank you' when she noticed the glass of vodka and very little tonic that I put in front of her. She took an unladylike gulp.

'Do you mind if I ask why you married Miles Linley?' I said, sitting down opposite her. 'I mean, honestly, *why*?'

She looked at me, and sipped her vodka, but still said nothing.

'Was it for the money and social status you judged he'd give you? The knighthood you could foresee even then? The advantages your children would enjoy? I'd guess at something along those lines and I wouldn't be far wrong, would I?'

'You don't know what you're talking about,' she said in an undertone.

'Oh, but I do. His promise to Eldritch, for instance. How could you let him break that?' Her momentary frown of puzzlement gave me my answer. 'You didn't know, did you? I suppose Sir Miles never thought you needed to know. He promised to get Eldritch out of prison at the end of the war, Lady Linley. That's why Eldritch withdrew his statement and said nothing at his trial. Because he took his old school friend at his word. More fool him.'

Most of the colour had drained from her face. She closed her eyes for a moment, then stood up. 'I'd like to go now. I . . . I have a coat.' She swayed and I jumped up, thinking she might be about to faint. But she recovered herself with a visible start. 'My coat, please,' she said, her voice by now barely a whisper.

I fetched it from the hall and helped her on with it. 'Would you like me to phone for a taxi?' I asked.

'That won't be necessary, thank you.'

'Eldritch is here, you know. In Antwerp. Do you want me to give him a message?'

She thought about that for a few seconds, then turned to look directly at me, as if to avoid any possible misunderstanding on the point. She shook her head. 'No message.'

FORTY-TWO

'She has gone, hasn't she?' van Briel asked, entering the lounge with exaggerated wariness to find me alone, sipping a second vodka.

'Yes, Bart. She's gone.'

'How was it?'

'Strange. I ended up feeling sorry for her.'

'Why?'

'Because I don't think she understood until now that all those sacrifices she made to get what she wanted may have ended up costing her brothers their lives.'

'You've got yourself into some heavy stuff, Stephen.'

'I know.'

'But soon it'll be over. Even your uncle thinks so.'

'You've spoken to Eldritch?'

'He phoned just before Lady Linley arrived. You can get him on this number.' Van Briel handed me a piece of paper with a number scrawled on it. 'He wants to know as soon as we hear they're letting Miss Banner go. Like I told him, it could take Bequaert most of tomorrow to decide he has to. But if this witness you say will show up does show up, it'll happen. For sure.'

Van Briel was right. Events played themselves out the following day as predicted. Also as predicted, they did so at a frustratingly slow pace. I alternated between short, aimless walks around Zurenborg and long, fretful pacings across van Briel's lounge. Eventually, he phoned me from the office to report that the Prosecutor's Office had thrown in the towel. New evidence (in the form of Tate's tame witness) meant Rachel was no longer regarded as the person most likely to have murdered Ardal Quilligan. And that meant they were going to let her go.

I phoned Eldritch right away. He picked up the receiver so quickly it was easy to believe he'd been sitting by it waiting for my call.

'Van Briel's going to drive Esther and me to Bruges to collect her,' I reported.

'That's good. You've done well, Stephen.'

'Oudermans will release the negatives to Tate at the same time.'

'And that will be that. Well, so be it. Give Rachel my regards, won't you?'

'Why don't you give them to her yourself? We'll be coming straight back to Antwerp.'

There was a lengthy pause, though what he needed to think about was unclear to me. His response, when it came, was typically ambiguous. 'We'll see.'

It was late afternoon by the time we reached the Palace of Justice in Bruges, where Rachel was waiting for us. Our reunion wasn't at all as I'd envisaged. She was strangely subdued and her mother's presence, not to mention van Briel's, as well as assorted poker-faced police officers', seemed to raise a barrier between us. She looked tired and drained, barely speaking as the bureaucratic details of her release were attended to.

Then van Briel reported a small but significant problem. Bequaert was nowhere to be found and he hadn't authorized the return of Rachel's passport – or mine. Whether this was a devious ploy or a mere oversight van Briel wasn't sure. Phone calls were made and messages passed. We sat in a crowded waiting room, drinking vending-machine coffee, incapable of saying much to each other, while he made a nuisance of himself on our behalf. Eventually, Rachel asked if I'd take her outside. Esther had the good sense to say she'd stay behind and fetch us if anything happened.

364

Night had fallen and I couldn't see Rachel's face clearly as we stood in the drizzle-smeared car park. I tried to kiss her, but she turned away so all I ended up doing was brushing my lips against her cheek. 'What's the matter?' I asked.

'Van Briel said you'd done a deal to get me out,' she replied, her voice distant and suspicious. 'Tell me what it was.'

And so I told her. I heard her suck in her breath when I recounted how and why I'd surrendered the proof that Desmond Quilligan had forged the Picassos. And I saw, despite the darkness, the solemn shake of her head as I explained why we had no choice but to accept defeat. I realized in that moment that Rachel did have a choice.

She'd gone on a very different journey from me over the past four days and had ended up in a very different place. The distance between us suddenly yawned in front of me. I loved her. And she loved me. I was sure of it. But I wasn't sure that our love would be enough to hold us together. 'There was no other way to save you, Rachel. Linley is untouchable. And that means your case against the Brownlow estate is unwinnable.'

'You found the proof,' she said incredulously, 'and you gave it away.'

'I traded it for your freedom.'

'You had no right to do that. It was for me to decide, not you. I've spent most of my life trying to lay hands on that proof. For the past year I've thought of nothing else. *And you gave it away.*'

'Listen to me, Rachel.' I tried to put my arm round her, but she recoiled. 'This is crazy. I—'

'That's what a lot of people said I was. Crazy. But *they* didn't believe me. It's worse . . . when someone who does believe you . . . when someone you trust . . .' Her voice fractured into a sob.

I reached out, but she pushed me away. 'I'm sorry,' I said. 'There was no alternative. You must understand that.'

'You should have consulted me.'

'How could I?'

'You knew I wouldn't agree. That's why you went ahead. You just wanted this over and done with.'

'That's not true. I did what I thought was best. I did the only thing I could think of to save you.'

'And yourself.'

'For God's sake, Rachel, there was no other way.'

'Yes, there was. There always is – if you look hard enough. But you didn't look, did you? Because you didn't want to find one.'

I knew this was her anger and frustration talking. Later, she'd come to see there truly had been no room for manoeuvre – no other way at all. But the knowledge did little to soften the blow of how disappointed she was in me.

'You betrayed me. I was relying on you. *And you betrayed me.*'

'No. I did what I had to do to get you out of trouble. And I did it because I love you.'

'*Love?*' She stared at me – and through me – as if I was a stranger. 'I can't talk to you any more, Stephen. Not now. Not after this. I have . . . nothing to say to you.'

Esther had already guessed what was wrong and was sorry, though unsurprised, to see my shocked and downcast look when I rejoined her in the waiting room.

'Rachel's greatest strength is also her greatest weakness, Stephen,' she said. 'She simply refuses to admit defeat, even when it's staring her in the face. She'll have sustained herself since her arrest with her certainty that eventually, somehow or other, she'll win.'

'I can't deliver that victory, Esther. No one can.'

'I know. But she can't accept that. Not yet, anyway. You're going to have to be patient with her. Don't let her push you away.'

'Maybe I should go back out to her.'

'No. What she needs now is time to adjust to the reality of the situation and to remember the things that really matter. Give her that time, Stephen. It's all you can do.'

I had little doubt Esther was right. But that didn't make it easy to follow her advice. It was van Briel who went to find Rachel, about twenty minutes later, with the news that Bequaert had finally been contacted and had approved the return of our passports. She came in with him, blank-faced and uncommunicative. The passports were delivered and signed for. We were free to go at last.

The drive back to Antwerp was tense and largely silent, van Briel's attempts at conversation fizzling out early. It was a tight squeeze for the four of us in his Porsche, but close was the last thing I felt to Rachel. She sat in the back with her mother and, whenever I glanced round at her, her expression was the same – an empty stare through the window into the surrounding night, where she could only have seen what I could see too: blackness.

We dropped Esther and Rachel at Zonnestralen. The parting was terse, almost perfunctory. Esther thanked van Briel and spoke of seeing me the next day, doing her best to compensate for the fact that Rachel said nothing at all.

'I'm sorry, Stephen,' said van Briel, as we drove the short distance to his house. 'She doesn't seem very grateful for what you've done for her, does she?'

'I thought she'd understand why I had to give up the proof, Bart. But I thought wrong.'

'She'll come round. Give her a little time.'

'That's what her mother said.'

'There you are, then. Mothers always know best.'

Several late-night vodkas blurred but failed to dispel the bleakness of my mood. The suddenness with which elation had turned to dejection left me shocked and bewildered. Remembering that I could ask no more of van Briel, I assured him I'd move out the next day, though where I'd be going I couldn't imagine. In truth, I couldn't imagine very much about my immediate future at all.

After a long and largely sleepless night, desperation drove me to appeal for help to the one person who might be able to persuade

Rachel I'd done the very best for her that could have been done in the circumstances.

Nimbala answered the phone and said Eldritch had gone out for a walk, which, since it was barely light, suggested he hadn't slept well himself. 'I'll have him call you as soon as he returns, Meneer Swan.'

'This is very important, Mr Nimbala. It's vital I speak to him.'

'Then, if you prefer, come here now.'

I did prefer. Nimbala's apartment was only about a mile away, in an Art Deco block overlooking the landscaped greenery of the Stadspark. I saw Eldritch going in as I approached and intercepted him before he made it to the lift.

'What are you doing here?' he demanded. Then, seeing the look on my face, his tone softened. 'What's happened?'

I explained during a slow circuit of the park. My plea was simple and direct. I'd helped him and now I needed him to help me. It meant he'd have to meet Esther, of course, which he'd gone to some lengths to avoid, but, as I saw it, only he stood any chance of making Rachel see reason.

'I doubt she'll listen to me, Stephen,' he objected.

'She certainly won't listen to anyone else. You can tell her exactly the sort of people we're dealing with.'

'Maybe. But—'

'I need you to try this, Eldritch. Is it really asking too much?'

He lit a cigarette while he thought about it, then said, 'You're actually lucky to have caught me. I went to see Marie-Louise yesterday after you'd left for Bruges. I invited her to go away with me and start spending my forty-five thousand.'

'She surely didn't turn you down?'

'No. But I wanted to leave straight away, whereas she insists on giving Esther at least a week's notice. She's supposed to be announcing it this morning. So, thanks to her . . . sense of duty . . . you got this chance to put me in the firing line.'

'Does that mean you'll do it?'

He sighed. 'I suppose so.'

I walked back with him as far as Tramplein. He headed on along Cogels-Osylei towards Zonnestralen, while I made for Velodroomstraat.

Van Briel was preparing to leave for the office when I arrived. He reckoned asking Eldritch to intercede on my behalf was a smart move and wished me luck with it. Generously, he added that I was welcome to stay another night if I needed to.

I had no idea whether I'd find myself having to take him up on his offer, incapable as I was of thinking so far ahead. The next hour or so consumed all my hopes and left no room for anything else.

Less than an hour had actually passed, though it seemed longer, when the doorbell rang. I had some idea I'd answer it to Rachel, or Eldritch *with* Rachel. But Eldritch was alone. And his expression was grave.

'What did she say?' I asked, dreading his answer.

'She wasn't there,' he replied, confounding me.

'Not there?'

'She left early this morning. She told her mother she was coming here. To patch things up with you.'

'But—'

'I couldn't come any sooner without Esther realizing she'd been lied to. She'd be beside herself if she knew. We need to make a phone call.'

'Who to?'

'Rachel's flatmate in London. She phoned her last night, apparently. That's the only clue I have to where she's really gone. And why.'

'United States Embassy.'

'Marilyn Liebermann, please.'

'Hold on while I try to connect you.'

Several seconds of silence, then a ringing tone. And then a voice I recognized. 'Grants and Bursaries.'

'Marilyn? This is Stephen Swan.'

'Oh, Stephen. I'm so glad you've called. I've been worried about Rachel since I spoke to her last night. I mean, it's great the Belgian authorities have cleared you two, but—'

'Why are you worried about her?'

'Well, she sounded, I don't know, sort of . . . Are you with her now?'

'No. In fact, I don't know where she is.'

'You don't?'

'What did she say last night?'

'Well, she told me the Belgian police had dropped all charges and let her go. I asked if she was coming back to London and she said yes, but she had to sort something out first.'

'What was that?'

'She said she had to . . . prove a point.'

'What point?'

'That no one is untouchable.'

'She said that?'

'Her exact words.'

'Did you ask her what she meant?'

'I never got the chance. She hung up. Does it make any sense to you?'

It did, reluctant as I was to admit it. It made perfect and terrible sense.

FORTY-THREE

If I'd thought about it, I might have recognized how strange it was, given his caution at other times, that Eldritch never once questioned what I proposed to do. Nor was there any suggestion he wouldn't accompany me. A crisis had come that we couldn't dodge or debate. Rachel meant to avenge herself on Sir Miles Linley. And we had to stop her.

But however fast we moved, we couldn't overtake her. There were several flights from Brussels to Heathrow she could already have left on and the earliest departure we were likely to make was at two o'clock. We hurried to Berchem station and set off.

'I should have known it was too good to be true,' said Eldritch as the train headed out through Antwerp's suburbs. 'I was confident I'd be able to talk Rachel round. Marie-Louise had just announced our plans when I got to Zonnestralen and Esther had reacted well, partly because a postcard from Joey arrived this morning telling her he was fine and she wasn't to worry. Then, when they told me where Rachel had supposedly gone, I realized . . .'

'I'm trying hard to believe she doesn't intend to kill him, Eldritch. I really am.'

'Keep trying. It could be true. Maybe she just wants to confront him.'

'But that wouldn't prove her point, would it?'

'No.' He looked me bleakly in the eye. 'It wouldn't.'

We reached the airport in adequate time for the two o'clock flight. The wait for it to be called gave me a chance to phone international enquiries. By then I'd overcome my reluctance to warn Linley of the threat Rachel might pose to him: it simply had to be done. But it couldn't be. As Eldritch had already anticipated, the Linleys were ex-directory.

The flight was less than an hour, but sitting in a cramped aeroplane seat with nothing to do but imagine ever more frightening possibilities turned it into an ordeal of tightly stretched anxiety. At last, we landed. We hurried through Customs and made straight for the car-hire desks.

It was the middle of a cool, still, grey afternoon when we reached Hatchwell Hall. I'd supposed Rachel might have used the same means to get there as we had, but there was no hire car parked in front of the house, which looked the very picture of moneyed domestic tranquillity. I began to wonder if we'd overreacted, or misinterpreted her words to Marilyn.

Eldritch voiced another possibility – 'Maybe he's not here and she went away disappointed' – and I prayed he was right.

I pulled at the doorbell and peered in through the glass. Nothing appeared to have changed since my visit with Rachel. Nothing about the place looked as if it ever changed.

'I might have guessed,' said Eldritch, gazing about him. 'This is exactly the kind of house Linley predicted he'd end up living in.'

I was about to ask when exactly Linley had predicted it, but the housekeeper loomed into view at that moment. She opened the door and frowned at me suspiciously.

'Well, my. First one, then the other.'

'What do you mean?'

'Your girlfriend was here a few hours ago. She never said you'd be following.'

'Where's Sir Miles?' Eldritch cut in.

'London. Gone for the day.'

'So, where's Rachel?' I asked.

'That'd be your girlfriend?'

'Yes,' I snapped.

She gave me a stern look, then an answer – of a kind. 'Well, I can't help you, anyhow. I told her where he was and she drove off.'

'What *exactly* did you tell her?' Eldritch asked.

'What she wanted to know. Sir Miles has gone to London. He often does. He has business to attend to there. He generally drives to Basingstoke and catches the train. So, like I told her, I imagine that's what he's done today. I couldn't say when he'll be back. He's taken the Bentley. She wanted to know that and all. And the colour and registration number.'

'Which are?'

'It's maroon, but if you think I have either the time or inclination to memorize registration numbers you're—'

'Where's Lady Linley?'

'She's away too.'

'When are you expecting her back?'

The housekeeper's mouth tightened. The question seemed to stump her. 'Well, I . . . I don't, er . . .'

'*Are* you expecting her back?'

The flustered look in her eyes suggested Eldritch was on to something. 'I can't help you any further. And I have work to do. This house doesn't clean itself, you know. If you have a message for Sir Miles, I'll see he gets it. Otherwise . . .'

'We may have got lucky,' Eldritch declared as I started the car and drove away. 'Rachel must have gone to Basingstoke to wait for him. That's why she wanted to know the make and colour of his car: so she could check it's parked at the station. If we can get there before his train does, we can stop her doing anything foolish.'

The speed I did on the drive scattered a good deal of gravel on to the recently trimmed lawn. But it was nothing to the speed I planned to do on the road to Basingstoke. We had a chance. But it would diminish with every moment that passed.

'Judging by the housekeeper's sudden outbreak of reticence, I'd say Isolde's left him,' Eldritch continued as we swerved out through the gates. 'Thorns have begun to sprout in Sir Miles Linley's rose garden. You'll be able to console Rachel with that thought, Stephen.'

'I hope so. I truly do.'

Basingstoke railway station was crowded with schoolchildren and workers knocking off early for the weekend. We hurried on to the platform for trains from London, where I turned left and Eldritch right.

With every step I wondered if I'd see her, glaring accusingly at me. But she wasn't among the waiting passengers, sitting on benches or leaning against pillars. It took me no more than a couple of minutes to establish that. As I reached the empty end of the platform beyond the canopy, I stepped to the edge and turned to see where Eldritch might be.

I saw him at once, standing apart and alone in the distance. As soon as he spotted me, he spread his arms wide and shrugged. He'd drawn a blank as well. I signalled for him to stay where he was and went to join him.

An announcement came over the Tannoy as I headed along the platform, prompting movement among the people around me. A London to Bournemouth train was due. The thought struck me then that if Rachel was lying in wait for Linley, she'd have to show herself now in case he was on this one. The same thought seemed to strike Eldritch. He started walking towards me.

We met near the ticket barrier. 'If she really means to attack Linley,' said Eldritch breathlessly, 'she'd have to be prepared every time a train arrives from London.'

'I know. But prepared how? And where?'

'We have to think what we'd do in her shoes.'

'Wait by his car, maybe?'

'No. He might see you before you saw him.'

'Wait in the booking hall, then. And follow him to his car.'

He nodded. 'That's more likely.'

I heard the rumble then of the approaching train. Glancing past Eldritch, I saw the blurred shape of it, speeding towards us. 'I'll check outside,' I said. 'You wait here.'

He nodded again in agreement. I turned and made for the barrier.

There were several people standing around in the booking hall and a dozen or so more queuing at the ticket window, but Rachel wasn't among them. I stepped into the adjoining newsagent's shop and looked around. She wasn't there either. The rumble of the train had dissolved by now into a jumble of rattling carriages and squealing brakes as it pulled into the station. I began to hope we were mistaken. Rachel had changed her mind. She'd seen reason. She must have done. I stepped back out into the booking hall.

And there she was, standing a few yards away, her back turned to me, her gaze fixed on the ticket barrier, through which latecomers for the Bournemouth train were hurrying. She was dressed as she'd been that first day I met her at the Royal Academy, in jeans, trainers and short mac, satchel looped over her shoulder. Her left hand was thrust into the pocket of her coat while with her right she grasped the flap of the satchel, as if about to open it.

Doors were slamming out on the platform now. Disembarking passengers began to spill into the hall, hurrying through to their cars and buses and homeward journeys. I watched Rachel scan their faces as they passed, searching and waiting for the one she wanted to see. I began to wonder what she had in the satchel – and what she planned to do if Linley appeared.

But he didn't appear. The rush of passengers slowed to a trickle. The last of the train doors slammed. A whistle blew. The final stragglers drifted through the barrier. The booking hall emptied. The train began to move.

'Rachel,' I said, stepping towards her.

She whirled round. Her face froze. 'Stephen?'

'Don't do it. Please.'

'Do what?' But her attempt to brazen it out was stillborn. As we stared at each other, pretence fell away. 'You shouldn't be here,' she said icily.

'I think I should actually. And—'

Suddenly, a bulky figure bustled through the barrier behind her. It was Sir Miles Linley, suited and overcoated and back from London. Eldritch was following him, glancing anxiously in my direction. Linley looked red-faced and angry, like a man breaking off from a quarrel.

In the same instant that Linley noticed me Rachel turned and saw him. And Linley's anger curdled into fear. Eldritch had warned him. But until this moment he hadn't taken the warning seriously.

Rachel flicked up the flap of her satchel and reached inside. As she pulled her hand out I saw the gleam of a blade. She took a stride towards Linley, a knife swinging into view.

She started to say something, but my charge knocked the breath from her mouth and slammed her to the floor. The knife slipped from her fingers and slid several feet away. There were cries of shock and dismay from onlookers. Rachel tried to push herself up, but I used my weight to pin her down.

'Let me go,' she gasped.

I saw Eldritch stoop smartly to retrieve the knife. He stepped back as others stepped forward.

'*Let me go.*'

So I did. I stood up and made a show of helping her up, grasping her arm tightly as I did so.

'It's all right, it's all right,' I said for the benefit of those gathering round us. 'Sorry, everyone. There's nothing to worry about. It was an accident.'

'Didn't look like an accident,' someone said.

'I thought I saw a knife,' said someone else.

I caught Linley's eye. He must have realized Eldritch and I had saved his life. But he had no intention of staying to express his gratitude. He turned and hurried out of the station.

Rachel took a step after him, but I yanked her back. 'Let go of my arm,' she cried.

'Yeah, why don't you do that?' put in one of the heftier and younger onlookers.

Suddenly, Eldritch was at our side. 'Listen to me, Rachel,' he said, quietly but urgently. 'If you force us to involve the police, we will. Do you want that? Think about it. You've only just been released by the Belgian authorities. Who's it going to look worse for? You or us?'

'Why are you trying to protect that man?' she snapped back at him. 'He ruined your life.'

'We're trying to protect *you*.'

'You shouldn't have interfered.'

'We had to, Rachel,' I said, pleading with her to understand. 'Linley isn't worth it. The Picassos aren't worth it. You have to give it up.'

'You two ought to stop hassling the lady,' said the hefty young man, stepping closer to us.

Rachel took a deep breath. 'It's OK,' she said, smiling stiffly at him. 'There's no problem. I'm fine. Everything's . . . fine. Honestly.'

The tension around us eased. The onlookers began to disperse, muttering amongst themselves as they went. Even the young man turned away with no more than a mumbled 'Please yourself.' They seemed to believe her. But I didn't. She wasn't fine at all.

'If it's any consolation,' Eldritch said to her, 'Linley isn't going to come out of this unscathed. Isolde's left him. She's discovered the sort of man he really is and she can't stomach it. Maybe their children won't be able to either, when she tells them, as I'm sure she will, what part he played in their uncle's death. That big house of his could soon seem very empty.'

Rachel closed her eyes. 'You think that's enough?'

'No. Of course not. But—'

Eldritch's words were drowned in a deafening roar and a shattering of glass. We all ducked, covering our heads as best we could, unable for the moment to imagine what had happened.

I'm not sure exactly how long it was before we learnt that a car bomb had exploded in front of the station, killing Sir Miles Linley instantly.

1922

FORTY-FOUR

On such a warm and windless afternoon, somnolence and quietude might normally be expected to prevail at Haywards Heath railway station. But this is no ordinary afternoon. It is the eve of the new academic year at Ardingly College, which stands in stolidly red-bricked readiness to receive new and returning pupils at its hill-top location a few miles north of the town. A sizeable number of those pupils are currently assembled in a baggage-clogged mass on the platform where the Horsted Keynes train, first stop Ardingly, is shortly expected. And they are neither somnolent nor quiet.

The fourteen-year-old Eldritch Swan has removed himself from the worst of the ruck and is sitting on his large, leather-strapped, steamer-stickered suitcase at the thinly populated far end of the platform. Though happy to give and take in the general spirit of schoolboyish squabbling, he finds most of his peers depressingly immature and prefers his own company during outbreaks of over-excitement such as this.

His aloofness from the fray confers upon him, despite his college uniform of Harris tweed jacket, stud-collared shirt, striped tie, grey trousers and black shoes, a distinct air of the adult in waiting. Yet he is in no sense a model pupil. The masters find him intelligent but lazy, adroit in argument but deficient in application, while his fellow pupils regard him with faint suspicion. He has no close friends. He is in no particular set. He cannot be readily classified as either a good egg or a bad sort. Even at fourteen, Eldritch Swan is something of an enigma.

A degree of order was brought to the jostling throng by the arrival of a group of prefects, who had just emerged from the station tea-room. A few sharp words and cuffed ears imposed their will to good effect, ensuring no words of complaint would reach the head-master concerning the boys' behaviour. Haywards Heath railway station was suddenly a calmer place.

One of the prefects who moved through the chaos of boys and bags like a breeze through a field of wheat was the highly respected senior, Miles Linley. Though shorter than several other prefects, he had a superior bearing and self-assured manner, not to mention a glittering academic record (that had him being groomed for Oxford) and a well-earned place in the cricket first XI and rugby first XV. He was generally expected to be named as head boy for the coming year. Unlike Eldritch Swan, he was the very embodi-ment of Ardingly's *esprit de corps*.

Linley acknowledged a few fawning remarks as he strode along the platform, but did not pause for longer exchanges. He appeared to have some pressing purpose in mind, and, oddly, that purpose took him to where Swan was sitting on his suitcase, twiddling his thumbs and staring into space.

'Swan, isn't it?' said Linley.

Swan looked up in some astonishment. He had no idea Linley even knew his name. He had certainly never spoken to him before. 'Yes,' he said, rising to his feet. 'That's me.'

'You'll be in the remove this year.'

'Yes. I will.'

'I've had my eye on you.'

'Have you?' This sounded bad. Swan did not crave the attention of Linley or any other prefect.

'I'll be needing a fag. And I thought of you.'

This sounded better – much better. A second year of general fagging duties, at the beck and call of any senior, was an irksome prospect. Only selection as a prefect's personal fag could earn Swan exemption, but he had not been prepared to do any of the sucking up which might have secured such a position. It was therefore a surprise, to say the least, that Linley should have considered him for the role.

'What do you say?'

'Gosh. Well, thanks, Linley. I'd, er . . . be honoured.'

'Splendid. We'll regard that as settled, then. Any questions?'

'I, er . . .' Swan hesitated.

'Why? That's what you're wondering, isn't it? Why in the world should I select you of all people to fag for me?'

Swan was indeed wondering that. But he did not deem it politic to say so. 'You must . . . think I'll make a good job of it.'

'You better had. But there are dozens of boys who'd do it just as well. No, no, young Swan. Or Cygnet, as I think I shall call you. I haven't chosen you because of your zeal and energy, in both of which departments you're reliably reported to be lacking. I've chosen you because you're a good deal cleverer than the other candidates and I don't care to have fools about me, even when all I require is the running of errands and the cleaning of my boots and shoes to a mirror-like finish. Who knows? There may be occasions, if you demonstrate your suitability, when I set you more demanding and indeed rewarding tasks. We shall see. As it is, I'll expect you to be at my disposal from tomorrow.'

'Very good, Linley. And . . . thanks very much.'

As Linley ambled back to the more densely populated middle of the platform, he was buttonholed by one of the other prefects, a tall and angular youth named Melrose.

'Was that Swan you were talking to?' he asked.

'It was, yes,' Linley replied, smiling superciliously.

'What did you want with him?'

'I've recruited him as my fag.'

'Swan? A rum choice, old man.'

'You think so?'

'The boy's a slacker. And too clever by half. You'll have trouble with him, mark my words.'

'*You* would have trouble with him, Melrose. I don't doubt that for a moment. I, on the other hand, won't. I shall enjoy managing young Swan. It'll add a little zest to life at the old place. Besides, if he doesn't come up to the mark, I'll simply get rid of him. I'm sure I shan't find that very difficult. If it proves necessary.'

Swan had watched Linley walk away and was still studying him as he chatted to Melrose. He had a shrewd and indeed accurate idea what Melrose, a prefect he had fallen foul of the previous year, might be saying. Yet he did not think Linley was likely to change his mind. His decision to choose Swan to fag for him seemed to have been carefully weighed.

Swan was sure he should feel flattered by this. Certainly there were others who would envy him. It was, in every respect, a stroke of good fortune. Yet something troubled him. Some sense he could not have put a name to told him that the advent of Miles Linley in his life was not necessarily to be welcomed.

The clunk of a signal being raised heralds the arrival of the train, shortly afterwards confirmed by the sound of the engine and the sighting of its plume of smoke in the middle distance. The boys of Ardingly begin to gather themselves and their belongings together. This interlude in the September sunshine will soon be over. No one present has any reason to suppose it will have consequences that will require many decades to reveal themselves. That is merely one of time's many invisible tricks, which it plays even as it passes.

2008

FORTY-FIVE

This year, had he lived, my uncle Eldritch would have been a hundred. Unsurprisingly, given his fondness for cigarettes and strong liquor, he actually died more than two decades ago, after what Marie-Louise described to me at his funeral as 'some very good years' with her on the French Riviera. It didn't turn out too badly for him in the end. And I smile whenever I think of him, which is probably the best tribute any of us can hope for.

I'm not far short now of the age Eldritch was when I first met him. In the thirty-two years since, our children, Rachel's and mine, have become adults, in one case with children of their own. Most of the people I encountered during those few hectic weeks in the early spring of 1976, when Eldritch did Rachel and me the great if unwitting service of bringing us together, are, like him, dead and buried.

Of them all, only Sir Miles Linley merited obituaries in the national press. The Provisional IRA claimed responsibility for the car bomb that killed him, though the official record of his years with the British Legation in Dublin hardly seemed to make him an obvious target for them. Perhaps they knew more than they were telling.

Who might have drawn their attention to him can only be guessed at. Moira Henchy did quite a lot of guessing at the time, but failed to uncover the truth. I've never come to any firm conclusion myself. Conceivably, his wife could have contacted the

IRA through former colleagues of her brother. But I couldn't quite convince myself she'd have gone so far as to do that. Then there was Eldritch. He must have served his time in Portlaoise prison alongside several IRA members. And what had he said to me in Antwerp? *'There's only one way to get the better of a giant: hire a bigger giant.'* I never summoned the nerve to ask him outright. I knew he'd deny it. I just didn't know whether his denial would be genuine. In my more cynical moments, I also wonder if Tate's bosses in London didn't simply decide Linley was more nuisance than he was worth. It would have been a fitting fate for him in many ways: to be betrayed by those he thought he could rely on for protection.

A few weeks after his murder, Simon Cardale contacted us with an unexpected proposal. He and Isolde Linley were willing to help Rachel pursue her family's claim against the Brownlow estate after all. With Sir Miles dead, Tate and his ilk no longer had any interest in the case, so there was nothing to prevent its revival and their testimonies, even without the photographs, would come close to the proof we needed. Isolde wanted to clear her conscience and realized she could never do so while that old injustice went uncorrected.

And so Rachel achieved what she wanted just when she'd finally accepted she never would. It hadn't been easy for us to feel our way back to how we'd felt about each other before her arrest in Belgium. There had been times, quite a few of them, when I'd doubted we ever could. But we'd managed it somehow. Love, I suppose, really does find a way. I was worried that reviving the law-suit would spoil everything all over again, but Rachel assured me she wasn't about to let that happen. She'd come to believe as well as to understand the truth of what I'd said to her just before the car bomb exploded that day in Basingstoke. Linley wasn't worth ruin-ing her life for. And nor were the Picassos.

In the event, the Brownlow estate settled out of court, paying her mother a sum of money about halfway between what the Picassos would have been worth in 1945 and what they were actually worth in 1976. That still represented a fortune, most of which she sank into a charitable foundation for Vietnam veterans with psychiatric problems. She asked Rachel and me to run it, with Joey's assistance. It turned his life around and, I'm proud to say, the lives of many like him. You could say it turned our lives around too. We've extended its remit to other wars since. It doesn't look as if it will run short of people to help any time soon.

Recently, some of the foundation's resources have been used for a post-war development project in the Congo. It's little more than a trial effort. The difficulties of operating in that part of the world are formidable. But it seems only right that some of the wealth Isaac Meridor took out of the country should find its way back, to do what good it can.

Earlier this year, I found myself near Haywards Heath, with time on my hands. On a whim, I diverted to Ardingly to take a look at Eldritch's old school. It was a wet day in half-term and the place was virtually deserted. Perhaps that was why the past felt so close at hand in its dusky cloisters and empty courtyards. If the fourteen-year-old Eldritch had come running round a corner ahead of me on some fagging errand for Linley, it somehow wouldn't have surprised me.

According to an advert I spotted on a noticeboard, a history of the college had just been published to mark its sesquicentenary; a copy was available for inspection at the senior school office. I wandered along and asked to see it.

Leafing through its glossy pages, I came across a section of potted biographies of eminent Old Ardinians, Sir Miles Linley among them. There, in a few paragraphs, was summarized a life of duty and attainment, tragically cut off when he should have had more years of his well-earned and honour-laden retirement to look forward to.

Needless to say, there was no potted biography – and no listing in the index – of Eldritch Swan. Some are remembered. And some are forgotten. But it isn't always the right way round.

AUTHOR'S NOTE

Malcolm MacDonald's mission to Dublin in June 1940 is a matter of historical record, as is Éamon de Valéra's subsequent rejection of a deal that might, just might, have secured what he claimed so passionately to desire all his life: a united and independent Ireland. But the Long Fellow, as his political career clearly shows, was a man who liked to say no.

A man who delights in saying yes, however, is my good friend Chris Allen, a style icon to all who know and love him, who generously shared with me his memories of a fag's life at Ardingly. I am also very grateful to Sven Lommaert for schooling me in Belgian police procedure. My thanks to them and to everyone else who helped me during the writing of this novel.